LOIS LENS[KI]

Author-Illustrator

Lois Lenski was born in Springfield, Ohio, the daughter of a [m]inister. When she was six, the family moved to a small Ohio village [w]here the rest of her childhood was spent. She came to New York, [st]udied in the Art Students' League for four years, and later studied [in] London, where she began illustrating children's books.

Miss Lenski's work soon became known for its originality, humor [a]nd charm, and in 1927 she wrote her first story, SKIPPING VILLAGE, [a]bout the little Ohio town of her childhood, and drew the pictures for [i]t. Then came A LITTLE GIRL OF NINETEEN HUNDRED and many de[li]ghtful stories and picture-books for younger children.

Miss Lenski now has a quaint and attractive studio in Harwinton, [C]onnecticut, adjacent to the delightful old 1790 farmhouse in which [s]he makes her home. Out of the history and associations of this old [f]armhouse, the little town, and its surroundings, and out of a study of [c]hildren's books of the past, of which she is an enthusiastic collector, [g]rew the story, PHEBE FAIRCHILD HER BOOK, and there also was written [a]nd illustrated her second story based on historical material—A-GOING [T]O THE WESTWARD.

Strawberry Bank 1732

OCEAN-BORN MARY

" 'You have broken my window!' he shouted. 'You have broken my window!' "

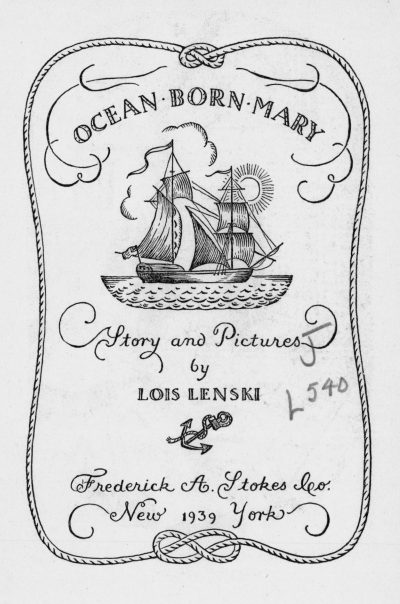

OCEAN·BORN·MARY

Story and Pictures
by
LOIS LENSKI

Frederick A. Stokes Co.
New 1939 York

7762

CONTENTS

ILLUSTRATIONS

Strawberry Bank

Chapter I

"WILL we soon be there, Ma?"

Through the dense New Hampshire forest, in the spring of the year 1732, two horses walked single file over a barely passable trail. The first carried a young woman dressed in homespun hood and shawl, with a sleeping child in her arms. Behind her, on the pillion, rode an eleven-year-old girl. Large basket panniers, piled high with farm produce, hung from the second horse's back. A tall, sturdy man, dressed in deerskin shirt and breeches, walked ahead, leading the animal.

"Will we soon be there, Ma?" The girl's voice sounded eager, though she yawned from lack of sleep.

"Yes, Mary, but you must learn to be patient," said Elizabeth Clark, her mother. She shifted the weight of the child in her arms slightly and her quiet voice echoed clearly through the empty forest. " 'Tis a long way to the Bank and the critters are slow. Think how far and how long it must be when Pa goes alone."

Huge trees pressed in on all sides, parting in front to let the slowly moving animals creep through and closing swiftly together behind. The panniers brushed against the low-hung branches and small bushes by the wayside. A fresh breeze stirred the thick boughs overhead.

" 'Tis a wonder we saved some of the potatoes for selling," said the woman quietly. "There are so many things we need."

"We have had a good winter and can well be thankful," added her husband. "As for the potatoes, they will bring a fine price as soon as men learn they are good for eating. We will still have enough left over for seed for this year's planting."

The horses moved slowly on, their hoofbeats thuding sharply in the damp stillness.

Elizabeth spoke again, thoughtfully: "Remember, James, to run a stick into the bung-hole of the molasses-barrel at Maggie McDonald's. To taste at the spigot is not enough."

"Yes, wife," answered her husband, dutifully.

"And when you select the dry codfish—even if they be Cousin Tom's—buy not the damp ones from the bottom of the pile, nor yet the little scrimped ones from the top."

"Yes, wife, I will remember," said James.

"I've been running over in my mind," continued

Elizabeth, "just what things we shall be in most need of. A barrel of molasses, half a quintal of codfish, half a barrel of mackerel. . . ."

"A bag of Turk's Island salt; don't forget that," interrupted James.

"Yes, the salt above all," answered Elizabeth. "We must have the salt. Snuff and spices we can do without, though I long for a whiff of cinnamon with all my heart," she added wistfully. "I hope we can manage four or five needles and then. . . . But I don't know how the horses can carry it all."

"Needles be not heavy, wife!" The tall man looked at her with a smile. "What else?"

"It is vain of me to even think . . ."

"What is't, wife? A piece of flowered brocade?"

"No, James, no," answered Elizabeth quickly. "I've long given up the thought of brocades and satins. They have no place in the wilderness."

"I know!" cried the bright-eyed girl, loosening her hold on her mother's waist. " 'Tis a chiny cream pot she wants and a new little foot-warmer to carry on to Meeting!"

"Hush, Mary!" said Elizabeth, as an embarrassed flush rose to her cheeks. "The thought did cross my mind that one day we might find a cream pot to match the old teapot I brought from Ireland; but I've done without one for so long, I doubt not I can do a while longer. 'Tis when I remember how cold is the Meeting House and how long are the sermons Pastor MacGregor preaches, 'tis then I wonder if we could not manage a wee foot-warmer. . . ."

3

"A foot-warmer it shall be!" cried James, merrily. "A foot-warmer first of all and perhaps a cream pot, too, even if it means fewer codfish. The season will be ripe, soon, for planting the corn, and with the field we burned off last fall, we shall grow enough to feed us well and a good bit over. If we have both corn and fish, we can ask for no more. So a wee foot-warmer it shall be, for you and the bairns!"

"We must put in more flax this year, James," said Elizabeth, in a shy effort to change the subject. "All the weaving brings a good price and more is always wanted."

"That we will," answered her husband soberly.

"Will we soon be there, Ma?" asked Mary again. "To Strawberry Bank, to Cousin Tom's?"

"Look, child, look," said Elizabeth, pointing ahead.

A sudden bend in the road revealed a faint gleam of light beyond the dark tree trunks. Mary looked up, doubting whether there really was a heaven above her. As she watched, the strip of sky grew bluer and the receding forest looked darker for its glowing brightness. The trees grew fewer and fewer and the forest path lay clear and plain ahead. Then, suddenly, they were out of the woods, and there was the blue arch above, dotted with white clouds, dazzling in their brightness. The trail turned into a road now, with open fields alongside.

The road was joined by another from the south, and together they became what was known as the King's Highway. A horseman galloped swiftly past on his way to Boston. Oxen and horses with loads of wood and produce made their tedious way toward the little seaport town. It was not long until Mary saw across the meadows a huddle of gray roofs among the trees, a line of towering masts against the sky and the blue, blue sea beyond.

Mary Wilson was no longer sleepy, though she had risen from her bed that morning at four. She sat up straight behind her mother and her heart beat fast beneath her linsey-woolsey gown. Her hands trembled and, though her mind was full of questions, she could not trust herself to speak. There was the sea, the beautiful sea. There was Portsmouth, known to all by its early name, Strawberry Bank, the town of boats and ships—boats and ships. They were there at last.

The horses followed the road skirting the south shore of North Mill Pond and passed Windmill Hill with its busy mill, where the town's cows grazed in surrounding pastures. Entering through the stockade gate, they trotted along King Street side by side until they came to the Parade, an open square in the center. Mary looked about her with a strange feeling of mixed bewilderment and joy. She saw the Meeting House, the fort and watch-house, interspersed with low, gray-weathered frame buildings.

How different it was from Nutfield! The amazing thing was that, no matter which way you looked, there was the sea. The town seemed to be surrounded by water on all sides, almost like an island. To be near the sea was all she wanted. Mary knew that no matter what happened, she would be happy—at Strawberry Bank.

They rode slowly down Market Street and the bustle

and confusion of Spring Hill Market soon engulfed them. Mary looked about her in astonishment. She had never seen such a large crowd before. The descent of the hill from Market Street was occupied on both sides by eager buyers and sellers. Rude sheds and open tables along the river's edge displayed vegetables, meat, fish, game and provisions of all kinds. Farmers, Indians, backwoodsmen, fishermen and townsfolk thronged the place.

James Clark tied his horses to a hitching rail and found a place in an empty corner, not far from the spring, whose vigorous flow of sparkling water brought every one sooner or later to its side. He opened his panniers and spread out his wares. A crowd gathered and he began to discuss the virtues and uses of that unknown vegetable, the potato.

The baby was awake now, kicking and crowing happily in Mary's arms. Elizabeth Clark opened her bundles and displayed her linen yarns and woven linens—towels and table-cloths. Bewildered, Mary stared about her.

"Lob—lob—lob—lobsters!" shouted a husky voice in her ear. An old man trundling a barrow of green, crawling lobsters passed by. He stopped, cupped his hand over his mouth, and called:

> "Who'll buy my lobsters? Yesterday
> They were deep down in Portsmouth Bay!
> Come, little maiden, buy one, buy!
> And you may suck his claws all dry!"

From a wherry with lateen sails, moored with many others at the adjacent wharf, a buxom fisherman's wife stepped up, carrying a basket, heavily laden with fish. She lifted it to her head and joined the throng, crying shrilly:

"Fresh cod and haddock! Look here, Ma'am, and see,
Here is your dinner, just drawn from the sea;
As fresh and as fair as your pretty young daughter,
They've hardly forgotten the taste of salt water."

Mary hardly knew which way to look, there were so many things happening at once. Two fashionable housewives appeared, followed by Negro slaves with baskets on their arms. Mary watched them make their selections, taste pats of butter, hold eggs to the light to see if they were fresh and feel chickens' breast-bones to see if they were tender.

"Verses!" screamed a sharp-voiced woman peddler, coming forward. "Essences and verses! Ballads tuppeny each—"*The Major's Only Son, Bar'bry Allen, Bar—bar—bar'bry Allen!* Essences, home-made essences?" The housewives turned away from her and disappeared in the crowd.

Then Mary heard her mother speaking. The first customer was a fine young lady, wearing a flowered calico wrapper, which fell in rich folds over her quilted petticoat. "This is Nutfield linen, is it not?" she inquired, unfolding a table-cloth as she spoke.

"Yes, Miss," answered Elizabeth. "We grew the flax and spun it ourselves."

"We?" the young woman looked down in surprise. "Do you mean the lass helped? Is she old enough to spin?"

"Yes, Miss, she will soon be twelve."

7

"Isn't that baby too heavy to hold?"

"Well, Miss," answered Elizabeth with a smile, "Mary's been tending babies ever since she could hold them. She has three brothers and this little sister."

"May I ask your name, my good woman?"

"Elizabeth Clark, Miss."

"Elizabeth Clark of Nutfield and Mary," repeated the young woman. "I will remember. I always prefer the Nutfield linens. I am Peggy Fayerweather. My father is a sea-captain. Perhaps you have heard of him?"

"A sea-captain?" cried Mary, impulsively, drawing a sharp breath. "Has he gone to sea?"

"Oh, many times!" cried Miss Peggy, laughing. "He has made so many voyages since I was a little girl, I could not count them all."

She looked over the pile of linens and made a selection, after inquiries about the price. Then she called her Negro slave who had been waiting at a respectful distance: "Samson, take these, please. Now we must find a plump duck for dinner. . . ." She turned away and was gone.

Mary clutched the kicking baby tightly and looked up at her mother. "Ma, she said her father is a sea-captain!" she cried, filled with a strange excitement.

"The Bank is full of sea-captains!" answered Elizabeth, shortly.

After various other purchases had been made, Mary's parents gathered their remaining goods together. Baby Ellen began to cry lustily. Elizabeth took her in her arms and gave her milk to drink. Just then an energetic, middle-aged woman came bustling up.

"Ah, Elizabeth, you are here," she cried. "I was just thinking about you and wondering when you'd come for Market Day again." She leaned over and embraced Elizabeth and Mary. "How these children do grow, Elizabeth!" she exclaimed. "Baby Ellen looks much like Mary did at the same age."

"I've come to stay, Aunt Becky!" cried Mary, with a proud air of importance. "I'm going to stay at Strawberry Bank and live here."

"Live here?" cried Becky Armstrong, in surprise. She looked at Elizabeth hastily. "You're not thinking of putting her out to me, are you? I've always been fond of Mary, but the almshouse is no place for a child, with all those fussy, crotchety old critters to live with."

"Never fear," said Elizabeth. "It's Cousin Jeanie. She sent a message by Silas Gregg to say that she's ailing again and could we spare Mary? Tom and the boys are off fishing to the Banks most of the time and she's left all alone with only the neighbors to come in now and then. She pines for women-folk and Mary's right handy, when she's told what to do."

Becky Armstrong looked down at the girl with penetrating eyes. "Yes," she repeated, " 'when she's told what to do!' If only Jeanie's not too weak-kneed to tell her. When you see her, tell her I said to send Jock with a quintal of codfish to the almshouse, day after tomorrow, if possible."

"I will," answered Elizabeth, "but we'll do all our

9

trading first. We calculate to spend tomorrow at Jeanie's and go home the day after. Don't you want to walk back to Maggie's with us?"

"I'll walk as far as the shop with you," answered Becky. "Then I must hurry home. The old uns will be waiting for their supper."

The two women walked together along the dirt street, visiting as they went. Mary followed leisurely behind. James loaded his panniers on his horses, mounted one of them and rode on ahead. In a short time they were back at the Parade and had passed the log gaol and arrived at Maggie McDonald's shop. Here Becky Armstrong was obliged to leave them, to return to her duties as Keeper of the almshouse, round the corner.

The little frame, one-story building had on one side a small-paned bay window, which bulged into the street and gave a curious lop-sided effect. It was partially balanced by an iron sign, crudely shaped into the form of a teapot, which swung clanking back and forth over the door, as if intent upon giving a blow on the head to any one so bold as to try to pass beneath. Beside the mill-stone doorstep stood a wooden pump, dripping at the spout. Two or three pin-feathery chickens who had been dipping their beaks into the water puddle below, scuttled noisily away.

"*Ting-a-ling! Ting-a-ling!*" The shrill little bell over the doorway of the shop announced the arrival of customers. Mary and her mother ducked under the sign and stepped inside. Maggie McDonald, a brisk young woman with a determined chin and a freckled nose, dropped her knitting and entered from the inner room.

"Marm Clark, is it not? Ah, yes, I remember you well. Are you just come from the country, Marm? And these are your children? Would you relish a cup of tea, Marm?" she inquired politely. "You are tired, no doubt, after your long journey."

Maggie McDonald's little box-like shop was enough to tempt the heart of every country woman who entered, with its gallant array of earthenware, cider mugs and milk-crocks. Behind the counter were boxes and barrels of staple groceries and molasses, and on the shelves above, small notions such as needles, brass thimbles, fishhooks, silver knee buckles and an assortment of herbs and spices. A long rope hung overhead, on which were arranged skeins of linen yarn, linen towels, gloves and mittens taken in trade. A large cheese, partly cut, reposed at one end of the counter, while the other end was graced with a small pair of scales for weighing snuff—that common luxury—by the copper's worth. A pleasant smell pervaded the room, a mingled combination of minty herbs, sweetness and spice.

Sign
of the
Teapot

Maggie McDonald led the way to the cosy parlor behind. On

11

the hearthstone before the fire could be seen several teapots, enough to provide tea for any imaginable number of callers, while an iron kettle boiled furiously on the crane.

"I hope you brought with you some bear's grease, Marm," said energetic Maggie, as she took the baby from Elizabeth's arms and laid her on the bed.

"Yes," said Elizabeth, "and snake root and gingseng, as well."

"They are useful, too," said Maggie, "but I've had so many calls for bear's grease. Great and small, they're all after it alike, from Madame Quackenbush down to poor old Goody Gregory. For general household use, 'tis more highly esteemed than aught else. When I rose from my bed at sun-up, I said to myself, some goodwife from the country will come today and bring me my bear's grease! And now you are here."

Maggie McDonald was a good talker and a fast one. The hot tea was soon brewed and poured and bannocks were brought from the cupboard. No one knew better than Maggie how to win the hearts of her customers and soon she was deep in the intricacies of trade and barter with Elizabeth Clark, while Mary sat and listened, missing never a word.

After tying his horses, James carried in the peltries and provisions. Then dutifully he stirred the hidden depths of several barrels of molasses with a stick, instead of turning on the spigot. After sampling several, he made his choice.

"I'll call for the barrel when we start for Nutfield, Marm," he announced from the doorway. Elizabeth and Mary came forward to hear. "I'll be going up to Master Wiggin's shipyard, now, wife," he added, "to see about the timber, while you and Maggie make up your minds about spices and cream pot and foot-warmer. I'll come back to Jeanie's as soon as I can. Don't forget the foot-warmer."

Elizabeth Clark absent-mindedly nodded her head, but she scarcely heard his words. She saw a row of large pewter plates on the shelf behind the diamond-shaped panes of the little bay window. She picked one up and held it in her hand, as through the open, upper half of the door, she watched James disappear down the street.

Her thoughts were far away. She looked at her daughter Mary as if she did not see her. She was living over again a scene on shipboard, during a storm on the mighty Atlantic. She saw herself, ill and miserable, lying in the crude berth, lashed fast to the wooden sides and watched over by Becky Armstrong—good, faithful Becky. She heard the captain's voice begging them to throw overboard their worldly goods, to lighten the cargo. She saw herself stagger to the rail and cling to it. She saw her two chairs, her trammel and hooks and Hugh's carpenter tools disappear over the side. She saw, as clearly as if it had been the day before, twelve fine, bright pewter plates, large and handsome like this one she held in her hand, twelve pewter plates which had been her mother's parting gift, disappear in the angry waves, one after the other.

"What is it, Ma?" asked Mary, wondering.

"Did you wish a pewter plate, too, Marm?" Maggie

McDonald was speaking. "There's nothing like a pewter plate . . ."

With an effort, Elizabeth came back to the present. "No . . . oh, no . . . I was just thinking. . . . They are exactly like some that my mother had in Ireland years ago." She turned away from the window and now her words came fast: "No, we have no need of them. James took some knots to the dish mill to be turned last week, and we shall have eight or ten new, wooden bowls when we reach home. Come, Mary, we must make haste and go now. Cousin Jeanie will be looking for us."

They bade Maggie farewell and she retired to her interrupted knitting. Elizabeth took the baby in her arms and they walked toward the door, the upper half of which stood open. But the way darkened suddenly and the vast bulk of a large man confronted them. He stood on the mill-stone, but did not come in.

Elizabeth Clark stood hesitating, baby in arms. With her right hand, she clutched her daughter's tightly. She trembled from head to foot, as if the chill of a wintry wave had struck her. The man's face, half-hidden by his long, black wig, was in shadow, his features were indistinct, and yet—there was no mistaking that form, that forward thrust of the neck, that hard gleam of the eye. She remembered the pewter plates again and knew at once who he was. Could a handsome pewter plate be a symbol of ill omen? How came he here and now? She dropped Mary's hand and her eyes sought the floor as she

opened the lower part of the door and tried to pass. She wished for wings to take her away, anywhere— only away.

But the huge bulk blocked her path.

And then the man spoke: "So it's you. We meet again."

Elizabeth Clark let go the door and pulled her hood down over her forehead. "I do not know you, sir," she said. "May I pass?"

"So this is Ocean-Born Mary!" said the man, quietly. "And Mary's mother. You *do* know me—as well as I know you."

There was no subterfuge. She would have to speak —say anything—to get away quickly. "Yes, this is

Mary." She spoke in a low voice to keep Maggie from hearing.

"Does she know?" asked the man.

"Yes, she knows," answered Elizabeth. "Mary, this is the man who saved your life, who saved our lives and your father, Hugh's. Will you thank him?"

Mary had heard the story from babyhood—the story of her birth on the ocean and of her miraculous rescue from death only by unexpected kindness from a black-hearted pirate.

She looked him full in the face and felt no fear.

"Thank you, sir!" she said, simply. "Are you a pirate? I never saw one before."

"Hush, Mary," said her mother, in great distress. "We must go." She held her baby close and once more she tried to pass, but was prevented.

"You have other children?" asked the stranger.

"My husband, Mary's father, died a month after we landed," explained Elizabeth. "A year later, I married again. A woman cannot live in the wilderness without a husband. I have four children besides Mary."

"You are keeping the green silk brocade?" he asked.

Without knowing why she did so, Elizabeth answered, "I am keeping it safe."

She saw the man looking intently at Mary. She pushed him aside with sudden strength and slipped out the door, dragging Mary after her. She was fearful for Mary as well as herself and was greatly unnerved by the meeting.

"Come, Mary," she cried. "We must go."

The Sign of Noah's Ark

Chapter II

THE next morning, Mary was up at sunrise. She
slipped on her clothes quickly and ran outdoors.
She stood on the rocky ledge and looked about her.
On Brimstone Hill, a rocky bluff on the southern
bank of Puddle Cove, stood a group of tiny, one-story
houses huddled together. Here, in the cottage nearest
to the water's edge, high above high-water mark, lived
Jeanie Martin, nearest of kin to Elizabeth Clark, with
her husband, Tom, and her two boys, Jock and Jamie.

The fishing settlement was a large one, well known
the country round. Scattered about, hit-or-miss, as
if thrown upon the shore by the waves, fishermen's
cottages lined the cove on both sides. Narrow criss-
cross paths with colorful names, Horse Lane, Puddle
Lane and Boat Lane, wound in and out. Fish-houses,

wharves and brush flakes crowded the water's edge.
Curious-looking fish-carts with a cask at one end for
a wheel and clumsy, home-made barrows stood about,
while drooping, brown fish-nets hung everywhere
over wooden racks to dry. Great iron kettles under
which driftwood fires had recently burned, stood on
the sheltered side of protruding rocks. The very air
was fishy, an honest reminder of an honest trade.

From the high ledge of Brimstone Hill, Mary looked
about her and felt as if she were on an island, for she
saw water on all sides. A short distance away, at the
entrance to Puddle Cove, she saw Swing Bridge, with
its hoist in the center for allowing large vessels to pass
through. Boats of various kinds were drawn up on

Brimstone Hill

18

the shores or lay at anchor in the cove. And there to the right, lay the Great Bay of the Piscataqua River, dotted with its numerous islands, and the Kittery shore beyond. Mary drew a deep breath. She felt the nearness of the ocean itself as she sniffed the salty tang in the air and listened to the screams of circling gulls.

A steep, winding path at her feet, doing service for stairs, led to the sandy terrace below. Here, on the gently sloping shore, Cousin Tom could beach his boats a few yards from his own door; and, in his own fish-yard, adjoining a fair-sized fish-house and wharf, dry his own fish on wooden flakes. As Mary looked to the left and saw Canoe Bridge stretching across Puddle Cove, little did she realize how familiar and well-worn a path it was to become.

Suddenly she thought of the dark shadows of the forest which engulfed the log cabin at Nutfield. She remembered the dark kitchen, lighted only by the small, greased-paper window. Here, there was light and sun and air. She breathed deeply.

"What are you looking at?" said a voice at her side. Mary jumped, startled. It was Jock, with his milk-pails.

"Oh, the cove and the harbor and . . . everything . . ." answered Mary, unable to explain. "Is Brimstone Hill an island?"

Jock laughed. "Sometimes!" he replied. "When the tide is high, boats can pass from the river into the cove, then into South Mill Pond and out into the river again! Sometimes the horses have to wade through two feet of water to get over Canoe Bridge."

"How far is it to the real ocean?" asked Mary.

"About three miles, I reckon," said Jock.

"Have you ever seen the ocean?" inquired Mary timidly.

"*Have* I?" cried Jock, laughing heartily. "Have I ever seen the ocean?"

Without deigning to give an answer, he led the way to the cowshed. Mary followed and watched him do the morning milking. Then he brought the cow to the margin of the bluff and tied her to a stake to graze on the scant grass between the numerous rocks.

After breakfast, at the fish-house, Jock loaded two baskets of fish onto a barrow.

"Want to go along?" he asked. "I have to deliver fish. First to Marm Cobbett's boarding-house for sailors—that's down on the waterfront—then to the Ark Tavern, to Landlord Drummond. Come along."

Mary needed no second invitation. She flew up the hill to the house and hurriedly fastened her hooded cape under her chin. A moment later she took her place at Jock's side. Across Canoe Bridge they went, then through such devious paths among the fishermen's cottages on the north side of the cove that she began to fear Jock had lost his way. He walked fast, pushing his cumbersome vehicle, whose wheels were made from solid sections of tree trunks. As Mary skipped trustingly along the dirt path at his heels, she plied him with questions.

"When will you take me fishing with you, Jock?" she asked.

"Can you row?" asked Jock.

"No, but . . . I'd like to go out in a boat and catch fish."

"Can you clean a fish?"

"No, but . . ."

"Then you can't go," said Jock promptly.

The heavy barrow bumped up and down over the rough path, but Jock did not stop to rest. He was dressed in a green baize shirt and old cloth breeches. His feet and legs were bare. His skin was reddened by sun and wind, and already he looked the counterpart of his fisherman father.

"Fishing's hard work," Jock went on. "Pa's taken me to the Banks with him for two trips now. I'm a 'cut-tail.' Do you know what that is?"

"No," answered Mary. "Tell me."

"I catch all my own fish," said Jock proudly, "and I cut a wedge-shaped bit from the tail of each one. In the sorting-out and counting-up at the close of the trip, Pa can tell just how many fish I caught. I get my share, just like the men. They call me a 'cut-tail.' "

"Oh!" said Mary, understanding only vaguely.

"That means I'm a real fisherman like Pa," announced Jock.

"Oh!" cried Mary again, duly impressed. " 'Cut-tail!' "

"Come along now, we must make haste!" admonished Jock.

"Oh, but Jock, there's so much to see . . ." begged Mary.

Suddenly they came out on Water Street and to Ocean-Born Mary, on this her first venture abroad, it was a step into a new and exciting world. She walked slowly and looked about, anxious to miss no detail of the busy scene before her. All through the narrow cross streets, the bustle and hum of life was heard. She saw the water-front, lined with wooden warehouses, and a row of wharves stretching out toward the center of the harbor.

Busy sounds met her ear—the blow of the cooper's mallet, the squeak of the timber saw, the shout and laughter of laboring men and sailors. She sniffed the air—a combination smell of tar, new canvas, spices and fish—and liked it. She saw the masts of ships, tall and slim, above and between the buildings, with half-reefed sails fluttering in the wind. She wondered if they had men enough in one vessel to wear all the jackets and trousers which she saw hanging on the ropes to dry. She gazed with wonder at the numerous vessels entering and leaving the harbor, sailing in every direction. Forgetting Jock and his errand, she stood still and looked and the sight was good to her sea-hungry heart.

Upon a wharf near by, there stood a dozen or more hogsheads of molasses, recently unloaded from a vessel arrived from Jamaica. Mary noticed a group of three boys, who had knocked out a bung and were running a stick into the hole and lapping up the molasses.

She ran over to join them. "Could I have a taste?" she asked.

The boys looked up in guilty surprise. "Ho!" cried

one, a tow-head. "Who are you? Where did you come from?"

"Ma—ry! Ma—ry!" called Jock from the distance. "Come along, Mary!"

"Could . . . could I have a taste?" asked Mary again, more boldly.

The boys looked at each other and shrugged their shoulders. They did not answer.

Mary leaned over, took the stick from the hand of one astonished member of the trio, pushed it deep into the bung-hole and pulled it out. Before they realized what she was about, she had put the dripping sweetness into her mouth and had sucked it off. Then she threw the stick down at their feet and ran.

"Ma—ry! Ma—ry!" Where are you?" came Jock's angry shout. In front of the log garrison house by the Town Dock, he stood beside his barrow, waving his arms wildly. He had delivered his fish at Marm Cobbett's boarding-house and come out again. In a moment Mary joined him, panting.

"When you go with me," scolded Jock, trundling his barrow on ahead as before, "you must not lag behind."

Mary said nothing. Down the front of her gown streaked a trickle of brown, sticky molasses which absorbed all her attention. She followed Jock blindly, sucking her fingers as she went. He turned left on Queen Street and soon came to the Ark Tavern at the corner of Ark Lane.

Jock entered by the rear door and delivered the fish to the fat Negro slave, Mammy Chloe, whose head was crowned by a huge turban.

"Who's dat gal?" asked Mammy Chloe, pointing at Mary.

"She's my cousin," answered Jock. "Her name is Ocean-Born Mary. She was born on the ocean."

"Born on de ocean! Land sakes!" cried fat Chloe. "Born on de ocean and still alive an' kickin'! Land sakes!" She looked at Mary as if she were some kind of queer fish that Jock had brought in.

"Can we go in?" asked Jock, pointing to an inside door.

"You sure can," answered good-hearted Chloe. "Here's gingerbread fer you, hot from de oven. Go right in. There's a heap o' sailor men in dere this

24

mawnin'. They come so early, they ain't give me no time to git the floor swept out. There's a painter-man in dere, a-paintin' the tavern sign. You kin watch. G'long in, both o' ye."

Jock pushed open the door which led to the bar-room and entered. Mary followed timidly. A settle had been pushed against the wall. Jock bade her sit on it and say nothing.

The wood-paneled room was dark and clouds of tobacco smoke filled the air. Several men sat at low tables, others stood about talking. Behind the fenced-off bar in the corner, Landlord Drummond was busily occupied, while black Cæsar moved back and forth bringing drinks and taking away mugs and glasses. The buzz and hum of conversation was punctuated now and then by a vicious blow of a fist upon a table or an angry shout.

In a corner by the window two men, young in years, sat at a table. One, with long, black, straight hair reaching to his shoulders, was busily painting a sign for the tavern—a verdant landscape in which stood Noah's ark upon a hill and a procession of fanciful animals about to enter. The second, a hatchet-faced man with eyes well-hidden under a low-hung tricorn hat, juggled pewter mugs with dexterity, keeping as many as five aloft at one time. A crowd gathered round and admiring comments flew back and forth. Jock crept up behind the others in an effort to see.

No one paid attention to Mary. She sat still and munched her gingerbread, completely screened from view by the high back of the settle. She could see nothing but the blank wall and her own feet on the sanded floor. In a few moments her curiosity got the better of her. She began to distinguish the men's words and she wanted to see as well. She stood up on the seat and peeped over the settle's high back.

The juggler and the painter kept looking in the landlord's direction. The juggler put down his mugs and the painter his brushes. The admiring crowd thinned out. The sign was turned so that Mary could not see it. She wondered if the picture was finished. The men seemed to be getting ready to go.

Then Landlord Drummond walked over. "What's that?" He spoke angrily. "A tree or an ark? Do you call that careful delineation?"

"The sign is completed, Landlord Drummond," said the painter. He stood up and made a graceful bow.

"Completed!" raged the landlord. "It is not completed until the ark looks like an ark and the animals look like animals. When you have completed the sign, I will cross off your reckoning on my book, but not before!"

"The light is very bad for painting, today, sir," begged the painter.

"You will not leave your seat until the sign is painted and your reckoning is paid," said the landlord firmly. "If you do, I will send for the constable."

The painter meekly resumed his seat, opened his box and took out his brushes once more. The juggler whispered a few words in his companion's ear and sat down opposite him, with a bored expression on his face. The painter began to paint again.

Mary turned her attention to the other men in the room. Two respectably dressed men at a table near by, were talking in loud voices.

"There are hundreds of gold and silver mines in Mexico and South America," asserted the first, who wore a white wig. "They are owned by the Spaniards and every Spanish ship is laden with uncounted treasures."

"I heard of a Spanish vessel," said his companion, "that was wrecked off the Bahama Islands, sunk one-half mile off the coast. A Boston sea-captain who was owner and master of a small craft, made a voyage to investigate the wreck. He took a goodly lot of gold and when he came home, everybody was eager to go after more of this sunken treasure, eager to pick up more gold from the bottom of the ocean. But alas! He could never find the exact spot again. Dozens of ships have gone down there hunting, but none have been able to find it."

"Bah! There's no such thing as Spanish treasure!" cried a man at the next table who looked like a merchant. " 'Tis these false tales of Spanish treasure which have made the sea unsafe for honest merchants!"

"You're right!" replied the first speaker. "Those fanciful tales are responsible for all our sea-robberies and for all the sea-rovers who have turned thieves and pirates. They all want to get rich by robbing and stealing."

"A man isn't safe to sail his vessel as far as the Gulf of Mexico," went on the merchant. "A pirate-thief suspects him of being loaded with Spanish treasure, sets upon him and plunders his cargo! Spanish treasure! A good excuse for dishonesty, robbery and murder!"

"*My name was Robert Kidd, when I sailed, when I sailed!*" came the merry voice of the juggler from the corner. He and his companion rose and turned the sign to face the room. From her point of vantage, Mary could now see two elephants making their way into the ark, followed by indistinct blobs. Were they bears or cows or what?

The painter laid down his brushes, opened his mouth and with the other men began to sing. All the pirates who had ever frequented the New England coast during the preceding fifty years, became blended in song into one composite type—Captain Kidd, hanged in England for his sins, just ten years before. The words resounded through the paneled room:

" 'My name was Robert Kidd, when I sail'd, when I sail'd,
　My name was Robert Kidd, when I sail'd;
　My name was Robert Kidd, God's law I did forbid,
　And so wickedly I did, when I sail'd.

I'd a Bible in my hand, when I sail'd, when I sail'd,
　I'd a Bible in my hand, when I sail'd;
　I'd a Bible in my hand, by my father's great command,
　But I sunk it in the sand, when I sail'd.

I'd ninety bars of gold, as I sail'd, as I sail'd,
　I'd ninety bars of gold, as I sail'd;
　I'd ninety bars of gold and dollars manifold,
　With riches uncontroll'd, as I sail'd.

Come all ye young and old, see me die, see me die,
　Come all ye young and old, see me die;
　Come all ye young and old, you're welcome to my gold,
　For by it I've lost my soul, and must die.' "

As the song ended, Mary saw the long-haired painter and the hatchet-faced juggler make a dash for the door, leaving paints, brushes and sign behind. Landlord Drummond saw them, too, and started after them.

"Come back! Come back!" he cried, in frantic haste. "The sign is not finished. The ark, the tree, the elephant—they are not finished. You must come back so I can cancel your reckoning!"

He ran to the door, wet-painted sign in hand. But the rogues were gone and he was confronted by a stranger.

"Here, lad," cried Landlord Drummond to Jock, who was standing near. "Fetch those two rogues back and I'll give you a shilling!"

Mary saw Jock run out and the stranger, a large, bulky man, wearing a long, black, curled wig, pass the landlord and enter the room, followed by several sailors. All eyes turned in his direction. He was a striking figure. He wore a long, black broadcloth cape and a red sash draped from shoulder to hip.

The stranger gave one glance about the room and doffed his plumed tricorn with a flourish. He took from his pocket a handful of gold pieces and, with a magnificent gesture, scattered them about the room. The men scrambled eagerly and picked them up. They examined the coins in surprised silence. Then from a corner came a hiss and the single word, "Piracy!"

The stranger took the challenge at once. In a loud voice he defended himself, shouting to the world in general that he had salvaged a wreck from the bottom of the ocean, a wreck full of gold bars and coins.

"Spanish gold!" came the sarcastic voice from the fireplace.

Fascinated, Mary watched the stranger as he removed his cape, found a seat at an empty table and calmly ordered a drink from the Negro slave. The sailors gathered about him and to them he talked. His voice was vibrant and his words seared themselves into the girl's eager mind. She was long to remember what he said.

He talked of his proposed voyage to the West Indies and asked for men to sail with him. He spoke of the dangers from the Algerines in the Mediterranean and pirates of the Spanish Main and boasted of his desire to combat them. With the backing of Governor Belcher and a carefully picked crew, he proposed to exterminate them. He would clean up His Majesty's seas and end piracy forever!

"What about the booty?" shouted a sailor.

"Why, Phil," cried another, astonished, "every one knows what you've been up to all these years. Why . . ?"

"Where did you get them pieces of eight?" cried a third. "Answer me that and I'll believe the rest!"

"Ah, sir!" came the sarcastic voice again from the fireplace. "Your plan is excellent, most commendable! But first, let me put a few questions. When did you arrive in port? What is the name of your ship, good sir? Have you not forgot to declare your cargo to His Majesty's Collector-General of the Port? What have you done with your lutestrings, lemons and tea, on which you paid no duty? Have you perhaps taken a pretty gift to Collector Quackenbush to blindfold his eyes? When are you off to Portugal with your illegal cargo of lumber and naval stores?"

The accusation came swift and sure, without a pause, as an arrow shoots from a tightened bow. That it hit its mark in a tender spot was proven by the uproar which immediately ensued. The stranger called his men upon the accuser at once. A scuffle took place as they rushed to obey.

"Order! Order!" cried Landlord Drummond, returning in frantic haste. "In my house, I must have order!"

Full of fear, Mary dropped down to her seat, out of sight—ready to flee to the kitchen if need be. But sudden silence in the room aroused her curiosity again. She stood up and peeped over the back of the settle.

At last she could see the owner of the scornful voice. He was a small, dark man with a large head—a head which sat with no neck on his high shoulders. He was a hunch-back. His opponents, the sea-captain's men, backed away from him, fearful. He walked out of the room, unscathed. At the door he turned and a single word rolled off his tongue with forceful bitterness: "PIRATE!"

The room was strangely quiet after his departure. No one spoke and gradually, a number of the men, singly and in groups, rose from their seats and left the tavern. The sea-captain sat down and took a drink. Mary suddenly wondered where Jock was. Had he returned or gone away without her? As her eyes traveled hurriedly over the room, they met those of the strange sea-captain, whose words, a moment before, had commanded the attention of all. He rose from his seat and came quickly toward the settle. The girl slipped down out of sight, trembling. The next moment the settle was moved out from the wall and there he stood before her.

"I thought I saw some bright eyes peeping. Is it you, Ocean-Born Mary?" He spoke in a low voice, not without gentleness. "What are you doing here?"

Not until this moment did Mary remember. He knew her name. He was the man that she and her mother had met on the doorstep of Maggie McDonald's shop.

"I came with my cousin," she replied, and her throat was husky and dry. "He's the fish-lad. He had to bring the fish."

"My child," said the sea-captain, "when I saw you

32

here just now, you made me think of my little sister. Her hair was red like yours and her name was Mary, too. She died in England twenty-five years ago . . ."

"Oh, sir, I'm sorry, sir!"

"No matter!" said the captain, hurriedly. "Tell me quickly. Do you live here? And your mother?"

"My home is in Nutfield, sir," replied Mary, "thirty miles inland. My parents live there, but I am staying at Cousin Tom Martin's."

"Tom Martin's?"

"Jock's father," explained Mary. "He is a fisherman. He lives on Brimstone Hill . . . by Puddle Dock, near Canoe Bridge."

"Brimstone Hill, oh, yes," answered the captain. "I will remember. Here is something for you." He put his hand in his pocket and the next moment pressed into her palm three shining gold-pieces. "Don't lose them," he said with a smile.

"Oh . . . sir . . ." cried Mary, overcome with surprise. "I don't think . . ."

The stranger closed her fingers firmly over the coins. "They are for you, Ocean-Born Mary."

"Oh, thank you, sir," cried Mary, filled with sudden happiness.

All her life, the word *pirate* had been a word to dread, a word filled with horror. But here was the very man—the pirate about whom she had heard so often—standing before her, not angry, not sinful, not wicked. Here he stood before her speaking in a kind voice with a gift in his hand. Mary was overcome with relief. Why should she have feared him?

"You're not a pirate any longer, sir, are you?" she cried.

"A pirate!" cried the man, angrily. "Who dares call me a pirate? Did you not hear me say that on my next voyage I go to destroy these outlaws?" Then in a softer tone, he added, "I promise you I am done with all that now. I am a changed man."

"I am glad to know you are an honest sea-captain, sir," said Mary, eagerly. "I hope you will have a good voyage when you sail to the West Indies, sir."

The man looked at her thoughtfully. Then he held out his left hand. On the first finger he wore a heavy, gold ring, richly ornamented with carving.

"Do you see that?" he exclaimed. "That's a magic ring to bring good luck! As long as I wear that ring, I will never go to the bottom of the ocean!"

"I'm glad of that, sir!" answered Mary. But he scarcely heard, for he had turned suddenly and was already making his way out the door. The next moment Jock stood beside her, pulling her arm. He was talking fast.

"I chased those two men all the way to the Town Dock," cried he, "but they got away."

"Did you run fast?" inquired Mary, absent-mindedly.

"Yes, but they ran faster," said Jock. "Now I won't get the shilling that Landlord Drummond promised me."

At the word *shilling* Mary suddenly remembered the gold coins. She opened her hand.

Jock stared. "Wh . . . where did you get those?"

34

"The sea-captain gave them to me," answered Mary. "The one who came in just as you went out."

Jock looked down in astonishment. "Pieces of eight! Spanish gold! Spanish gold! What for?"

Mary did not know how to explain it herself, so she did not answer. All the way home, Jock puzzled his head as to why a strange sea-captain should bestow upon a country girl a handful of gold. To all his excited questions, Mary answered never a word. She closed her lips in a firm line and she clutched the gold-pieces in her hand.

That evening in Jeanie Martin's kitchen, the two families crowded about the table and ate a supper of fish-chowder and potatoes. In one corner of the room, Jeanie lay in her bed, watching all that went on with her bright eyes. In another, deaf old Sandy, her aged father, was weaving at a small loom. He stopped only long enough to take a hasty bite of food and then returned to his work. Jeanie's two boys, Jock and Jamie, gulped their food standing, then sprawled on the hearth, listening to their elders. Jamie whittled out a boat from a scrap of wood, while Jock painstakingly mended his father's fish-net.

"I met a splendid captain at the shipyard today," said James Clark. "Phil Babb—Captain Philip Babb was his name. I sold him my white pine timber for delivery in June, when he sails to the Mediterranean. He let me have a sack of salt . . ."

"Is that his brig Nick Wiggins is building?" asked Tom Martin, from his corner within the shadow of the large fireplace.

"No," said James. "I inquired about that. Merchant McFarland is owner and Anthony Fayerweather is captain and part-owner. A beauty she will be—Nick Wiggin's best."

"A fine ship," added Tom briefly, taking his pipe from his mouth and relighting the tobacco with a hot coal from the hearth.

"Captain Fayerweather?" asked Mary, who was drying the supper dishes at the table near by. "Did you say Captain Fayerweather, Pa? Why, that was his daughter we saw at Spring Hill Market, Ma . . ."

"Hush, child, don't interrupt," said Elizabeth.

The room was quiet for a minute or two, then old Uncle Sandy resumed his weaving with strenuous thumps.

"I went to Cooper Nutley's at Pipestave Cove," continued James. "I got an order for pipe-stave lumber, too. He said this same Phil Babb would be needing them and others as well, so now I'll be busy with more work than I can do."

"Phil Babb!" grunted Tom Martin, shaking his head. "'Pears to me like I've heard of him before and not good, either."

"Do you mean he's dishonest?" asked James.

"Well," Tom went on slowly, "I can't seem to remember just what 'twas I heard, but I reckon he ain't to be trusted."

"Ain't to be trusted?" cried James hotly. "What do you mean, man? He's trusted me with a sack of salt already! What do you mean?"

"Just—what—I—said!" replied Tom slowly and emphatically. "I can't understand why you would sell your timber to a man like that. I can't understand you, that's all! Why you waste all your strength and energy, felling those trees and hauling those logs to feed and warm your family . . ."

"Oh, Tom," cried Jeanie from the corner. "Don't start quarreling the first thing!"

"This New England coast is rocky and won't grow a thing," Tom went on firmly. "The sea is full of fish, to be had for the taking . . ."

"Fish!" shouted James angrily. "You want to make a fisherman out of me, you . . . you . . . you red-faced lobster! A fisherman, bah!"

"James, James," implored Elizabeth. "Do we have to hear this every time we come? Can't we have a pleasant evening once?"

The thumping of the loom in the corner did not stop for a moment, for the old man was so deaf he could not hear a word of the argument. But Elizabeth noticed Mary standing in the middle of the floor as if rooted to the spot, all else but the blustering words of the two men forgotten. She spoke sharply: "Mary! To your work!"

The girl jumped. The wooden bowl in her hands fell to the floor with a resounding thump. She leaned over and picked it up guiltily. Then she went on with her work.

Tom's ruddy face glowed redder than ever in the firelight, as he leaned back and said in a loud voice: "Think of all the good timber you waste! Here, 'thou mayst reap without sowing!'"

"Who wants to?" retorted James. "I love the feel of the earth on my hands, I love the seeds, I love to fell trees, to plow and plant and sow and reap! I hate fishing and always will! I hate the smell of fish, the taste of fish, the sight of fish . . ."

"James! James!" "Tom! Tom!" called the two women.

" 'Tis an honest trade and not without God's blessing," shouted Tom Martin, angrily. " 'Twas the apostles own calling!"

The two boys dropped their work and, like Mary, looked on in silence. They had heard words like these before. Was it only a tiff or was it a real quarrel? *Thump, thump, thump,* sounded the busy loom in the corner.

"I notice you eat plenty of my fish!" shouted Tom, scornfully.

"I notice you eat plenty of my corn!" cried James, with equal scorn.

"And you put a fish in every hill to make your corn grow!" sniffed Tom. "Even the Indians know that people cannot live without fish!"

"That reminds me," said James in a quieter tone. "Can you let us have half a quintal of codfish and half a barrel of mackerel to take home with us? I'll give you an order on Maggie McDonald's shop against those peltries I brought in."

Before he had finished speaking, Tom Martin broke out in a loud roar of laughter which filled the small house, and the quarrel was over. "I told ye so! I told ye so!" he cried, slapping James heartily on the back.

"Come, now," said Elizabeth, bringing a pitcher of cider. She filled two mugs to the brim. "Have a drink."

The two men picked up their mugs sheepishly, drained them, looked at each other and laughed again.

The next morning early, Mary stood on the door-step of Jeanie's cottage and listened to her mother's parting words. Then she waved good-by, as she watched the horses walk across Canoe Bridge, turn a corner and disappear from view. For a moment, she felt bereft and her heart was flooded with loneliness. She picked up her apron and dried her eyes with it. Then she heard Cousin Jeanie calling and ran indoors to obey.

James Clark stopped at Maggie McDonald's for his molasses as he passed through the town. With strong strips of bark, he lashed the two small barrels—fish and molasses—fast to the pack-saddle, one on each side of his horse's back. He tied the sack of salt on top. At Elizabeth's side hung a pannier, well-loaded with store commodities, those things which only the seaport town could supply—spices, snuff, needles and most important of all, a cream pot and a tin foot-warmer.

The horses walked slowly westward along King Street, passed out the stockade gate and disappeared beyond Rock Pasture.

New Friends

Chapter III

JOCK'S fish barrow was a familiar sight in Strawberry Bank. Up and down through the narrow
streets he went two or three times a week, de-
livering fish to regular customers. Every moment that
Mary could spare from home duties she spent trudging
at his heels. Each trip through the town was an exciting adventure.

One morning they stopped in front of the almshouse on Back Street. Jock blew a loud blast on his
fish-horn. *Toot-toot-toot*, it echoed down the street.
"This is where Aunt Becky lives," he announced.
"The old uns eat fish every day."

Mary looked up in wonder at the bleak, two-story
building. Out of the front door clattered a thin-
faced woman with two wooden pails. She hurried 'to

the pump in the roadway, filled her pails and splashed back with them into the house.

"Who's that?" asked Mary, staring.

"That's one of the old women," answered Jock. "Her name's Tilly Jenkins. She's the quiet one."

Two tall sassafras trees in the dooryard were making feeble efforts to send forth green buds in the April sunshine, but the long, dead-topped grass beneath them showed no signs of life.

"Why is she quiet?" asked Mary.

"Because she never has anything to say," answered Jock. "Hetty Atwood's the noisy one. When she shouts for Aunt Becky, you think the roof is coming down."

"Who are the others?" asked Mary.

"Oh, there's Jinny Miller, the queer one, Goody Stubbs and Goodman Bascom, Uncle Rufus and others. They are all poor people who have no homes of their own, so the town lets them live here and sets them to work if they are able. They have to wash their face and hands at least once a day."

The almshouse, one of the few two-story buildings of which Strawberry Bank was able to boast, was built in 1716 and had the distinction of being the first pauper work-house in America or any other country. It stood in a large garden plot, fenced in across the rear by the Town Stockade. A row of granite tomb stones marked the location of a small burying-ground at one side.

Mary followed Jock round the house to the back door. Beyond a huge wood-pile and several sheds, she saw an old man chasing a pig and a flock of chickens. He waved his cane and shouted in a cracked voice. Jock opened the back door and the next moment Mary found herself in the kitchen. The thin-faced woman who had brought in the water pails was now leaning over the open fire, stirring a mixture in a huge pot. The ceiling and walls above hung thick with all manner of iron utensils, drying herbs, peppers and vegetables. A plump, tousle-headed woman sat at a table, peeling turnips. She looked up, recognized Jock and screamed loudly, "Marm Armstrong!"

"She's the noisy one," whispered Jock, nudging Mary's elbow.

Soon Aunt Becky came bustling out. "So Jock brought you along, Mary!" she exclaimed. "Now that you know the way, you must run in often. I mean to keep my eye on you." She emptied the fish into a wooden firkin. "Come into my room for a few minutes. Jock, you run out and help Uncle Rufus catch that pig!"

The almshouse was a busy place. Its halls and rooms smelled of soapy water and cabbage. In rooms bordering on the central hall, Mary saw two women scrubbing floors, two others spinning flax and three old men busily weaving sail cloth. Their thumping looms made a noisy clatter. In another room, several old men were engaged in the useful occupation of picking oakum. Old tarred ropes were being untwisted into loose hemp to be used for calking the seams of ships, to prevent leaking.

Aunt Becky's room was in the little lean-to at the

rear and had two windows looking out on the garden. Aunt Becky sat down in an armchair by the fireplace and motioned Mary to a low ladderback opposite. "How is Cousin Jeanie?" she asked.

"She is much better, Aunt," answered Mary. "She said seeing her own kin-folk made her better at once."

"And have they gone, your Pa and Ma and the baby?"

"They left at sun-up Friday," said Mary.

"Now, tell me this, when is your Pa going to build that new log cabin?" Aunt Becky's voice had a sharp ring, as if she were tired of being patient.

"I don't know, Aunt," said Mary. "He says he has to sell the timber, so he never has any to use himself."

"Bad management, bad management," sniffed Aunt Becky. "James always was a trifle weak. How are the boys?"

"Johnny had tooth-ache and Sammy stomach-ache and . . ."

"And Georgie, what did he have, small-pox?"

"No, Aunt, Georgie was well when I left. But Ma was hoping he wouldn't fall into the brook or run away and get lost or . . ."

"Who's staying with them while your Ma's away?" asked Aunt Becky.

"Sukey Gregg came and Ma says she can trust her, she's so sensible."

"Well, she'll have her hands full a-chasing after those scalawag boys," said Aunt Becky. "Why, last summer when I was at Nutfield, they nearly drove me frantic. I was that glad to come home again to the

Bank, I made up my mind I'd never go away again—not even to see Elizabeth. Now, another thing, what does your Ma mean, a-sending you away from home like this?"

"I . . . don't . . . know, Aunt," answered Mary, taken aback by the suddenness of the question. "She said . . . Cousin Jeanie needed me."

"But do you intend to help Cousin Jeanie all you can?"

Mary stirred uneasily, for Aunt Becky's eyes seemed to look through and through her. "Yes, Aunt," she answered meekly. She thought for a moment, then went on, gaining courage. "Ma knew I wanted to come. Why, Aunt Becky, all my life I've wanted to come to the Bank!"

"You have? Dear me, what for?"

"Why, Pa always talked about it when he came home, and . . . about the sea . . . and the boats . . ."

"And do you like it, now you've come?"

"Oh, Aunt Becky! It's wonderful!"

"What? What's that you say? Wonderful? Tush! What nonsense!" cried Aunt Becky. "One place is as good as another to be in, so see that you mind your duty and take care of poor Jeanie, who can't stir out of her bed. But I've often wondered myself why your Ma went to that God-forsaken wilderness to live . . ."

"Marm Armstrong! Marm Armstrong!" came a strident call from the front hall.

"That's Hetty again. What does she want now, I wonder?"

As Mary rose hastily from her chair, she stumbled over an iron trivet on the hearth. She regained her balance quickly, but as she did so, a clatter of ringing metal was heard.

"Good gracious, what was that?" cried Aunt Becky, in alarm. "I heard something fall. Did you drop something?"

"Yes, Aunt," said Mary, hastily.

Mary saw the three coins roll in different directions, like sunbeams across the sanded floor. She ran quickly from one to the other and picked them up. She held them tightly in her hand, wondering why she had brought them.

"What is it?" asked Aunt Becky. "What are they?"

Mary opened her palm obediently. It was damp and sticky. Upon it lay three gold coins. Their edges were rough and uneven, but the wrought designs upon them glowed with a ruddy brilliance.

"Laws sakes!" cried Aunt Becky, in shocked surprise. "Gold! Pieces of eight! How came you by these?"

A Spanish "Piece of Eight"

showing both sides of coin

Before Mary had time to speak, Jock entered the room without ceremony. "I caught the pig for Uncle Rufus," he cried, "but not until after it had rooted up the cabbage bed." Then he saw Aunt Becky looking at the coins in Mary's hand. "A sea-captain gave them to her," he explained. "A sea-captain at the Ark Tavern, looking for sailors to man his vessel. *He* gave them to her, Aunt Becky."

"Marm Armstrong! Marm Arm—strong!" came the shrill call from Old Hetty again. The tousled head appeared suddenly at the door. "Hit's a gem-man to see yer, Marm."

"I'm coming," answered Aunt Becky, sharply. "I'll be there in a minute. But first let me tell you this, child. Keep away from the water-front. Don't talk to any sailors or sea-captains. Go to Cousin Jeanie's and stay there. Jock, make haste, now, and take Mary home with you. . . ."

The door opened and a gentleman walked in. "She's in there, sir," said Old Hetty, who then closed the door and disappeared.

"Oh . . . good morning, Mr. McFarland!" said

Aunt Becky, regaining her self-possession in a moment. "I'm right glad to see you, I'm sure."

Daniel McFarland, Scotchman, was a person of no small importance in Strawberry Bank. Besides being a wealthy merchant and former sea-captain, he was a member of the King's Council, First Select man of the town and Overseer of the almshouse. His portly form was adorned with plum-colored velvet coat and breeches, his wrists were hung with lace ruffles and his shoes were ornamented with silver buckles.

"I happened to be passing on this fine spring morning," he announced, "so I thought I would look in, Madam Armstrong. I have already made a hasty inspection of the building, while awaiting your leisure. Everything seems to be in order. The inmates are busy, well-fed and contented. The house is spotless to a fault. Your management is excellent."

"Thank you, sir," said Becky Armstrong, with becoming modesty. "If there are any suggestions, I shall be happy to hear them."

"There is one thing, Madam . . ." said Mr. McFarland, with a gentle cough. He reached to his coat-tails, withdrew a silken kerchief and mopped his brow. As he did so, his eye fell on the two children, who stood, waiting respectfully, in the corner. "Ah!" he cried, in some confusion, "I thought . . . we were alone." He looked at Jock and Mary again. "The fisherman's lad, is it not?" he asked.

"Yes, sir, Jock Martin, sir," said Jock quickly.

"But the lass . . . I do not know her," Mr. McFarland went on.

"How fortunate you happened in just now," said

Becky Armstrong. " 'Tis the Wilson child, of whom I have already told you. Her name is Ocean-Born Mary. She was born on the ocean and christened by a pirate, who was kind enough to save not only her life, but the lives of all those aboard, including your humble servant. 'Twas when Mary's parents and I came from Ireland eleven years ago, sir. Each year, on the anniversary of our rescue, a thanksgiving service is held in Nutfield, sir, where most of the passengers of that ill-fated voyage are now living. It is a Scotch-Irish settlement, sir, as you know."

Daniel McFarland looked down at the little girl before him. He saw a child of pure Scotch blood, hair reddish, eyes blue tinged with green, freckled face and determined chin. She was dressed in a striped linsey-woolsey gown, reaching to her toes with a white kerchief crossed over her breast. Her speckled homespun cape hung in loose folds from her shoulders and her hood, falling back, formed a dark halo for her ruddy hair.

The man's eyes studied her fair face earnestly.

"She has a familiar look," he said, with a puzzled air. "Is it possible I have seen her before? Nutfield? You say her family lives in Nutfield and the name is Wilson?"

"Her own name is Wilson, but her step-father's name is Clark—James Clark," replied Becky Armstrong. "He is a lumber man."

"Ah! Clark! Now I remember," said the merchant. "Yes, Clark of Nutfield. 'Twas from him I bought my ship's timbers. I remember it well. I stopped over night in his cabin—'twas nigh two years ago.

48

There was a lovely young woman and a group of small children. Ah, yes, the red hair! How could I forget that? But she has changed in two years—changed and yet she is the same. 'Ocean-Born Mary!' Child of the deep! What a beautiful name! I hope, my child, you will be known by that name as long as you live. God has been very good to you."

"Thank you, sir," said Mary, dropping a curtsey.

The merchant leaned over and took her right hand in his own. "I have a little daughter just your age," he said. "I wish you two might know each other. You are visiting here?"

"She is living with Jock's mother for some time," answered Becky Armstrong. "We expect to see her often."

"My child," cried Daniel McFarland, impulsively, "will you come and see us tomorrow, at four in the afternoon? I want you and Judy to be friends. Can you not come?"

Mary looked from Jock to Aunt Becky, hesitating.

"Why, yes," said Aunt Becky, answering for her. "Cousin Jeanie can spare you for a short time and Jack can show you where Mr. McFarland lives."

"That is splendid," said the merchant. "We will be looking for you."

Mary looked up, trustfully. "I will come, sir," she said.

The next afternoon at four o'clock, Mary appeared at the door of Merchant McFarland's home. A short distance above the McFarland wharf, at the corner of Chapel Street and Graffort Lane, stood the finest

The Home of Merchant McFarland

mansion in Strawberry Bank, a three-story brick building with a gambrel roof and luthern windows. Behind the house was an orchard of apple and pear trees, and a garden where primroses, daffodils and other spring flowers bloomed in profusion.

On the doorstep, black Peter, the Negro slave, was engaged in polishing the brass knocker until it shone. "Did you want to see some one?" he asked.

"Yes, please," gulped Mary. "Mr. McFarland, please."

"Mister McFarland?" asked Peter. "What you want ter see dat fine gem'man for? Hain't got no fish in your pocket to sell, has ye?"

"No—o," said Mary, frightened. She was about to turn and run when the door opened and Merchant McFarland appeared.

"Why, here you are!" he cried eagerly. "I'm glad you did not forget to come, Mary."

To black Peter's surprise, he took the girl by the hand and invited her to come in. Within the great hall, a wide stairway with carved baluster and a polished mahogany rail, led to the rooms above. A clock stood upon the landing, against a brightly colored wall. Mr. McFarland entered a side room, which was enriched with wood paneling on the walls. A group of people were laughing and talking about the Dutch-tiled fireplace.

"Judy, I've brought some one to see you," announced Mr. McFarland.

Judy stopped laughing and came forward. She was a plump girl of thirteen, taller than Mary, with dark hair and rosy cheeks. She wore a handsome short-gown of flowered silk, over an embroidered petticoat, and her sleeves had lace ruffles at the elbows.

"This is the little girl that Madam Armstrong told me of," explained her father. "Ocean-Born Mary is her name, because she was born on the ocean."

"Why, little Mary of Nutfield, you never told me that!" cried a young woman in flowered chintz who stood near by. "I know you already. 'Twas last Market Day I bought the linen of your mother. But you never told me you were born on the ocean."

Standing awkwardly in the middle of the floor with all eyes fixed upon her, Mary heard the friendly words with relief. "Oh!" she cried, looking up and recognizing the speaker, "you are the sea-captain's daughter!"

"Yes, and the sea-captain's daughter's name is Peggy Fayerweather!" laughed the young woman, who looked but little older than young Judy today. Her seventeen years sat lightly upon her fair form and golden hair. "You may call me Peggy. And who do you think this is?"

A ruddy-faced, middle-aged man was pointed out.

"I don't know, Miss," said Mary, embarrassed. All the people were looking at her again.

" 'Tis my father, the sea-captain himself!" cried Peggy, gaily. "The one who took so many voyages!" Every one laughed.

"Oh!" cried Mary, as she made a hasty curtsey.

"Where did you find her, Daniel?" asked the merchant's wife, a dignified, kind-looking woman, dressed in silvery gray.

"At the almshouse, of all places! I knew you would want to see her, so I insisted upon her coming," answered her husband. "I remember her well at Nutfield. She's step-daughter to James Clark, who furnishes my ship timbers."

"What a striking child!" said Madam McFarland softly.

"'Ocean-Born Mary!'" cried Captain Fayerweather. "What a curious name! Was she really born on the ocean? I've heard of others. There was Oceanus, son of Stephen Hopkins, who was born on the *Mayflower* and John Cotton's son, Seaborn, but I never heard of a girl before."

"Well, now you've heard of Mary, Captain," said the merchant. "Besides being born on the ocean, she owes her life to a wicked pirate."

"What! Pirate adventures, too?"

Daniel McFarland told the story of the pirate in a few words.

"But, sir," spoke up Mary, forgetting her shyness, "he's a real sea-captain now. He has a vessel of his own and he's looking for sailors to man it. . . ."

"What! Here at the Bank?" cried the captain.

"We saw him last week, sir," said Mary. "Jock and I saw him at the Ark Tavern and he told me so."

Merchant McFarland looked at Captain Fayerweather and frowned. Both men knew that a great deal of illegal trade was carried on by sea-captains who were clever enough and dishonest enough to evade

His Majesty's laws. They knew that the sea was full of rovers who endangered every voyage of an honest merchant ship, and the long, unexplored and uninhabited coast line offered convenient hiding places for the pirates. The merchants of Strawberry Bank could not have pirates plundering and destroying their ships and what made them very angry was the fact that they did not know whom to trust. They were quite sure that some of their own neighbors were quietly fitting out pirate ships and sending them off after their vessels. It was very difficult to say just who were the thieves and who were honest men.

"What is this sea-captain's name, Mary?" asked Merchant McFarland, sharply.

"I don't know, sir," said Mary, trembling.

"Would you know him again if you saw him?"

"I think I would, sir," said Mary, as her eyes sought the floor.

An uncomfortable silence filled the room. Then Miss Peggy spoke, to relieve the tension: "You should see the beautiful table-cloth I bought from Mary's mother. It is Nutfield linen and Mary and her mother raised the flax and did all the spinning."

"I have often heard of the Nutfield linens," said Madam McFarland, quietly, taking Mary's hand in her own. "Did you weave the table-cloth, too?"

"No, Ma'am," answered Mary. "The women do the spinning and the older men do the weaving. Old Uncle Jemmie at Nutfield does all our weaving. The men used to weave in Ireland and in Scotland before that. All the Scotchmen weave fine linen."

"The settlement at Nutfield is not Scotch, but

Scotch-Irish," explained Merchant McFarland, "about one hundred families, I understand. They are of pure Scotch blood and Protestant, being descendants of a colony which migrated from Scotland to Ulster, Ireland, about 1612. For a number of generations they lived in Ireland, surrounded by the Irish but not mixing with them. They were the heroic defenders of Old Londonderry against the troops of King James the Second. After suffering considerable persecution, this group, Mary's parents among them, came to America ten or twelve years ago. Little Mary here is of good fighting blood, aren't you, Mary?"

"Aye, aye, sir!" cried Mary, laughing.

"Well, Mary," the merchant continued, "in a week or two, I must make a trip to Nutfield, to see about more ship timbers. Your Nutfield trees make the finest ships afloat. If you are homesick for your mother, I'll take you back for a visit."

"Thank you kindly, sir," said Mary.

"The new ship! Oh, Father, that reminds me," cried Judy, beaming. "You interrupted us when you came in just now. We were talking of the ventures we wish to take in the new ship. Do you know what I long for most of all? A little Dutch keeking-glass to see myself in. I was thinking, too, of a new pair of shoes and a pair of new-fashioned silver candlesticks."

"Daughter," answered the merchant, patting her curls fondly, "you may look in the well for want of a mirror. Old shoes may easily be mended and as for silver candlesticks, we have already a goodly store."

"And Peggy wants a little Dutch keeking-glass, too," added Judy, laughing.

"But, ladies," cried Captain Fayerweather, "what is your investment? How will you pay for these luxuries? If, like the other great ladies in the Bank, you make commercial ventures, you must first bring your investment."

"We thought," spoke up Peggy, bashfully, "we would pack up all the discarded snuff-boxes, buckles and glove-strings we could find, pack them in a box and deliver them to the captain of the vessel with orders to sell them . . ."

"And return the proceeds in produce to the best advantage!" laughed her father. "Or, to bring you two little Negro slave girls from the Barbadoes? Is that what you would like, Peggy?"

"No, no!" cried Judy and Peggy together. "Dutch keeking-glasses we wish and . . ."

Just then, black Peter entered the room, announcing new arrivals. Mary looked up and saw two Indians walk in. They were tall, handsome fellows and in their arms they carried the enormous antlers of an elk. Mary recognized them as Nutfield Indians and ran to them at once. "Why, Lean Wolf," she cried, "how strange to see you here!"

The Indian looked at her in equal surprise. "We bring gift to Big Chief," he grunted.

"How are Blackbird and papoose?" asked Mary.

"Blackbird want needle," said Lean Wolf, bluntly.

"She wants a needle?" repeated Mary with a laugh. Then she turned to Madam McFarland. "They're always wanting and asking for things," she explained.

"They make their own needles from a small bone in a deer foot, but they like ours better. Could you spare one, Ma'am? Ma always tries to give them what they want."

"Yes, of course," said Madam McFarland. She sent black Peter to fetch one.

Meanwhile, Standing Elk, the second Indian, had presented the antlers. Merchant McFarland explained: "I've known these two red men for a long time. We've been in the fur trade together for many years. They never fail to make me a present when they come to the Bank. Of course, you've all seen their portraits."

He took the antlers into the hall and pointed out the spot where he expected to hang them. The Indians seemed satisfied, the needle for Blackbird was produced and they took their silent departure. As soon as the door was closed, Judy beseiged Mary with questions.

"We see them often," Mary explained. Then she told of their friendliness, how Lean Wolf had taught her to make sweet-fern brooms and braid osiers for baskets, how Standing Elk often helped her grind corn with the tree-trunk mortar and pestle. They were always hungry, and whenever they stopped in, were given food. Blackbird was a greedy squaw, always demanding something. It seemed strange to see the two men here, in a civilized house, so far from their wild surroundings. And strange, too, to be here herself, thought Mary, so far away from the log kitchen at Nutfield.

The others were listening to what she was saying

about the Indians, but suddenly she choked and could not speak. She stood silent before them and the tears ran, unbidden, down her cheeks. All in a moment she was overcome with homesickness and she wondered why she had left her mother.

Then a plump arm stole round her waist and she was drawn gently out of the room, away from the others, into the hall.

"Come, I will show you something." It was Judy who spoke in a comforting voice. Mary followed up the stairs where she led.

There were gorgeous wall paintings in the stairway. Judy explained them as they looked. There, on a life-sized horse, rode Governor Phipps, first royal Governor of New England. In the corner sat a lady at a

flax wheel, interrupted in her work by a hawk lighting amongst a flock of chickens. Near by was a Scripture scene, depicting Abraham offering up Isaac, with the angel and the ram, and in the distance, a busy city scene.

Mary forgot her homesickness and everything else. She clapped her hands with delight.

"Oh, but I haven't shown you the best part," said Judy, pointing. At the head of the first flight, on the broad space at each side of the stair window were the portraits of two Indians, life size, highly decorated. "Do you know who they are?"

"Lean Wolf and Standing Elk!" cried Mary, in amazement. "Why, they are alive!" The realistic representations filled her with happiness. She touched the wall with her hand.

"They are painted on the wall," explained Judy.

"I know!" cried Mary. "Like the Sign of Noah's Ark at the tavern. A man with long, straight black hair was painting it. Jock and I watched him. Did he paint these, too?"

"No," laughed Judy; "the man who painted these had yellow hair and a queue! I remember him well, though I was only three at the time."

Judy put her arm about Mary's waist again and the two girls laughed merrily.

A Ship from England

Chapter IV

"GOOD news! A sail! A sail! A copper for good news!"

Mary followed at the heels of a group of boys who were racing swiftly through the streets.

"What is it? What is it?" she called. "Jock, tell me, what is it?"

"A sail!" shouted Jock, pointing out to the bay. "A ship from England! It's coming into port and will soon tie up at the dock."

The boys dashed madly on, heading for counting-houses, taverns and shops to spread the news. Long before the incoming ship had reached the Narrows between Trefethren's and Peirce's Islands, the boys were collecting coppers from interested merchants, as the reward for the news they brought.

Mary ran out on a wharf, held up her hand to shade her eyes and looked. Above the cluster of islands, she saw a white-sailed ship approaching—a cluster of top-masts sweeping along, the hulk hidden by dry land. A ship! A ship from England! She ran back to Water Street and hurried north.

"Hear all! Hear all! Hear all!" sounded a thunderous voice, followed by the lusty ringing of a bell. A queer-looking man appeared suddenly round the corner of Queen Street. He was short and fat and had bow-legs. He stopped, took a firm grip on the clapper of his bell and opened his mouth.

Mary stared in astonishment.

The upper part of the man's face folded itself into thick wrinkles, as he shouted: "Hear all! Hear all! Hear all! His Majesty's Commissioner of Imposts announces that the good ship, *Olive Branch*, sent out by the Admiralty to obtain masts, has arrived in Portsmouth harbor, bringing cargo and passengers. She will anchor today at the Town Dock. Hear all! Hear all! Hear all!"

The call was ear-splitting and its effect was immediate. Windows in near-by houses were thrown out with a jerk and heads were thrust forth. Doors sprang open and men, women and children rushed into the street. Every one seemed excited and every one hurried.

Jock appeared suddenly, a copper in each hand.

"Who's that?" asked Mary, pointing toward the man with the bell.

"That's Nicky Newton," answered Jock. "He's

Town Crier. He calls all the news—funerals and auctions, articles lost and found, missing children and things like that. But a ship from England—that's the best news of all!"

"Oh, is it?" cried Mary.

Jock was gone again. She stood for a moment, listening to the Town Crier's voice bellowing loudly down the street. She watched him disappear round the next corner. Then she ran after Jock in the direction of the Town Dock.

Already the wharf was alive with bustle and excitement. From every direction the townsfolk hastened, eager and breathless. A ship from England was the newspaper of the day, for it was the only source of news from the outside world. No one wanted to miss it. Among the crowd were merchants, magistrates, ministers, tradesmen and shop-keepers, apprentices, journeymen and citizens. Backwoods settlers clad in furs and deerskin brushed against elegant ladies in richly embroidered petticoats. All eyes turned expectantly toward the bay.

Mary made her way through the crowd, stepping on buckled slippers and pushing aside stiffly padded skirts. She reached the edge of the wharf and found a wooden post to hold to. She kept her eyes fixed on the white sails which grew larger and larger as she watched.

The great ship slowly rounded the point of Pierce's Island and made its way up the harbor, bearing the English flag proudly on its mast. Several small boats put out from shore to welcome the incoming vessel.

After a long, tedious period of waiting, it drew up to its pier. The *Olive Branch* was a beautiful ship. Her bow crouched low in the water and her stern, elaborately carved and incrusted with gilding, rose high above it.

Mary held her breath as the excitement began. Sailors on deck let loose the windlasses which released the anchor ropes and let the anchor rattle to the harbor bottom. Other sailors threw ropes to those who had already jumped ashore, to make the ship fast to the piles and snubbing posts on the dock. The crowd was pushed back to make way for the cargo and the unloading soon began. Strange-looking, dark-skinned seamen who chattered in foreign tongues, carried forth boxes, bales and bundles or threw them on the wharf in great heaps. Merchants and shopkeepers began to search for their supplies and question shipmaster and mate regarding their orders.

A young sailor brought a pile of bundles and dropped them near where Mary stood. He sang gaily as he worked:

> " 'A sailor's life's a life of woe,
>   He works now late, now early,
>   Now up and down, now to and fro—
>   What then? he takes it cheerily . . .' "

When Mary heard the English words, she peeped out from behind her post. "Did you have a good voyage?" she asked timidly.

The sailor looked up and smiled. "Two storms," he replied.

"Did you meet any pirates?" asked Mary.

"When we were in the Mediterranean Sea, we sighted a ship which our captain took for an Algerine corsair. He put us into a fright and alarmed us beyond reason. But all our fears went for nothing, for the vessel sailed away from us the moment she saw us. Afraid of us, I reckon." The youth shook his head, as he went on: "All the seas are terribly infested. But how do you know about pirates?"

Before Mary could answer, a tall gentleman who had suddenly appeared beside her and who had overheard her questions, spoke up sternly: "Child, why are you idling here?" His eyes were unfriendly and his tone was harsh. "A lass of your age should be occupied. Have you no knitting? No spinning to do? A lass is very idle who cannot spin a thread to catch a fish. Are you not ashamed to waste your time upon a public wharf?"

"Yes, sir," said Mary, as she curtsied politely.

"Go to your home at once, lass, and let me never see your face in a public place again."

"Yes, sir," answered Mary, with another curtsey.

She looked at the sailor who stood listening behind the strange man's back. The sailor winked at her, then started whistling loudly as he continued his work. Mary walked away through the crowd.

She knew the reprimand was deserved and she felt guilty, but the sailor's wink gave her courage. She remembered what Jock had said: "A ship from England—that's the best news of all!" This was her first opportunity to witness the arrival of a ship from England and it seemed a shame to go home. Cousin Jeanie had been much better in the morning; in fact, she was up and dressed. A huge pile of barrels beside the frame warehouse offered a solution. Mary crept behind them. It was a perfect hiding place.

Two men were talking near by. Mary listened with interest.

"Do you see the tall, dark man over there with those sailors?" asked the first, pointing to the man who had just spoken to Mary. "Do you know who he is?"

"Yes," answered the other. "That's the Honorable David Dunbar, Lieutenant-Governor of New Hampshire. And I know what they are unloading, too.

The gifts from Queen Caroline for the new Queen's Chapel. I hear that the Queen has sent two Bibles, a silver christening basin and two handsome mahogany chairs for the Governor's pew!"

"Yes," retorted the first, sharply. "Trappings of royalty! Why are the Governor and the Lieutenant-Governor better than honest men? Why should they sit in a pew raised above the rest? Why should they have red plush curtains festooned above them, bearing the royal coat of arms? Are they so much better than ordinary men?"

"But, surely we owe allegiance to our mother country," said the first. "I believe . . ."

The two men moved away and Mary heard no more. After a short interval, she saw the Lieutenant-Governor himself leave the wharf, followed by several well-laden retainers. She came out again into the open, breathing freely.

She was just in time to see the passengers disembark from the *Olive Branch*. A murmur of admiration arose from the crowd as a distinguished gentleman stepped ashore. He was followed by three men-servants in elegant livery, weighed down with many bundles. Mary forgot the Lieutenant-Governor and his reprimand in this new excitement. She listened to the whispers of the people: "A nobleman, indeed!" "A wealthy aristocrat!" "Whom can His Lordship be seeking in Strawberry Bank?"

Mary stared with the others. She had never seen such fine garments before. The stranger wore a gold-laced coat of purple velvet, a long embroidered waistcoat, scarlet breeches and silk stockings of snowy white. Upon his powdered wig was perched a gold-laced hat, adorned with a sweeping plume. His delicate fingers, hidden beneath a shower of lace ruffles at his wrist, grasped firmly a gold-headed cane. He held his nose aloft, as if to breathe the purer air above.

The little procession left the dock and moved slowly up Water Street. Mary hurried along in front of the crowd. The distinguished stranger approached a large mansion-house at the head of the docks. Mary knew it was the home of Captain Fayerweather and Peggy. He ascended the steps and tapped the brass knocker smartly. In a moment the great front door was opened by unseen hands and His Lordship disappeared within. The people stood about gossiping, reluctant to go. Mary listened.

"Captain Fayerweather is receiving a distinguished caller today!" a voice was saying. "His name is Lord Peabody. He is betrothed to the Captain's daughter."

"What!" cried a woman, whom Mary recognized as Maggie McDonald of the Sign of the Teapot. "She's only a child. His Lordship must be forty if he's a day."

" 'Tis true, 'tis true!" repeated the first speaker. Mary pushed forward and saw that he was the hunch-backed man whom she had seen at the Ark Tavern. His voice, as he went on, had the bitter tone which she remembered so well. "A sea-captain who travels over the face of the globe, may pick and choose for his daughter."

Maggie McDonald shook her head, as if unwilling to believe what she heard.

"Is it true, Marm McDonald?" asked Mary, anxiously, at her elbow.

"Law sakes, you startled me, child," answered Maggie. "I hope it is not true, but Master Pecksniff usually knows whereof he speaks."

Mary looked into the man's face, which because of his hunched shoulders was but little higher than her own. His black hair was drawn tightly into a queue, his dark eyes darted about eagerly as if anxious to miss nothing. His nose was long and pointed. He stared at her angrily as if he resented her interruption. Then, ignoring her completely, he continued his conversation with the shop-keeper.

"A goodly store of drugs has the *Olive Branch* brought," he said; "rhubarb, wormseed, senna, mace, cloves, pepper and alum; also plants, seeds and roots enough to cure every ache and pain in the Bank."

"Ah, Master Apothecary," exclaimed Maggie. "What would we do without Old England? 'Twas a long list of things I ordered for my shop—silver and pewter ware, buttons, pots, candles, hardware, ironware and window glass! Now my customers may no longer complain that my supply is low."

The two parted at the corner. Maggie McDonald turned up Graffort Lane, followed by several men, trundling her merchandise in barrows, while her companion walked on alone.

"Hunch-back! Hunch-back!" cried a group of

boys, darting out from behind a building. "Poke-Nose, Peck-sniff, Poke-Nose!"

The ill-shaped man turned and faced them resentfully. The boys retreated, throwing stones in his direction.

Mary followed at a safe distance. Master Pecksniff! Master Pecksniff! She said the name over and over to herself. The hunch-back was Master Pecksniff. He kept the apothecary shop. He sold drugs and medicines to make people well. After the boys had disappeared, she walked behind him a few paces, wondering at his queer shape and ill-natured voice.

Master Pecksniff approached his shop, a small building with a bay window in front. A sign swinging at one side showed a painted mortar and pestle. A ladder stood propped over the window and a man stood near the top. Mary drew nearer to watch. He held a carved wooden head, which he was screwing to a wide ledge.

Master Pecksniff watched, too. He rubbed his hands together and whispered pleasant words to himself: "Ah ha! Hippocrates—my lord and master—the great Greek physician and apothecary—what a hero to emulate!"

The man on the ladder was youthful and had a friendly smile. He looked down eagerly. " 'Tis a good likeness of the great Hippocrates, is it not?" he inquired, addressing Master Pecksniff. "You are pleased with my carving, are you not?"

Mary looked at the apothecary. How could he help but be pleased? The carved head looked very handsome above the window. How wonderful that this young man could carve a life-like head from a log of wood! She waited for the apothecary to speak.

But he did not answer the carver. He continued to rub his fat, stubby hands together, staring ahead as if he saw and heard no one, muttering to himself. He stepped forward suddenly toward the door of his shop, laughing and chuckling. He jostled against the sloping ladder. The ladder slipped, tottered for a moment and fell with a noisy clatter. It knocked into the bay window and brought down a shower of broken glass.

"Oh!" cried Mary, putting her hand to her mouth. There lay the young carver, helpless on the ground, his right foot under the ladder. She stared at him, speechless.

"Hey! Hey! Who's making all the noise down there? Ye're not Indians, be ye?" shouted a shrill, cackling voice.

Mary looked up and saw a thin-faced woman leaning out of an upper window. She wore a ruffled night cap, which flopped up and down over her forehead, and she gesticulated with long, skinny arms which were bare to the elbow.

Mary looked at the apothecary, vaguely expecting help. Still laughing and chuckling, Master Pecksniff had opened the door of his shop and was about to enter. Then he turned and looked at the awkward scene of his own carelessness. Instead of offering to help, he pointed to his broken window and advanced, shaking his fist.

"You have broken my window!" he shouted. "You have broken my window!"

Mary ran to the carver and bent over him. "Are you hurt?" she cried anxiously. She lifted the ladder off and helped the young man to rise.

"Not badly," he said in a low voice.

"Be ye Indians? I say, be ye Indians?" cackled the old woman from the upper window. "Why don't ye go away and leave us in peace? Be off with ye, be off with ye! Shoo—oo!"

"If you please, Master Pecksniff," began the carver, quietly, "the charge for carving the head of Hippocrates is one pound, ten shilling. . . ."

"The charge, indeed!" shouted the apothecary, furious with anger. "Look at the glass you have broken! English window glass from London! Broken to a thousand bits! One pound, ten shillings, eh? Well—wait till you get it!"

Master Pecksniff entered his shop and slammed the door behind him. The casement window above also closed with a sharp thud. Mary and the carver were left alone in the street.

"Oh, sir," cried Mary, "won't he pay you what he owes you?"

"It appears not," said the carver sadly.

"Perhaps he will change his mind," suggested Mary, "when his anger has had time to cool."

"Perhaps," said the carver.

"May I help you, sir?" asked Mary. "Lean on my shoulder and I will take you wherever you wish to go."

"You are very kind," said the young man. "My

shop is only a short distance—down on the water's edge. If I walk slowly, I think I can manage. I shall try not to lean on you too heavily."

"Never mind that, Master . . . but I do not know your name, sir."

"Greenwood," said the young man, smiling, "Nathaniel Greenwood."

"Do not hesitate to lean on me, I beg of you, Master Greenwood," repeated Mary. "I am very strong."

"Are you, Miss . . . ? But I do not know you, either," said the carver. "I have not seen you before. I should have remembered the color of your hair."

"Mary Wilson, sir," said the girl, looking downward, "though sometimes I am called Ocean-Born Mary."

"'Ocean-Born Mary!' How came you by that name?"

As Mary explained, she found Master Greenwood an agreeable person to talk to. She liked the way the wrinkles danced about his eyes when he smiled. She noticed that his green cloth coat was patched and his sleeves were worn into holes at the elbows.

By slow stages, limping painfully, Master Greenwood reached his shop with Mary's help. They crossed a wharf and entered a small log building. Mary helped Master Greenwood to a chair. She followed his directions, built up his fire and heated some water. Then she tore some cloths into strips, bathed and bound up his sprained ankle. Not until he was resting comfortably did she look about the shop.

A rear door stood open, overlooking the water. From where she stood, a ladder descended and a small boat was moored below. She saw the *Olive Branch* and other boats and ships at near-by wharves.

Within, the floor was deep in shavings and chips, which formed a soft carpet for the feet. Great blocks of wood of various shapes leaned against the walls. Several carved ornamental pump-heads and wooden urns for gate-posts and doorways sat about the room. On the carver's pine work bench in the corner, lay an array of tools—chisels, gouges and mallets.

"Look in the corner there, Mary," said the carver. "Take off that covering and see what is beneath."

Mary did so and a row of carved wooden figures met her gaze. Some were men and some were women and a few were animals. Mary felt the soft wood and followed the shapes with her hands.

"They are beautiful," she said. "They are alive!"

"Ah! You love them too! Just as I do!" said Master Greenwood with a pleased smile.

"I've seen logs in Nutfield all my life," said Mary, "but I never knew there were people living in them until now."

"Yes," answered the carver, "the shape of the log determines the character of the figure. And the opposite is also true. When I decide to make a certain figure, I must search for the log. I must find exactly the right log. No other will do. Sometime when I am carving, you must come and watch me."

"When your ankle is well again," added Mary. She looked about the room, puzzled. "But where do you eat and sleep? You don't live here?"

"No," said the carver. "I live across the way at

72

Marm Cobbett's boarding-house for sailors. I'll call one of the boys as they pass to help me over, so don't worry about that. I went to Master Wiggin's ship-yard yesterday and saw a new ship a-building," he went on. His pale face lighted up with the joy of remembrance. "Ah! What a beauty she is! How I would love to carve a figure-head for her prow!"

"Was it Merchant McFarland's?" asked Mary.

"Yes," said the carver, "and Captain Fayerweather is the master, I hear."

"I know his daughter, Peggy!" exclaimed Mary.

"You do?" asked the carver, eagerly.

"Yes," answered Mary. "And Judy McFarland, too. I go with Jock sometimes when he takes fish to their homes."

"Could you bring Miss Peggy to see me sometime . . . I mean to watch me carve?" asked Master Green-wood.

Mary suddenly remembered the great English lord who had called at the Fayerweather mansion and the rumor which coupled his name with Peggy's. She hesitated, realizing that she had only the slightest ac-quaintance with Peggy.

"I could . . ." she answered slowly, "but I do not know when I shall see her again."

"I just thought . . . she might possibly . . . be in-terested in wood carving," said Master Greenwood.

"Oh, yes, I am certain she would be!" answered Mary, with assurance.

"And now," said the carver, "before I forget, there

73

is a little girl whom I want you to visit. Do you know the Sign of the Teapot?"

"Oh, yes, sir," cried Mary. "That's Maggie McDonald's."

"The log gaol is just this side of the Teapot," explained the carver. "The little girl's name is Susannah Winslow. Her father is the gaoler and they live in the wing at the side. She has only a few friends and has been ill for many weeks. She grows lonely staying in bed all day long. Will you go and see her?"

"Yes, sir," said Mary. "I can stop in sometime when I go to Maggie's."

As the setting sun dropped behind the darkened roofs of the town, Mary opened the door of the little shop.

"You won't forget to come back and see how my ankle is getting along, will you, Mary?" asked the carver.

"I'll come every day until it is well," answered Mary.

"And after that, too?"

"Yes, after that, too."

Good, Strong Bed-Cords

Chapter V

MARY stood by the well in front of the alms-house. She set her filled pail down with a splash. She leaned against the pump, dreaming lazily. It was a warm, sunny afternoon in late May.

She thought of the new bed she was to have at Cousin Tom's. A real bedstead, made of wood, with bed-cords laced across to hold the straw-tick and coverings. It would be more comfortable than sleeping on the hard floor. She had started out at noon with a bag of spun thread. Cousin Jeanie's instructions were to take it to Master Griggs' ropewalk and exchange it for bed-cords. It was a delightful errand, for it meant a long walk through the center of town and all the way out to North Mill Pond.

Mary made several calls along the way. She stopped at the Ark Tavern kitchen to get a piece of fresh gingerbread from Mammy Chloe. She stopped in at the Sign of the Teapot to bid Maggie McDonald good day. Here she left her bag while she ran over to see Aunt Becky for a minute. But she had not been able to leave the almshouse as soon as she expected. Uncle Rufus had a fever and Tilly Jenkins was down with lumbago. Aunt Becky was short of help, so Mary was immediately set to work. Water had to be carried, floors had to be scrubbed and various errands done.

Mary was filling the water pails one at a time. She sat on the edge of the watering trough and looked down. She forgot the new bed and the bed-cords as she looked at the reflection of her face in the water. The bottom of the wooden trough was dark, spotted here and there with green moss. Mary had never thought of her looks before. She was surprised to see how brightly her eyes sparkled in the dark, clear water. She pursed her mouth, opened it and smiled broadly, to study the changing reflections. How wonderful it would be to have a tiny little mirror—small enough to carry wherever she went! She thought of the little Dutch keeking-glass that Judy had talked about.

"Ma—ry! Ma—ry! Come here at once!" Aunt Becky called, but her words fell on deaf ears.

Mary put out her tongue and made faces at the water. She thought of Peggy and Judy and their ship's ventures. It was a long time since she had seen Judy. She wondered when the merchant's new ship would be built and ready to sail.

"Ma—ry! Ma—ry!" came the call a second time. Aunt Becky could call almost as loud as Hetty Atwood, the noisy one.

Mary heard the call clearly. She came back to life with a start. She stooped to take up the water pail at her feet. On the ground beside it, she saw a small object, beautiful and shining bright. She picked it up. When she brushed off the mud, it shone brighter than ever. It was a little oval box of silver, with an engraved design on the top. Mary lifted the hinged cover. There was nothing inside.

"Ma—ry! Ma—ry!" came the call again, more impatiently this time.

Mary grasped the silver box firmly in one hand and the pail in the other. She hastened into the house.

"Mercy on us, lass!" exclaimed Aunt Becky. "If we always had you to bring water for our tea, we'd die of thirst." She took the pail from her. "Now, heed," she went on. "Go to the barn and saddle old Tibby. I'll help you load on those sacks of grain. Ride out to the windmill and ask Uncle Job Watkins to grind the corn. Make haste. We need some meal for hasty pudding and I want you to scrub the hall floor before you go home."

A few moments later Mary rode out King Street into the Highway, astride the almshouse nag. Crippled in one leg and lacking a shoe, the animal moved with a curious, lop-sided motion. Through the stockade gate the horse hobbled along and entered Rock Pasture. She followed a well-worn path through the tall, uncut grass to the hill where the windmill stood. A strong wind was blowing and its huge arms were circling steadily.

"Hey! I'll help you there, wait a minute!" A tow-headed boy bounded over the field from his seat on a huge rock, where he had been watching a herd of cows. He lifted the sacks down and carried them into the mill. He came out in a few minutes and sat down on the stone doorstep. His hair was long and unkempt and his nose was covered with freckles.

"Uncle Job," he pointed backwards with his thumb, "he's the miller. He'll take care of it."

Mary looked at the boy and remembered she had seen him before. Promptly she sat down beside him. "What's your name?" she demanded.

"Joey Moseley," said the boy, eyeing her sharply. "What's yours?"

"Mary Wilson," answered Mary.

The boy glared at her. "*I* know," he said, in an accusing tone. "'Twas you stole a lick of molasses off the stick that day on the wharf."

"Yes," answered Mary, complacently. "I like molasses."

"Where do you come from?" asked Joey.

"I live at Jock Martin's. Do you know him?"

"The fish-lad? Yes."

"Are those your cows?" asked Mary.

"The town's," answered Joey. "I'm cow-herd."

"Oh!" exclaimed Mary. "Are you supposed to be watching them?"

"Well," answered Joey, slowly, "I've trained my dog to do that. His name's Frisky. See him over there?" Mary nodded. "If one of those cows sets foot out of Rock Pasture, Frisky goes after 'em and brings 'em right back."

"What do you do?" demanded Mary.

"Oh, I just sort of keep one eye on Frisky, in case she forgets," explained Joey. "You see, I'm a town officer, appointed by the First Select man. I get two shillings a season for each cow. That's because I'm cow-herd."

"You do?" asked Mary, in surprise. "How many cows are there?"

"Twenty, sometimes more."

"Why, that must be a lot of money," said Mary. "What do you do with it all?"

"Nothing," said Joey, crossly. "They usually pay it in corn and my mother feeds it to the family."

"Have you a family?" asked Mary.

"Nine children," said Joey with a frown. "Jim and John and I go out to work every day and that leaves six little ones. And one cow. That's her over there, the spotted one. Dandelion's her name. She lives in one room and we live in the other."

"Do you like having so many brothers and sisters?" asked Mary, thinking of her own in Nutfield.

"Too many," said Joey, briefly. "I don't like being cow-herd, either. That's why I let Frisky do most of the work."

"I saw you at the dock when the *Olive Branch* came in," said Mary. "Was Frisky taking care of the cows for you then?"

"Yes," answered Joey. "There's nothing to see out in Rock Pasture and I get tired. Once in a while I have to go down to the wharves to see what is going on. I like water better than land. I'd rather ride in a boat than on a horse."

"So would I," added Mary, softly.

"You?" asked Joey, contemptuously. "Girls can't go away to sea."

"I don't care," asserted Mary. "I've always lived in the woods and I'm tired of it. I like the ocean better."

Joey was thoughtful for a moment, then he changed the subject. "Do you know what I saw one day, while I was sitting right here, doing nothing?"

"No," answered Mary. "I thought you said nothing happened."

"Well, one time, something did," exclaimed Joey. "I saw Governor Belcher come up the King's Highway! Right up the Highway over there as plain as day. He rode all the way from Boston. He's Governor of the provinces of Massachusetts and New Hampshire. Did you know that? The roads are so bad for traveling, he can come only about once a year. You never saw so many fine horses and men ride together. They trotted two in a row before and after the Governor. *His* horse pranced the liveliest of them all. And all the men were dressed in splendid clothes with gold lace and plumes. It was worth being a cow-herd to see it. You never saw anything as fine as that, did you?"

"I saw an English lord who came over on the *Olive Branch*. He wore gold lace and plumes, too . . ." began Mary.

"But he's not the Governor!" ejaculated Joey. "Why, even Lieutenant-Governor Dunbar isn't half as grand as Governor Belcher. I'll tell you something. Everybody, even Dunbar, is afraid of Governor Belcher."

"Are they?" asked Mary. "Why?"

"Because whatever he says they have to obey. Lieutenant-Governor Dunbar has to obey, too, though he doesn't like to."

"I don't like Lieutenant-Governor Dunbar," said Mary.

"Do you know him?" asked Joey, staring.

"Yes," said Mary, "all I want to know."

"What's that in your hand?" asked Joey, suddenly.

Mary opened her fingers and displayed the silver snuff-box.

"Oh!" cried Joey, astonished. "Where did you get that?"

"I found it by the well in front of the almshouse," said Mary.

"One of the paupers must have lost it!" laughed Joey, kicking up his heels. "No," he added, seriously, "it must have belonged to some fine gentleman." He turned it over and handed it back. "What are you going to do with it?"

"I'll keep it till I find the owner," said Mary.

Just then, Uncle Job, the miller, brought out the sack of meal and loaded it on the back of patient old Tibby. Mary mounted and rode away. Joey stared after her, puzzled. Then he ran toward the large rock, climbed nimbly to the top, stretched out on his stomach and began lazily counting the cows.

Old Tibby, besides being lame and unshod, was nearly blind. But she knew her way to the windmill and back as well as if she could see. At the corner of King Street and Back Street, Mary slipped down to the ground, gave the horse a few slaps and cried, "Go home, Tibby, go home!"

Tibby turned the corner as obediently as if she had had a rider. Mary watched until she saw the horse turn into the almshouse yard. She decided that the bed-cords needed immediate attention. She had not forgotten Aunt Becky's last words. She knew it would be more fun to visit a ropewalk than to scrub floors.

With Tibby and the bag of meal safely out of sight, Mary felt free again. She looked at the silver box in her hand. Its beauty gave her a comfortable feeling.

She started leisurely in the direction of the Parade. As she passed a small, one-story house, its front door burst open and half-a-dozen children came running out. They all had tow-heads and blue eyes.

"Give it back! Give it back!" they shouted, as they chased the smallest of their number.

This agile infant, whose age could not have been more than three, ran at once to Mary, looked up with a glance of complete confidence and hid himself in her full-gathered skirts.

"Whatever is the matter?" asked Mary.

"He took our piece of cheese," said a six-year-old girl. "Ma said we were to divide it."

Mary pulled the infant from his hiding-place and asked to see the cheese. The grimy little fingers opened, revealing a piece so small as to hardly deserve the name. Mary had had plenty of experience dealing with situations of this kind. She counted heads. "One, two, three, four, five, six! But if we break it into six pieces, there will be only a crumb for each. Why not let baby . . ."

"His name is Ichabod!" said the somewhat larger sister.

"Why not let little Ichabod have it?"

No sooner was the decision made than the infant popped the cheese into his mouth and a chorus of howling protests rose from

the others. A frowsy-haired woman, with a bedraggled apron and a worried look, rushed out of the house,
scolding. She carried a switch in her hand, and at the
sight of it, all the children disappeared as if by magic.
The woman vanished, too, and the door closed behind
her. Mary was left standing alone in the path. It had
all happened so quickly that she laughed to herself.
Then she remembered the bed-cords again.

She crossed the street, went into Maggie McDonald's
shop on the corner and came out with her bag of
thread. She stood before the window for a few moments, her nose pressed against the glass. The pewter
plates were gone now and the window was filled with
a display of buttons, laces and English woolens.

Mary walked on, absent-mindedly. She was about to
pass the log gaol next door when she remembered the
words of Master Greenwood, the carver, and her promise to visit the little sick girl. This was as good a time
as any. The bed-cords could wait.

Although she had passed it many times, Mary had
scarcely noticed the gaol before. She looked at it now
with interest. It was a strongly built log building, a
story-and-a-half high, with a wing at one end. Its
thick, oaken door was studded with heavy nails and
its tiny windows were darkly hidden behind mill-saw
gratings. Mary wondered if any criminals were con-
fined within, but she saw no signs of life. The carver
had said that the gaoler's family lived in the wing, so
she approached the side door and knocked timidly.
She dropped her bag on the doorstep.

No answer came. She knocked again. After a few

moments, she turned to go. Then the door opened and a sad-faced woman asked her to come in.

"Susannah . . . Susan—nah," she stammered, feeling strange.

"Susannah is in here," said the woman kindly. "Come and see her."

A little girl of ten years lay in a curtained bed which almost filled the room. Her face was very pale, and her golden hair was outspread over the pillow. Her hands lay listlessly on the cover-lid but her eyes brightened considerably as she looked up.

"Here is a little girl to see you, Susannah," said Marm Winslow. She left the two girls together and went back to the kitchen.

Mary and Susannah were friends at once, as soon as the name of Master Greenwood was mentioned. Susannah brought out a wooden monkey on a stick which he had carved for her. Then she began asking questions. Before Mary realized it, she was telling how she happened to come to the Bank and all the adventures she had had there. Susannah felt, after listening, as if she had done the same things herself. Her eyes glowed with a fresh brightness and she smiled happily.

Mary then told about the little children at the house on the corner and their piece of cheese.

"They are the Moseleys," laughed Susannah. "There are nine of them all together and they are always getting into some sort of trouble."

"Moseley?" inquired Mary. "Is there one called Joey, who is cow-herd?"

"Yes," said Susannah. "Their father is a very jolly

man, always laughing and joking. He is a ship's carpenter at Master Wiggins' shipyard. Jim is apprenticed to a joiner and John to a ropemaker, while Joey is cow-herd. The little boys are Jacob, Josiah and Ichabod and the little girls are Mercy, Patience and Thankful. They come to see me every day. I don't know what I should do without the Moseleys."

The girls were laughing cheerfully, when Marm Winslow entered with a bowl of hot broth.

"Madam McFarland came with a basket of good things yesterday," Susannah explained, after taking a sip. "Broths and jellies and bannocks and other things. She has a daughter, Judy . . ."

"Oh, Judy is my best friend!" cried Mary.

And now the two girls had another bond between them. They both knew Judy and loved her. They talked of her for awhile, then Mary showed Susannah her new-found treasure, the silver snuff-box. The sick girl took it in her thin hands and rubbed her finger over the engraving. "It is beautiful," she said.

A sharp knock came at the door and Susannah trembled. She thrust the silver box hastily into Mary's hands. She heard her mother open the door.

"Oh, Mary!" cried Susannah, drawing her close. "It is Master Pecksniff and I am afraid of him."

Mary put her arm about her. "Do you mean the apothecary?" she asked.

"Yes," whispered Susannah. "Father wants him to come to make me well. He gives me bad-tasting medicines and I always feel worse after he's gone away."

"There! there!" soothed Mary. "Perhaps he'll see

how much better you are today and not give you anything."

Before she had finished speaking, the hunch-backed man entered the room, carrying a black leather bag, followed by Susannah's mother. He was talking briskly about the recent arrival of new drugs from London.

Master Pecksniff saw Mary at once. "Who are you, lass?" he asked, glaring.

"Mary Wilson, sir," answered Mary, with a curtsey. The sound of his voice made her heart start beating quickly. She wondered if he remembered their former meeting.

"Where do you live?" he asked, gruffly.

"At Tom Martin's, sir, at Brimstone Hill."

"The fisherman's?"

"Yes, sir."

"What are you doing here?"

"I . . . I . . ." stammered Mary, quite unprepared for the question.

"The little girl just came to visit for half an hour, sir," explained Marm Winslow.

The apothecary was thoughtful for a moment, resting his chin in his palm, studying Mary intently. Then he turned to Marm Winslow: "May I suggest, Marm," he said in a decided tone, "that your daughter have no visitors after today?"

"But, Master Pecksniff," protested Marm Winslow, "I cannot see that it does Susannah any harm to talk to a little friend. It might even help her to forget that she is ill."

"Your daughter," said the apothecary, "is too ill to have visitors." The apothecary turned to Mary and asked, sharply, "You would not wish to make Susannah worse, would you?"

"Oh, no, sir," cried Mary, in distress.

"Very well, then, you may go."

Looking back over her shoulder, Mary saw tears in Susannah's eyes. She bade her and her mother a hasty farewell, and hurried out. She closed the door softly behind her and picked up her bag from the doorstep. She wondered how her visit could possibly have done Susannah harm. How could such a man, even if he were a doctor and knew all about mixing medicines, make a sick child well? The memory of the carver's accident came back to her with sudden force. Did Master Pecksniff delight in hurting people?

Then she remembered the bed-cords again. She

turned up Vaughan Street and ran, her skirts flying.
Soon she reached Master Griggs' establishment.

She stood on the doorstep, reluctant to go in. The
buzzing of saws and the pounding of mallets reached
her ears. There was the shipyard nearby on the water's
edge, with the new ship a-building. She wanted des-
perately to go and see it, but she thought of the bed-
cords again. She had put them off too long already.
She promised herself that she would run into the shipyard for just a moment, but first she must get the
bed-cords. She opened the door.

The ropewalk where ropes were made was a low
building, nearly one thousand feet in length. Long
ropes required plenty of room for laying and spinning.
As Mary entered the door at one end, the building ex-
tended so far away from her that the men at the
opposite end looked as small as ants. The whirling of
the wheels filled the dusty room with a drowsy, hum-
ming sound.

Mary looked about her with interest. A circle of
men and boys sat in a corner hackling flax and hemp
by combing the fiber straight over a board, studded
with sharp, steel teeth. They talked and laughed together as they worked. Mary approached them, but
they appeared not to notice her.

She saw two rope-spinners going down the long

Master Griggs'
Ropewalk

walk together. They had bunches of hemp wound round their waists, the ends of which were attached by hooks to the wheel near where she stood, which was being turned by an apprentice. The two men walked slowly backwards, away from the wheel, feeding the fiber slowly to make the yarn as they went. When they reached the end of the walk, they joined their yarns together. Each then began a new yarn and returned to the other end of the walk. When a sufficient number of yarns were spun, they would be twisted into strands and the strands into ropes. Heavy coils of finished ropes, of varying thicknesses, hung from pegs and were piled up along the walls.

Mary wished she had remembered which one of the Moseley boys was a ropemaker's apprentice, so she could ask for him. "Please, sir . . ." she said timidly, addressing the circle in the corner. "Please, sir . . ."

One man seemed to be telling a story: "Cap'n Eb looked from his chamber window one dark night, when he saw a tall form all clothed in white, with two great white wings a-wavin'. He shouted to it. . . . What d'ye want, lass?"

The interruption made the story funnier. The men roared loudly as the speaker rose to his feet. He was tall and thin and walked with a shambling gait.

"Are . . . you Joey's brother?" asked Mary, uncertainly. Then, realizing her mistake, she cried, "I mean . . . are you the ropemaker?"

"She wants to know if I'm Joey's brother," said the man to the others, who roared in reply. Then to Mary, he said, "Master Griggs is my name."

"Oh, then . . . here's a bag of spun thread for you,

sir," said Mary, "ready to be laid up. Marm Martin sent it, and says she will take it out in bed-cords—good, strong bed-cords."

"Good, strong bed-cords?" said the ropemaker, with a twinkle in his eye. "Who's so heavy they need good, strong bed-cords? Who's getting a new bed, lass?"

"I am, sir . . . I mean . . ." said Mary, in confusion, "the new bed is for me, so I won't have to sleep on the floor, sir."

The listening men laughed heartily.

"I'll give you good, strong bed-cords, lass," laughed Master Griggs, "fit for bouncing!"

The men roared again.

Mary waited uncomfortably while the ropemaker went to fetch the cords. By the time he returned, the men had forgotten her and resumed their conversation.

"What are all the ropes for?" asked Mary, gaining courage.

"Why, where are you from that you don't know?" asked Master Griggs. "The backwoods?"

Mary nodded.

"Just as I thought," he went on. "They're for ships, of course. Have you never watched the Honest Johns on a vessel pull at the ropes? Have you not seen all the new ships a-building in the yards? But of course you haven't if you live in the woods."

"Oh, yes, sir, I have, sir," cried Mary eagerly, as she took the cords in her hands. "I've seen . . ." She started to tell about Merchant McFarland and his new ship but the ropemaker turned away. With a parting glance at the two spinners, who, like spiders, were still walking backwards, Mary went out the door.

She knew the men were only teasing, but she was glad to get away from them. She put the coil of bed-cords about her neck and looked at the silver box in her hand. It gave her a strange kind of satisfaction.

Suddenly she noticed how late it was. The sun would soon be setting behind the trees on the other side of North Mill Pond. The buzzing clamor of the shipyard had ceased. The workmen were getting ready to go home. It was too late to visit the shipyard to-day. Disappointed, she walked quickly homeward.

As she crossed Canoe Bridge, she saw figures near the fish-house. She stopped to look. Cousin Tom's boat was drawn up on the shore and he and Jock were busy taking care of their day's catch. Jock, in the boat, carelessly tossed the limp and slimy fish upon the shore with a pitchfork. Cousin Tom split them open with a sharp-pointed knife, beheaded them and threw them into a basket. Mary watched, fascinated.

Cousin Tom spat upon his whetstone and began to sharpen his knife. "Want to help?" he asked, eyeing the girl, with a grin.

"No," said Mary, turning to go quickly. She called back over her shoulder, "Cousin Jeanie wants me."

"Hey, lass!" called Cousin Tom. "Did ye fetch that fish-net?"

"What fish-net?" asked Mary.

"From Master Griggs, the ropemaker. Jeanie sent ye with the bag o' thread, didn't she?"

"Yes, Cousin Tom," said Mary, "but she told me to fetch it in bed-cords. . . ."

Cousin Tom frowned blackly. "Bed-cords?" he

92

shouted. "What do she want bed-cords for? 'Tis a new fish-net I'm a-needin' this day!"

Mary ran up the hill and into the house. She never ceased to be frightened of Cousin Tom when he was angry. She sat down on a chair, breathless.

"What be the matter, lass?" asked Cousin Jeanie, kindly.

"Cousin Tom said I should 'ave fetched a fish-net and not the bed-cords!" cried Mary, tearfully.

"Now, don't ye fret, lass," said Cousin Jeanie, patting her on the back. "I know how to manage Cousin Tom. And a new bed ye shall surely have, for ye've lain on the hard floor long enough."

How good Cousin Jeanie was! Not a word about being away all afternoon. Not a question about what had kept her for so long. Mary set to work with a will to prepare the supper.

When Tom came into the house, Cousin Jeanie spoke to him and his anger faded away at once. All evening he worked with Jock by the firelight, making the new bedstead for Mary—setting up four posts and fastening them together with two side-boards and two end-boards. Jock had brought the lumber from the sawmill the day before. When the bedstead was completed, Mary helped Cousin Jeanie lace the cords back and forth. That night for the first time since she came to the Bank, Mary slept in a comfortable bed. While she dozed off to a restful sleep, her hand clutched a silver snuff-box, under her pillow.

Goat Island

Chapter VI

"MAKE haste, Mary, if you're going along!" called Jock.

Mary came flying down the steep hill and climbed over the side of the wherry. A cord of firewood filled the flat bottom of the boat to overflowing and the only empty space was the small seat at the bow. Mary doubled up her knees and crowded in.

Jock pushed the boat off, threw his woolen cap into Mary's lap and bent to the oars. His eyes gleamed brightly out of his bronzed and ruddy face and his hair flew loosely in the wind. The boat leaped out upon the water at his pull, as if anxious to be off.

"When are you going to learn to row?" asked Jock.

"Some day," answered Mary absently.

The morning air was fresh and sweet after the

shower of the evening before. Old Uncle Sandy, Jock's
grandfather, stood on the ledge of Brimstone Hill shaking his head as he watched the children go. According to his prediction, the rain was not over and the day
would end in showers. As the boat slid away, he put
his pipe in his mouth again, returned to the house and
resumed his weaving.

Jock rowed eastward through Puddle Cove, quickly
leaving the fishermen's wharves behind. His wherry
passed under Swing Bridge and emerged into that
broad, deep, still basin called *the Pool,* which reached
from the upper end of Great Island to the town of
Portsmouth itself. The islands and shores on all sides
provided generous anchorage for ships, especially for
the mast ships which made annual voyages between
England and the Piscataqua, for ship-timber and masts
could be had here in greater abundance than in any
other part of New England.

Both wind and tide had risen and the current was
strong. But Jock rowed sturdily and held the wherry
steady, without undue exertion.

It was a new and entrancing world which Mary
entered, as Jock's wherry moved across the harbor.
At last she was on the water which she loved so much.
She looked about feverishly and tried to see everything at once. She saw the banks clothed in fresh,
spring green and dotted with wharves and buildings
which grew smaller and smaller at each stroke of the
oars and shifted position rapidly as the boat glided
swiftly away. She saw boats and ships sailing to and
fro, bound upon unknown but fascinating errands.

She was amazed at the stillness of this water-world and the clearness of the echoes which followed the slightest sound. She was so absorbed in what she saw that she had no time or inclination to express herself in words. She could only drink in the whole delightful scene.

She saw Mast Cove on Peirce's Island on one side and Shapley's Island on the other, as they moved swiftly along. Rounding the lower end of Peirce's Island, they left the town behind. The boat moved more slowly through the narrow channel, between rocky ledges, and the sun came out hot and bright. It was only a few moments more until Jock pulled up on a rocky shore and beached the wherry on Goat Island.

"That's where she lives," said Jock, "in that little hut up there." He dropped his oars, jumped on the beach and pulled the wherry up on the sand. "There are her lobster pots," he added, pointing to a pile of crates on the sand, "and that's her boat. She takes it out just like a man."

Goat Island, only three acres in area, was one of the smallest in the harbor. A little log hut was perched on its rugged cliffs, to which a steep path wound up from the shore.

"Go on up and talk to her," said Jock, "while I unload the wood. Then I'll come up and see about the calf."

Mary started up the path. The little island appeared to be nothing but rocky cliffs, thrust upward from the waters of the bay, and worn smooth by the constant washing of the waves. There was but little grass and not a single tree. When she reached the top, Mary looked about her and saw water on all sides. What a wonderful place it was! Goody Gregory must love the sea, too.

As she followed the path toward the hut, she saw a cow, several goats and a small flock of sheep nibbling grass between the rocks. She wondered where they could find enough to eat. As she came closer, she noticed a bobbing form ahead—a little bent figure covered by a shawl. It was Goody Gregory herself. She had a small spade in her hand and was cutting squares of sod from a grassy patch. As she worked she sang a quavering tune:

> " 'Ewie with the crooked horn,
> May you never see the morn;
> Every day you steal my corn,
> Ewie with the crooked horn.' "

Mary waited until the song was ended. Then she said, shyly: "Good morning, Marm!"

Apparently the old woman did not hear. She bent over and lifted a heavy sod. She placed it on a pile of others to dry. Then she took up the spade and resumed her digging. She looked very small and frail to be working so hard. It seemed impossible that she could ever handle a boat, as Jock said.

"I can do that for you, Marm," ventured Mary, sympathetically.

"Who wants ye to do it?" came the ungracious reply.

She had heard, after all. She was not deaf, although she looked old enough to be. She went on with her work. Mary waited impatiently, standing first on one foot and then on the other. She wished that Jock would come.

Goat Island

At last the old woman stopped digging and lifted her face. Like a wrinkled, brown, rotted apple it peered out from under the gray shawl, lighted by quick-moving, sparkling gray eyes. One glance only she gave the new-comer, then started briskly toward her house. "Come along," she muttered, grudgingly.

"It must be nice to live all alone on an island," said Mary, in a polite attempt at conversation.

The old woman did not reply. She stalked steadily on ahead.

"What do the critters eat?" began Mary again.

"Grass, of course."

"Between the rocks?"

"Yes," said the old woman, turning round with a mischievous cackle, "that's why their noses are pointed!"

"Pointed?" inquired Mary. Then she saw the twinkle in the old woman's eye and she laughed aloud. "But in the winter-time?"

"Hay!" said the old woman.

"Where do they get hay?"

"I cut it for them."

"But there's no room for a scythe between the rocks."

"I use a knife," said Goody, chuckling and cackling to herself as if it were a huge joke.

"Do you grow flax and hemp?" asked Mary.

"No, I grow sheep," said the old woman.

"But what do you do for cloth?"

"Wait till I show you," said Goody, abruptly.

The little hut was small and bare, but had a look of comfort. A turf fire blazed on the hearth and a kettle simmered gently. The old woman put a pipe in her mouth, filled it with tobacco and lighted it with a coal, which she picked up with a pair of tongs.

"Is that what the sods are for?" asked Mary. "To burn in the fire?"

"Turfs, child, turfs," answered Goody Gregory, puffing vigorously.

"We burn wood. It must be funny to live without trees," said Mary, thinking of Nutfield. She looked at the floor which was bright with sunshine from the open door.

"Plenty of wood on the mainland," said the old woman. "Forty years ago, the forest came right down to the shore and a man could cut his trees and build his boats in his dooryard. But times have changed. Now, he has to go twenty miles inland for timber."

"I know," said Mary. "My home is in Nutfield. My father cuts timber and brings it to the Bank and sells it there."

"Yes, yes," said Goody Gregory, settling herself in her chair. She took a few whiffs of her pipe and smiled. "I know all about you."

"You do?" asked Mary, wondering.

"Yes, Ocean-Born Mary," said the old woman, looking the girl full in the face. "You were born on the ocean and saved by a pirate!"

"Why, who told you?" asked Mary, anxiously. "How do you know?"

"Never mind who told me. Come here, let me tell you something," said Goody.

Mary thought she had never seen so kind a face, as she came nearer, unafraid. She sat down on a low stool before her. The old woman put down her pipe and took Mary's hands in her own. She spoke in a gentle voice:

"Ocean-Born Mary, you will live by the sea for a time and then return to the woods. You will always be a friend to those who befriend you. You will live a long life—nigh onto a century—and all your life, you will be a marked person. People will talk of you, build up legends about you, some true and some untrue, but all your life, Ocean-Born Mary, you will be a marked woman. Yes, and longer. After you are dead, after your long, kind, useful life is over, people will talk of you still, for many generations."

Mary trembled as she listened. The old woman held her hypnotically to her words. It was the first time she had ever thought of the future. It seemed wonderful that Goody Gregory should know of things which had not yet happened. Mary's trust was complete. She had no inclination to doubt her words.

"Will I go back to the woods?" she asked anxiously.

"Yes, child," said Goody. "You will live only a short time at the Bank, so make the most of it. Dip your hands in sea-water while you can. Remember that whatever happens, you will always be a friend to those who befriend you. The rest of your life will be spent far away from the sea—but you will love it the more for having lived with it here."

"Will I be unhappy there? In the woods?"

"What ever you have to do, you will do," said the old woman. "That is all I can say."

"But I don't want to go . . ." implored Mary.

"Not yet, not yet!" soothed the old woman. "The time has not yet come. When it does, you will be ready to go, yes, happy to go. You will never forget the sea. You will remember it to your dying day. Come," she said, rising from her chair, "come and see my wool wheel and loom."

She led the way into an adjoining room and pointed out the wool spinning-wheel—almost twice as large as the flax wheels to which Mary was accustomed. The loom, too, was much larger. Mary ran her hand over the piece of soft, gray flannel which was in the making.

"And you don't have a man to weave it for you?" she asked.

"I weave it myself," said Goody. "Better than any man. I raise the sheep, shear them myself, spin the wool, weave it and wear it."

Meanwhile, Jock had unloaded the wood from the wherry and carried it in armfuls up the steep hill to Goody's woodpile. As he straightened his back and looked about, he caught sight of the mast of a ship in the cove at the other side of Goat Island. Knowing well there was no wharf there and not even a good landing-place, he was puzzled. He ran to the door of the hut and called, "Ma-ry! Ma-ry! There's a brigantine down in the cove. Let's go and see her!"

"What's that?" cried Goody Gregory, sharply, as she hustled to the door. "What's that ye say?"

Jock pointed and Mary and the old woman looked from the doorstep.

"'Tis nothing!" said Goody, dismissing the matter. "There's a spring down there and sometimes a boat stops for water. That's all."

"But they've careened her. She's lying on her side for cleaning and repairing!" protested Jock.

"I'll fetch the calf for ye now," said the old woman, sternly. "Can you take her in your boat? Can ye row careful so ye won't drown the poor thing?"

Jock and Mary followed the woman across the rocky pasture to a small shed. As they passed the sheep, she pointed to one and said, "There's the ewe with the crooked horn." She began to hum the song under her breath: "*Ewie with the crooked horn . . . may you never see the morn . . .*"

In the shed they found the calf beside its mother and soon it was roped and lifted into the boat. Mary climbed in and Jock took the oars, while the air rang with the piteous bawling of the mother cow. The old woman peered at the two children earnestly until they rounded the point and passed out of her sight.

"Let's go round to the other side," suggested Jock, "and see whose boat it is. Goody can't see us if we keep close to shore."

Jock rowed vigorously. It was not long until the wherry came near to the cove. Jock was right. A small brigantine lay upon its side on the shore while its bottom was being scraped and calked. She was being made ship-shape for her next voyage.

"I never saw her before," said Jock, shaking his head. "I don't recognize her."

Mary stared at the scene in the little cove with straining eyes. Why had Goody Gregory said it was only a boat stopping for water? Why did she so obviously not wish them to know there was a brigantine in the cove? As the wherry came near, the figures of men could be seen, holding oiled torches, burning barnacles off the ship's bottom. Mary spied a large man wearing a black cape and a plume in his hat. He was talking to two sailors and giving them orders. Mary did not need to be told who it was.

"Oh, Jock, let's go back," she cried. "Don't let them see us."

"I'd like to have a look at her prow," insisted Jock, "just to see if I know her."

"You don't know her, Jock. Come, let's turn round and go home."

"I can almost see . . ." said Jock.

"Jock, Jock!" cried Mary, in distress. Just then she noticed the calf. "Oh, look at the calf! She's choking!"

Neither of them had paid attention to the calf, which in its struggles had become entangled in its ropes. Jock dropped the oars and leaned over the calf to release her. Mary saw her chance. She changed seats quickly, took the oars, turned the boat about and began to row away from the cove as fast as she could.

Jock looked up in amazement. "What are you afraid of?" he demanded.

"Nothing," said Mary, breathing hard.

"Why are you rowing so fast then?"

"To get the poor calf home before she chokes."

"But I thought you didn't know how to row," laughed Jock.

"I'm learning fast!" said Mary, grimly.

Mary did not like to admit that what she had seen in the cove was upsetting. The calf was a convenient excuse, for she particularly wished to avoid a meeting with Captain Babb while Jock was with her. Then the whole thing was very strange. Did Goody Gregory know Captain Babb and was she trying to protect him?

Mary had still another reason for wanting to get home quickly. Their stay on Goat Island had taken much longer than she had expected. The sun was already high in the heavens and Judy McFarland had promised to take her to Nicholas Wiggin's shipyard in the afternoon. She had sent word by Jock when he delivered fish yesterday. Goody Gregory's words came back to Mary vividly as she rowed—"You will live by the sea for a short time, so make the most of it!" Cousin Jeanie was growing better daily. What

if Mary should have to go back to Nutfield without
seeing the shipyard and Merchant McFarland's new
ship? A driving force within her sped her on. The
oars dipped up and down as smoothly as if she had
been rowing all her life.

Although the palms of her hands were covered with
blisters by the time she jumped out of the wherry at
Brimstone Hill, she forgot about them as she helped
put dinner on the table and washed the dishes afterwards.

Judy was waiting at the gate in front of her home
when Mary came up, panting.

"Oh, I'm so glad you've come," said Judy. "I was
beginning to think something had happened."

"I wouldn't let anything happen," said Mary, "to
keep me from seeing your father's new ship."

Arm in arm the two girls started out. Up Fore
Street they walked, crossing over at Russell. Here
they descended the hill, passed the ropewalk and entered the shipyard. As they drew near they heard
the resounding thuds of mallets and the rhythmical,
musical song of the cross-cut saw. They smelled the
sweetness of the newly cut timber, mixed with the
freshness of the salt air.

In the timber-yard lay numerous trunks of massive
trees, which for untold years had waved their branches
in deep forest along the sea-coast. Now, they lay
waiting, ready to be made into living vessels to sail
triumphant through wind and wave. As Mary looked,
she seemed to hear the crash of falling trees in the
forest at Nutfield, the clamor and shouting of the

timber men as they sawed and chopped and hauled on the snow-covered ground.

"I'm glad that Nutfield trees are used for ships," she said aloud.

"So am I," answered Judy. "Father won't use anything else."

Several teams of oxen were dragging logs down the rough road to the shipyard at the water-front. The two girls followed and soon came to an earthen saw-pit, where a large log was being slowly ripped into plank. They watched quietly. Two men sawed with a long, vertical handsaw, one above and the other, sawdust-covered, in the pit below.

After watching a few moments, the two girls walked on. They passed several small sheds and Judy explained that all structural plans were drawn out to scale on the floor of the mold-loft and that these patterns were used for shaping the ship's timbers.

"Come, let us go and see Father's ship," cried Judy, disregarding several smaller boats which were being

built. "These are 'the ways,'" she explained, "from which the vessel will be launched." She pointed out two huge timbers, laid on a groundwork of solid oak blocks which ran parallel to each other from the shore to the water's edge.

The two girls stepped up on the staging and looked down upon the keel resting on the ways. They saw its long out-curving bow line and its upright stern-post. They saw the shipwrights working busily, talking and laughing. Some were sawing out ribs while others were fastening the shaped ribs to the keel. Already the curving timbers suggested the shape of the finished brig. The new ship, a mere skeleton, lay there, graceful and full of promise.

"Do you know Joey Moseley's father?" asked Mary. "Is he working on the new ship?"

"Oh, you mean Doc Moseley," said Judy, with a laugh. "He's over there. He's not a doctor, but every one calls him Doc. He's always joking and making the men laugh."

Mary saw a fat, jovial man inside an open shed, surrounded by others. From within came a constant chipping sound, interrupted by frequent roars of laughter.

"They're clipping out tree nails or 'trunnels' from oak sticks," explained Judy. "They are used to fasten the planking to the frame."

"How long does it take to build a ship?" asked Mary.

"Oh . . . quite a long time," answered Judy, carelessly.

"When will this ship be ready to sail?" asked Mary.

"Hush!" whispered Judy. "Say not a word. Here comes Master Nicholas Wiggin himself. He's master builder. He has built several ships for the Royal Navy!"

A short, sturdy-looking man, wearing a plain blue cloth suit, appeared. His brow was furrowed and his mouth was closed in a hard line. He walked about the frame-work and studied it carefully, while the shipwrights dropped their work and waited. Now and then he spoke a quiet word to a workman, who saluted in respectful silence. After a thorough inspection, the master builder walked rapidly away. Not until the shipwrights saw him re-enter the door of the mold-loft, did the buzz of work and conversation begin again.

Mary had not forgotten her question. She felt she must know the important day when this new ship would take to the water. Her heart beat with a bursting impatience. "How long will it take till she's ready?" she asked again.

"Well," said Judy, "it will be about two months before the planking is started, for it takes a long time for the carpenters to get the plank ready. After the hull is finished, the masts must be stepped in and the rigging set up and rove and then, at last, the ship will be launched."

"How long will it take to do all that?" persisted Mary.

"All summer, probably," answered Judy.

"All summer?" cried Mary, her heart sinking.

"Yes, perhaps longer," answered Judy, cheerfully.

A feeling of despair rushed over Mary. What if she should have to go back to Nutfield and miss it all! A great sob rose in her throat and she tried to choke it back.

"In the meantime," went on Judy, merrily, "we must plan out our ventures. Father says I can take one if Peggy does. Come, let us go down to the counting-house and see about them."

"Oh . . ." said Mary, uncertainly, "I don't think . . ."

"Nonsense! Come along!" ordered Judy. "It's on

our way home and we may as well stop in. Father likes to have me come. And if you've never been in a counting-house . . ."

No, Mary had never been in a counting-house. She must see as much as she could while she had the chance. The girls hurried back to town and soon reached the McFarland Wharf near the Town Dock.

The front door was locked, so Judy led the way into the door of the warehouse. The interior was dark and the floor was deeply stained with oil. Great bundles and bales of stored merchandise protruded mysteriously from the shadows and there was a curious mixture of smells. Judy opened a door and a ray of light streaked down from above to light the way. The girls climbed up the steep, narrow back stairs and entered the counting-room. There was no one there.

"When Father's here, talking to merchants and skippers, I have to keep silent," explained Judy. "I just sit in the corner and listen. That's how I know all about ventures."

"I wish I knew all about ventures, too," said Mary, wistfully.

"Oh, I can tell you," exclaimed Judy, cheerfully. "Come here and see. I know all about cargoes and ports and voyages. Father discusses all his voyages with me. He shows me his books and tells me all about his profits and losses during the year. He says I'm almost as good as a son and he's got over wishing he had one instead of me!"

The counting-room was small, with two windows overlooking the wharf and harbor. A great mahogany desk against the wall was crowded with leather-bound books and papers.

Judy picked up a bill of lading, a paper many feet in length which lay on the desk. At the top was the name of one of her father's ships which had sailed to England several months before. It listed its cargo, destination and the "adventures" which various people in town had taken. These were small speculations entrusted to the captain by boys and girls, sweethearts, brothers, mothers and wives of the crew, to be sold by the captain and the profits brought home to the investors. Mary learned to her surprise that any one who wished to risk a venture could sign his name with the amount of money or goods he wished to give and state what he wished to receive in return.

Judy held up the paper and read aloud:

"Shipped by the Grace of God in good order & well conditioned, by Daniel McFarlands on their acct. & risque, in & upon the good Brig called the *Friendship*, whereof is master under God for this present voyage Robt. Thornton, now riding at anchor in the River Piscataqua and by God's grace bound to Barbadoes and London, England."

"Now I'll read you some of the ventures," Judy went on:

"ON BOARD BRIG *FRIENDSHIP* PORTSMOUTH TO LONDON, 1732:

Memorandum of Mme. Sairey Moseley's Adventure: Please to purchase lay out 9 chickens 1 female which I send by you, Vizt: One Tureen 14 by 10 Inches; Calicko for 1 collar & 1 hat for Boy felt with buttons nif anything more Lay it out in Rice & you will oblige.

Memo. Thos. Barney's Adventure: Please to lay out 3 bushels potatoes in 1 lb. tea, 2 oz. indigo & the rest shugar; & 1 good pair sleeve buttons for myself Brass.

Memo. Landlord Drummond's Adventure: 6 Sheets of Paper & 3 Pipes & I have sent half a Guinea.

Memorandum of Mme. Pecksniff's Adventure: Please to purchase 1 doz. cotton caps in 2 sizes to sample & 1 pair spectacles, & invest remainder in nutmegs or spice as you think best. Please do for me as you do for your own and oblige."

Mary listened, incredulous. The thought of the silver snuff-box came unbidden, to her mind. "The captain will buy Marm Pecksniff's caps for her in London?" she asked.

"Yes," answered Judy, "and invest the remainder in such a way as to bring a profit. Peggy and I are going to write: 'Please to purchase 1 Dutch keeking-glass, small, to fit the hand . . .'"

"What shall you invest?" interrupted Mary, her heart beating quickly.

"Oh, some old snuff-boxes and buckles and . . ."

"Would a silver snuff-box do instead of money?" asked Mary.

"Of course, silly . . ."

Heavy footsteps sounded on the stairs and a stern voice called, "Hey! What are you doing up there?"

Mary looked at Judy with frightened eyes. An old, bewhiskered man, with a wooden leg, entered, gruff and angry.

"Get along out o' here!" he shouted, shaking a knobbly cane. "Yes, yes! I know ye're the merchant's darter, but I say, git along! This ain't no place fer gals, nohow. Yer Pa told me ter close up shop fer 'im."

The girls stumbled down the stairway, filled with dismay.

"That's Old Cap'n Pete," explained Judy. "Sometimes when he's not cross, he tells wonderful tales about all the things that happened to him at sea. But he's cross most of the time, now, because he's crippled with rheumatism and too old to go to sea and nobody wants him for a skipper. Father lets him sweep out the counting-room and do odd jobs for him."

Mary was surprised to see when they came out on the wharf that it was nearly dark and rain was falling heavily. Old Uncle Sandy was always right about the weather. She remembered his prophesy of the morning, as she and Jock had started for Goat Island. It seemed a long time since then and so many things had happened. What a wonderful place was Strawberry Bank! How could she ever bear to leave it? She bade Judy a hasty farewell and they parted at the corner. Then she ran down the street as fast as she could go.

Chapter VII

"RAKE away the ashes, Mary, and blow the fire with the belluses," said Aunt Becky. "Now fill that heavy iron pot with water fresh from the well. Then pull the crane forward and hang it on to heat."

The little cottage on Brimstone Hill seemed strangely empty without Cousin Tom and Jock. Two days before, the fishing fleet had sailed to the Newfoundland Banks, to be gone for an indefinite period—until they could bring home a good catch. Cousin Jeanie was worse and had taken to bed again. Jamie had taken the wherry and gone fishing along the shore. Aunt Becky, who had come to Brimstone Hill to spend the day, leaving the almshouse in care of Tilly and Hetty, had taken things in hand at once.

After doing up the morning work and making Jeanie comfortable, she sat down in a chair beside the bed. Mary staggered in with the pot of water.

"Oh, won't you please tell us, Aunt?" she begged.

"But what about the bag pudding?" answered Aunt Becky, rather more pleased at Mary's eagerness than she cared to admit.

"I'll make it at once, once the water is heated," said Mary. She lifted the heavy pot to the crane and then sat down on a stool at Aunt Becky's feet. "Cousin Jeanie and I will both be as still as mice."

"But you've heard it a hundred times before," laughed Aunt Becky.

"I've heard Ma tell it," said Mary, "and now I want to hear you."

"Do tell it again," begged Cousin Jeanie in her gentle voice. "I never tire of the story and now that I know Mary, it means so much more."

Aunt Becky settled her skirts and leaned back in her chair. "I shall never forget that dreadful voyage as long as I live," she began, "nor the last words of Elizabeth's mother, as we embarked at Lough Foyle. 'Go and God be with ye all but Becky Armstrong, and she'll be smart enough to take care of herself and Elizabeth, too!' Deary me, the poor woman must have known what was going to happen."

Aunt Becky was silent for a few moments. She always made this impressive pause at the beginning. It was a dramatic story and she liked to make the most of it. Mary listened, wide-eyed.

"The passage of eight weeks was stormy and our ship

was small and crowded. We had not been out but a short time till she sprang a leak and we had to put back. Setting sail again, we met heavy weather at once and from the first day out, we were nearly jolted to death. Small wonder we were so sea-sick. When she sprang another leak, we threw overboard everything we could to lighten her—Hugh's carpenter tools and the household furnishings, iron and pewter-ware. This left us with only clothing and provision for our passage.

"In mid-ocean the storm came which carried away the ship's rudder-head and fore-topmast. We knew there was trouble ahead when we heard the sailors hammering down the hatches and putting up the dead lights. The wind blew harder and harder and the waves rushed over the vessel like a deluge and flooded the cabins. All the chicken coops and nine hogs-heads of fresh water were torn loose from their moorings and washed overboard. I can hear yet the melancholy sound of the rattling of the sails and see the poor Johns, wet through to the skin, pulling at the creaking ropes. All was confusion within the cabin, with chairs, joint-stools, chests, bales and bundles float-ing and the water almost up to our beds. The storm increased in violence, all hands were called and the ves-sel rose and fell on the rocking waves like a chip of wood. It seemed a miracle that her planks should hold together at all. But at last the skies cleared, the wind died away and our terror came to an end. After it was all over, the broken parts were somehow repaired and we began to take heart again.

"Then one day we saw a strange ship which got us into a fright. All through the day we watched it come nearer and nearer. We had been so battered to pieces by the storm, we had no strength left to meet another trial. Elizabeth lay in her bed like a statue, pale and white, but patient always. I took the new-born babe in my arms and tried to warm it by a feeble fire which I had managed to kindle by first drying out some sticks of wood before a candle flame.

"Then, suddenly, I knew that something had happened. I knew that boats had come alongside and men were swarming upon the deck. I could hear heavy treads on the deck and sharp words interspersed with oaths. I could hear women's voices crying out in fright. I wondered where Hugh was, but I knew my place was at Elizabeth's side. I made up my mind to save the life of the babe at the risk of my own.

"I had not long to wait. I heard the tramp of heavy boots on the stairs; the door opened and a burly man entered. He had long black hair, a red sash across his shoulder and a sword in his hand. His hard face was flushed with brutality. I can see him yet. I knew at once that we were in the hands of pirates and that he was the pirate captain. Quickly I laid the babe at Elizabeth's side and advanced to meet him. I said to myself, 'Becky Armstrong, now is the time to show what you are made of.' I fully expected to be killed the next minute, defending Elizabeth and her child. But he pushed me aside roughly. He looked at the babe beside its mother and a change came over him where he stood. His hard face softened and his voice was as gentle as a woman's when he spoke. He asked a question or two and I told him the child was a girl and had been born the night before. Elizabeth said nothing, but her eyes asked pity.

"He leaned over and took the child in his arms. 'I christen thee Ocean-Born Mary!' he said huskily. 'If you will call her by this name, the name of my beloved mother and little sister,' he said to Elizabeth, 'I will not disturb you.'

" 'I will, sir,' said Elizabeth gratefully, in a frightened whisper. 'And thank you for your kindness.'

"Without another word, the pirate put the child down, turned and went up the steps, while Elizabeth and I waited in breathless silence, wondering what would happen next. In a few moments he was back, carrying in his arms a bolt of rich, green silk brocade.

" 'Let Ocean-Born Mary wear this on her wedding day!' he said with a bow and was gone again.

"There was little worth taking on a poor emigrant ship and that little he left alone, nor did he harm a soul. He called his men and returned to his boat. How we all rejoiced that night, Hugh and Elizabeth, the captain, mate and all the passengers and crew. As the pirate's boat disappeared from view, we fell on our knees and thanked God for his goodness and mercy. And every night until we came to land we did the same.

"The rest of the voyage was free of storm and mishap, but our food supply was sadly diminished. We lived mostly on potatoes and musty crackers. But the babe seemed to thrive and Elizabeth regained her strength day by day.

"You both know the rest of the story, how Hugh sickened suddenly in port of a strange malady and died there, leaving Elizabeth a sad, young widow; how she married James Clark and went to Nutfield to live; and how she has kept for Mary all these years the pirate's green brocade, because of the promise she made that day. I suppose, Mary, they will scarcely hold the thanksgiving service in Nutfield this year—now that you are no longer there."

"I suppose not," said Mary, regretfully, remembering the feeling of pride and elation it had always given her to be the center of attention.

Becky Armstrong bustled over to the fire and began to poke it energetically, to hide the emotion which the story never failed to rouse. "But that is no reason, I'm sure," she added sternly, "why you shouldn't thank God each day for your safe deliverance. And ask Him to stifle your pride and make you meek and humble."

"Yes, Aunt," said Mary, obediently.

"Now, the water's come to a boil; let us see about the bag pudding. We must heat this milk—deary me, who's making all that noise out there?" She went to the open window and looked out. The words of a rollicking song came into the room clearly:

" 'In Scotland there dwelt three brothers of late,
   Three brothers of late, brothers three,
And they cast lots, to see which of them
   Should go robbing all on the salt sea, salt sea;
And they cast lots, to see which of them
   Should go robbing all on the salt sea . . .
                          all on the salt sea!' "

"Who is it? What is it?" cried Mary, running to look.

"Go and measure out the meal, Mary," said Aunt Becky quickly. "It's only a crowd of drunken sailors. Why they have to put their boat in here, is more than I can understand." She closed the window.

Following instructions, Mary brought out the great wooden bowl and stirred Indian meal into a quart of boiling milk, making a stiff batter. To this she added ginger, salt, molasses and more meal. Under Aunt Becky's watchful eye, she stirred and rolled and mixed and pounded the ingredients until they held together.

But still the song came through the closed window. Every word could be heard clearly:

" 'Put back!' he cried, 'and square your main tack,
   Come sail down under my lee;
Your gold we'll take from you, your ship we'll let drift,
   And your bodies we'll sink in the sea!
Your gold we'll take from you, your ship we'll let drift,
   And your bodies we'll sink in the sea!' "

Louder and louder came the song, followed by a fumbling knock at the door. "I'll put an end to this nonsense," said Aunt Becky, marching toward the door. "Knead your pudding well, Mary," she said with a backward glance.

Aunt Becky opened the door and took in the situation at once. The dense fog of the morning had lifted and she saw that a strange ship had passed through Swing Bridge and had dropped anchor in the cove. A boatload of its men had pulled up on the gravel beach below and two of them stood before her on the doorstep. Mary could see them from where she stood.

"Please, Marm, the Captain sent us . . . the Captain said . . . could we fill up our water casks at your well, Marm?" asked the first, who had a hatchet face.

"No," said Aunt Becky, with determination, "you may not. If you take one drop of water from that well, you do so against my wishes and you will suffer the consequences."

"Thank you, Marm," said the second, whose hair was long and black. "And the Captain, he wanted to know, Marm, is there a lass here called Ocean-Born Mary?"

"Who?" cried Aunt Becky, in surprise. She seized a broom and started out the door, after the men, with her petticoats flying. "Be off with you! Be off with you! I'll give you just half an hour to get that brigantine of yours out of Puddle Dock and out of Portsmouth Harbor!"

The men retraced their steps with all speed, laughing and singing as they went. From the bottom of the hill, their song could still be heard:

> " 'Bad news, bad news I bring to old England,
>   Bad news I bring to thee;
>   Your rich merchant ship is now cast away,
>   And your mariners sunk in the sea!
>   Your rich merchant ship is now cast away,
>   And your mariners sunk in the sea!' "

Mary stood stock-still, her hands in the pudding dough. Aunt Becky returned to the table and began to talk about the pudding as if there had been no interruption. She showed Mary how to season and roll and pound the mixture. A pat here, a toss there and the pudding was at last as round as a ball. Mary tied it up in the cloth and put it in the pot to boil. Then she stood by the fireside and waited nervously.

Soon another knock came at the door—a blustering, noisy, resounding knock, as if the person who knocked knew no fear. Aunt Becky advanced with a determined look on her face. She opened the door and there on the doorstep she confronted the man whom she most hated and feared, the man who had caused her the greatest suffering she had ever known. She recognized him at once. He was the pirate and the captain of the brigantine in the cove below. Out of a corner of her eye, she saw a line of sailors behind him, bringing empty water casks and setting them down by

the well-curb. She heard their jokes and laughter.

"Madam!" said the captain, bowing low. "You will allow us, I am sure, to fill our casks at your well. We are about to embark on a long voyage to foreign lands."

His lips seemed to move automatically, as if saying a speech which he had prepared beforehand. His lips formed the outward words, but it was his eyes which betrayed his surprise. Although it was more than ten years since they had met on the emigrant ship in the middle of the ocean, Philip Babb recognized Becky Armstrong as readily as if it had been but yesterday. He would have known her anywhere, for she had scarcely changed at all.

Her answer came like a flash: "I forbid you to touch a drop of water from that well."

Ignoring it, he went on, unabashed. "A lass by the name of Ocean-Born Mary lives here, does she not?"

"There is no one here by that name," came the unhesitating reply.

Becky Armstrong trembled from head to foot. She had just relived the whole experience in the telling of the story, and now, as in a bad dream, the perpetrator of it all stood before her. She slammed the door shut with all the strength she could muster, put up the bar, then sat down weakly in a chair. She dropped her head in her hands, but only for a moment.

"What's the matter? What is it? Who is it?" cried poor Jeanie, in great agitation, from her bed.

"The devil himself!" ejaculated Becky, when she could find words. "That pirate captain is still alive and has come to Puddle Dock. His brigantine is anchored out there in the cove. With all the ports in the great, wide world to choose from, he has to come here." Then she added, after a glance out the window, "His men are filling their casks at the well."

Mary had not moved from her place on the hearth. Her eyes were fixed on the bag pudding in the pot, but she saw it not. She knew by the sound of his voice that it was the pirate who stood at the door. She did not need to be told. She had heard him speak her name and she wanted to let him know that she was there. She remembered his friendliness at the Ark Tavern. But at the same time, she understood, as never before, Aunt Becky's undying hatred for the man. Her feet were glued to the stone hearth and she could not move.

When she heard the door slam, she looked up. She saw Aunt Becky move quickly to the window to watch. She heard Aunt Becky's words: "They have filled the casks. They are wrestling and pummeling each other now. . . . They are in no hurry to carry the casks to the boat. . . . They are arguing among themselves. . . . The captain is being rowed out to his vessel . . . he climbs aboard. . . . The sailors are leaving; they are going the other way, across Canoe Bridge, to town, to town! They have gone and they have left the casks sitting by the well! Now is my opportunity . . ."

Mary saw Aunt Becky unbar the door and go out. She ran to the window and watched nervously, with dry lips. She saw Aunt Becky hasten to the first cask, bend her tall, straight figure and calmly tip it over.

Bang, bang, rackety bang, it went down over the rocky cliffs, spilling the water and breaking the barrel to pieces. The second and third casks followed. What a dreadful thing to do and how unlike Aunt Becky to do it! Soon all twelve were shattered to bits on the gravel beach below and Aunt Becky returned to the house.

"How's the pudding?" she inquired, calmly.

The answer came sooner than she had expected—in a loud explosion. The pudding burst the confines of its bag and spattered and hissed in every direction.

"Deary me!" cried Aunt Becky, as she stared. "The likes of that never happened to me before. Did you fill the bag too full or forget to tie the pudding string, Mary? When a bag pudding bursts," she shook her head sadly, "it means no good, no good to any one."

Mary could not help thinking about the pirate and his broken casks. She wondered what he would say when he found them. She kept a close watch, but she saw no signs of life about the ship in the cove and the sailors did not return. She felt sorry for the pirate and wanted to tell him that she was right there in the kitchen when he came. She wanted to explain that Aunt Becky hated him and that was why she had said what she did and had broken the casks. She wondered how she could find the pirate to tell him these things. She thought of rowing the wherry out to the ship, but Jamie had not returned. When, a little later, Aunt Becky scolded her for looking out of the window and then asked her to go to the Sign of the Mortar and Pestle to fetch some medicine for Cousin Jeanie, Mary knew it was only an excuse to get her safely away from the pirate.

The apothecary's shop was locked. Old Marm Pecksniff leaned out of the upper window and talked a while, but she did not know where her son had gone. As Mary turned toward home, she remembered again the pirate and his casks. When he found them broken to bits, he would have to buy new ones. What a happy thought! He would need new pipe-staves to make new casks and he would go to Cooper Nutley's to get them. Perhaps he was there right now! Why hadn't she thought of it before?

It did not take long to reach the cooper's shop which was in Pipe-stave Cove, near the saw-mill at the north end of town. As Mary walked into the yard, she caught sight of a longboat drawn up at the wharf and several strange-looking sailors loading on bundles of pipe-staves. She wondered if the longboat belonged to the pirate, but she had no way of knowing.

Cooper Nutley's shop was a busy place, where large quantities of lumber were split into pipe-staves for making 'pipes' or hogsheads, which according to the English law of weights and measures, held two barrels or sixty-three gallons each. A number of men were working busily. Mary watched them from the doorway. First they split out the staves, then they put them together with heads and hoops. Other men took them apart and put each lot in a bundle, ready for shipping to Barbadoes, where other coopers would remake them into casks for rum and molasses.

Mary looked about, but saw no one resembling the

pirate. She began to think she had come on a wild goose chase. She was about to leave the yard, when she saw a huge raft floating down the river, loaded with large timbers. She listened to the shouting of the timber men and watched them guide the raft to the saw-mill wharf and fasten it to the mooring.

"Hello, Mary," said a familiar voice at her ear. Mary turned and was surprised to see Joey Moseley.

"Why, Joey," she cried, "what are you doing here? Why aren't you watching your cows?"

"Hush!" exclaimed Joey. "You never can tell when there's a Select man about! Frisky's getting too fat—needs more exercise. Besides, something always happens at a saw-mill. That's why I came away."

Mary and Joey walked out on the wharf and watched the timber men as they unloaded a pile of logs on the shore. Then the men walked lazily up the street in the direction of Deer Tavern.

"There! Now they've gone," said Mary. "They probably won't unload the rest till tomorrow. We may as well go home."

"Oh, no," cried Joey. "Wait a bit. Something is sure to happen. Hear those men talking over there? They sound angry."

A group of men had gathered about the logs which had just been unloaded. The two children moved closer and sat down upon the logs where they could hear.

"There ain't no sense to this Pine Tree Law," said a ropemaker's apprentice, "a-holdin' out on the best trees for the King."

"Where's he a-goin' to git his masts, if he don't git 'em here?" asked a young fisherman. "All the trees in England have been chopped down already."

"I have land of my own," said a cocky little backwoodsman, "and I regard all the trees on it as my own property, whether they're marked or not. I'll chop 'em up into pipe-staves if I feel like it."

"Before a man clears his land," said a shop-keeper with an air of authority, "he must pay Lieutenant-Governor Dunbar to send one of his deputy-surveyors to come and mark the King's trees with the Broad Arrow."

"I know it," snorted the backwoodsman bitterly. "I've seen it. I've watched him make it—three cuts through the bark with a marking-hatchet, like the barbed head of an arrow or the track of a crow. But," he added with a laugh, "it's mighty easy to shave it off!"

The King's Broad Arrow

The listening men laughed, showing their sympathy.

"Better not try shaving off the Broad Arrow! Better not try cutting down the King's pines!" Mary recognized at once the warning voice as that of Master Pecksniff. Why had he closed up his shop and come here?

"No, I wouldn't shave off the Broad Arrow," said the woodsman, backing down. "But Dunbar can't prevent me from clearing all the trees round the biggest pines, or from setting a fire for a 'burn' that would likely kill them in burning off my land."

"No, he couldn't touch you there," said the shop-keeper.

"Couldn't he?" asked Master Pecksniff with a chuckle.

Just then two men entered the saw-mill yard and made their way swiftly across the wharf, from which they jumped down onto the raft.

"Oh!" cried Mary, "there he is!"

"Who?" asked Joey.

Just when she had given up looking for him, she saw the pirate. That must have been his longboat filled with pipe-staves, after all.

"Why, that man in black there on the raft. He's . . . a sea-captain, and . . ." She looked more closely at the second of the new-comers. "Well, if it isn't Silas Gregg—Sukey's Pa!" she exclaimed, in astonishment.

In a flash, she understood. She remembered that her father had spoken of selling his pine timbers to a sea-captain by the name of Philip Babb. That must be the pirate's name—Philip Babb. Her father must have had Gregg bring the timber to town for him, as he sometimes did. She watched the two men as they talked together on the raft. Her faith in the pirate increased, as she realized that her father trusted him.

"Do you know him?" asked Joey.

"Yes, he's Sukey's Pa," said Mary, absent-mindedly. "He has the land next to Pa's in Nutfield. Sukey comes to spin for us sometimes. I wonder how Sukey is . . ."

"Listen!" said Joey. The men behind them were talking again.

"Each tree's worth a hundred pounds," said the backwoodsman. "Why should we give them to the King?"

"It's the biggest ones the King wants—those that are three feet through," said the ropemaker's apprentice.

"Twenty-four inches will do," said the fisherman, "if measured one foot off the ground when standing. Let's take a look at this raft timber and see if it's marked."

The two men approached the pile of logs where the children were sitting and bent over.

Impulsively, Mary kicked out her foot. "You needn't measure them!" she said, defiantly. "They belong to my Pa and he wouldn't try to cheat the King. He's an honest man."

The men looked up at her and burst into loud guffaws.

"Hush, Mary," warned Joey.

The men went on with their measuring.

"They'll pass all right," said the first.

"Smart lass that!" laughed the other, as they walked off.

"Somebody might remember that I'm cow-herd," added Joey.

But Mary was not listening. She saw that Master Pecksniff had heard the remarks. She saw him dart forward and look at the logs sharply. Then he called his Negro slave, who was waiting near at hand and spoke a few words in his ear. The Negro hurried away and the apothecary walked about with an unpleasant smile on his face.

"Why did he look at Pa's logs like that?" asked Mary, anxiously.

"Who?" asked Joey.

"Master Pecksniff."

"Oh, you mean Poke-Nose!" laughed Joey. "He's always poking his nose in other people's business. That's why it has grown so long. Did you notice?"

Cooper Nutley, owner of the cooper's shop and saw-mill, came bustling up. "If this fellow's trying to sell marked timber," he shouted, waving his fists, "he'll soon find out he can't do it at this saw-mill. I'll send for Dunbar himself!"

At the word "Dunbar," the men showed their dislike of the man in angry shouts: "Dunbar's not honest!" "Dunbar lets his surveyors mark trees that are already down!" "Dunbar abuses and threatens the people!" They shouted and argued loudly. The commotion increased and other people came running up to see what was wrong.

"I want to see Sukey's Pa," said Mary, climbing down from her perch. "I want to ask how Sukey . . ."

The men had now left the raft and climbed up on the wharf. Mary could see Silas Gregg's head towering above the others. The pirate must be beside him. She must explain about the water casks.

"Oh, don't go," begged Joey. "Let's listen to Old Poke-Nose. Whenever something happens, Poke-Nose is always there."

Mary changed her mind and stayed where she was.

Master Pecksniff had mounted a barrel and was apparently trying to quiet the crowd.

"Good people," he said in an unctuous voice, "let me remind you that Lieutenant-Governor Dunbar, in his office of Surveyor-General of the Woods, is a faithful servant of the Crown. It is his duty to obey His Majesty the King and carry out all his commands."

Pecksniff then pointed out Silas Gregg and addressed him in a loud sarcastic tone: "Have you not come to the wrong place with these trees, sir? Should not this timber have been taken to Mast Landing? Are not these masts for His Majesty's royal navy? If you had been really clever, sir, you would have sawed them into narrow boards so that they might not be direct evidence of illegal cutting!"

"These trees are not marked, sir!" replied Silas Gregg, hotly. "They are not mine; they belong to my friend and neighbor, James Clark of Nutfield, and I speak for his honesty as I do for my own. The surveyor has been through Clark's land and has marked all the mast trees, which are still standing. I, myself, can vouch for that. These trees," pointing to the logs on the raft, "are less than twenty-four inches in diameter. They have been ordered by a sea-captain for export to the West Indies and it is my duty to deliver them." He looked round to ask Philip Babb to attest the fact, but the man had disappeared.

"You are right, sir!" cried Mary, standing up on the logs and shouting so all could hear. "These trees belong to my Pa and he is an honest man."

Silas Gregg was startled to see Mary, but grateful

132

for her support, little though it was. The crowd tit-
tered, then turned to make way for important arrivals.
Four men rode up on fiery horses and quickly dis-
mounted.

"That's Dunbar and his men," whispered Joey, with
a tug at Mary's elbow. "Now things are going to happen. Just watch."

"What does he want?" asked Mary, suddenly cold
with fear. "Why has he come?"

"Oh, somebody sent for him, I suppose," said Joey.
"Poke-Nose, like as not."

Mary had seen the apothecary send his slave away on
a hasty errand. Was it possible he had sent for the
Governor?

"I must go," whispered Joey, hastily. "If Dunbar
sees me here, he'll have me punished for leavin' the
cows. But didn't I tell you, something always happens
at saw-mills, especially when Old Poke-Nose is there?"

The next moment he was gone. Mary thought of
his words as she watched the swift proceedings. Dunbar sent his three surveyors to measure the trees on the
raft. After doing so, one of them returned to speak a
few words to the Governor, who nodded in reply.
Then the men took their hatchets and marked Broad
Arrows on the tops of the logs, so that they could be
plainly seen from wharf and shore. A murmur ran
through the crowd. The Governor mounted the logs
to speak. The people fell back, silent. They hid their
resentment and listened respectfully.

"It is our happiness," said Dunbar in a loud and
pompous voice, "to live under the protection of a

Prince who is the best of Kings and an indulgent Father, and we are continually reaping great advantage from the trade with our mother Kingdom. When we consider these things, I hope this Province will never be wanting in their loyalty and obedience to His Majesty and upon all occasions show their dutiful dependence on the Crown of Breat Britain."

He went on to speak of the King's need of masts and other timbers for the ships of the royal navy. He asked the people for support. He told them that the King wished to encourage the cutting of masts for this purpose, by offering a bounty of one pound a ton, which meant one pound for fifty cubic feet of rough or forty cubic feet of hewn lumber—to be paid in gold. Here he stopped for applause from the crowd. A bounty, hurrah!

He spoke of the King's desire to increase the manufacture of Naval Stores—turpentine, rosin, tar, pitch, linseed oil and oakum—all those raw by-products so essential in the building and maintaining of wooden sailing vessels. He mentioned also a bounty for raising hemp for rope-making.

"I am commanded by the King," he said in conclusion, "to take effectual care that the several acts of Parliament relating to the Royal Woods be strictly observed, and by the help of my deputies, to prevent its wanton destruction. I warn you that all offenders therein will be brought to condign punishment and I remind you once more of your respect and duty to your King." Pointing to the raft, he added, "I claim these trees in the name of His Majesty the King!"

Dunbar stepped down, called his men and gave them orders to remove the raft to Mast Landing at once, there to transfer the timber to the waiting mast ship, the *Olive Branch*. The crowd began to scatter, some to witness the seizure of the raft, others to leave the yard.

"But, sir," protested Silas Gregg, in one last effort to try to save James Clark's timber, "these trees are not of the required size!"

Dunbar turned with a smile. "My men have measured them," he said. "They are a scant twenty-four inches, 'tis true, but they are more than twenty-three. You have chosen carefully, my friend!"

Mary looked about distractedly for Philip Babb. Even the water casks were forgotten for this more important matter. If only he would step forward and say that he was a legitimate sea-captain and had bought the logs from her father, Dunbar would understand and it would make everything right. But Philip Babb was nowhere to be seen. Was he, like Joey, afraid of Governor Dunbar?

Mary ran to the Governor's side. She felt no fear, for she was moved by a sense of loyalty to Philip Babb as well as to her father. "But, sir," she cried, "my father is an honest man! He has sold these logs to a sea-captain, who was here just now, but has been called away. You cannot take them for the King! They are sold!" All the indignation which she felt was poured forth in her high, shrill voice.

"Tut, tut! Who is this?" exclaimed Dunbar, looking down with piercing eyes. He put his hand under Mary's chin and tipped it up, sharply. "Lass, have I not seen you before? Why are you idling here? Have I not told you not to let me see your face in a public place again?"

Nutfield

Chapter VIII

"WHICH shall I take and which shall I leave?" said Mary to herself. In one hand she held the snuff-box and in the other the three gold-pieces. After careful deliberation, she put the snuff-box back into its hiding place—an old earthen pot behind the cow-shed. She covered the pot with a flat stone, so no one would notice it. For weeks her treasures had been hidden there and whenever she had been able to spare a moment from other things, she had come to the ledge to spread them out and enjoy them.

She carried the gold-pieces into the cottage and wrapped them up in her small bundle of clothing. Daniel McFarland had not forgotten his promise to take her home for a visit when he went to Nutfield and the appointed day had arrived.

"Will you promise to bring me back with you, sir, when you come home again?" asked Mary anxiously, before she mounted the pillion. Ever since her visit to Goody Gregory's, Mary had felt that she might at any moment be torn away from Strawberry Bank. It was like tempting fate to go home—even for a visit, though she longed to see her parents, brothers and baby sister.

"If I came home without you, Mary," said Merchant McFarland with a laugh, "Judy would send me straight back to bring you."

The long ride through the forest brought back to Mary the memory of that day in early April when she had first come to the Bank. The trees were out in full leaf now, and birds were fluttering from bough to bough. The heat of the June sun could scarcely penetrate the dense masses of foliage, and the merchant's horse trotted steadily along in the cool and quiet solitude. Mary talked freely to the merchant of many things and felt as if she had always known him. For he was, indeed, one of those understanding individuals who took rare delight in listening to the words of a child.

With a tavern stop for the night, the long journey came to an end at noon on the second day. In front of the Clark cabin, Mary slipped down from the horse's back, stiff-legged and tired. As she looked about her, the familiar place was girdled round with a queer strangeness, as if she had never observed it carefully before. Opposite the low log cabin, a clear and sparkling brook rumbled boisterously over the rocks and disappeared round a bend. On one side, a plowed field stretched away into the forest, ready to be planted with seed corn. On the other side, two sheds were fenced in close to the house for the animals, while a small potato garden wound in and out among the stumps. All about, dark, menacing and fearful, stood the heavy forest, blotting out the sun. Mary shivered as she looked.

"Mary, Mary!" "How are you, Mary?" "I did not forget you, Mary." The family came running out, excited and eager. James and Elizabeth Clark greeted the merchant respectfully. Mary kissed her father and fell into her mother's arms. Then the three little boys pulled her into the cabin, plying her with eager questions while the merchant and James walked away into the forest.

The log house had two rooms and a lean-to and its furnishings were of the simplest. It had not changed at all. There was the little treadwheel with its distaff and spindle for flax spinning. There was the great fireplace stretching across one end of the room, large enough for the whole family to warm themselves in; and the lug-pole with its iron pot in which a piece of venison was simmering. There in the ashes were potatoes roasting—everything was just the same, as if Mary had never been away at all. It was a comfortable feeling to be at home again.

And yet, as she talked to her mother and told her all that had happened, Mary seemed to see, beyond the depths of the dark, forbidding forest, the bright sun shining on the blue sea in Portsmouth harbor. And in her heart she knew, as never before, that she must return to Strawberry Bank.

In the late afternoon, the two men came in from the forest where they had been inspecting trees.

"There won't be a stick of timber left in the ship-yard," Merchant McFarland was saying, "once my new brig is launched. I can give you a substantial order for ship-building timbers."

The timber used in building ships had to be cut two years before use and allowed to season in the interval. As the seasoned timber kept on hand in the shipyard was used up, green timber had to be brought in to take its place.

"I would be glad to have your order at any other time, sir," replied James Clark, as they gathered about the fireplace. He paused, glancing nervously at his wife. "But the fact is, I am inclined to go into the mast business."

"The mast business?" cried Elizabeth, looking up.

"It is more and more difficult to sell timber without being suspected," explained James. "I sent in a raft-load by Silas Gregg last week and Governor Dunbar seized it for masts, though the trees were all under-sized."

"Is that possible?" asked Merchant McFarland, in surprise. "I have heard rumors of Dunbar's dishon-esty, but I thought it was only idle talk."

Mary was listening with all ears. She wished she could tell all about the seizing of the timber. And yet it would be difficult to explain Philip Babb's disappearance at the critical moment. Yes, it would be better to say nothing. She listened again.

"He's a hard master, sir," said James Clark, "to say the least. His men antagonize every one they meet with their high-handed methods. I remember well when they came to mark the trees in Nutfield. They boasted in such an ugly way, they excited a strong prejudice against them."

"They walked into this house without invitation, sir," added Elizabeth, "and gave me orders to prepare food for them. When I could not provide what they asked for, they swore they would tell Dunbar."

"Too bad, too bad," answered McFarland. "I believe Dunbar is a loyal servant of the King, but his task is a difficult one and requires the utmost tact and consideration."

"It would seem to me that the best way to avoid difficulty," James went on, "would be to cut masts for Dunbar and take the bounty which he offers. Silas Gregg says it is one pound for every ton of timber and it is paid in gold."

"But we have no need of hard money, James," said Elizabeth, who had been listening quietly. She turned to Mr. McFarland as with genuine pride she explained more fully: "We spin and weave all our garments. We knit all our stockings. While my husband is not a shoemaker, he makes all our shoes. We make our own soap and candles and we boil down sugar from the sap of the sugar-trees in the woods. We grow our own corn to make our bread and cakes and to feed our live-stock during the winter. What need have we of hard money? To buy tea and spices and some imported goods, you will say. Yes, but we can get those things any day by sending a pile of furs or some linen yarn, to Strawberry Bank."

"But isn't gold money good for anything, then, Ma?" burst out Mary, anxiously. She held out her hand, displaying the three gold-pieces which she had brought from the Bank.

"Child!" cried Elizabeth, in a shocked voice. "How came you by these coins?"

"A man . . . gave them to me, Ma . . ." said Mary, suddenly ashamed, though she knew not why. "He was . . . a sea-captain . . . I think. . . ."

"Have you been talking to a strange sea-captain?" asked Elizabeth sternly, remembering the encounter in Maggie McDonald's shop.

"I have been thinking, sir," James Clark went on, slowly, hardly noticing the interruption, "that it might be a profitable thing to cut mast trees and take the bounty."

"The mast ships keep on coming into port and it is Dunbar's duty to fill them with masts," said the merchant. "Where can he get them, if loyal citizens will not help?"

"But the trees are of immense size, James—too large for you to handle—and the cattle are small and not strong enough," protested Elizabeth.

"If all the men in the neighborhood went together," suggested Mr. McFarland, "the work would not be too heavy."

"That is just what we are planning to do," announced James, full of keen anticipation and delighted to have the merchant's approval. "We expect to spend the summer cutting masts for next winter's hauling. Silas Gregg says that if we peel the bark off, it will keep the worms from spoiling the trunks. By early November, we can have a great number of masts and other timber ready to haul to the river on the first snows. Then they can be floated down by the freshet in the spring."

"But who will plant the corn and take care of it?" asked Elizabeth, greatly disturbed, "while you are away in the woods so long?"

"We will not need to plant corn," said James, enthusiastically. "We will have plenty of money to buy it next year. The season is so backward, the corn should have been planted long ago. It seems useless to bother now. The flax, the peas and the potatoes are already in. That is all we shall need."

"If we grow no corn, what will the critters eat?" asked Elizabeth soberly.

"In haying-time, I will come home," answered James, "and mow all the wild grass in the meadows and stack it. That will be plenty of hay to feed the cattle all winter."

"Who will kill the game? Who will take bear, raccoons, beaver and deer? How will we get enough to eat?" Elizabeth went on, anxiously.

"Johnny is nine now," said James, sternly. "It is time he began to help."

An uncomfortable pause followed. Then Merchant McFarland spoke: "I am sorry about the ship timbers,

Clark. I'd calculated on getting them here . . ."

Little Georgie came running in. "Indian! Indian!" he cried, pointing out the door.

"Go and see who it is, Mary," said Elizabeth. "It's probably Lean Wolf's squaw."

"Why are the Indians so friendly here?" asked Merchant McFarland. "I've had dealings with some of them for years, without trouble of any kind, but I have heard of a number of massacres up in Maine."

"We think it is due to Pastor MacGregor's friendship with Marquis de Vaudreuil, the French Governor of Canada, sir," said Clark. "The two men were educated in the same school and became fast friends. The Governor has a great deal of influence with the Indians and it is evident that he has told them not to disturb the Scotch-Irish settlers in Nutfield. They seem to hate the English most, for there has been trouble on all sides of us."

"Then, too," added Elizabeth, "we try always to treat them with consideration, and that may have helped. We have lived her for ten years and have never found them anything but friendly."

"It's Lean Wolf and Blackbird, Ma," called Mary from the door. "They want to come in."

Without waiting for an invitation, Lean Wolf entered, followed by his squaw, who carried her papoose strapped on her back. Blackbird took the child off and set it upon its board against the wall.

"Indian hungry," said Lean Wolf.

"Squaw want thread," added Blackbird.

Mary went to the pot on the crane and filled two

large bowls with the stewed venison. Then she brought a corn-cake and broke it to pieces.

"There goes our supper," said James in a vexed tone.

"But they're tired and hungry, Pa," said Mary. "They've been walking a long way." She knelt on the floor before the Indian baby and gave it spoonfuls of milk.

"They always know where to find food," added James.

"We still have potatoes," said Elizabeth in a low voice.

The Indians squatted on their heels before the fire and ate greedily. As soon as the food had disappeared, Lean Wolf told Merchant McFarland, his friend and benefactor, that he and Standing Elk expected to bring a load of furs to the Bank the following week.

"Squaw want thread," said Blackbird with a grunt.

"Blackbird wants her thread, Ma," said Mary, bringing her mother's spinning-wheel and setting it before her. Elizabeth set to work at once to spin the coarse, strong thread which she had promised the Indian woman.

"What does she want it for?" asked the merchant.

"She uses it for stringing beads and lacing moccasins," explained Elizabeth. "It is stronger than deer-sinew for either purpose."

As Blackbird crouched on the floor and watched the spinning, her face broke into a broad smile. Like all the Indian women, she never ceased to be amused by the sight of those curious implements of the white woman—clock reels, hand-cards for hackling flax and spinning-wheels.

The Indian baby began to cry, puckering its face up like a shriveled brown apple. Blackbird rose to her feet, picked up a gourd full of cold water and dashed it into the infant's face. Its cries stopped immediately and the squaw returned to the table. As she laid the gourd down, she saw three bright, glittering objects lying on the table. Her nimble fingers could not resist the temptation. With her broad back turned toward the people in the room, she picked the gold-pieces up quickly and hid them inside her clothing.

Then she grunted to her husband, giving a signal which he readily understood. Lean Wolf picked up

146

the thread and left the house without ceremony. His squaw fastened the papoose to her back and followed, neither showing any signs of gratitude for the hospitality which they had received.

"Oh, Ma!" cried Mary, as soon as the Indians were out of sight. "My gold-pieces are gone! I laid them right here by the gourd."

"Blackbird took them, of course, when she threw the water in the baby's face," said Elizabeth. "That's why she left so abruptly. No Indian can resist a loose shining object."

"What! Gold-pieces!" cried James, in astonishment. "Do you mean to say you had gold-pieces and you allowed those wretched Indians to steal them, after eating up all our supper?"

Merchant McFarland put his arm about Mary's shoulders, when he saw the tears rolling down her face. "If they were given to you by the sea-captain you told me about, Mary," he said, kindly, "it is much better that the Indian squaw took them. They were tainted gold and they would never do you any good. Of that I am certain."

"If I thought that Mary spent her time talking to sea-captains and taking gifts from them," said Elizabeth, "I should not willingly let her return to Strawberry Bank."

"I am sure Mary will not do anything that she shouldn't, will you, Mary?" said Mr. McFarland. "Judy would miss her sorely, if she did not return."

"Oh, please let me go, Ma," begged Mary, frightened at the sudden turn which the conversation had taken. The loss of the gold-pieces was nothing compared with her fear of not being allowed to go back. "Cousin Jeanie is worse and needs me," she cried. "There's only Uncle Sandy and Jamie and they can't do much about the house."

"Yes, I reckon Jeanie needs you more than I do," said Elizabeth reluctantly, "but I hate to think what an evil place a seaport town can be. You will be certain to keep an eye on her, will you not, Mr. McFarland?"

"With the greatest of pleasure," laughed the merchant, "and with wise little Judy's help. Mary could not be in better hands than our own, I assure you."

The journey back to Strawberry Bank took three days, for Merchant McFarland had several errands to accomplish on the way. He stopped at Exeter, Durham and then at Dover, where his factory for rolling iron bars was located. Here he saw a load of bar iron, some of which would be needed for his new ship, placed on a boat and shipped down the Piscataqua River.

Mary rode on the pillion behind the merchant, chatting happily. She talked freely of her life at the fisherman's cottage and told him about her frequent visits to Susannah, the little sick girl at the gaol. She found him a responsive companion and enjoyed the whole journey, for she knew that every beat of the horse's hoofs brought her nearer and nearer to her beloved Strawberry Bank.

"Do you know Master Greenwood, sir?" she asked,

as they followed leisurely along the banks of the river, southward.

"Who is he?" asked Mr. McFarland.

"He is a wood carver and has a shop on the water-front, not far from the Sign of the Mortar and Pestle," explained Mary. "He is a newcomer at the Bank. He carves beautiful figures out of logs of wood, the most beautiful figures in the whole world. And he wants, more than anything else, to carve a figure-head for your new ship."

"Does he, indeed?" laughed Mr. McFarland. "How does he know about it?"

"Oh, I told him, sir," answered Mary, seriously. "That is, he saw it first and I told him it was yours. I told him it is going to be the finest ship that Master Wiggin has ever built and that's why he wants to do the figure-head. Everybody's talking about your new ship, sir. Didn't you know that?"

"I suspect that you and Judy are doing the most of it," laughed the merchant. "Judy cannot possibly keep a secret."

"Oh! Is it supposed to be a secret?" asked Mary, in alarm. "I did not realize that, sir."

"No, no, never fear," said the merchant. "It's quite all right. A new ship cannot be kept a secret, no matter how hard we may try. Now, who is this figure-head carver and is he a friend of yours?"

"His name, sir, is Master Greenwood and . . ."

"Can you take me to his shop?"

"Oh, yes, sir, I can, sir," exclaimed Mary, delighted

beyond measure. "You'll like him, I know, sir, because . . ."

"Why will I like him?"

"Because I do, sir, so very much."

"And Judy? Will she like him, too?"

"I am sure she will, sir."

Entering town, the merchant rode at once to his home, where Judy came joyfully out to greet the returned travelers. Black Peter took the horse to the stable and the merchant and the two girls set out for the carver's shop on foot.

The door stood open and Mary led the way. Master Greenwood was still limping slightly, although the ankle was no longer bandaged. He still wore his green cloth coat with patches on it and holes in the elbow. And he still had dancing wrinkles about his eyes when he smiled.

"This is Merchant McFarland, sir," said Mary, shyly. Her voice showed that she was overcome somewhat by the seriousness of her errand. "He is building . . . he is going to build . . ."

"Never mind, Mary!" laughed the merchant. "I will explain to Master Greenwood. Ocean-Born Mary has told me about your splendid carving and I have come to see it, sir."

Soon Master Greenwood was showing all his carvings and explaining intricate details of his work. And both Daniel McFarland and his daughter felt as if they had known him all their lives. Then the merchant sent the two girls out on the wharf while he talked business with the carver. He looked over the row of carved figures in the corner and expressed interest in one, a woman who represented *Britannia*.

"I want the finest figure-head it is possible to get," said the merchant. "I offer the highest compensation, but I wish the best workmanship available."

"I shall be glad to undertake it, sir," said the carver, with becoming modesty. His shaking hands were the only outward sign of his inner emotion. This was a commission such as he had dreamed of all his life. A figure-head for the prow of the merchant's ship would travel to the ends of the earth and be seen in many foreign ports. It would bring him further orders from all the sea-captains and merchants who saw and admired it. His future was settled. No more pump-handles and gate-posts to keep the pot a-boiling!

"I will undertake it, sir, on one condition," said the carver, his pale face flushing.

"Do you hesitate?" asked the merchant, puzzled.

"On one condition, sir," the carver went on, his excitement increasing: "that no one see it until it is completed."

"Er . . . er . . . I do not know . . ." said Merchant McFarland, "whether that is practicable . . . or possible."

"Then, sir, I do not wish to undertake it," said Master Greenwood, emphatically. "I cannot do my best work with an audience spying upon me."

"Oh, you have misunderstood me," cried Mr. McFarland, with a hearty laugh. "I was only wondering how we could ever keep Mary and Judy out! They are in the secret already and they would feel deprived . . ."

"As for Mary and Judy," laughed the carver, "I can never do my best work without their constant supervision. I am sure of that. It was the general public I meant, sir."

"How can you keep them from knowing?"

"I can bar my door, sir."

"But will that not make them more curious than ever?"

The two girls came bursting in.

"Is it all arranged? Is it all arranged?" cried Mary.

"Why do you talk so long without letting us hear?" cried Judy. "Mary and I could have arranged this little matter in half the time."

"What little matter?" asked her father, teasing.

"Why, the figure-head, of course!" cried Judy. "Mary and I think that Peggy will make a beautiful *Britannia*."

"Peggy Fayerweather?" asked Mr. McFarland. "So she will. We must ask the Captain. But Master Greenwood says he intends to bar the door to keep people out."

"May I come in a boat and climb up the ladder to the back door?" asked Mary, promptly.

"Yes, and you may bring Judy along," said the carver happily. "By the way, I saw Susannah this morning and she has been missing you while you have been away at Nutfield. You'll stop in soon and see her, won't you?

"Oh, yes," answered Mary. "I have so much to tell her—about Blackbird and the gold-pieces and everything!"

The carver stood in the doorway and shaded his eyes from the afternoon sun as he watched the three go up the street together.

"What a kind, thoughtful child Mary is!" he said to himself. The feeling of discouragement which had enveloped him in the morning had completely disappeared. He felt as if he could dance and sing and shout from the housetops. He knew that now at last he had the opportunity to do his best work—an opportunity laid on his doorstep by no one else than Ocean-Born Mary—bless her!

On his way to the shipyard, the merchant stopped in at a low weather-beaten shed, with a sign over the door which read "Sail Loft." Sniffing the odor of tar and canvas, Mary and Judy followed. Mr. McFarland discussed the matter of sails for the new ship with Master Montgomery, the master sailmaker, who assured him that splendid progress was being made.

"I know all about sails," said Judy confidently, leading the way about the room, while Mary followed. "First, the master sailmaker determines the dimensions and they cast the pattern—the shape and length of

each individual cloth necessary to make up the various sails. Then the cutter cuts out each sail, cloth by cloth, in regular order, numbering them one, two, three, four and so on. They are all cut now and the workmen are sewing them together."

She pointed to the busy sailmakers, each sitting on a sailmaker's bench, surrounded by his tools, with his lap and feet enshrouded in billowing sail canvas. Mary watched in amazement, as they joined the cut pieces of sail-cloth carefully, making double flat seams with strong, waxed twine, as neat and handy as semp-stresses.

One of the men spoke up. "We use a funny kind of thimble!" he said, with a twinkle in his eye.

"It's called a 'palm'!" interrupted Judy, eagerly.

The man held up his hand. "That's so we can push the needle through the stiff canvas more easily," he explained. A heavy piece of leather was strapped around his palm, leaving thumb and fingers free. On the palm-side, just below the thumb, a piece of metal with indented needle holes was inserted.

"After all the pieces of canvas are joined," Judy went on, "some strengthening pieces have to be added, the hemming is done and then the outside edge is bound with a bolt-rope."

"Why, Judy," laughed her father, stepping up. "You know more about these things than I do. Come, girls, it is time to go."

Merchant McFarland was hungry for a sight of his new ship and anxious to see what progress had been made in his absence. From the sail-loft, he walked with the two girls to the shipyard. They went directly to the ways, where they examined the ribbed skeleton carefully. Word was sent to Master Wiggin, the builder, who immediately appeared, and the two men were soon engaged in the discussion of technical details, while Judy listened eagerly.

Mary waited, understanding very little. Suddenly she saw a familiar figure in the distance, standing in front of the ropewalk. Leaving Judy and her father, she ran to make sure. Yes, it was the pirate. At last, she would have a chance to talk to him and alone. Philip Babb. Philip Babb, she must not forget the name.

She came up, flushed and panting. All the things she had been wanting to say rushed into her mind at once —the water casks, the words of Aunt Becky, the logs from Nutfield . . . .

Sail-maker's "Palm"

"Why, Ocean-Born Mary, are you here?" the man asked, with a smile.

"You are . . . you are . . . a real sea-captain, aren't you, Mr. Babb?" The words burst out before she realized what she was saying.

"Who says I'm not?" he glared, defiantly.

"You are sailing soon, are you not, Captain Babb? You wanted logs for your cargo or were you intending to have the timber sawed up into lumber? And what can you take instead and what do you intend to bring back? And there's that sack of salt you let Pa take. I'd like to know so I can tell people when they ask me."

"What are you babbling about, my child?" asked the burly man.

"I was right there all the time, Captain Babb, only Aunt Becky doesn't like you because . . ." but she could not give the reason why Aunt Becky did not like him.

"Listen, child," said Philip Babb, earnestly, "rest a moment and catch your breath and then perhaps I can understand what you are trying to tell me."

"They'll see us," cried Mary, in haste. "They'll be calling me back any minute and I don't want them to know . . ."

"What do you want to tell me, Ocean-Born Mary?"

"I lost the gold-pieces you gave me, sir, and I'm very sorry the Indian squaw took them."

"Is that all?" asked the pirate, reaching into his pocket. "Here are some more for you. . . ."

"Oh, no, sir, please, sir. Ma and the merchant said the gold was tainted and would do me no good, sir," cried Mary, with a look of fear on her face.

"They did, did they?" The man glared again.

"I would have to go back to Nutfield if I took them, sir," continued Mary. "I don't want them, sir, but thank you very much. And I'm not to speak to sea-captains any more, sir, and I won't unless it's necessary."

As she spoke, Mary seemed to see the little earthen jar empty of its bright and shining gold-pieces and her heart felt heavy for her loss. They had been so beautiful to look at and to touch. Then she remembered the silver snuff-box. She knew that Captain Babb was soon to start on a voyage. Perhaps he would take it for a venture and exchange it for a little Dutch keeking-glass like Judy's and Peggy's. If he was willing to give her gold-pieces which she did not want, he might be willing to bring her a keeking-glass which she did want.

"Would you . . . would you, please . . ." she gulped and swallowed. It was very hard to ask for something for herself.

"What is it you want, Mary?" asked Captain Babb. "I will be glad to do . . ."

"Mary! Who is this?" came the stern voice of Merchant McFarland at her side. He and Judy had approached while she was talking. Philip Babb must have seen them coming. Why did he not warn her?

The pirate showed no fear at all, as he glared at Merchant McFarland and the merchant glared back.

"What do you want with this child?" demanded McFarland savagely.

"May I not speak to a friend?" sneered Babb.

"This child is not a friend of yours," said the merchant, "while she is under my protection."

"Are you not my friend, Ocean-Born Mary?" asked Captain Babb.

It was a cruel test. Mary hung her head, shame-faced. After a moment she raised it, flushed with earnestness and sincerity.

"Oh, sir," she cried, taking Merchant McFarland by the hand, as if he had been her own father. "Won't you please try to understand? He is a sea-captain who is going on a voyage . . ."

"I understand well enough," said the merchant, gruffly.

"Oh, Judy," cried Mary, "please try to make your father understand!"

Merchant McFarland understood only too well. The moment he set eyes on the man, he knew that he was not a legitimate sea-captain as Mary so earnestly believed. He knew that he was engaged in the illegal trade which the King was trying to suppress. He recognized the man as a native of the town for many years past, always going away for long absences, but always returning again, ever more bold and daring, to the place of his birth. It was bad enough to have the Algerine pirates to face, let alone your own plantation neighbors turned pirate. And yet, how clever the man was, to carry on his dishonesty for so many years without being caught! Surely the time would come when he would be brought to justice and punished for his crimes.

Merchant McFarland understood clearly the man's

power over Ocean-Born Mary. That he was the pirate who had saved her life as a babe, he had not the slightest doubt. The girl knew it and in return was offering her lifelong devotion and gratitude, to be used by this villain to cloak other evil. The merchant stared at the man's face keenly, to stamp his brutal features on his mind, that he might always recognize him in the future, for Ocean-Born Mary's sake. The face was full and round but hard and firm. The brows were heavy and black; they covered the deep-set eyes when he frowned. A searing scar from left ear to chin stood out white against the coarse darkness of the skin. Yes, he would always remember that face.

"What are you doing in this shipyard, sir?" he demanded angrily. "Does Master Wiggin know he is honored by a visit from . . ."

"Philip Babb, sir," said the pirate, bowing low, with mock courtesy. "Captain Philip Babb is my name and I have as much right in this shipyard as you have, sir." Then he added in a sarcastic tone: "I have heard of your new ship and I have just taken a look at her. Will you not be afraid to entrust so frail a bark to the perils of the sea, sir?"

"Just what do you mean by that?" demanded Merchant McFarland, his blood running cold at the insolence of the man's veiled threat. In that movement, he knew that the man was capable of the worst.

"Oh, sir," cried Mary. "He is my friend and he has been kind to me . . ."

"He doesn't look like a kind man," said Judy frankly, having missed nothing of the challenge of angry words. "He looks very cross to me. I would not want him for a friend."

"Come, Mary," said the merchant, grasping her firmly by the hand. "We must go quickly. Come, Judy."

They walked rapidly down the grassy path and turned the corner. Philip Babb stood where he was and looked after them thoughtfully. Then he burst into a hoarse, taunting laugh.

No one spoke for a time. The merchant knew he must warn Mary of the dangers of seeing the pirate and put her on her guard, but this was not the time to speak. He began to talk of other things quietly: "I hope, Mary, that the Puddle Dock fishermen will come back from the Banks with plenty of fish and get them dried in time for the first voyage of my new ship. I shall need a good many tons of codfish of all three sorts—merchantable for the Catholic countries of Europe, middling cod for use on the merchant vessels and refuse cod or 'Jamaica fish' for the Negroes in the West Indies."

"Yes, sir," said Mary, politely. She walked along, slowly, her hand in the merchant's, but she did not hear what he said.

Chapter IX

" 'In Lim'ric City . . . he was brought up,
And Dub . . . lin was his station;
He fell in love . . . with a nice girl,
Her name was Bar' . . . bry Allen.

When he took sick . . . and very ill,
He sent for Bar' . . . bry Allen;
But when she came . . . was all she said,
'I fear, young man . . . you're dyin'!' "

IN A corner of the market place, Jane Hawkins, the
verse peddler, sang her mournful ballad. She
paused frequently, to call out in a shrill voice:
"Ballads, tuppeny each, verses, ballads, tuppeny each!"
Old Uncle Sandy and Ocean-Born Mary made their
way slowly through the market crowd, taking turns

pushing the fish-barrow. At last they reached an empty corner and there took up their stand.

"Fresh cod, mackerel, halibut, eels,
  More choice than a King has served at his meals,"

cried Mary over and over again. She had learned that it was necessary to attract attention in order to sell her wares.

Since Cousin Tom's and Jock's departure with the fishing fleet, Jamie managed to bring in a catch daily, which provided enough for the family's food and some over for selling. This surplus Uncle Sandy brought to the market each Market Day and sold with Mary's help.

Two rollicking young fellows took up a stand near by. They had a variety of things to sell—unusual things which were not often seen in Spring Hill Market. The thin-faced man with the triangular hat pulled low over his eyes, arranged various bundles and bottles on a small table. The round-faced man, with straight, black hair, reaching to his shoulders, spread out a fine array of linens and silks.

"Lemons, raisins, right this way!" shouted the first in a nasal voice. "Oil, soap, wine, the finest made!"

"Lutestrings, best quality lutestring silks, in plum-color, cinnamon and laylock!" called his partner. "Linen, Nutfield linen!"

At the word 'Nutfield,' Mary pricked up her ears and stared at the men. One glance was enough to prove to her that these men had never set foot in Nutfield in all the days of their lives. Their faces had a dark, brownish look as if they had come from a southern climate. And yet they looked strangely familiar, too. Had she ever seen them before and where? She watched them more closely.

The hatchet-faced man picked up a handful of lemons and began to juggle them. Like a flash, the scene in the Ark Tavern came back to Mary in all its vividness. He had juggled pewter mugs then instead of lemons. And the long-haired man was the painter, of course, who had run away without completing Landlord Drummond's Noah's Ark sign.

"Mackerel? Is this good mackerel? Cod sold out? What? Whoever heard of such a thing? Well, eels then. What, no eels? These mackerel are only spikes, blinkers and tinkers—all too small. I like something to put my teeth into. A good cod is hard to beat. . . ."

Mary had to give her attention to her customer, Marm Pecksniff, finicky and talkative. It seemed strange that she should talk so much about fish, look them all over and not buy anything. Was she just waiting for her son? Mary thought she saw the apothecary beyond in the crowd.

"Which will you have, Marm?" she asked politely. But Marm Pecksniff had turned to a country woman on the other side and was discussing buttermilk and pot-cheese balls.

Then Mary saw that Peggy Fayerweather had come and was buying linen from the two dark-skinned men. Her Negro slave took the roll and placed it in the basket which he carried.

"Oh, Peggy!" cried Mary.

Peggy walked over to where Mary stood by her barrow.

"Oh, Peggy, you haven't . . ."

"Haven't what?" asked Peggy.

"You haven't bought linen from those men, have you?"

"Why, yes," answered Peggy. "You know, Ocean-Born Mary, I love Nutfield linen best and I need new aprons."

"But that's not Nutfield linen they're selling," whispered Mary. "Those men have never been in Nutfield."

"They haven't?" cried Peggy in alarm.

"Let us see it, to make certain," said Mary, quietly. "Uncle Sandy can tell us." Mary knew that she could recognize Nutfield linens and hollands anywhere—brown, white, speckled, striped or checked. And Uncle Sandy, who had spent his long life weaving them, could certainly make no mistake.

The briefest of examinations was sufficient. Uncle Sandy peered sharply at the linen with his watery eyes and felt it between his fingers. Then he shook his head, saying, "This is not Nutfield linen, Miss."

"Not Nutfield linen?" cried Peggy. "Then the men must take it back and return my money."

"Ah, no, my dear young lady," said a low-toned, smooth-tongued voice at her side. "Be not so hasty! We all know that there are great frauds and deceits being practiced in this Province by the selling of foreign linens under pretense that they were made at

Nutfield, and that the credit of the Nutfield manu-factory is being rapidly undermined."

Yes, it was Master Pecksniff. Had he been lingering in the crowd, waiting for the right moment? He stepped forward and immediately took the matter of the linen into his own hands.

"It is our duty," he went on, "to bring to justice those deceitful persons who are imposing foreign and outlandish linens upon an innocent public."

"Oh, Master Pecksniff, I would prefer simply to re-turn the linen," cried Peggy in distress. "I would not wish to have the men punished on my account."

"My dear Miss Peggy, it is your duty." The apothecary pulled her to one side and spoke seriously, in a low voice. "The matter is not so small as you seem to think. I have been on the trail of these men for some time. They are selling, not only illegal linen, but lemons, soap, oil and other goods, imported from Portugal and Spain, on which they have paid no duties. Of this I have been assured by Collector of the Port Quackenbush. They have broken His Majesty's Navigation Acts by exporting naval stores, which our mother country needs, to her enemies, France, Spain and Portugal, and then smuggling into our ports all manner of prohibited goods. It is a matter serious enough to be brought to the attention of the Board of Trade. At the very least, they are dishonest. Your father is the honest captain of a merchantman. Such men as these and their captain are his bitter enemies and can cause him infinite trouble. You will be loyal to your father, will you not? You will stand witness for the illegal linen, will you not?"

Peggy hesitated, thinking quickly.

"Oh, Peggy, please don't!" cried Mary, anxiously. She knew not why she spoke, except that an instinctive feeling told her to beware of the apothecary. No good would come, she felt certain, of giving him support. He took delight in hurting people and he would hurt Peggy, too. "Oh, don't!" she begged again.

The apothecary frowned angrily.

"Why, Mary!" cried Peggy. "I am surprised that you would support evil practices such as this, especially when it affects your family and neighbors in Nutfield so vitally. Of course it is my duty to do as Master Pecksniff advises."

With a look of triumph on his face, the apothecary gave a signal to some one in the crowd.

"Look who's coming!" screamed Jane Hawkins, who had been enjoying the proceedings. "Somebody's been and told the Justice about it! Well, I never!"

The constable came up with a warrant. Master Pecksniff had planned his strategy carefully. Before the two dark-skinned strangers realized they were suspect, a crowd advanced, surrounding the constable, a tall, thin man with a beetling brow, carrying a long, black tipstave, the emblem of his office. After a few moments of confusion, the juggler and his companion were led away to the office of the Justice of the Peace, Deacon Puddington, for trial. Peggy and Uncle Sandy were taken along to act as witnesses. Mary looked after them, waiting a while for customers. When none came, she ran to the shore, and quickly dumped out all the unsold fish into the water. Then she took up the empty fish-barrow and followed.

The little front room in Deacon Puddington's tiny house was filled to capacity by the persons involved in the trial: the magistrate—the Deacon himself—the culprits and the witnesses, not to mention Master Pecksniff. The curious bystanders had to look and listen through door and windows. To their disappointment, the trial was soon over.

By the time Mary came up with her barrow, Peggy and Uncle Sandy had gone and she saw the constable leading the two culprits away in the direction of the Parade, surrounded by the noisy crowd.

> " 'There was a ship sailed for the North Amer-i-ky,
> Crying, O the lowland low . . .
> There was a ship sailed for the North Amer-i-ky,
> And she went by the name of the Golden Van-i-ty,
> And she sailed from the lowlands low . . .' "

The song, in rich, resonant tones, came clearly over the babble of the crowd as they moved along.

"Who is singing?" asked Mary, full of wonder.

"Those wicked, sinful men," answered Marm Pecksniff.

"Where are they going?"

"To the log gaol by the Meeting House." Marm Pecksniff had not looked in at the Deacon's window for nothing.

"Will they have to stay there long?" asked Mary. She remembered little Susannah Winslow lying ill there in bed. If the prisoners sang there in the gaol, it would be company for her.

"Till after Meeting next Sabbath."

"And then?"

"They will have to sit in the Town Stocks for three hours at noonday! Ha ha!"

"What for?" asked Mary.

"As an example and warning to the loose-minded!" said the woman in a solemn, significant tone.

"What is the crowd hooting for?" asked Mary.

"Because the men are guilty and have been brought to justice!" said the old lady, vindictively. "Ah! When I was young," she went on, cackling with relish, "there was some one whipped every day at the town pump, and the cage at South Mill Pond was always full—stocks, pillory and all. But times have changed. . . ."

"Was every one so bad then?" asked Mary, innocently.

"Why, no!" snapped Marm Pecksniff in a sudden passion. "We were better than most, for we let no sin go unpunished."

The following Sabbath dawned clear and bright. From the moment she first opened her eyes, Mary felt that it would be an eventful day. As she sat on the narrow bench in the Meeting House, she fidgeted restlessly. The day was warm and the room was close and musty-smelling. Then her attention was caught by the entrance of a beautiful young girl, dressed like a woman in a fashionable gown. Mary had never seen its like before. It was made of paduasoy of marvelous fineness of texture and beauty of design and it was trimmed with gold lace. According to the latest fashion, it had great, padded hips upon which the young lady rested her arms, bare to the beruffled elbows. She had to turn sideways to enter her seat. All the people in the Meeting House turned and stared at her.

Mary dreamed and dozed as the meeting continued. Then at last it was over and she stood outside with the others. The front of the Meeting House, severe in its plainness, was covered with written notices of important town matters—town meetings, sales of cattle and farms, prohibitions regarding the sale of guns and liquor to the Indians and notices of marriages and vendues. Great dark splotches on the wood indicated the places where heads of wolves had been nailed to the outer wall, for the purpose of securing a bounty for their captors.

Mary stood near a group of women whom she knew and listened to their comments as the young lady appeared. "Just see how her hoops do spread her skirts in ample volume! Like a fishing smack in full sail!" whispered Susie Cobbett.

"They are so large, she was obliged to enter the door crab-wise, pointing her out-thrusting flanks end foremost!" added Granny McKeen.

"If Almighty God should make a woman in the same shape her hoops make her," snorted Marm Pecksniff, shaking her head with disapproval, "everybody would call it monstrous."

"But what a different matter when it's the latest London fashion!" said Susie Cobbett. "Eh, Maggie?"

Maggie McDonald, who of all the townsfolk should know of such matters, replied without hesitation: "Yes, indeed. 'Twas Lord Peabody came from London on the *Olive Branch* and brought them for a gift to

Miss Peggy Fayerweather, his betrothed. It has been told me by a reliable authority."

"Has the wedding date been announced?" asked the women eagerly.

Mary could scarce believe her ears. Was it Peggy? She approached the fine lady and was amazed to find it was she.

"Oh, Peggy, is it true what they are saying?" she cried.

"Are they speaking of my new gown?" asked Peggy, spinning about lightly. "Do they not think it beautiful?"

"They are saying that Lord Peabody . . ." but Mary could not finish the sentence.

"Bother Lord Peabody!" laughed Peggy. "He brought only the hoops. Father ordered my new gown in London! Tell me how you like it!"

"Oh, it is beautiful," cried Mary, "but you look so different, I scarcely know you."

Judy and her parents now joined the two girls and together they started homeward.

The hot, midsummer sun beat down upon the little seaport town, with its low, frame buildings and its narrow streets. It beat down upon the Parade with its watch-house, town pump and place of punishment. As the church-goers started homeward, they stopped with one accord at the southeast corner of the Meeting House. Here sat two men, awkward and uncomfortable in the town stocks. The heat of the noon-day sun beat down upon their bare heads pitilessly and great drops of sweat rolled down unhindered. They did not move hands or feet, for these were set firmly locked in wooden bonds and they seemed not to hear the shouts and jeers of the people or note their wondering stares. Their legs and bodies ached from the tight clamps, but they sat patiently, waiting for the minutes and hours to pass.

Mary, Peggy and the McFarlands stopped with the others. Mary saw the two men stare boldly at Peggy, then speak to each other under their breath. Undoubtedly they recognized her as the person who had testified against them.

Peggy, too, noticed their stares as she looked, all her happiness over the new gown faded away. "They have been punished on my account," she cried in distress. "Oh, why did I listen to Master Pecksniff?"

"You did the right thing, Peggy," said Mr. McFarland. "You must not be guided by sentiment. If these evil practices are not put down, they will lead to worse crimes."

"Oh, let us go away quickly," begged Peggy, with tears in her eyes. "I cannot bear to look at the wretched men."

"You must not be too cowardly to look," said Mr. McFarland, kindly but firmly. "Look well, children," he said to Judy and Mary. "Allow this scene to sink deeply into your minds and hearts. These men have received the just rewards of their deeds—dishonesty, greed, deceit and worse."

Mary and Judy walked closer.

Mary looked at the two men in consternation. Without their hats, she hardly recognized them. She stared, unconvinced. Yes, the thin, hatchet-faced man was the juggler, but the other? His face was full and round, his head was entirely bald and—his ears were cropped!

"Do you miss my wig, Ocean-Born Mary?" the man asked brazenly, noting her confusion. "I'm sorry, but the gaoler took it off and refused to give it back!"

"Ha, ha, ha, ha, ha!" laughed both men.

Mary and Judy looked at each other in dismay. They knew well the meaning of cropped ears—only the worst of crimes were punished by cropping the ears. The man had worn his wig of straight, black hair to his shoulders to conceal the fact that he was a deep-dyed criminal. Mary shuddered.

"Do they know you?" asked Judy, in surprise. "I heard one of them call you by name."

"He is the peddler who painted the Noah's Ark Sign at the tavern," explained Mary. "He wore a black wig then. Is he the same man who painted your walls?"

"Father," cried Judy, "is not the man on the right the artist who painted our walls?"

"No, child, no," said the merchant. "Our artist was old enough to be this man's father. What foolish notions you do have! Do you think I would employ a criminal?"

"Do come away, Mary," begged Judy. "Father and mother are waiting."

"Stay for a moment," begged the crop-eared peddler. "I want you to do something for me."

Earnestly Judy begged Mary to come away, only to meet refusal.

"The men are so hot, sitting there in the sun," exclaimed Mary. "I would like to get them a drink of cold water."

"Oh, no, Mary, they are wicked men. You must not go near them," cried Judy, running to join her parents.

The townsfolk passed on one by one, leaving Mary alone, still staring at the criminals. Suddenly she saw half-a-dozen little Moseleys approach the town pump in the middle of the Parade with pails in their hands. She ran hastily, snatched a mug from little Ichabod's hand, regardless of his wailing protest, and filled it with water. Surrounded by the staring children, she brought it to the peddler to drink. She filled it a second time for the juggler. Then she handed it back to little Ichabod and sent the children home.

"You are Ocean-Born Mary, are you not?" asked

the peddler, as soon as they were gone. "You live at Tom Martin's on Brimstone Hill, do you not?"

"How do you know?" asked Mary, suspicious.

"Never mind that now," replied the man. "I must talk quickly before some one comes. You saw us when we brought the water casks, did you not?"

"Was that you?" countered Mary. "Singing the ballads?"

"Yes, the captain sent us to see if you lived there."

"I was there," said Mary. "And I saw you once before, too."

"Where?"

"At the Ark Tavern," said Mary. "*He* was juggling pewter mugs and *you* were painting the Noah's Ark Sign. Why didn't you finish it?"

"I was in too much of a hurry. Now, listen. You know where the captain's ship is anchored, don't you?"

"Captain Babb's?" Mary hesitated. "Ye—es."

"You can row a wherry, can't you?"

"Ye—es."

"Will you take a message to him for us?"

"I . . . don't . . . know."

"I'll tell you what it is and you must promise you won't forget. It's easy," said the crop-eared peddler. "Tell him that you saw Mink and Weasel in the stocks and he's not to sail till we get there. Now, what are you going to tell him?"

"That I saw Mink and Weasel in the stocks and he's not to sail till you get there. Is he sailing soon?"

"Not till we get there, we hope!" said the peddler, looking at the juggler. They both burst into loud guffaws.

"Are you both pirates, too?"

"Who said we were pirates? Will you go and tell him?"

Just then a tall, serious-looking man, dressed in sober black, came round the corner of the Meeting House and approached the stocks with a noiseless tread. He stepped forth beside Mary.

"You see here, my child," he began in a solemn voice, "two men caught in their wickedness and brought to punishment. Let this be an example to you, to teach you the dangers of evil and wrong-doing and to give you a wholesome regard for goodness, industry and right living. One must labor without ceasing that good may overcome evil."

Mary recognized at once the awe-inspiring voice and figure of Parson Flint. She waited respectfully until he finished, then darted swiftly away. As she ran, she heard his deep voice behind her, chiding the men in the stocks, but she did not look back.

It was late afternoon before Mary could leave the cottage. She went out on the ledge and shaded her eyes. She saw the pirate's brigantine in the distance, riding at anchor. A few days before, the ship had been moved to an anchorage near Swing Bridge, still within Puddle Dock. She knew the ship's distinguishing marks and recognized it clearly.

She went out behind the cow-shed, uncovered the little earthen jar and took out the snuff-box with a smile of determination. It was to be an eventful day, after all. She ran down to the beach, cast off the painter and climbed into the wherry. She struck off rapidly with the oars and rowed toward the mouth of the cove. The day was clear and the water was still. The gulls circled overhead, screaming shrilly. She made swift progress and soon came alongside the brigantine.

The ship displayed no colors of any sort, but Mary noticed that all sails were ready for setting. On the stern, she saw the name *Marygold* carved and blazoned in gold, and the captain himself, standing above, looking down. He seemed to know her at once, for he shouted directions, then let down a rope ladder from the main bulwarks. Mary climbed up and he set her on her feet. A network of shadows from the ropes above crossed the sunlit deck. Three sailors, lounging near by, were singing lustily:

" 'Go tell the King of England,
Go tell him this from me,
Though he reigns King o'er all the land,
I will reign King at sea . . .
Though he reigns King o'er all . . .' "

The song stopped abruptly as the men stared at the newcomer.

"Ocean-Born Mary, what brings you here?" asked Captain Babb, taking his long pipe from his mouth. He looked strangely huge and imposing. He glanced swiftly at the sailors, then back again. His voice had not the gentleness of former meetings and he frowned as he spoke.

"I just wanted to see you today, sir," said Mary, nervously. "I was to give you a message . . ."

"A message?" frowned Captain Babb.

"I was to say that I saw Mink and Weasel in the stocks, sir . . ."

"In the stocks, are they? The rascals! Serves 'em right. Listen, men," cried Babb, "Mink and Weasel are in the stocks!"

The men burst into roars of laughter, rose lazily and sauntered nearer, still staring at Mary as they might have stared at some strange kind of fish. The captain pointed them out by name—Rat, Squirrel and Turtle.

"And you're not to sail till they get here, sir," Mary added.

"Not to sail till they get here?" roared Babb. "Hear that, men?"

Rat, Squirrel and Turtle roared again, "Haw, haw, haw!" and the noise filled Mary with sudden fear.

"Those two jolly rogues can jolly well take care of themselves!" cried the captain.

"You won't sail without them, will you, sir?" asked Mary, earnestly.

"I'll sail when I've a mind to," answered the captain, harshly.

"Will that be soon, sir?" persisted Mary.

"What makes you so curious, lass?" asked Babb, with a chuckle.

"I just wondered, sir . . . if you take ventures . . ." said Mary, timidly.

"Sometimes," admitted Babb, "if they're the right sort." The men roared again.

"Would this do for a venture?" asked Mary, holding out the snuff-box.

The three sailors crowded up to see. Squirrel, a sullen man with a broken nose, reached out and took the

" 'Ocean-Born Mary, what brings you here?' asked
Captain Babb."

box with a swift, greedy motion. "Does this belong to you, Miss?" he asked.

Turtle, an old man with long whiskers, took it from him. "Where did you steal this, Miss?" he asked with a wink.

"I'll take it!" yelled Rat, whose eyes were small and squinting. He snatched roughly. "I'll take it!"

"You will, will you?" shouted Captain Babb, in a thunderous voice. He took the box from Rat and gave him a sturdy kick. The youth stumbled, tripped over a coil of rope and fell backwards down the hatchway. The sailors chuckled gleefully.

"Oh!" cried Mary, in alarm. "Is he hurt, sir?"

"Twenty tumbles won't hurt a tough Rat like him," answered the captain, putting the snuff-box in her hand.

"Why did you kick him, sir?"

"Haw, haw, haw, she wants to know why did you kick him sir!" roared the men.

"To teach him manners!" snorted Babb, angrily. "Come, I want to show you something." He led the way. They climbed the poop ladder and descended to the cabin by the companionway. Philip Babb motioned Mary to a seat, then unlocked a small chest. He brought out a leather case, which he tossed into Mary's lap. "Open it and look," he ordered.

Mary laid the snuff-box down. She slipped the little gold latch and opened the case. It was a beautifully painted miniature. A pretty, young girl looked up at her with bright, shining eyes. She held a doll in her arms. It had bright, staring eyes and a flaring skirt.

"How beautiful!" said Mary, softly. "Who is it?"

"My little sister," answered Captain Babb. "Her hair was red like yours and her name was Mary, too."

The man's face softened and Mary felt as she looked at him, what a simple, good-natured man he was.

"What is that in her arms, sir?" asked Mary, looking at the miniature again.

"Her poppet!" answered Babb. "She always had it with her, she loved it so. She would never give it up."

"Oh!" said Mary. "It would be nice to have a poppet to hold in your arms and take to bed at night, just like a baby . . . I wouldn't give it up, either."

"Have you never had a doll or poppet to play with?" asked Babb.

"Yes, sir," cried Mary, eagerly. "I made one out of a towel once and stained its cheeks with checkerberry juice, but my little brothers tore it up."

"Oh, ho! Is that so?" said Babb, thoughtfully. "Well, when I come back from my next voyage, I'll bring you one."

"A . . . a . . . you don't mean—?" stammered Mary.

"I'll bring you the finest poppet I can find in Europe, with a silk brocade gown, ear-rings in her ears and a gold necklace round her neck!"

"Oh, sir!" cried Mary, puzzled. "Do you mean for a venture? If I trade in my snuff-box?" She handed it out eagerly. "Could I get . . . a poppet?"

"I mean I will *give* you one," said the pirate, gruffly. "Keep your snuff-box, I don't want it. I'll give you a poppet for your very own."

"For . . . my very . . . own, sir?" asked Mary, scarcely able to comprehend his meaning.

"Yes, to keep. Would you like that?"

Mary grasped the man's hand impulsively and looked up at him with eyes full of trust. Surely this was the height of kindness and goodness. "Oh, sir . . . I would be like your little sister, sir." She glanced at the miniature where it lay, open on the table. "I would never give it up. I'm sorry little Mary died, sir."

A loud snort was heard. "That's why every blessed ship he takes has to have her name changed to *Marygold!* Bah!" shouted Rat, maliciously.

The three sailors had been eavesdropping on the deck above and could contain their disgust no longer. They burst out in loud guffaws over the sentimental conversation they had just heard. Philip Babb shook his fist and, furious with anger, ordered them away. Looking up, through the skylight, Mary saw their squinting eyes, their scarred faces and their leering smiles. She trembled violently.

"Sentimental, I calls it!" shouted Turtle.

"What's he brought that gal aboard for?" mocked Rat.

After their voices had died away, Philip Babb opened a box and emptied a handful of treasures into Mary's lap,—gold chains and necklaces, pearls, gems and precious stones which shone like stars. While she examined them, he climbed up the companionway, leaving her alone.

Mary looked at the jewels in her lap and was overcome by their beauty. Where had they come from? How did the captain happen to have them? Of course, a sea-captain could buy anything he liked in foreign lands. But was he an honest man? To whom did these belong? She dropped the gold chains with a sudden fear. She shuddered and rose to her feet. The gems and jewels fell to the floor and rolled in every direction. They were hateful, not beautiful. Then Mary was overcome with uneasiness. She looked about the room and saw that she was alone. Was the vessel moving or was she dreaming? She thought she heard the "Yo-heave-ho" of the sailors getting up their anchor. No, she must be dreaming. She looked at the jewels and necklaces on the floor and stooped to pick them up. A sudden lurch came and she knew.

She picked up the snuff-box hastily. She climbed up the companionway with all speed. She saw Captain Babb standing by the helmsman, quietly giving short commands. She ran to his side.

"Oh, sir!" she cried out in dismay. "You are not sailing now, are you?"

"You were anxious enough for me to sail a moment ago," said Babb gruffly.

"Oh, please let me off, sir," cried Mary. "I must row back in the wherry. Stop the boat, sir, quickly."

"Get out of my sight!" shouted the captain, with a sharp oath. "Did I ask you to come aboard this boat? What business have you to be here anyway? Do you think I can change my plans just for you?"

The captain no longer had a look of kindness on his face. He turned a deaf ear to Mary's pleas. She walked away from him, hopeless, feeling that she had lost a friend. She stood by the rail with her face turned toward home. The tears rolled slowly down her face.

Swing Gate stood open, where the ship had passed through. The expanse of water between her and the shore grew greater every minute and the little huddle of buildings that made up the town grew smaller as she watched. She saw Goat Island, with Goody Gregory's hut nestling among the rocks, swing slowly past, like the other islands in the harbor. The sun went down in the west and dusk descended gently, blotting out familiar landmarks. Night came and with it, dampness and chill. When she could see no more, she curled up on a pile of sail-cloth near the main hatch and her heart beat heavily in her breast.

The real truth of the situation stared her in the face. Why had she come? All day she had been conscious of the fact that it was July 28, her birthday. Aunt Becky had said that the service in Nutfield would not be held in her absence. She had felt she must see the pirate to-day—on the twelfth anniversary of that eventful happening in mid-ocean. She had seen him, it is true, but she had had no opportunity to mention the day, and it was obvious he had forgotten. Her birthday meant nothing to him.

Then, too, her impulse had been one of kindness, an instinctive desire to help those outcasts of society whom every one condemned and whom no one else would help. Bitterly she regretted it now, when she saw to what her kindly impulses had brought her. She had had faith in the captain's innate goodness, because he had once saved her life. Now, for the first time, she was confronted by his wickedness and cruelty, which blotted out the good. The knowledge of the truth stabbed her like a sharp pain. She knew now that what every one said was true—the juggler and the peddler, like their captain, were dishonest men. She knew she should never have set foot in the captain's vessel. In frantic fear, she wondered where they were taking her—when she would ever see her loved ones again. Although she knew nothing of pirate voyages, the prospect filled her with horror. She thought of Merchant McFarland's words 'just rewards,' and she knew that she had brought this deserved punishment upon herself. She tried to think of some way out of her difficulty, but no solution came to her mind.

Finally, she dozed off to sleep. It seemed a long time afterwards when she was rudely wakened by the be-whiskered old man, Turtle. Her legs were stiff and her hands were cold. She shivered as she stumbled to her feet, clutching the snuff-box tightly in her hand. Everything was dark now, except the feeble light from a lantern hanging at the mast head and a single star in the night sky.

The old man pulled her roughly and shoved her toward the rail. She saw a rope ladder hanging over the side and she climbed down obediently. When she put her foot down in the boat below, she was surprised to see that they were near land. Where were they? Was it an island? One of the Isles of Shoals? She began to ask questions, but Old Turtle bade her hush. She saw that she was in a gundalow and a wherry—was it her own?—was tied on behind. As they moved away, the ship's great hulk loomed up black against the pale night sky. Mary saw a lantern cross the deck and she heard orders given in a voice that she knew—a voice that could be kind and could be cruel.

Chapter X

"ALL'S well! One o'clock and fair winds! All's
we—e—ll!" sounded the call of the night
watchman through the dark streets of Strawberry Bank.

Four long hours before, the melancholy tones of the
nightly curfew had rolled out of the steeple of the
North Meeting House, warning the townsfolk dutifully to their beds. Through the unpaved, narrow and
unlighted streets, the night watchman made his tedious
rounds, holding his lantern ahead, so that its rays might
guide his steps. He saw no robbers or revelers in the
streets, he heard no noise or roistering to break the
peace. Only the sound of his own footsteps and the
sharp thuds of his staff on the ground. He opened his
mouth and called again: "One o'clock and all's we—
e—ll!"

"But this is the Town Dock!" cried Mary in dismay, from her seat in the gundalow. "I told you I live at Puddle Dock—away south of here."

"The captain's orders was to put ye out at Town Dock," insisted Old Turtle, in a stubborn tone which settled the matter. "I always obeys the captain's orders."

The gundalow came alongside the wharf. The tide was low and it was difficult to see in the darkness. The old man motioned Mary toward the ladder and she climbed up on to the wharf. She heard him below in the darkness loosening her wherry and making it fast to the dock. In a few moments he stood beside her.

"One o'clock and all's well!" came the watchman's cry, suddenly close at hand. The scattered rays of a lantern in an uplifted hand streamed across the wharf.

"Here, hide!" said Old Turtle in a husky whisper.

He pushed Mary behind a barrel and himself disappeared inside an adjoining shed. Mary looked after him but could not see where he went or hear his footsteps.

The flashing rays of the lantern came closer and closer, exposing every nook and corner. Mary's heart throbbed with fright. The light stood still. Had the watchman seen something? Was he turning to go? No, the light came forward. It fell on the fold of Mary's linsey-woolsey skirt which protruded beyond the barrel. The next moment, the man's hand grasped her firmly by the shoulder and pulled her forth. The lantern glared brightly at her. She was suddenly conscious that she was dirty and unkempt. She hid her face in her hands, ashamed to be seen.

"What are you doing here, lass, at this unseemly hour?" shouted the watchman, angrily. "Was that your boat I heard splashing out there? Where have you been? What have you been doing?"

Mary hung her head. The words would not come. It was all so difficult to explain, it was better to say nothing. Suddenly the thought entered her mind that the watchman might take her before the Lieutenant-Governor or Parson Flint. How dreadful that would be. She darted out from under the man's elbow and started to run. But he was too quick for her. He caught her and pulled her back.

"No, ye don't, lass!" he cried. He pushed her in a corner, held up the lantern and stared in her face.

"The old man," began Mary, hoping to deflect the watchman's attention, "went in there." She pointed to the shed.

"What old man?" asked the watchman, distrustfully. "Now ye know, lass, there warn't no old man with ye. Ye rowed up in that wherry yourself and ye can't tell me different. I heard ye and I seen ye. Ye're just talkin' 'bout an old man so's ye kin run away from me agin."

Mary hung her head again. What was the use of trying to explain? The tears came, though she tried to hold them back. Then she heard voices and she trembled, wondering what was coming next. Oh, if she had only not listened to those men in the stocks, this would not have happened. She would at this moment have been comfortably asleep in her new bed at Cousin Jeanie's.

The watchman heard the voices, too. He waited,

listening alertly. More people abroad in the middle of the night. Strange happenings, these. And yet it was time something happened. The nights had been long and monotonous lately and he felt a trifle guilty about accepting his shilling a night, unless a fire or thieves or some other disorder happened now and then to make it worth while.

"Oh, here she is!" cried a woman's voice. The tone was aggravated, yet relieved. "I knew I should find her somewhere, even if I had to traipse the whole town over. Mary! What are you doing here at this time of night?"

Mary saw at once that it was Aunt Becky with Jamie at her side, holding a lantern. They both had upset and frightened looks on their faces as if something out of the ordinary had happened. And truly nothing more out of the ordinary could have happened than this—a walk abroad in the middle of the night, ending at the water-front.

Mary turned away from Aunt Becky, filled with shame.

"So this is where you are, Mary," Aunt Becky went on. "Cousin Jeanie could not sleep because you had not come home. She was so worried, she sat up till long after curfew, waiting. Then she sent Jamie to the almshouse, thinking you might have come to see me. Jamie and I set out at once and have been hunting for you ever since."

"Where have you *been*, Mary?" demanded Jamie, angered that she did not answer.

Mary burst into tears.

Ben Snuffer, the watchman, recognized the Keeper

of the almshouse at once and doffed his hat politely. Becky Armstrong was a woman who commanded respect wherever she went.

"Shall I say anything about it, ma'am?" he asked, deferentially. "Will not the Select men make a fuss if I don't notify 'em?"

"How will they find it out if you don't notify them?" asked Becky Armstrong, sharply.

"True, that's true, ma'am," squeaked the watchman, shaking in his boots. He had heard that this woman ruled the almshouse with a rod of iron and it might be as well to please her. "And besides, what's the use of knockin' 'em up at two o'clock at night—er, I mean in the mornin'? The thing's done and can't be undone."

"You have seen nothing, Master Snuffer!" said Becky Armstrong, severely. "The lass is the daughter of a friend of mine. She is under my protection. I am taking her at once to my home. Have you any objections, Master Snuffer?"

"None at all, ma'am! None at all!" squeaked the watchman, considerably relieved to have the matter taken out of his hands.

"Remember, Master Snuffer," continued Becky. "You have seen nothing. You have heard nothing."

"I have seen nothing, ma'am. I have heard nothing. May I bid you good evening—or should it be good morning, ma'am?"

"Good evening, Master Snuffer!" said Becky Armstrong. "Jamie, you run along home now and tell your mother that Mary is safe in my hands. I will send her home tomorrow."

"Yes, Aunt Becky," said Jamie.

"Jamie . . ." called Mary, faintly.

"What is it?" asked Aunt Becky.

"The wherry . . . is there . . . at the dock," Mary went on. "I thought Jamie might like . . . to take it home. . . ."

"The wherry?" grunted Jamie, astonished. "Have you been out in the wherry?"

"Go and find it, Jamie," ordered Aunt Becky, severely. "You may as well row it home."

"Yes, ma'am," said Jamie, as he stumbled off in the darkness.

The familiar town seemed strange and lifeless at night. No groups of lively sailors or backwoodsmen dawdled before shop doors or warehouses, rollicking with gaiety and laughter. Doors and windows were covered with shutters and even the taverns were barred and bolted against visitors. The wooden signs above the doors swung back and forth disconsolately, with ominous creakings. All the sounds of busy work were stilled. Mary walked along at Aunt Becky's side, filled with a strange discomfort, as if she had never seen the place before.

"All's well! Two o'clock and fair winds! All—l—'s we—ll!" came the sonorous call of the night watchman behind them.

When they reached the almshouse, Aunt Becky sent Mary to bed without a word. Mary's sleep was restless. The snores of the women inmates in the next room disturbed her no less than her own thoughts. At daybreak, she woke, disappointed and disheartened over her adventure. She had failed to send the silver snuff-box off for a venture and she had no faith in the pirate's promise. She took the box out from under her pillow and looked at it. Then she heard the blast of a horn from without and it reminded her of Joey Moseley. A sudden inspiration seized her. She rose and dressed quickly. Snuff-box in hand, she crept out of the house. In the kitchen, Tilly, the quiet one, was already starting the fire. Mary slipped by, unobserved.

Down King Street to the Parade she ran in the bleak dawn. There at the corner of the Meeting House, she saw Joey Moseley with his dog, Frisky, scampering about his feet. Joey blew loud blasts on his horn which resounded through the empty streets and cows were coming toward him from all directions. After having been milked, they had been turned out of their barns by their owners, to go to meet the cow-herd. Some browzed lazily on the grass by the roadside, others stalked promptly with heads up to the meeting place. Among them were Maggie McDonald's Spotted Moll, Deacon Puddington's young heifer, the Moseleys' Dandelion, Brownie and Queenie belonging to the Ark Tavern and many others.

Joey waited a few moments, then tramped sturdily along the center of King Street in the direction of Rock Pasture, following the cows, while Frisky darted about barking furiously at their heels.

Mary joined him behind the herd. "Hello, Joey," she called.

"What are you doing out so early?" asked Joey.

"Joey," cried Mary, breathless, "when you go to sea, will you do something for me?"

"Yes, of course," answered Joey, promptly.

"Will you take my silver snuff-box for a venture and exchange it for a little Dutch keeking-glass?"

"To be sure," answered Joey, obligingly.

"Well . . . here it is, then, Joey."

"Oh, I don't want it now," answered Joey. "I might lose it out in the pasture. Keep it till I go. Listen, do you want to know a secret?"

"Oh, yes, Joey, please tell me," begged Mary.

"I'm going to ship on that new brig of Merchant McFarland's, with Captain Fayerweather. He's a fine captain and . . ."

"Oh, Joey, I'm so glad. And you won't forget my snuff-box, will you? I must hurry back now."

"Don't tell anybody!"

"I won't, Joey."

Mary ran happily back to the almshouse, with a weight off her mind. At last she had found a way to take her venture. Then suddenly she remembered Captain Babb's promise. The unpleasantness of the adventure faded away. Would he bring her a poppet as he had said? A poppet and a keeking-glass, how wonderful that would be! Mary's heart felt light again as she dreamed of the future. She slipped into the almshouse and was quietly setting the table for breakfast when Aunt Becky appeared.

"I feel as if I'd been up all night," said Aunt Becky, "what with Goody Stubbs coughing and Goodman Bascom snoring loud enough to lift the roof." Then she turned to Mary. "No rest for the wicked, I've often heard it said, and I'm inclined to believe it's true."

Mary began to wonder. Had Aunt Becky forgotten

the water-front episode or was she just making it clear that she did not wish to have it mentioned?

"Have you combed your hair this morning, Hetty?" asked Aunt Becky.

Jinny and Uncle Rufus and Old Jemmy, who were taking their places at the table, began to chuckle with laughter.

"Merchant McFarland, the Overseer, came yesterday and put in his complaint at last," explained Aunt Becky. "He doesn't like tousled heads and he wants Hetty to keep hers combed!"

"Why don't ye cut it off and save all the trouble?" asked Jinny, the queer one.

"I combed it slick!" announced Hetty, in a loud voice. "I poured a pan of melted grease over it to keep it smooth."

Mary joined in the roar of laughter which followed. Hetty did indeed look like a stranger, with her well-greased locks.

"Now, Uncle Rufus," announced Aunt Becky, when breakfast was over, "do you and the men make haste and finish those yokes. We must put them on the pigs today so we can turn them loose. They'll root up the whole garden, soon." The men hurried out obediently.

No, Aunt Becky never forgot. After dispatching her morning duties with her usual promptness, she took Mary into the lean-to room and questioned her. Mary told her story as briefly as possible.

" 'Twas probably the Isles of Shoals where he took you—I haven't a doubt," said Aunt Becky, reflectively. "Those islands are a secure refuge for rovers like him who infest our coasts. They can refit their ships there, hide their booty, carouse as much as they please and snap their fingers at the hand of the law. If he went there, he's probably at sea by now. Judging from the looks of things, he's been making preparations for some time. I don't like to wish any one evil, but I'll feel satisfied as soon as I know that wicked man is at the bottom of the ocean."

"Oh, but Aunt Becky," cried Mary, "he did save our lives!" It was on the tip of her tongue to add also that he had promised to bring her a poppet, but she stopped short.

"One good impulse can never atone for a lifetime of wrong-doing," said Aunt Becky, sharply. "It was a great risk you ran, to set foot on his vessel, and your guardian angel was there by your side, I haven't a doubt."

Mary was puzzled and alarmed by Aunt Becky's attitude. Why did she blame Captain Babb for it all? Why did she not scold and get it over with and the punishment as well?

"He's related to the Old Gentleman himself," Aunt Becky went on. "That's why you are not responsible. I will arm and protect you against him the best way I know. Come, let us go to the Sign of the Teapot."

As they started out the door, they noticed a commotion in the yard. Jinny, the queer one, had taken two pails of skim milk and poured it into the trough for the pigs. The pigs rushed away from the men who were yoking them and began to drink the milk. In a moment the trough was empty and they began to run wildly about. They broke down the gate and rushed out into the street. Old Jinny cackled and laughed with glee as she watched.

"They are not yoked! They are not yoked!" screamed Uncle Rufus, waving the wooden yokes helplessly in his hands.

"We must run and catch them quickly," called Aunt Becky, "before the hog-reeve gets them."

Everybody started after the pigs, Mary, Aunt Becky and all the old men and women. A wild commotion it made, but in an incredibly short time, all the pigs were caught and yoked.

"You let somebody else feed the pigs next time," said Aunt Becky to Old Jinny.

"Yes'm, 'twas the milk did it, not me, Marm," said Old Jinny, with a grin, as she walked meekly back into the house.

Mary and Aunt Becky made their way round the corner to Maggie McDonald's shop. "I'll buy you a hornbook," said Aunt Becky, as the bell on the door of the shop tinkled merrily. "Then you'll be safe."

Mary looked up, more puzzled than ever.

Maggie McDonald brought out from under the counter a pile of hornbooks at request. Aunt Becky picked one up and studied it carefully. It was really not a book at all. It was a thin piece of wood about three by five inches, upon which was a printed paper, covered with a transparent sheet of yellowish horn, fastened down along the edges by tacks in a strip of brass.

"It's about time the poor child had one," sniffed Aunt Becky, full of scorn. "No one would think of it but myself. Here's your criss-cross row," she went on, pointing to the crosses in the two upper corners and the alphabet between. She held it down so Mary could see. "Here are your *a b abs* and this is the Lord's Prayer."

"I'll give you a thread to hang it by," said Maggie, interested as always. She laced a strong linen thread through the hole in the handle at the bottom of the hornbook.

"What is it for, Aunt?" asked Mary.

"To teach you to read and spell," answered Aunt Becky, soberly. "And this immortal prayer," she went on, "is a holy charm before which will flee all unholy ghosts, goblins and even the Old Gentleman himself to the very bottom of the Red Sea." She fastened the string to Mary's belt, letting the hornbook fall at her side, to hide among the folds of her skirt. "Now, my child," she concluded, breathing a sigh of relief, "at last you will be safe."

At Aunt Becky's bidding, Mary started at last for home. Her feet dragged reluctantly. She forgot all her happiness over the poppet which the pirate was to bring, and was ashamed of herself for having caused Cousin Jeanie so much worry. She knew that Cousin Jeanie would not scold and that made it all the harder to face her.

As she crossed over Canoe Bridge and climbed up the rocky path, she heard Jamie whistling in the fish-house. Then voices—women's voices in the cottage. Mary walked slowly round to the back door and went in. Old Uncle Sandy was weaving sail-cloth at his loom, just as always. Cousin Jeanie lay in her bed, pale and ill, and on a chair beside her, sat Old Marm Pecksniff.

"I'm here, Cousin Jeanie," said Mary, approaching the bed.

"Come and kiss me, dear," said Cousin Jeanie.

That was all, not a word of reproach. How good Cousin Jeanie was! Mary knew that her own mother would never have been so forgiving. She bent over and kissed her, and as she did so, the hornbook knocked against the bedstead.

"What is this, Mary?" asked Cousin Jeanie.

"A hornbook that Aunt Becky bought for me," answered Mary. "She wants me to wear it all the time. It's to teach me to read and spell."

"You'd a far sight better stay to hum and keep out of mischief!" snorted Marm Pecksniff.

"Go and pare some potatoes, Mary," said Cousin Jeanie, "and put them on to cook for supper."

"Potatoes? What be they?" sniffed Marm Pecksniff, suspiciously.

Mary brought her apron full of potatoes and showed them to the woman.

"You don't eat them things, do ye?" she cried in a shocked voice.

"Oh, yes," answered cousin Jeanie. "They're a staple food in Scotland where we come from. We brought the seed from there years ago. You can roast them in their skins in the ashes or pare and boil them in water. They're good to eat with fish and for feeding stock of all kinds."

"Well, I never!" ejaculated Marm Pecksniff. "I heard of a man who planted some once. He cut off the tops of the plants and ate 'em for greens. He said they tasted dreadful, so he pulled them up by the roots and threw them out."

"Then he threw out the whole of his crop!" laughed Jeanie.

"In Nutfield," explained Mary, starting her paring, "we put them in a hole in the ground in the spring-time. Then in the fall, we dig it open and find a whole hill full of potatoes from the one that we put there."

"In Nutfield!" exclaimed the old lady with a frown. "Did you say in Nutfield? Where's that?"

"About thirty miles west," said Mary, "out in the King's woods."

"Mary's parents live there," added Jeanie.

"Are there Indians out there?" asked Marm Pecksniff, apprehensively.

"Oh, yes, Marm," answered Mary. Then, seeing the black look which came over the visitor's face, she added cheerfully: "But they are our friends. They are not dangerous. We see them often."

"No Indian is ever a friend of a white man!" said the old lady, soberly. "Remember that."

"Why, we give them a corn-loaf when they're hungry or a piece of tobacco and they sometimes bring us venison or the hind leg of a beaver. Ma spun some thread for Lean Wolf's squaw while I was at home . . ."

"Never trust an Indian," said Marm Pecksniff, obstinately. The tears came to her eyes and she appeared to be greatly disturbed. "They will eat your bread and cut your throat afterwards."

"Mother says we must feed our fellow-creatures when they are hungry," said Mary, "and warm them when they are cold. . . ."

"If you had ever lived through what I have lived through, child, you would not talk as you do; no, nor your mother either," said Marm Pecksniff, with vehemence. "I can remember when the Indians used to come and peep in at the windows of our houses, right in this very town. That was less than thirty years ago, when we built the Stockade to keep them out. The Plains Massacre was nine years before that. I lived out at Portsmouth Plains then."

"Were you . . . were you . . . in it?" asked Mary, faintly.

"Was I?" asked Marm Pecksniff, bitterly. "I was only a young woman then and all my children were born afterwards. There! Take a look at that, child!" She lifted her cap and wig and revealed a silver plate in her bald scalp. "That's where an Indian wounded me with a tomahawk, after removing my scalp," she went on, cackling with relish. "No, it don't hurt a bit; besides I've got used to it."

"Would you like to tell us about it?" asked Cousin Jeanie, thinking that the telling might ease the poor woman's mind.

"I can remember it all as plain as day," said Marm Pecksniff. "We had heard news of trouble at Dover and we were anxious. Just before dawn we awoke to see the light of our burning barns. The Indians sounded their war-whoop and set upon our houses. The women and children fled to the garrison-house, while the men fought with such implements as came to hand. I spoke a word to my poor slave, Dinah, and then we ran. When it was all over, my husband and friends found me midway between our house and the garrison. They took me up for dead. We always built the garrison-houses with an overhang, so we could pour boiling water down on their necks. But we didn't get there to do it. Oh, dear, oh, dear, there were two little girls whose names were Betsy and Nancy and three fine young men and my poor Dinah, who died that day . . . and others . . . oh, dear, oh, dear . . ." sobbed the poor woman.

"But that's all over, now," comforted Mary. "You're not afraid any longer, are you?"

"We have plenty of forts and garrison-houses still standing," said Cousin Jeanie. "They haven't been used for over twenty years, so it scarcely looks like danger."

"Ah!" said Marm Pecksniff, drawing a long breath. "It's all very well to have a garrison-house and plenty of boiling water. But," she added in a forbidding whisper, "what if you cannot get there on time? I ask you, what if you cannot . . . ever . . . get there?"

"Fetch Marm Pecksniff some barley broth, Mary," said Cousin Jeanie, quietly.

Mary filled a bowl and set it before the distressed woman.

Marm Pecksniff was easily distracted from her grief. She stirred the broth with her spoon for a moment, then lifted it up and stared at it. "Why, ye Scotch folks puts barley in it and calls it barley broth, don't ye?" she exclaimed, with all the candor of a child. "Now, we English, we puts beans in it and calls it bean porridge! Think of that!"

"Mary! Ma-ry!" called Jamie from the beach below.

Mary ran out the open back door to the ledge and looked.

"The fishing fleet has come back! The fishing fleet has come back!" shouted Jamie.

There was Puddle Dock full of fishing boats and over all the buzz and stir of excited activity. Mary could see Cousin Tom's boat plainly and there he was with Jock unloading. She ran back into the house.

"Oh, Cousin Jeanie," she cried, "the fishing fleet's come back, and they're unloading already."

HORN BOOK

Chapter XI

"OH, YOU are up!" cried Mary, happily. As she entered the room, she saw that the little sick girl was dressed and sitting up in a chair.

"I sometimes sit up," said Susannah, proudly, "and today I've been walking, too."

"I'm so glad," said Mary. "I've brought you something to make you quite well, Susannah!" She held a covered earthen dish in her hands. "Cods' livers, and you eat them for their oil."

"Do they taste fishy?" asked Susannah, with a laugh.

"Yes, a little. Goody Gregory came over while we were curing the fish that the men brought home," Mary went on. "She helped us spread the fish on the flakes. 'Twas she who told me about the oil. 'Their livers eaten,' she said, 'are a good medicine to restore them that have melted their grease.' When I told her that you were ill, she bade me fetch them. If you wish I can bring you some often."

"You are very kind, Mary," answered Marm Winslow, taking the dish. "I am going over to the Teapot for a few moments, children. I shall be back directly."

As the door closed after her mother, Susannah said, "Do tell me about curing the fish, Mary." Still as pale and thin as ever, the little sick girl leaned back in her chair contentedly. A happy smile passed over her face and lighted it with a warm glow.

"Oh, yes!" exclaimed Mary. "It is such fun. The men take pitch forks and throw the fish from the boats into great piles on the shore—all wiggly and squirmy. Then Zeb Tulley—he's the Cutter—cuts their throats, rips open their bellies and hands them to the Header. That's Cousin Tom and you should see how fast he works! He takes out the entrails, detaches the livers and breaks off the heads. Then he hands them to Tim Coddle, the Splitter. Tim takes out the backbone, splits the fish open and hands them to Joe Tuthill, the Salter. Joe salts them and piles them up in a pile, where they have to lie for from ten to twenty hours."

"I wish I could watch it all!" said Susannah, wistfully.

"Perhaps you will, if you eat the cods' livers and keep on growing better," cried Mary. "It's great fun, but hard work, too. The sun shines so hot down there on the beach, it makes blisters on your nose. Everybody goes barefoot. All the men laugh and joke and the fish-heads go flying about—oh, it's fun!"

"What do *you* do to help?" asked Susannah.

"After the fish are salted, we wash them carefully," Mary went on. "I work with the women—Aunt Lyddy Tuthill, Marm Coddle, Granny McKeen, Goody Gregory and all the children. Then we spread the fish out on the flakes to dry in the sun. It takes three or four weeks for this, depending on the weather, and every day we have to turn them, pile them in fagots and then spread them out again. When they are completely cured, they are ready for market."

"Will your Cousin Tom sell them at Spring Hill Market?" asked Susannah.

"No," answered Mary, "the dried fish are for shipment." Then she added with an air of pride, "These have all been ordered by Merchant McFarland for the first voyage of his new ship. How many fish do you think Jock caught?"

"I couldn't even guess," said Susannah.

"They were all marked by wedges in the tails," explained Mary. "That's why the fisherman call him, 'cut-tail!' When they measured them, Jock's share turned out to be three quarters that of Cousin Tom's. He acts like a man, too, since he's come back with the fleet. He won't pay any attention to me at all."

"Would you like to see me walk, Mary?" asked Susannah.

"Yes, yes," cried Mary, eagerly, "if you're certain it won't tire you."

"If I do a little every day, I will soon grow stronger, Mother says," replied Susannah. She rose to her feet, took a few, uncertain steps, then walked steadily across the room.

"That is splendid, Susannah!" cried Mary.

She followed close behind, hoping she would not fall. Susannah walked from one room to the other until she had explored the whole of the tiny house. Then she sat down and rested.

After a few moments, she said boldly, "Now I shall show you the gaol, Mary. Have you ever seen the inside?"

"No," answered Mary, shrinking back. "But, is it . . . do you . . . what will your father say?" cried Mary, in a frightened voice.

"There are no prisoners, now," replied Susannah. "I used to go in often and I know where Father keeps the keys."

"Won't you get too tired, Susannah?" cried Mary, in alarm.

"It will take only a minute and then I shall rest again," said Susannah, confidently.

With a bunch of large keys in her hand, she approached a door which opened out of the kitchen. She separated one key from the others and unlocked it. As the door swung open, Mary noticed that it was made of two heavy thicknesses of oaken planks, banded between with plates of iron, and that the outer surface was heavily studded with iron nails. The light from the kitchen streamed into the dark interior, but, as the two girls entered, they could scarcely see. They groped their way, hand-in-hand, and Susannah pointed out the four dark cells, bare and empty save for a narrow wood bench in each. The cell doors of bar iron were also secured by heavy locks and Susannah held out their respective keys. Pointing to the crevices be-

tween the bars which were banded with blades of mill saws, Susannah explained, "Father has to pass the bread and water through here."

"Is that what they have to eat?" asked Mary, overcome with awe and fear. "Bread and water?"

"Yes," said Susannah, in a matter-of-fact tone. She approached a trap-door in the heavy, plank floor. "There's the dungeon below," she added. "The worst ones are put there, in irons."

"In irons?" asked Mary, weakly.

"Yes," said Susannah. "Chained so they cannot move. But not many of them go there."

The words of Merchant McFarland and Parson Flint regarding evil and wrong-doing came back vividly to Mary's mind. Then she remembered that the peddler and the juggler had spent three days in these very cells.

She shivered to think she had imagined them singing in such a place.

"Come," said Susannah, "there's nothing more to see."

She led the way out and the light in the kitchen seemed very bright. Susannah closed and locked the heavy door and hung the keys on their usual hook. It was a comforting thing to lock away out of sight those dreary cells of squalor and gloom.

"I think I shall . . ." said Susannah, but her voice faded weakly away.

Mary turned quickly, but she was too late. Susannah had fallen to the floor in a faint.

"Oh!" cried Mary, looking down at her helplessly. "She should not . . . have walked so much . . ." Then, realizing that Marm Winslow was away and there was no one else in the house, she added, "What can I . . . do?"

She answered her own question by setting to work with determination, half pulling, half lifting Susannah toward her bed. Fortunately, the distance was not great and she managed somehow to raise her. Then she ran for water and began to bathe the pale, pale face and fan it with a cloth. At last, the eyelids fluttered and a heavy sigh came from the parted lips.

"Susannah! Susannah!" cried Mary, in great distress. "Are you all right, Susannah?"

"Oh, I . . . am . . . so tired," came the halting words.

But it was enough for Mary and it relieved that first dread that Susannah might never waken. Feverishly, she removed the sick girl's clothing and laid the coverings over her. She continued bathing Susannah's face until her eyes opened.

"Did I frighten you?" asked Susannah. "I thought I could get back to my bed, but everything turned black before me." She leaned back among her pillows contentedly. "Bed feels good sometimes," she added.

The outer door opened and Marm Winslow came hurrying in. "I am sorry I stayed so long . . ." She stopped short, when she saw her daughter in the bed. "Oh, my child, my child, what is it? Has anything happened?"

"She wanted to show me how she could walk," explained Mary, "and she fell in a faint."

"It was nothing, Mother," added Susannah, in a weak voice. "If one walks, one must expect a tumble now and then."

Joseph Winslow, the gaoler, a thin-faced man with a stern look on his face, entered the room and glanced sharply at his daughter. "Wife," he demanded, "is not Susannah looking pale?"

"Perhaps a trifle, Joseph," said Marm Winslow, in a low tone.

"What is this?" the gaoler asked, lifting the cover of the dish which Mary had brought.

"Mary brought some cods' livers for Susannah," replied Marm Winslow.

"Cods' livers?" asked the man. "Has Master Pecksniff ordered cods' livers for Susannah?"

"No, Joseph," said Marm Winslow, "but . . ."

"Is not Master Pecksniff providing the proper drugs for Susannah?"

"He gives her drugs daily . . ."

"Goody Gregory says, sir," explained Mary, anxiously, "that the reason why all the fishermen's children are so plump and well nourished is because they eat cods' livers, sir."

"Master Pecksniff is our doctor, not Goody Gregory," said the gaoler, harshly. "The livers are apt to make Susannah worse, wife. Ask Master Pecksniff before you give them to her." Then he stared at Mary as if he had not noticed her before. "Wife! Did Master Pecksniff say that Susannah is well enough to have visitors?"

"Why, Joseph . . . er . . ." began Marm Winslow, nervously. "It won't hurt her a mite to talk to a little girl like Mary . . ."

"She is worse today; you can see that for yourself," said Joseph Winslow, severely. "Did Master Pecksniff say that Mary might come?"

"No, Joseph, but . . . I will ask him. I am looking for him any minute now."

"Mary must go home at once," said the gaoler sharply.

"Why, Joseph," cried Marm Winslow, unhappily, "they always have such a happy time together."

"The child is worse," said the gaoler. "Are you blind, wife?"

Mary rose hastily from her chair. "Good-bye, Susannah," she said, with a lump in her throat. "I hope you will soon be . . . better."

"I am sorry to have you go, Mary," said Marm Winslow, sadly.

"You need not come again," said Joseph Winslow, gruffly, "until Master Pecksniff gives permission."

"Yes, sir," answered Mary with a curtsey.

The door closed sharply behind her. Mary knew that both of Susannah's parents were suffering from dread anxiety. The gaoler did not mean to be unkind. He wanted only the best for his child—a return to health and strength. If only he would listen to Goody Gregory instead of Master Pecksniff!

Mary looked up, to see the black-caped figure of a small man approaching her. She knew at a glance that it was Master Pecksniff. He walked with a stooped motion like no one else. Marm Winslow had been expecting him. Thankful that she had escaped in time, Mary turned the corner and avoided a meeting.

The days following the return of the fishing fleet had been busy ones for all the fishermen and their families at Puddle Dock. The great haul of fish had been salted and dried in record time. Mary had enjoyed helping and yet it had been exacting, for it meant regular hours of work instead of her usual, careless freedom. She was hungry again for a sight of the town and her friends.

The stiff salt wind blew freshly up from the bay, as Mary hurried through Queen Street down to the water-front. Her short red hair flew out loosely behind her white cap. Her feet moved as if on the lightest wings and her skirts billowed softly in the breeze.

The little, wooden door of Master Greenwood's shop was barred and bolted. The shutters on the window were closed tight. But Mary knew how to get in. She ran to the end of the wharf, climbed down into a wherry which was moored there and rowed swiftly to the back of the shop. She made the wherry fast and climbed nimbly up the ladder. She poked her head in at the door and called, "Here I am, Master Greenwood!"

"Why, Mary, is that you?" cried Peggy Fayerweather.

It was Mary who had first brought Peggy to the carver's shop at his own request. Peggy had not only become deeply interested in wood carving, but had willingly agreed to give him sittings for the figurehead, and the two were already on the way to becoming fast friends.

"Oh, Mary!" cried Judy McFarland. "I'm so glad you've come."

Mary stepped in at the door and looked round. At one end of the shop Peggy and Judy were talking to an old sea-captain who sat on a wooden bench. His skin was well-seasoned by long exposure to the weather and his long white hair was brushed back and tied with a black ribbon.

"But I thought," cried Mary, staring, "you didn't want visitors!"

"I don't!" said Master Greenwood, coming forward. "Only my special friends are wanted, Cap'n Pete, Judy, Peggy and you."

"But . . ." cried Mary, staring at the sea-captain again, and wondering if it could possibly be the man who had chased her and Judy out of the countinghouse. He had a pipe in his mouth, upon which he was puffing vigorously, and as she looked down, she saw that he had a wooden leg. It could be no other.

"It's all right," explained Judy, putting her arm about the old man's shoulder, "Cap'n Pete isn't cross today. His rheumatism's better, and he's promised to tell us how he lost his leg and got the wooden one."

"Wall, I ain't so sartin," began the old man, taking his pipe out of his mouth. "I jes' wanted ter see this here figger-head, I did. Ye see, ye can't sail 'thout no figger-head and I thought as how Cap'n Fayerweather orter have the finest one in the land, seein' as how it's Merchant McFarland's ship, so . . ."

Mary looked toward the other end of the shop. There, in the half-shadow, she saw the unfinished figure of a woman, clothed in flowing garments, carved out of wood. The afternoon sun filtered through a small, high, dust-covered window and touched the raw wood here and there with a glowing warmth.

"Oh!" cried Mary, overcome with delight. "It's Peggy herself!"

Master Greenwood had returned to his seat on a high stool, before the large, seasoned pine log which was securely braced to the floor. He held a chisel in one hand and a wooden mallet in the other. His eye was fixed on the sweeping curve of the grain in the wood. He touched it lightly here and there, cutting wisely and tenderly, modeling the shape as easily as if it had been soft clay.

Mary held her breath as she watched. Like the others, she looked on in silence. The figure seemed to grow before their eyes. What if the tool should cut too deeply? What if it should slip for a hair's breadth? But no, it was secure in the carver's hand, and he, the artist, forgetful of all else, lost himself in his deeply loved work. Mary sat down on a log and watched every movement.

After a time, Old Cap'n Pete began to speak in a low tone. " 'Tis a dreadful thing when a ship loses her figger-head," he said solemnly. "It happened once to the good barque, *Swallow*. 'Twas many a year back, but I'll never fergit till my dyin' day. During a storm in the night, we heard her a-bangin' agin the ship and we knew we'd never git back to port without her —if she should be lost in the stormy waves. All sailors believe that the figger-head brings either good or bad luck. If damaged in any way, the ship will fare badly. So I climbed out on the bowsprit and hung by my toes like a monkey—I war a young man then, and more nimble far than most—while I screwed her tight agin. And that's why we didn't go down to Davy Jones's locker that v'yage. No, we come back home agin safe and sound."

"Was that the voyage, Cap'n Pete, when you lost your leg and got the wooden one?" asked Judy.

"No, child, no," said the old man, impatiently. "I'm a-talkin' 'bout figger-heads now." He spat noisily into the saw-dust in the corner.

"Was the *Swallow's* figure-head as beautiful as this one?" asked Mary, pointing toward the carved figure.

"I don't jes' rec'lect what she looked like," said Cap'n Pete, "but aye, I reckon, she war handsome, too."

"Do the sailors think the figure-head is like a guardian angel to protect them?" asked Mary, earnestly.

"Something like that," mumbled Old Pete, chewing hard on his pipe-stem. "Only if somethin' goes wrong, they blame it all on the figger-head, too."

"You'll have to behave yourself, Peggy, when you're fastened to the prow of Father's ship," laughed Judy. "Take good care of the sailors and bring them all back safe."

"Just think how far and fast I shall travel," laughed Peggy, "leading the good ship where she should go. The waves will wet my hair and wash my face when it storms. I shall talk to the porpoises and the whales. And whenever we come to a foreign port, I shall be the first one there!"

"And the first one home again, too, we hope," added Nathaniel Greenwood.

"How will she look when she is all finished, sir?" asked Mary.

"The lower part of the lady's figure will be white," explained the carver, "with trimmings of silver on the edges. The upper part, blue, edged with gold. The lady's shoes will be blue with silver buckles . . ."

"Just like mine!" interrupted Peggy.

"And her hair streaming down her back will be raven black!"

"Just like mine!" added Peggy.

"Just like Miss Peggy's," repeated the carver, softly. "How could I have made her without your help? Come, now, the kettle is boiling, ready for tea. Let's taste Judy's bannocks and see if they are as good as she says they are. She makes it her duty to keep me from starving."

"Why, you know, Master Nathaniel Greenwood," said Judy, accusingly, "you never stop your work long enough to eat, and your cheeks are growing thinner every day."

"Food for the soul is quite enough," laughed the carver, "but here, let me taste one of these bannocks."

A plate was passed and soon everybody was munching on the delicious flat cakes. Judy made the tea and the afternoon became a sociable occasion.

Peggy and Judy talked eagerly of the new ship which was to be launched as soon as the figure-head was ready and of their intended ventures. Mary listened with a detached aloofness. Now that the arrangements for her own venture were made, she smiled with tolerance as the two girls argued back and forth.

"Why, Mary!" cried Judy, suddenly remembering. "You haven't put down your venture. Aren't you going to take one?"

"I've already arranged for mine," said Mary, with a tilt of her red head, an expression of pride.

"You have? What is it? Do tell us," cried Peggy.

"It's a secret, I cannot," answered Mary.

"Has Mary taken a venture?" asked Master Green-wood. "Then I think I shall take one, too. I shall invest the gold guineas which I am to receive for my figure-head in the West India trade, with Captain Fayerweather in the new ship. Are you willing?"

"Yes, yes, yes!" cried all three girls at once.

"And now at last," announced Judy, with a wave of the hand, "Cap'n Pete is going to tell us how he got his wooden leg."

"Wall," began the captain, in a grumbling, but good-natured voice, "once when we was down in the West Indies in Trinidad, I had the fever and I jes' laid round most anywhere and sometimes somebody'd offer me a drink of water. One time I woke up out of my doze, but I war too weak to open an eye. All to once I heerd the Cap'n and the rest of the boys who was a-standin' over me, say that I war dead . . ."

"But that's not how you lost your leg!" protested Judy.

"The mate brought a piece of canvas," went on Cap'n Pete, with a twinkle in his eye, "and covered me over. They waited a bit, sayin' they'd let me get cold first. Then they went away. I had heerd it all. Wall, the canvas warmed me up, instead, and I come to and crawled out back into the fo'castle. Pretty soon they come for the funeral, with long faces and tears in their eyes, but there warn't no corpse! Haw, haw, haw! I fooled 'em. From that day on, I began to git better, and they ain't never drowned me yet! Haw, haw, haw, haw!"

"But what about your wooden leg?" cried Judy, while the others laughed.

"Oh, that?" cried Cap'n Pete, stamping it briskly on the floor. "Why, a pirate shot it off, with his wicked little cannon! Haw, haw, haw! Now, I must be movin'. I've got to go and shet up your Pa's countin' house, I reckon."

The old man bent his rheumatic knees and rose to his feet. He knocked the ashes from his pipe and walked to the door, his wooden leg tap-tap-tapping sharply on the floor. Master Greenwood bade good-bye to his guests and opened the door. Cap'n Pete took Peggy on one arm and Judy on the other and began to sing lustily:

> " 'I'll go no more a-roving,
>   With you, fair maid;
> A-roving, a-roving.
> Since roving's been my ruin,
> I'll go no more a-roving,
>   With you, fair maid.' "

"Aren't you coming, Mary?" called Judy, looking back.

"Not yet!" answered Mary. "Good-bye!"

"Master Greenwood," said Mary, as soon as the door was closed, "did a pirate really shoot off the Captain's leg with a cannon?"

"Nobody knows how he lost it," laughed the carver. "He's always promising to tell, but never does. It might have been a pirate at that."

"Do you think all pirates are bad at heart?" asked Mary.

"They must be," said the carver, seriously, "or they could not do the things they do."

"Could a pirate change into an honest merchant-man?"

"It is possible, of course," answered Master Green-wood, "but not likely. It's pretty hard for a leopard to change his spots."

"But if he said he was through with pirating . . ."

"If he meant what he said, then he could do it."

Mary smiled thoughtfully. Nathaniel would be-lieve in Captain Babb, too, if he knew. The carver watched her, but did not press her with questions. He knew that she would tell him what was troubling her when she was ready to do so.

Mary sat down on the wooden bench. "Now, let me have your coat," she demanded. The carver took it off obediently, and handed it to her. From under her neck-kerchief, Mary brought forth a needle and from her pocket a small skein of green worsted. She set to work to darn the holes in the sleeves while Master Greenwood looked on, in agreeable surprise.

"Why, what is this?" he cried, picking up the piece of wood which dangled at her side. "A hornbook? You have not told me you are being educated, child!"

"Aunt Becky bought it for me . . ." explained Mary, "for a certain reason . . ."

"To learn how to read and spell is an excellent reason," said Nathaniel, "as Madam Armstrong has undoubtedly found out."

"Even if you're a girl?" asked Mary, timidly.

"Yes, even if you're a girl."

Mary lifted her head and looked at the carver again.

"Master Greenwood," she said, hesitatingly, "I think I know why you eat so little. Did you ever get your money for the head of Hippocrates?"

"Why, no, Mary," said the carver. "I've never asked for it."

"Why haven't you asked for it, sir?"

"Because I do not wish to see Master Pecksniff or speak to him," said Master Greenwood, simply.

"Master Pecksniff is giving drugs to Susannah every day," said Mary slowly, "but she isn't getting any better."

"Have you been to see her?" asked the carver, thinking guiltily of his own neglect of the child, caused by his long hours of carving.

"Yes," said Mary. "I was there today and was surprised to see her up and walking. Then she fainted and her father thought she was much worse. I took her some cods' livers because Goody Gregory said they would be good for her."

"Do you mean the old woman who lives on Goat Island?" asked the carver. Mary nodded. "I know her well. She comes round sometimes and cleans up the shavings and chips out of my shop and takes them away in her boat."

"Mr. Winslow said that Susannah shouldn't eat the livers unless Master Pecksniff says she can and he won't say she can when he hears I brought them, because he doesn't like me."

"Never mind, lass," said the carver, putting his arm about Mary's shoulder. "You must not worry about Susannah. Perhaps nothing will make her really better. We can only visit her now and then and try to bring her a little cheer, while she is still with us."

"But Mr. Winslow sent me away because Master Pecksniff says that Susannah must not have any visitors."

"Does he say that?" asked the carver, frowning deeply.

"Why does Master Pecksniff hate me so?" cried Mary.

"He hates the whole world, lass."

"Marm Winslow says that Susannah is always better when I come."

"Of course," said the carver. "Let me think for a minute."

Mary looked again at Master Greenwood's kind, thoughtful face, then she resumed her darning. If the apothecary had paid for the head of Hippocrates, the carver would have had a new coat to wear.

"You are not afraid of the apothecary, are you, Mary?" asked Master Greenwood, with a determined look in his eye.

"No, sir," said Mary, feeling suddenly brave and courageous, "not really, though I don't like it when he speaks crossly."

"Nor do I," answered the carver, sympathetically. "But sometimes we are willing to endure, are we not? Especially when we can give happiness to others?"

"Yes, sir," said Mary, trustfully.

"Well, then, you will go to the Winslows' often," said Master Greenwood. "Take Susannah her cods' livers whenever you can. I'll warrant she'll have a better chance with you and the livers than she will with Pecksniff and his drugs. If the apothecary is there, when you enter the house, you can leave quickly, can you not? Without words?"

"Yes, sir."

"If he comes while you are there, or if Mr. Winslow asks you to go, you can go. And if you should meet Master Pecksniff on the street, you can go away, can you not?"

"I can run very fast, sir," said Mary, with a smile.

"Very well, then. You and I will act as if Master Pecksniff did not exist and we will give Susannah what happiness we can. Ah!" cried the carver, with a shudder. "How I would hate to be an apothecary, always pouring pills and potions down people's throats and waiting to see them die! Stalking through life perfumed with assafoetida! There in his smelly little shop he stands, amid his odd-looking, poisonous vials and jars, taking out his herbs and drugs and mixing them together with his mortar and pestle! Always grinding! Always grinding people's lives away!"

"What did you say, sir?" asked Mary, alarmed at the strange whispers coming from the carver's mouth.

"My child, forgive me!" said Master Greenwood, recalled to the present by Mary's question. "I was only thinking aloud. Run along now and do not forget Susannah."

Mary had need of all the courage and bravery she had mustered by her talk with the carver. She had gone but a short distance from his shop, when the apothecary darted out from a doorway, as if he had been lying in wait. His chin hung low upon his bulging breast and under the low point of his tricorn hat, his black eyes flashed with ill-concealed fury. He spread his feet apart and, blocking the way, confronted Mary.

"Have you seen Susannah Winslow today, Miss?" he demanded in a voice of thunder.

"Yes, sir," said Mary. Her voice was plain and clear, but her heart thumped wildly.

"Have I not told you she is to have no visitors?"

Mary looked at the little man with unwavering eyes. As she listened to his words, she tried to read in his face the reason why he hated her so much.

"You have, sir!" she replied, with a curtsey.

"Do you expect to obey my orders?" the man demanded.

But he spoke to the empty air. Before the last word was out of his mouth, Mary had disappeared round the corner. Knowing that safety lay only in flight, she did not waste a moment.

"Here, you . . ." cried Master Pecksniff, clutching at the air in the place where the girl had been. "Here, I say . . ."

The "Golden Arrow"

Chapter XII

THE day of the launching of Merchant McFarland's new ship came at last—a bright, crisp morning in early September. Mary had slept but little the night before. Always, at the back of her mind, lay the remembrance of Goody Gregory's words, the prophetic warning that her days in Strawberry Bank might soon come to an end. Now, at last, she knew that she was to be permitted to see the launching and her heart was glad.

Cousin Jeanie was up again and well enough to go, accompanied by Aunt Becky. But eager Mary could not wait for them. She took a piece of corn-bread in each hand and started out before the sun was three hours high. She was determined to miss nothing.

She passed Master Greenwood's carving shop by. Its

door and window were barred and bolted and she saw no signs of life. She knew that the figure-head was no longer there. On the preceding day she had seen it, swathed in heavy wrappings, carefully carried by a group of shipwrights and laid in a longboat, beside the wharf. She had watched the carver, with a strained and anxious look on his face, climb aboard. He spoke to Mary absent-mindedly, but scarcely seemed to notice her. She knew that he would not rest content until the figure-head was safely hoisted to its mortise on the ship's prow and bolted securely. Standing silent on the wharf, she had watched the men row the longboat out into the bay and had seen it disappear round the bend in the direction of Master Wiggin's shipyard.

Now, she gave but one glance at the carver's shop and hurried on through the narrow street. She had not gone far before she met Joey Moseley.

"Did you leave Frisky to take care of the cows?" she asked.

"Hush!" said Joey, frowning, "somebody might hear you. You don't suppose I would miss a launching, do you?"

"Hardly!" laughed Mary. "Do you want to take my snuff-box now? I'll go and fetch it for you."

"Oh, no," said Joey. "The ship won't sail for weeks." He dashed off to join Jock Martin and a group of boys who were waiting for him.

The shipyard was thronged with people when Mary entered. Coming from all directions were farmers, backwoodsmen and townsfolk with their families.

Everybody was there from Lieutenant-Governor Dunbar and Deacon Puddington down to the smallest fisherman's child.

Mary ran to the water-front to see the ship. Although the launching would not take place until high water at eleven o'clock, everything was in readiness. Under the bowsprit, a heavy canvas was fastened with ropes to conceal the figure-head, already in place. The waiting ship, resting upon her cradle of supporting timbers, looked gaunt and unclothed without her masts and sails. Her bottom, painted white, glared brightly in the morning sun, offset as it was by the sharp black above. Mary saw shipwrights walking about, admiring the grace and symmetry of her lines. She saw laborers pouring buckets of whale oil on the ways, under the stern, at the water's edge. The keel had been laid only five short months before, and now like a bird, full-fledged on the edge of its nest, the ship was ready for flight. How sad and empty it would be when she was gone!

A light breeze had sprung up which sent small clouds scurrying across the blue sky and whipped up white caps in the bay. Mary stood at the water's edge idly watching sailboats in the harbor, as they rocked and dipped on the waves. Two lumbermen near her began to talk. Mary recognized one of them as the cocky little backwoodsman who had boasted of defying the King on the day that the Governor seized the mast timber.

"Ah!" said he, pointing his finger toward the ways. "That ship's timbers will be rotten and worm-eaten before the year is out. I've been told they were felled in the full of the moon."

"Yes," answered his companion, "at full moon, the trunks would be full of sap and 'tis sap that causes decay. If cut on the day of the new moon, timbers cannot rot, but will last forever."

"The ways," continued the first man, still pointing, "will never stand the weight of her. They will crack like two wooden splinters."

Mary walked rapidly away. She did not wish to hear more. The men's words sickened and alarmed her. Then when she looked ahead, she saw Master Pecksniff in her path. She stopped still where she was. She saw the apothecary's Negro slave come running up, with a look of fear on his face.

"Oh, massa!" he cried, "I jes' seed a woman a-carryin' an empty pail across Cap'n Fayerweather's path, and the Cap'n . . . the Cap'n . . ."

"Well?" cried Master Pecksniff, rubbing his hands together, "what did the Captain do, Pompey?"

"Why, massa, he done turned quick and went t'other way, and when I seed his face, 'twas as white as a ghost! Look! Right thar he goes, massa, and yonder's the woman, too, a-carryin' the empty pail!"

The frightened Negro pointed his finger and both Master Pecksniff and Mary looked in the direction indicated. There was Goody Gregory walking briskly across the yard, and beyond her, Captain Fayerweather talking to Master Wiggin, the ship-builder.

"It means bad luck, massa," cried the Negro in a

trembling voice. "The new ship will be sunk, sure, massa! It's bad luck, bad luck!"

The apothecary chuckled under his breath and walked away with his slave. Mary stared after them, wondering. Was it true? Even if Master Pecksniff believed it, did that make it true? Suddenly a friendly voice called to her and Mary knew it was Goody Gregory. The old woman's gray eyes sparkled with good humor and kindness as she approached.

"Ah! Ocean-Born Mary!" she cried, taking her stubby pipe from her mouth. "I know you are happy today. You have remembered my words to dip your hands in sea-water while you can? You are happy, I know, because this is your first launching."

"Yes, Goody," answered Mary, politely. Her eyes sought the ground as she spoke.

"Why, what is it, Ocean Mary?" cried the old woman. "You do not look at me. You are not happy today? Has some trouble befallen you?"

"I have heard . . . them say . . . dreadful things," stammered Mary.

"Who has said dreadful things?" asked the old woman.

"Oh, Goody!" cried Mary, staring and pointing with her finger at the pail on the woman's arm. "It's . . . EMPTY . . . just as the Negro said. . . ."

"What do you mean, child?" asked Goody.

"He said . . . the Negro said . . . that it was a bad sign!" Mary blurted out the whole truth candidly.

The old woman understood at once. "Surely you are too wise, Ocean Mary," said she, "to believe the words of a foolish Negro. Listen not to gossipings and light-winged rumors which breed evil. Be wise, my child. And be happy today, of all days!"

As Goody Gregory patted her on the back and smiled reassuringly, Mary felt a tremendous relief. After a final word, the old woman bobbed nimbly down towards the water-front and Mary saw her climb into her small boat, which was filled with chips of wood, and row away.

Cousin Jeanie and Aunt Becky were talking to Jane Hawkins, the verse peddler, not far off. Mary ran to join them. Maggie McDonald and several other women crowded up, all eager to see that Jeanie Martin was well again and able to be out.

"Oh, look!" cried Jane Hawkins, shrilly, pointing to the crowd which was assembling near the new ship. "There's Parson Flint."

Mary looked with the others at the tall, black-clothed figure.

"Why, to be sure," said Maggie McDonald; "he never misses anything."

"I thought his wife looked pindling last Sabbath," said Becky Armstrong.

"Oh, but . . ." cried Jane Hawkins, holding her hand to her mouth, as her two eyes opened wide in alarm. The eager women put their heads together over Mary's own. "Why, didn't you know—a minister's always unlucky, the seafaring folks say. If there's one on board, it bodes foul weather. And the sailors never dare mention one by name. The word itself is unlucky."

The women looked back over their shoulders, fearfully.

" 'Tis true," said Jeanie Martin, shaking her head sadly. "The fishermen believe it, too."

"Yes, I've heard it many a time, from the sailors," added Susie Cobbett, the keeper of the sailors' boarding-house.

"Sailors believe a lot of nonsense!" snapped Maggie McDonald.

"Do you reckon it bodes ill for the new ship?" asked Granny McKeen, in a frightened voice.

"Why, sartain sure!" cried Jane Hawkins. "You just wait and see what happens."

"Nonsense!" snorted Becky Armstrong. "I don't believe such foolish notions, not when Daniel McFarland owns the ship and Anthony Fayerweather sails her! Come, Jeanie, let us go and see her." The two women walked away.

"Is it true, what they say, Aunt?" cried Mary, following.

"Of course not!" answered Aunt Becky. "How a good Christian man on land can harm a ship at sea is more than I can comprehend. Now, if 'twas those wicked pirates the women were worrying over, that would be another matter."

Mary turned away, greatly disturbed. All these dread prophecies and the pirates, too. How could the new ship ever face so much evil? She hurried at once to the ways. Close by the ship, in a small group, she saw the merchant, the captain, Madam McFarland, Judy and Peggy—all waiting expectantly. The girls were dressed in their best brocades, but Mary scarcely noticed them. She walked up to the two men.

"Mr. McFarland . . ." she cried, in a broken voice.

"What is it, Ocean-Born Mary?" asked the merchant, looking down. "I am so glad you've come. Do you want to mount the deck to ride down the ways with Judy and Peggy?"

"I wanted to tell you and Captain Fayerweather . . ." gulped Mary.

"What's this? What does little Mary want?" asked the Captain. "We haven't much time. If she wishes to go up, it will be all right, I dare say. Nobody will notice her."

"Oh, no, sir, I don't wish to go, sir," said Mary, looking from one man to the other. "I just wanted to tell you what the people out there are saying." She pointed to the crowd and drew a deep breath. "The apothecary's Negro slave . . . saw a woman with a pail . . . and the ship's timbers might rot, sir, if the ways . . . don't break down, and Parson Flint's there, too!"

"What are you trying to say, Mary?" asked Merchant McFarland, patiently.

"Why, why, they say it's unlucky, sir, and the ways are going to break under her and . . ."

The two men looked at each other and nodded slightly.

"She says," repeated the merchant, with a smile, "that our fair brig is doomed before she is even launched."

"It would not be a launching," laughed Captain Fayerweather, "if the gossips and busybodies did not predict ill. I'll trust the *Golden Arrow* to live it down, Mary, as many another good ship has done."

"And so shall I!" added the merchant, gazing at the brig, fondly. "She'll make a fortune for us in the West India trade, I haven't a doubt."

"Then, sir, you do not think she is in danger?" asked Mary, uncertainly. "The ways won't break down, sir?"

"You need not be anxious, child," said the merchant. "Come and help Judy and Peggy with the launching."

"No, sir, thank you, sir, I'd rather not," said Mary, hastily.

"Do come, Mary," cried Peggy, hurrying up.

"We want you, Mary," added Judy. "You're not afraid, are you?"

Mary looked down at her plain gown of brown linen, then up at Judy's shining brocade. She backed away, instinctively.

"No, I'm not afraid," she said. "I want to watch from below, that's all." She did not like to mention that she must be the first to see the figure-head.

She hurried back and found a place on a small rise of ground at one side of the shipyard. From there, she watched the two girls mount and appear above on the deck of the ship. Beside them, near the rail, she saw the captain, the merchant, the carver, the master ship-builder and several other men take their places.

The waiting seemed to Mary never-ending. She stood first on one foot, then on the other. Suddenly, a wave of excitement passed over the crowd as a shout rang out from beneath the ship. All eyes were at once directed toward Master Wiggin at the bow, who waved a bottle aloft in the air. Mary's heart began to pound.

The "Golden Arrow"

"As her stern touched the water, the waves parted in a wide spread to receive her."

An answering signal came from below, followed immediately, by the thud-thud-thudding of the heavy mauls and the clatter of the supporting blocks as they were knocked out of position and the hull settled down on its cradle.

A breathless silence held the crowd. Not a word was spoken as the people waited in suspense. Then a resounding blow was heard and the last block fell and lay still.

"Now!" cried Master Wiggin, passing the bottle quickly to Miss Peggy Fayerweather's waiting hand. As the ship quivered with its first breath, Peggy broke the bottle of rum over the bow and a crash of broken glass was heard. "I christen thee the *Golden Arrow!*" she cried, and her rich, young voice was carried out on the breeze to the crowd below and a great shout went up. Mary jumped up and down on her feet and cried aloud with the others.

And then the miraculous, the incredible happened. The ship began to move. It was awake, alive. First, so slowly that Mary could not discern its motion except by looking at objects on the shore and watching them glide past. She held her hand before her mouth, expecting something to happen. She could scarcely breathe as she kept her eyes fixed on the *Golden Arrow*, and saw that the ways did not break beneath her.

"Hooray! Thar she goes!" cried an old man in front of the crowd, rushing forward. It was Old Cap'n Pete with his wooden leg. He shouted at the top of his lungs.

Mary stared at his wooden leg, the leg shot off by

a pirate's cannon. In that moment, there came vividly into her mind, a swift vision of a hundred black-faced men swarming over the rail of a ship, and one, their leader, tramping down the stairs, where two women with a babe waited, helpless with fear. What if the *Golden Arrow* should fall into the hands of pirates? What if the *Golden Arrow* should never come back? Mary shivered and hid her face in her hands.

She was called back to the scene before her by another mighty shout from the throat of Master Wiggin. She looked up in time to see Master Nathaniel Greenwood give a brisk pull on the rope in his hand, which released the canvas below him, unveiling the figurehead to the light of day. Again a spontaneous shout went up from the crowd, followed by a murmur of admiration and awe.

Mary stood, transfixed. She knew she had never seen anything so beautiful. Above the prow, the image stood, wooden but yet alive, clothed in colors of sharp brilliance, heightened here and there by edges of silver and gold. It was like Peggy Fayerweather and yet different. There was a far-away look in the boldly staring eyes, a straining eagerness for all that the future might bring; and more than that, the solemn dignity and pride of a woman sure of herself, wise in understanding and skilled in the ways of the world.

The words of Old Cap'n Pete came back to Mary clearly, as she looked. Surely this radiant image would be a guardian angel and keep the ship from harm. She would take her away with goodly freights on long voyages and by grace of fair winds and good weather, bring her home safely, too. And if danger arose, she would right it, keeping faith with the sailors who trusted her so well.

The ship's pace, meanwhile, had increased, as she slid softly down the well-greased ways. As her stern touched the water, the waves parted in a wide spread to receive her. The hull dipped, quivered and then stood still. The *Golden Arrow* was safely launched and the land would know her no more.

Mary saw the crowds make their way out of the shipyard. But she waited until the longboat brought back the launching party. Just as she had hoped, Master Greenwood lingered behind the others. He stood on the shore, looking at the *Golden Arrow* lying at anchor in mid-stream, with her figure-head gleaming in the sunlight. Mary came up behind him and took his hand in her own. No words were spoken, for each understood the other.

The days that followed were full of excitement. The *Golden Arrow* was floated down the river from the shipyard to be rigged at the rigging dock, where her masts, yards, booms and gaffs had been previously assembled. After the masts were stepped in, the work of rigging began. A procession of fifty men, walking two abreast, passed through the streets, bearing on their shoulders the great rope cables from Master Griggs' ropewalk. Mary scampered along beside them, with the other children, laughing and shouting. Windows and doors were opened as they passed and men and women gazed with admiration. The rigging was soon accomplished—a score of men clambering aloft like spiders spinning their webs of rope.

Then came the loading of the cargo at the McFarland dock. Pig-iron and stone were placed in the hold for ballast, then ton timber, logs of eight, ten and twelve feet in length, hewn square for easy stowage. Huge bundles of pipe-staves and headings, tree-nails and bolts, and great piles of timber clapboards were brought from Cooper Nutley's shop. Tom Martin and his fishermen neighbors brought a vast quantity of dry fish in casks and raw fish in bulk to be stored in the hold. Farmers from the country brought wheat, pease, pork and beef, while Indians appeared with furs— moose, beaver, otter and bear. Long strings of laden horses and oxen filled the streets leading to the wharf for many days.

The *Golden Arrow,* at first riding high on the water, sunk lower day by day, until her shining white-painted bottom was entirely submerged. At the main hatchway stood a man, checking the in-going cargo, as sailors and laborers hauled it in. Incredible confusion reigned on the wharf, as the day of departure drew near.

On the day when the *Golden Arrow* was to sail, Mary hunted for Joey Moseley, snuff-box in hand. She went to Rock Pasture first, but he was nowhere in sight. Uncle Job Watkins told her that he had not seen him since he brought the cows at dawn. Mary hurried to the McFarland wharf. She was surprised to see that the *Golden Arrow*—the beautiful brig of the days before—resembled nothing so much as a farmyard. She laughed as she came near. On the deck were horses, oxen, sheep, pigs, mules, chickens, geese and turkeys. The air was filled with a medley of crowings, cacklings and stampings. A huge haystack was piled up almost to the lower yards.

"But the critters!" cried Mary, in astonishment, as she met Judy coming toward her. "What are they for?"

"They're to be sold in the West Indies," explained Judy. "Peggy's father says he can get good prices for them, if he can get them out safe. But if a bad storm comes, the waves will soon clear the decks."

"And wash them all into the sea to be drowned?" cried Mary.

"Unless they can swim to shore!" answered Judy, with a grin.

"I should think it would be better to leave them at home!" murmured Mary.

"A jolly fine merchant you'd make!" laughed Judy.

"Oh! I almost forgot," cried Mary. "Do you know where Joey is?"

"No," said Judy. "Captain Fayerweather's gone to get his papers and then Mother's coming and Peggy's grandmother and they'll be off."

"So soon?" asked Mary. "Then I must find Joey."

"The Captain's gone to see Collector Quackenbush," Judy went on. "He's Collector-General of the Port. He has to prepare the clearance papers and the Captain has to pay a fee."

"What papers?" asked Mary.

"The papers which give the ship a good character," said Judy. "Then he is free to sail."

"Oh!" said Mary, understanding only vaguely.

"Some men enter and leave a port without papers," explained Judy. "That's called smuggling. Those two men that we saw in the stocks brought in their lemons and linen from Portugal without declaring them to Collector Quackenbush and paying the necessary duties. That's what pirates do. It's called illegal trade."

"Yes, I know," said Mary, in a low voice. "But have you seen Joey?"

"Do you mean the cow-herd? He's out at Rock Pasture, no doubt," answered Judy, with little interest.

"I must find Joey!" repeated Mary.

"But don't go away," begged Judy. "They'll be leaving soon and we want to bid the ship good-bye."

"Yes, I know, but I must find Joey."

"Why, what do you want with him?" asked Judy.

"I cannot tell you till I find him," shouted Mary, as she went flying off. "I . . . I beg your pardon, sir!" she cried the next moment, when she saw that she had bumped into a tall, dignified man. "I was hunting for Joey, and . . . I . . . thought he might be here . . . somewhere."

"Joey who?" asked the man.

"Joey Moseley, sir!" answered Mary, breathless.

"Do you mean the lad who is cow-herd?"

The emphatic tones made Mary look up into the man's face. She gasped when she saw that it was Lieutenant-Governor Dunbar. She made a hasty curtsey.

"He said, sir . . . he would take . . . I mean, he's going to . . . but I promised I would not tell, sir!"

"He's here, then, is he?" asked the Governor.

"Oh, no, sir, he's out at Rock Pasture, sir," cried Mary, hastily, biting her lip, "watching the cows."

"A flogging he shall have," said the Governor, sharply, "as soon as I lay hands on him. Tell me at once where he is hiding, lass."

"I do not know, sir!" cried Mary, truthfully.

"And what have I told you about showing your face in public?"

"Mary, Mary, do come now, the Captain is back and . . ." called Judy, running up.

"I must go, sir, and see the ship, sir," cried Mary, backing rapidly away from the Governor and making repeated curtsies as she went. The Governor took rapid strides in the same direction.

Mary forgot both snuff-box and Joey in her excitement, as she joined Judy and Peggy and they made their way through the crowd to the place where their elders stood. After a period of tedious waiting, they watched the *Golden Arrow* swing slowly from her moorings out into the harbor.

The *Golden Arrow*, under the command of the experienced master, Captain Anthony Fayerweather, was to proceed with her freight to the West Indies, thence to Spain or to the Mediterranean for a return cargo, perhaps stopping at London on the way. The people on the wharf waved their kerchiefs and shouted good wishes for a prosperous voyage, while tears streamed down many faces. Mary and Judy put their arms about poor Peggy and sobbed with her, in her grief at parting with her father. They did not move from the dock until the ship had passed beyond the islands and disappeared from sight. Then Merchant and Madam McFarland took Peggy and her grandmother to their home.

The crowd scattered quickly, leaving Mary behind. She looked down at the snuff-box in her hand and the tears rolled down her face. She had not taken a venture on the *Golden Arrow* after all. Then she remembered. Joey had said he was going to ship on the *Golden Arrow*, but he had never appeared. Where was Joey?

Mary left the dock and hastened to the Moseley cottage. Dusk had begun to fall, when she saw three straggling cows trailing slowly homeward through the long grasses on King Street. She recognized them at once—Maggie McDonald's Spotted Moll, Landlord Drummond's Queenie and the Moseley's Dandelion. Where was Joey? Had he forgotten to bring home the cows? He would be in for a flogging if the Governor knew.

"Joey! Jo—ey!" she called, running out through the stockade and viewing the King's Highway.

But no answer came—only an empty echo. The remaining cows came straggling home, one by one. Mary retraced her steps, stopped at the Moseley cottage and walked in.

"Where is Joey, Marm Moseley?" she asked.

"Land sakes, don't ask me!" answered the frowsy-haired woman. She looked as bedraggled and worried as ever, as she sat before a small fire in the grate, with three of the smallest children on her lap and the others on the floor at her feet.

"I like you!" said little Ichabod, advancing shyly, with his finger in his mouth.

"He wasn't down at the dock when the *Golden Arrow* sailed today, and he's not out at Rock Pasture because all the cows are coming home alone," said Mary.

"Well, I reckon he'll turn up in time," said Marm Moseley with calm composure.

The outer door was pushed open and in came Frisky, with her tail down. She crept to the hearth with a guilty motion and lay down quietly. A loud moo was heard outside the door, as Dandelion begged to come into the adjoining room, which was her stable.

"See! There's Frisky!" cried Mary, hoping to prove Joey's absence.

"Frisky, Frisky!" cried all the little Moseleys. They tumbled off their mother's lap and began to pommel poor Frisky, who growled fiercely in self-defense.

The outer door opened again and Joe Moseley, senior, came in. His jovial look was gone. Sober and dejected, he sat down quickly, without noticing the presence of a visitor.

"Joey's gone," said Marm Moseley, mournfully.

"Mebbe you'd better notify the town-crier or the night watchman or somebody."

" 'Tain't no use," answered the man, slowly. "Joey's went and shipped before the mast . . . on the *Golden Arrow*. Joe Winslow, the gaoler, told me. Governor Dunbar had him and the constable out huntin' to find him. When they found him stowed away on board, the Captain said he'd take him, and the Governor said, 'Let him go. Mebbe he'll make a better sailor than a cow-herd.' "

"What's the matter, Pa?" asked little Ichabod.

"Joey's gone to sea," replied his father.

The news seemed to stun the listeners for a moment. Even Mary, who had known Joey's intentions for so long, could hardly believe it. Marm Moseley began to wail and moan and all the children crowded round her, weeping in chorus. "Joey's gone! Joey's gone to sea!"

Mary slipped out the door unobserved.

The Silver Snuff-Box

Chapter XIII

ONE day in early November, Mary sat by the milk-crocks and waited while Maggie McDonald poured cups of tea for her customers in the back room of her shop. Mary sniffed eagerly, wondering whether it could be gingerbread on the plate which was being passed. But the scent of herbs and spice filled the shop and she could not be certain. She looked down at the snuff-box in her hand.

"Aye, but haggis puddin's the best," asserted Old Granny McKeen. "First we take a sheep's stomach and carefully clean it and then we fill it with the heart, liver and various parts and boil it and serve it up . . ."

"Ye Scotch are queer folks to eat the likes o' that," retorted Marm Pecksniff. "Now roast beef and Yorkshire pudding is more to my taste."

The women's voices floated pleasantly into the front room and Mary became more and more hungry as she listened. She laid the snuff-box on the bench beside the milk-crocks. Suddenly the little bell tinkled and who should walk in but Old Goody Gregory.

"Ah! Ocean Mary!" she cried. "It is good to see you again."

"Can I do something for you, Marm?" asked the proprietress, appearing promptly from the room in the rear. Then she added, "Why, Mary, I didn't know you were waiting."

Goody Gregory opened a large roll of wool cloth and spread it out on the counter. It was a beautiful piece, as smooth and soft as velvet and it was dyed a brilliant scarlet.

"What a handsome color!" exclaimed Maggie, feeling of the cloth with her hand. "What did you color it with, Goody?"

"The leaves and blossom of a plant I found," replied the old woman, ambiguously.

"What plant was it?" asked Maggie, full of curiosity.

"Can't say. Don't rec'lect," said Goody briefly.

"Is the color fast?" asked Maggie.

"Ye needn't worry 'bout its fadin'," said Goody. "I'd like some provisions, Marm—corn, molasses, beans, tea, barley—and don't forget the tobacco for my pipe. How much will you give for it?"

Maggie McDonald hesitated a moment, looking at the cloth with genuine admiration.

A smile passed over the old woman's face as she put

her hand on Mary's shoulder. "It's time to lay in my winter provisions," she said. "I'm not like a squirrel —I'm no good at finding nuts. But I can weave a fine piece of cloth; aye, Mary? You haven't forgot that loom of mine, have you?"

"Oh, no, Goody," responded Mary. "And I think the cloth is beautiful."

"But, Goody," said Maggie, slowly, "I cannot buy this."

"Cannot buy it? What do you mean? How am I going to eat this winter?" cried the old woman in dismay.

"I'm allowed to sell only imported wool—wool made in England and brought over in English ships. That's the King's orders," said Maggie, firmly.

"But you've bought my cloth before!" protested Goody.

"They are watching us more closely now," said Maggie, in a voice so low it could not be heard in the next room. "There are spies, like hawks, who see everything and report."

"But I must sell the cloth or starve!" cried the old woman. "Surely they'll never notice if you take it just this once."

"I happen to know . . ." began Maggie. Then she looked down at Mary. "What is it you wanted, Mary? I did not mean to keep you waiting so long."

"I'm in no hurry, Marm," said Mary. How could she leave until Goody's fate was settled?

"I happen to know I am being watched," Maggie went on. "I would like to help you, but I do not dare. Do you raise your own sheep?"

"Yes, Marm. I've always had sheep."

"You'd better sell them at once," warned Maggie, "before the authorities come and kill them. Why don't you weave linen? The Lieutenant-Governor has had orders from the King to offer a liberal bounty for raising hemp and flax and weaving canvas and fine linen. There's Old Uncle Sandy at the Martin's. He weaves sail-cloth and helps supply the sail-lofts."

"I have no land to cultivate," said the old woman sadly. "Neither hemp nor flax will grow on my rocky island and sheep will." She hesitated, then asked again, in a stubborn tone, "What's it worth?"

"I tell you I cannot buy wool cloth!" cried Maggie again. She raised her voice, as her patience came to an end. Her desire was to do this as kindly as possible, but the old lady made it difficult.

"Is that woman selling home-made wool cloth?" cried Marm Pecksniff. She had heard Maggie's words and she put her head in at the door. "It's agin the law, I tell ye! I'll notify my son!" She sailed in angrily and shook her fists before Goody Gregory's nose.

"Mary, you'd best run along home. Tell me what it is you want, and I'll get it for you," cried Maggie, who knew well that the child was not missing a single word of the argument.

"U-um-m," grunted Mary. "I'll go in a minute, Marm."

"But what did you want, Mary?" cried Maggie, considerably vexed.

"A quarter pound of tea for Cousin Jeanie, Marm," said Mary. Being pressed, she was obliged to answer, but she had no intention of leaving the shop just when things were getting exciting.

"I'll tell my son ye're a-breakin' the law, Goody Gregory, and he'll report ye mighty quick," Marm Pecksniff went on. "Ye're a law-breaker just like that wicked pirate son of yours. Blood will tell, every time. *Captain* Philip Babb he pretends to be, when everybody knows his real name is *Pirate* Babb. No wonder he doesn't dare set foot in this port—he knows he's a law-breaker, same as his Ma!" With these words, Marm Pecksniff returned to her cup of tea and could be heard chatting volubly to the other women on the subjects of pirates and prohibited wool.

Maggie quietly weighed out the tea for Mary. The girl watched with staring eyes. The news was incredible. Was Captain Babb really Goody's son? It was possible, of course, that Goody might have been married twice. That would explain the difference in their names. In a flash, Mary understood several things which had puzzled her since her first visit to Goat Island. She knew now how Goody had happened to know her identity and all the facts about her before their first meeting. She knew now why Goody had shielded Captain Babb, when he careened his brigantine on her island. Suddenly the knowledge brought a tremendous relief, for if he were Goody's son, he could not be a wicked man.

She looked up. "Where can I sell it then, Marm?" she heard Goody asking quietly.

Maggie McDonald mentioned the other shops in town, but said again that she was certain none of them would buy the cloth. The old woman rolled it up slowly and, without a word, made her way out of the shop. Mary hurried after her and began to speak eagerly.

"But Captain Babb is a rich man, Goody!" she cried. "If you'll only let him know, he can give you everything you want. There's no need of selling the cloth at all!"

The old woman stopped still in her path and faced the girl. "I'll have none of his gold!" she answered, in a strained voice.

"But if Captain Babb is your son, as Marm Pecksniff says," cried Mary, "you should let him help you. He has so many gold-pieces he throws them away! Who should help you, if not your own son?"

"He is my son, I am sorry to say," replied the old woman, sadly, "my own flesh and blood. I brought him up in the path of virtue, but he has strayed far from it. His way is not my way, but I love him still. I will help him when he needs help, but I will take nothing from him. I would rather starve than take one penny of his tainted gold."

She turned abruptly and hurried off down the street, leaving Mary standing, bewildered. The girl stared after her for a moment, then she saw two Indians enter the shop with loads of beaver skins on their backs. She recognized them as Lean Wolf and Standing Elk from Nutfield and followed them in. Forgetting Goody and the pirate for a moment, she began to talk to the Indians, in the hope of hearing some news of her family.

"How are Blackbird and papoose?" she asked.

The first Indian smiled. "Blackbird sick," he

grunted. "Eat all day too much. She buy sweetmeat with gold money. Stomach, big pain."

"Ugh!" added Standing Elk. "Squaw howl all night."

"Did she buy sweetmeats with my gold-pieces?" asked Mary, smiling in spite of herself.

"Papoose eat sweet too," Lean Wolf went on. "Blackbird and papoose howl all night."

"That's too bad," responded Mary. "Blackbird should not steal money that does not belong to her."

"Lean Wolf sell furs," announced the first Indian, looking at the proprietress.

"Want tobacco," added Standing Elk.

"Let me see what you have," said Maggie McDonald. "Open your packs."

Having now finished her cup of tea, Marm Pecksniff put her head in at the door again, looking for the woman who was breaking the law. She sniffed once or twice and smelled the peculiar Indian odor. She saw the dark forms, with their backs turned toward her, leaning over their packs. Indians meant only one thing to her, danger and death. Now at last had come the moment for which she had been waiting so many years. She did not hesitate. Silently, with all the stealth of the red man she hated, she crept behind the counter and seized a hatchet. Her eyes opened wide with terror and her face was blanched with fear, as she moved forward step by step.

It was Maggie McDonald who saw her first. "Help!" shrieked Maggie. "Help! She'll murder them!"

Maggie was behind the counter, too far away to do

anything. Mary heard her words, but her legs were paralyzed. Only for a moment, then they obeyed her swift thoughts. She had only to take a step.

Closer and closer crept the enraged woman, hatchet uplifted. Suddenly she drew back her arm, prepared to sink her weapon in the skull of the nearest Indian. At that instant, Mary stepped behind her and grabbed her elbow. The hatchet flew from her hand, but instead of hitting an Indian, fell to the floor and stuck quivering in one of its broad planks.

Breathing hard, Marm Pecksniff turned and looked at the girl with a strange light in her eye. "Well, if 'tain't Ocean-Born Mary, as sure as I'm alive! Oh, my dear," she cried, leaning on Mary's shoulder, "I feel faint, oh, I do feel faint."

Meanwhile, the Indians had jumped up in self-defense. Seeing Mary's quick action and realizing that the sudden danger was over, they resisted their impulse to attack the enraged woman. When Mary looked again, they had slipped silently through the door and were gone, leaving their packs strewn over the floor. She was glad to know that they had escaped. The women from the inner room bustled forth and filled the air with screams and cries.

Marm Pecksniff seemed to have forgotten the Indians entirely. She leaned on Mary and sobbed and cried, "Fetch my night cap for me, child. Take me home. I want to go to bed. Take me home."

Maggie and the other women looked at Mary expectantly. Mary saw fear in their eyes and knew that she could manage Marm Pecksniff better than they. There was nothing else to do, so she led the woman slowly out of the shop and down the street to the water-front.

When they reached the apothecary shop, Mary did not wish to go inside, but the old lady insisted. Mary hoped she had forgotten Goody Gregory's wool as completely as the Indians, but it might be well to make sure.

"Fetch my night cap for me, Mary! I want to go to bed," cried Marm Pecksniff, crying like a child.

As they entered, Mary saw Master Pecksniff standing behind the counter, surrounded by his numerous vials and bottles. He was busily grinding drugs in a mortar with a pestle. "Who's there?" he cried, without looking up.

"It's me," said his mother. "I saw Goody Gregory

255

at Maggie McDonald's shop," she began at once, "with red wool cloth to sell." No, she had not forgotten. "That woman's raisin' her own sheep and breakin' the law and I told her so. She weaves wool cloth. That's why she lives all alone out on that island. She's not loyal to the King. Fetch me my night cap, child. I'm tired."

"What's this? Is it true?" cried the apothecary, briskly.

"It's true enough, ain't it, Ocean-Born Mary?" The old lady patted her on the back. "You were there and saw it, too, and heard it all. Didn't you, Mary? Now, there's a good child, run and fetch . . ."

"Did you, Mary?" demanded the apothecary.

Mary was a truthful child and could only say yes, even though she knew she was a traitor to do so.

"Good child!" cried the man, looking at her with approval for the first time. Then, hoping to find two culprits instead of one, he asked, "Did Maggie buy it?"

"No, sir," said Mary. "She said it was against the law."

"Ah, but then she can testify against the old woman for making the cloth and trying to sell it. I'll report it! I'll go to the Sign of the Teapot and get Maggie's evidence first. Then I'll go to Justice Puddington and get a warrant for the constable. This will mean being set in the pillory or a whipping at the town pump. We'll kill those sheep and eat them. You come along with me, Mary. I shall need you, too."

"No, you shan't take her," cried the old lady, fretfully. "She's going up to my room with me, and she's going to fetch my night cap and help me to bed. I've taken a fancy to Mary."

But they were both disappointed, for when they looked round, Mary was gone.

What a fortunate escape! Once outside the stuffy apothecary shop, she breathed more freely, and thought of the dreadful thing about to happen to Goody Gregory. Mary regretted her part in it, and yet, Marm Pecksniff would undoubtedly have told the same story, whether Mary had gone in or not. At least, she would not be obliged to testify against her. What, oh, what could she do to avert this calamity? She knew she must find help and she turned instinctively toward the carver's shop.

Mary's talk with the carver was brief. Ten minutes after she entered the shop, a row-boat carrying two muffled figures left the wharf and a half-hour later, Mary and Master Greenwood were in Goody Gregory's hut on Goat Island. They found the red cloth lying on the table, and Goody Gregory, in her despair, was easily convinced of the necessity of quick action. When they left a few moments later to row back to town, a large bundle lay in the bottom of their boat. It contained bats of unspun wool, skeins of wool yarn and other pieces of wool flannel, besides the bolt of red cloth. The boat carried also four bleating sheep. Mary and the carver disembarked quickly and carried the bundle and the sheep up the back ladder into the carver's shop.

"Oh, I'm so happy!" cried Mary. "Now they won't punish her. How surprised Master Pecksniff and the constable will be when they cannot find a thing!"

"They'll be very angry, I haven't a doubt!" said Nathaniel with a laugh.

"If Merchant McFarland will only buy the sheep and the cloth as you say," Mary went on, "then Goody can get a flax wheel and loom and start weaving linen. Ma will bring her all the flax she wants from Nutfield. I'll tell Judy about it. Her father will do anything she asks."

"No, I shouldn't mention it to Judy," cautioned Nathaniel. "I shall go to Madam McFarland first, but not at once. I shall wait until the excitement has died down a bit!"

"Just think!" cried Mary, laughing. "If the Mc-Farlands buy the sheep, they will have enough barley broth to last all winter and roast mutton and haggis pudding every day!"

"Goody is in need of provisions, I am sure," said the carver, thoughtfully. "Perhaps Madam McFarland will send her some."

"You haven't forgotten my snuff-box, have you?" cried Mary. "That reminds me, I must hurry and go to Maggie's at once."

She bade the carver a hasty good-bye and set out. She felt quite certain that the silver snuff-box would still be on the bench by the milk-crocks, where, in her haste, she had left it. She smiled to herself as she thought of her plan. She hurried along and her footsteps made clear marks behind her in the snow.

It was early November and heavy snows had already fallen. It seemed a long time to Mary since the *Golden Arrow* had sailed away, taking Joey along. Fortunately, the cows needed no cow-herd in the winter-time.

The town was very quiet after the excitements of the fall and summer and Mary wondered how it would be when the real winter came. As she made her way up Graffort Lane, a strange commotion filled the air, cries and shoutings from many throats, and she wondered if she were dreaming again of the launching. But no, it was real.

King Street was full of people and a notable sight met her eyes. A long procession of forty yoke of oxen reached from the Sign of the Teapot almost to the stockade gate. Over the packed and beaten snow, on heavy sled runners, the beasts drew a huge mast, four feet in diameter at its base and nearly a hundred feet in length. The shouts of the drivers following along the side, coupled with those of the bystanders, filled the air and the runners creaked and groaned under their weight. The afternoon sun shone warm and golden, but the air was crisp and chill.

The *Olive Branch* had long ago returned well-laden to England and other mast ships had come in her place. Sometimes as many as seven lay at anchor at one time in the Pool near Mast Landing, waiting for the accumulation of government timber, masts, bowsprits and yards. During the summer months, the landing had been a busy place, as the huge timbers came floating down the Piscataqua River from her tributaries. One final mast ship, waiting to complete her load, was expected to sail before permanent cold weather. From certain inland areas, without rivers, large masts could be hauled directly to the town on the first heavy snows.

Mary stopped before the door of Maggie McDonald's shop. The proprietress came out and stood beside.

"Oh! It's Pa!" Mary cried aloud, recognizing the leader. "It's the men from Nutfield! They've hauled a log all the way to the Bank instead of to the river." She ran out into the street. "Pa! Pa! Oh, Pa!" she cried. "I'm so glad to see you, Pa! It's me, here I am, Mary!" When she saw she could not get his attention, she came back to the shop.

"He don't see ye, lass, he's too busy," comforted Maggie. "It's a mighty big task to handle one of those big trees."

"Yes, it is," agreed Mary. "They have to break out the road with empty sleds first, when the snow is deep. Then they go over the road and fill in the hollows and shovel out the high places, to make it as level as possible. When it freezes, it makes a hard, smooth road all the way to the river. How strange they should have come all the way to the Bank! I never knew Pa to do it before."

"Probably the river is frozen already," suggested Maggie, "and he didn't want to wait for the spring freshets."

Mary was thoughtful for a moment. "Yes, that must be it," she replied. "He needs gold-pieces—to buy things for winter for Ma and the bairns, and the river froze, so he had to come all that long way. How tired the men and the critters must be! Pa's going to work at masts all the time now. He likes it better than farming."

"Is that so?" asked Maggie. "Well, I'm right glad to hear it. The King needs masts for his ships."

"Hooray! Hooray! Hooray for the King!" shouted a group of boys. "Masts for the King!" "Masts for the royal navy!" "We can't get along without our mother country!" came the cries from the crowd.

Mary thought again of the trouble at Cooper Nutley's saw-mill, weeks before, over her father's unmarked timber. It must be right, after all, to obey the King and cut his masts.

"How they do shout!" exclaimed Maggie. "How they all do love their King!"

Mary listened to the cries of approval coming from all sides. The people were loyal subjects of their King, willing and anxious to obey his laws. How could they get along without him and the mother country? Then, suddenly, she thought of Goody Gregory and stubborn rebellion rose up in her heart. Why could not a good woman be allowed to make her living off a few sheep? What difference did it make to the King far away in England? Why should she be severely punished because he had said something and called it a law?

"They're stopping now," said Susie Cobbett, stepping up briskly, full of the latest news. "They'll be going to the Ark Tavern for refreshment and rest. Then they'll be received by Lieutenant-Governor Dunbar. I hear they've brought their bushel of potatoes—that's the annual quit-rent from Nutfield, to acknowledge that they received their charter from the King and are his faithful subjects."

"They've brought the Governor a gift, too, no doubt," added Maggie. "Probably a handsome piece of the finest Nutfield linen. They give him a gift each year about this time."

Susie Cobbett passed on, to spread her news.

"Why should they give him a gift, Marm?" asked Mary, frankly.

"He stands in the place of the King, child," answered Maggie, in a tone of respectful awe. "And they'll get their pay in gold—the bounty's a liberal one, everybody says."

"Does the King have to *pay* his people to make them obey?" demanded Mary. "You said he'd offered a bounty for growing flax and hemp, too. Is that the way to get people like Goody Gregory to do what they do not want to do?"

"Hush, child," replied Maggie. "You must not speak disrespectfully of the King. The chief reason why the King has sent his people to live in this new country is to create a market here for the surplus of England's goods. If every one here weaves woolen cloth, no one will buy cloth made in England. It's too bad Master Pecksniff isn't here. This sight would do his heart good."

Mary looked up at the shopkeeper and wondered if there was just a hint of sarcasm in her tone.

"Did you . . . did you, by any chance, Marm," began Mary, timidly, "tell Master Pecksniff about Goody's wool cloth?"

"Why, no, child!" cried Maggie, indignantly. "His mother told him, of course. He came here and pestered me with questions and a heap of good it did, for he learned nothing from me. I wouldn't harm the poor soul a mite. Master Pecksniff will soon find out, if he hasn't already, that he cannot wrap *me* around his little finger!"

Just then, Mary happened to remember where the apothecary probably was at that very moment—out on Goat Island. She burst into a hearty laugh and kept on laughing.

"Why, what's so funny, child?" cried Maggie, beginning to smile herself, though she might have laughed, like Mary, had she known how completely the apothecary had been outwitted. "It seems to me I've seen you here all day long. Don't you want to take your tea and run now to see your Pa?"

"Not just yet, Marm," said Mary. "I have something to do first. Oh, I forgot to ask. What became of the furs the Indians brought?"

"The Indians came back again," said Maggie. "I had the furs all picked up and we made our trade. You were a smart child to save them from that wretched woman. She would have killed them, she hates Indians so."

The excitement in the street had now quieted down, so Mary followed Maggie into the shop. There were no customers now and the snuff-box lay on the bench, undisturbed. Mary hesitated, then held it out to the proprietress.

Maggie McDonald took the snuff-box in her hand and looked at it with considerable surprise. "Where did you get this, Mary?"

"I didn't steal it, Marm!" cried Mary, on the defensive.

"I know you wouldn't do that," said Maggie, with a trusting look.

"I found it," explained Mary, "and I thought you might know who lost it. I've asked everybody I've seen, for weeks now, and no one knows whose it is."

"No," said Maggie, with assurance, "I never saw it before. It is English silver. Here are the initials on it —P S P. How long have you had it, child?"

"All summer," said Mary. "I found it last May, soon after I first came to the Bank."

"And no one has had a silver snuff-box cried in all that time. It's evident they have forgotten it," said Maggie.

"Then it's mine to do with as I like, Marm?" asked Mary, eagerly.

"I should think so, child," answered Maggie. "Somebody's paid a pretty penny for this, I'll warrant. Only the rich have money to throw away."

"How much is 'a pretty penny,' Marm?" asked Mary.

"Well," said Maggie, holding the snuff-box at a distance and surveying it meditatively, "it might be worth a guinea and again it might not."

"Then," said Mary promptly, "I'll take some corn, molasses, beans, tea, barley . . . and please don't forget the tobacco!"

"What!" cried Maggie, in astonishment. "You don't mean . . ."

"I'll take it out in provisions, please," said Mary in the same sharp tone which she had heard other customers use.

"But it's not worth more than ten shillings and sixpence, if taken in provisions," answered Maggie, soberly. "You see, I run the risk that the owner may come and demand the snuff-box back again. I'm running a great risk to take it at all."

"Will ten shillings and sixpence buy corn and . . ."

"I have no corn to sell," said Maggie, seriously.

"Will it buy molasses, beans, tea, barley and quite a lot of tobacco?" persisted Mary.

"It will," said Maggie, and it did. When Maggie heard for whom the provisions were intended, she measured generously. Mary never saw her snuff-box from that day, but she parted from it without a pang.

The bundle was so heavy that she had to borrow Maggie's barrow to carry it down to the carver's shop. There she met Goody Gregory according to the pre-arranged plan, and she and Nathaniel Greenwood listened to Goody's story. The constable and the apothecary had indeed paid her a call as expected, but they found no sheep to kill and no criminal to set in the pillory. They had gone away considerably annoyed. The apothecary shook his fists in fury, complaining bitterly that he had been led into a trap. When Mary told that Maggie McDonald had refused to give evidence, they all knew there was nothing more to fear from the apothecary. As Mary left them, both Goody Gregory and the carver thought of her unselfish goodness and their hearts were filled with gratitude.

That evening at the Martin cottage, James Clark told of his desperate effort to arrive in time for the last mast ship with his mast. He had to have gold for his family's winter needs. He could not wait until spring. He displayed his gold-pieces and told of the splendid reception at the home of Lieutenant-Governor Dunbar. As he sat contentedly by the fire, Mary stood beside him, her arm affectionately about his shoulders, drinking in every word. How good it was to see Pa again!

"What are you going to do with all your gold-pieces?" asked Cousin Tom, duly impressed.

"Spend them, of course!" laughed James in reply.

The next morning, James was absent. At midday, he returned and his voice had lost its gaiety. "There's no corn to be bought in this town," he said bitterly.

"How about fish, then?" asked Tom.

"I want corn, not fish."

"Then why didn't you grow some?" shouted Tom.

"I've been lumbering for masts," answered James.

"Didn't you plant any corn?"

"Masting's hard work," growled James. "I can't do everything."

"Well, now you've got your gold-pieces, go and spend them."

"I told you before, there's no corn to be had," cried James. "All the settlers have given up farming and have gone into the mast business. Nobody in our vicinity planted corn. Those who haven't a surplus on hand will fare badly."

"Maybe some will be brought in to the stores and warehouses from other towns," suggested Jeanie.

"It doesn't look that way," said James in a down-hearted tone. "All that has been harvested must be in by this time. I went to Merchant McFarland and Merchant Pomeroy and to all the warehouses as soon as I found there was none at the shops. I've scoured the town and cannot find a grain. If they have any, it is well hidden."

"How about fish, then?" persisted Tom.

"I hate the sight of fish, the smell of fish and the taste of fish," snorted James, angrily.

"It's not so bad when you are hungry, James," said Jeanie gently.

"See where your lumbering has led you?" jeered Tom.

"This is what we get for being loyal to the King! Masts for the King! Bah!"

James Clark returned to Nutfield with two barrels of fish and a bag of salt. He did so, much against his will, for he knew his family had to have something to eat. As Mary watched him go, her eyes were wet with tears. She said to herself, "What will Ma and the bairns do without corn?"

Dutiful, Industrious Child

Chapter XIV

MARY sat on a low stool before the fire in the almshouse kitchen, hornbook in hand. Her face was red and flushed from the heat. "A b, ab, e b, eb, i b, ib, o b, ob, u b, ub," she recited aloud. Then she paused.

Above the fire, hung by strong, hempen cords from pegs in the brick chimney, were four large joints of mutton, sizzling and crackling. Mary basted the first, then gave the cord a twist to send the roast whirling and passed on the second joint. By the time she had twisted the fourth, the first had stopped whirling and was ready to be basted again. Turning the spit was monotonous work, especially when it had to be accompanied by a dreary chant of meaningless syllables.

"A b, ab, e b, eb, i b, ib, o b, ob," she began again, cheerlessly.

"Don't mumble, child," scolded Aunt Becky. "Say them out loud and plain, as if you meant them. I never see that hornbook but what I think of that wicked pirate. Thank goodness, the charm is working, and he hasn't been seen since the day I bought it. The thought of him is enough to spoil more than a good supper, so I hope, by now, he is safe at the bottom of the ocean."

"Ah! What a delightful odor! It invigorates the appetite!" said a tall man, looking in at the door. "And a dutiful child is indeed a pleasant sight to see."

Mary rose from her seat and made a hasty curtsey.

"Thank you, Parson Flint," answered Becky Armstrong. "None could be better than Ocean-Born Mary."

"She is the child of whom I have heard, the child of misfortune, born on the great deep?" As he asked the question, he lifted his long nose and looked down the sides, while his deep-set eyes inspected Mary from head to foot.

"You have heard correctly, sir," said Becky Armstrong, briefly.

"Turning the spit, I see. Well, well," the parson went on, "as the branch is bent, so is the tree inclined. I am certain she has you to thank for her habits of industry and learning, Madam Armstrong!"

"I try to do my duty, sir," answered the woman, closing her lips in a firm line.

As the intruder disappeared and the door closed, Aunt Becky rattled her wooden bowls and iron spoons angrily. "I'll cook for the gentlemen once a year if I must," she said under her breath, "but if any more of them come prying into my kitchen this day, I shall not be responsible for the consequences." Then she added, aloud, "Mary, turn the spit! The joint is burning! And mind your hornbook, too. Hetty, run down cellar and fetch up a basket of potatoes and you, Tilly, stir up the corn-cake. Deary me, there'd be no supper at all if I did not keep right after everything. How those men can eat! We'll cook up enough to feed an army and there won't be a crumb left over."

Mary's syllabic monotone began again, to the hissing and spurting of the whirling joints, and the kitchen settled down to its regular rhythm of work. Mary had grown accustomed to wearing her hornbook dangling at her side and to the noise it made as it bumped about. It was fortunate that the string was so strong, or she would have lost it long ago. She sometimes left it at home, but on the days when she was certain to see Aunt Becky, she never forgot it. For she knew that Aunt Becky had taken it upon herself to direct her education and there was nothing to do but submit. She was quite unaware of the real truth, that each day her eager mind was filling itself with knowledge and understanding, without the aid of so-called learning.

It was a gala day—the day of the annual supper to the fathers of the town. The almshouse was decked out in its best and all the rooms were thrown open for inspection by overseers, town officers and guests. The floors had been thoroughly scrubbed with soap and water, and sprinkled with the cleanest sand obtainable. Fresh fires burned on the hearths. The rooms of the inmates were spick and span and the old women and men likewise. Not a cobweb was visible, not a fly-speck on a window-pane.

A large table stretched the full length of the room called Union Hall, where the town business was usually transacted. The table was covered with hand-woven linen tablecloths, borrowed from the wealthiest matrons in town. It was to be a Scotch meal, with barley-broth, haggis, sheep's-head, roast mutton and blood-puddings. Merchant McFarland, first Select man, and always a generous person, had furnished the sheep himself.

The joints were done at last and the hornbook cheerfully forgotten, as Mary, dressed in a fresh linen gown, began to lay the table. The McFarland silver ware and plate had been lent for the occasion and it gave Mary pleasure to look at it and touch it.

The men had arrived and were exploring the house. They put their heads in at the doors of the inmates' rooms and exclaimed over their cleanliness and comfort. They talked to the old men and women and examined the works of their hands—their spun thread and linen yarns, their pieces of woven linen and sail-cloth, their sacks of oakum. They wandered into Union Hall and out again, when they saw that supper was not yet ready.

"Here, Mary," cried Aunt Becky, her face flushed and her eyes shining under stress of excitement, "take these pewter plates and . . ."

"Ah, Madam Armstrong," said a man's voice at her side, "your management is perfect. I wish to congratulate you. The inmates are to be envied their happy, contented life."

"Thank you, sir," said Becky Armstrong, tipping her head slightly.

Mary saw that it was Lieutenant-Governor Dunbar and curtsied. The man looked down at her where she waited. "Have I not seen this lass before?" he asked.

"This is Ocean-Born Mary, sir," answered Becky, proud to be able to bring the girl to the Governor's attention. "She was born on the ocean and christened by a pirate."

"So that is it!" replied Dunbar, thoughtfully. "That explains a great deal."

Mary looked down at the floor, suddenly embarrassed.

"A pirate, did you say, Madam?" asked the Governor, frowning.

"Yes, indeed," answered Becky. "He saved the lives of all on board an emigrant ship, twelve years ago, including myself and many of the Nutfield settlers."

"The story has been brought to my attention. And you have lived through such an experience and still live to tell the tale, Madam?" The Governor eyed the woman sharply.

"We can never forget it, sir," she answered, simply. "And we hope we are not forgetful of God's mercies."

Dunbar paused a moment, then burst out fiercely: "To think that such things are allowed to go on! These outlaws shall be punished for their outrages against His Majesty's ships! Such a villain as you speak of . . ."

"But he saved our lives, sir," cried Mary, impulsively.

272

"Surely a man cannot be really wicked if he did that. . . ."

"An outlaw once is an outlaw still!" growled the Governor, gruffly.

"Oh, but he's not an outlaw any more, sir!"

Mary was conscious that Aunt Becky was making motions to her behind the Governor's back and warning her to hush, but she could keep still no longer, even though she feared Dunbar more than any one she knew. She was convinced that Philip Babb was a misjudged and misunderstood man, because he had never received due credit for the one good act of his life. If no one else defended him, she was determined to do it herself.

She clutched the pile of pewter plates tightly. "No, he's not an outlaw any longer, sir," she cried, staunchly. "He's an honest sea-captain, now, sir."

"Now?" asked Dunbar, puzzled.

"I saw him at the Ark Tavern . . . it was several months ago, sir . . . he sailed soon afterward for the West Indies."

"So now, I suppose it's about time for him to be coming back, with more dastardly crimes to boast of, eh?" growled the Governor, crossly. "Madam Armstrong, has this child been seeing the pirate you told me of and carrying on conversations with him?"

"She has, sir . . . I am sorry . . . " came the reluctant words in a low tone from Becky Armstrong's lips.

"Madam," the Governor continued, turning his back toward Mary, "I have seen this child many times idling about the wharves on the water-front. Such behavior ill becomes one of her age. I understand she is

under your protection. I ask you to see that her morals
be improved, her freedom curtailed, and that she be
kept within doors and be taught habits of useful industry, and also—to hold her tongue."

Mary heard only the sentence predicting the pirate's
return and it sent her brain reeling. It had been a long
time since she had thought of Captain Babb and she
had grown accustomed to his absence. But now, the
Governor's words made his return seem imminent.
She thought again of the miniature of the little girl,
holding the poppet. Would he come back again? And
would he remember to bring her 'the finest poppet in
all Europe'?

The Governor, meanwhile, had finished his conversation with Madam Armstrong. As he turned toward
the table, he noticed the hornbook hanging at Mary's
side. He picked it up, glanced at it sharply and murmured, "Ah ha!" He turned it over and let it fall.
Then he went to join the men who were streaming in
to take their places.

"Hurry! the plates, Mary!" cried Aunt Becky, in
distress. It was plain to see that she was upset, but
whether by reason of the mention of the pirate or the
Governor's parting words, Mary could not tell.
"They're a-taking their places and, deary me, we're
not ready!"

The candles shone with a brilliant light and supper
progressed in good order, served by Hetty and Tilly,
with Mary's help. The men looked different, somehow, in the candlelight, as if they had thrown away
their every-day faces and put on new ones for this

special occasion. Even the apothecary, who sat at the left of the Governor, looked almost kind. Every one was polite and in good humor as they ate the well-prepared food and enjoyed it.

Mary saw at once that Master Greenwood was there —at the far end of the table. She heard snatches of conversation as she passed back and forth. She heard the remarks on the general condition of the almshouse and the excellent way that it was managed. Then, as this matter was settled, the men talked of other things. She heard the apothecary congratulate the Lieutenant-Governor on the safe departure of all but the last of the mast ships. She heard Merchant Pomeroy say that he was glad to learn that the backwoods settlers had come to their senses at last and begun to take the bounties for mast-cutting.

"Did you hear the approving shouts of the people when the large masts were hauled through the streets?" asked Dunbar. "That shows where their sympathies lie."

"Why, sir," cried Merchant McFarland, "you do not doubt the loyalty of the people, do you?"

"There have been rumors . . . there have been rumors," said the Governor, pettishly, as if he did not care to continue a disagreeable subject of conversation.

"By the way, sir," Parson Flint broke in, "just what progress has been made on the new Queen's chapel? Will it soon be ready to house Her Majesty's splendid gifts?"

But the unpleasant subject would not be downed.

"Is it true," asked the carver, from the far end of

275

the table, "that a bounty is to be paid to encourage linen weaving? Is no one to be allowed to make wool cloth? How are we to keep warm in the winter-time?"

His words brought back again to Mary the whole experience with Goody Gregory. Mary trembled to think that he dared to mention the matter openly.

"Every English ship is bringing wool from England," came the ready reply from Collector of the Port Quackenbush. "English wool is far warmer than that made in the colonies."

A general laugh followed.

"If every person found guilty of making wool cloth were publicly whipped," added Master Pecksniff, maliciously, "it would put a stop to the practice soon enough."

"You are a man after my own heart, sir," said Dunbar. "I see that you have the blood of the lion and the unicorn in every vein."

The apothecary flushed with the unexpected praise and began to eat greedily. "Ah! What delicious mutton and sheep's-head!" he cried. "I do not think I ever ate better."

"Delicious! Utterly delicious!" cried Deacon Puddington, the Justice.

"Do you like it, sirs?" asked Master Greenwood. "I'm so glad that you do." He looked at Mary, standing opposite, and winked. Then he faced the apothecary and went on, in a serious voice: "If a woman were convicted of weaving wool cloth, sir, what would be done with her sheep? Would they be killed and eaten? Would not such criminal sheep be poisonous and choke a man at the first bite?"

The apothecary was about to answer the question in all seriousness, when the assembled men began to roar with laughter. He snapped his mouth shut with vast annoyance, realizing that he was being made game of. He looked at his plate and resumed his eating.

"Take heed, apothecary! It may be poison!" cried Merchant McFarland, with a twinkle in his eye. Master Pecksniff stopped his well-laden fork halfway to his mouth and laid it down hastily.

The men roared again. An understanding look passed from the merchant to the carver. The apothecary looked at him, too, with a savage glare, yet touched with wonder at the audacity of one to whom he had not paid an honest debt.

"Why not try a bounty on pitch and tar, sir?" asked Merchant Pomeroy, after the laughter had died down.

"The settlers refuse to manufacture them," growled Dunbar.

"Allow me to differ with you, sir," objected Collector Quackenbush. "They produce naval stores enough, but they sell all they produce to Portugal, Spain and France illegally and ignore their own mother country who needs them."

"It's like the wool weaving," said Merchant Pomeroy. "The people do it, just to annoy the King deliberately and to disobey his laws."

"I hope, gentlemen," said Lieutenant-Governor Dunbar, solemnly, taking up the challenge, "with the cooperation of Governor Belcher of both provinces, to divert and turn the people's labor and thoughts from working up their own wool, in which they seem to have made some progress, to the raising of naval stores.

It is the wish of the Crown to encourage employment upon tar, hemp, iron, spars, masts and the building of ships, to prevent the colonists from running into woolen manufacture, so that they may continue to wear cloth made in and brought from England. I hope, also, with the help of Governor Belcher, to take steps to stop illegal trade between this country and the Mediterranean countries and the looting of honest merchantmen by outlaws. Every pirate who disobeys the navigation laws shall hang by the neck!"

Bump, bump, bumpety bump! A platter of roast mutton fell out of Mary's limp hands and hit the floor. The phrase 'hang by the neck' was more than she could bear.

"Oh, do allow me, please!" cried the carver, jumping up from his chair. He picked up the joint, replaced it on the platter and handed it back to Mary, whispering, "Mutton, eh?"

Mary's alarm over the pirate's possible fate vanished at once. Giggling, she hurried back to the kitchen.

"But are not these measures oppressive, sir? Will they not encourage the people in active resistance against Great Britain? Is it wise to make so many restrictions?" asked Merchant McFarland, tolerantly. "And can we enforce them if we do? With Governor Belcher seventy miles away in Boston? Suppose a pirate should infest our coast and we had advice of him in a harbor where we could surprise him in twelve hours? Must we wait two days for Governor Belcher's reply to give us permission to act?"

Dunbar scowled, then spoke up in a determined

voice: "I am the Chief Magistrate of New Hampshire during the absence in Massachusetts of the Governor of both provinces. I can call my Council to act . . ." He paused.

A scuffle was heard in the outer hall, followed by excited shouts from the inmates and the cry of Becky Armstrong: "They are not to be disturbed, I say!"

The door burst open and all the men turned to look. A disheveled man, panting and almost overcome with fatigue, entered. He wore the laced badge of his office and the men knew at once that he was a King's surveyor, one of Dunbar's men. He looked about, distracted, then seeing the Lieutenant-Governor, approached quickly. He doffed his hat and spoke in an agitated voice: "There's been a riot, sir, at Exeter. . . ."

"What? What?" cried the listening men, rising to their feet.

"A riot over the timber, sir," the surveyor went on, "at the public house of Samuel Gilman. I took my men, sir, to remove the timber according to your orders. The owner threatened us, said the people held 'The Pine Tree Law' in contempt, sir. . . ."

"This is rebellion!" snorted Dunbar, angrily. "We'll put it down in short order. Then what happened?"

"We paid no heed to the owner, sir," said the surveyor. "We went into the tavern to refresh ourselves, before loading the timber on the boat. Suddenly, without warning, a great number of ill-disposed persons, disguised as Indians . . ."

"Indians, ha!" cried Dunbar. "If they think they can hide their identity, they are mistaken!"

"They burst in upon us, attacked and beat us unmercifully," the surveyor continued. "Others, outside, cut the rigging and sails of our boat and made a hole in her bottom."

"Outrageous! A dishonor to His Majesty's province!" cried Merchant Pomeroy.

"Not finding ourselves safe in the house," the surveyor went on, "we retreated to the boat and pushed off, without realizing that she was damaged. In a moment we were in danger of sinking. With difficulty, we regained the shore and hid ourselves till this morning. Then I came on foot at once to the Bank, sir."

"A flagrant insult to the King!" exclaimed Master Pecksniff, rubbing his hands together gleefully.

"Outrageous! Incredible!" cried Collector Quackenbush.

But it was noticeable that many of the men, including Merchant McFarland, received the news in silence and made not a word of comment.

"It is a conspiracy against me, by evil-minded persons," cried Dunbar, in anger, "to prevent me from doing my duty to the King. I shall call a meeting of the Council at once. We will issue a proclamation commanding all magistrates to assist in discovering the rioters and we will offer a reward for their apprehension."

"The President of the Council is here, sir," said Master Pecksniff, eager for immediate action.

Captain Giddings, a grave-looking man, with a stubborn jaw, had been silent most of the evening. He stepped forward and faced the Lieutenant-Governor with folded arms, and it was easy to see that he was the man's bitter enemy. "There is no need to call a meeting, sir," he said, grimly.

"Ah, yes," cried Dunbar, looking at him with half-closed eyes, "I have noticed that you call meetings when *you* deem it necessary. And in my own house, too, during my absence and without my knowledge. Am I then only a cipher?" He paused, then went on more slowly: "I order you to call a meeting of the Council. The major part of the men are present here and we can attend to this matter at once."

"Even if a meeting were called, sir," said Captain Giddings, stonily, "the major part of the Council believes that no proclamation could be issued except by Governor Belcher. It would be useless, sir."

"How, then, can we call these rioters to account?" demanded Dunbar, completely out of patience.

"I do not know, sir," replied Captain Giddings.

"I see," said Governor Dunbar, looking round at the tight-lipped faces. "Are you all then against me? Are you defending these law-breaking timber men? I see it all plainly now. It is a conspiracy against me to aid the people in the defiance of their King." He dropped his hand in a hopeless gesture.

"But, sir, why not appeal to Governor Belcher at once?" asked Master Pecksniff at his elbow.

"Action is needed immediately, sir," cried the King's surveyor, "to bring the rioters to account. If we wait two days, it will be impossible."

"Call an express," said Dunbar, turning his back on

the assembled men. Pecksniff left the room obediently. Dunbar turned to Becky Armstrong, who stood listening in the doorway. "Madam," he said, "will you kindly fetch writing materials?"

Aunt Becky and Mary hurriedly brought pen, ink, paper, sand-box and sealing-wax. The letter was quickly written by the light of a flickering candle, while the unsympathetic men looked on. In a short time, Pecksniff was back with the express—a man who carried messages on horse-back over long distances. The letter was signed, sealed and placed in his custody, with orders for the greatest possible speed. He left the room quickly.

It was an unpleasant ending to Becky Armstrong's supper. The Lieutenant-Governor started to leave the room immediately, followed by the surveyor and a few of his close friends. Master Greenwood stood by the door waiting for them to pass.

Mary ran to him at once. "Oh, Master Greenwood," she cried eagerly, "I'm glad the surveyors didn't get the timber, aren't you?" Then to the King's surveyor, she put the question: "Did your boat sink, sir, after they made the hole in her bottom?" Her voice rang out high and clear and every one heard, including Governor Dunbar.

He stopped abruptly, pushing the surveyor aside. "Here's that lass again!" he cried in a loud and angry voice. He knew well that her plain words echoed the growing sentiment of the people against him and the truth rankled and hurt. "Have I not given orders that this child should be restrained?" he demanded.

The remaining men crowded round to hear.

"This meddlesome child has caused me untold annoyance and trouble," added Master Pecksniff at Dunbar's elbow. "She delights in putting her finger in everybody's pie!"

"You mean mutton, don't you, Poke-Nose?" came a cry from the rear, but no one knew who spoke.

"Why, what's all this, Mary?" asked Merchant McFarland, kindly. "You have had a long, hard day. You must be tired and ready for bed."

"Why, it is the same dutiful, industrious child I saw in the kitchen," exclaimed Parson Flint, crowding forward. "I commended Madam Armstrong on her successful upbringing."

"Yes," added the carver, with a bright smile, "I have never seen a more unselfish child!"

With a look of contempt directed toward the men

for trying to defend her, Governor Dunbar took Mary by the arm and gave her a vigorous shaking.

"Madam Armstrong!" he called, "will you please teach this child to hold her vicious tongue?" He looked round, but Madam Armstrong was nowhere to be seen and his question fell on the empty air. He stalked out angrily, the other men following.

At last they were all gone but Nathaniel Greenwood. He looked at Mary mischievously, saying: "How does it feel, lassie, to be shaken by the Honorable David Dunbar, Lieutenant-Governor of the Province of New Hampshire and Surveyor-General of His Majesty's Woods?"

"I didn't mind a bit," laughed Mary, "and I'm still glad the surveyors didn't get the timber, aren't you?"

"Yes, child," said Nathaniel. "And I'm glad we made Poke-Nose eat Goody's mutton, too. How angry he would be if he knew!"

They both laughed heartily.

Chapter XV

"MA-RY! Ma-ry!" called Jock. His voice had a distressed sound as if he were in trouble. Mary ran to the cow-shed on the ledge. The air was cold and a strong east wind blew in from the bay. She held her shawl close about her thin shoulders.

The cow-shed door was open and, inside, Jock knelt on his knees. "The cow's dead," he said, in a queer, muffled tone.

The cow lay on the ground, stiff and cold. She would never graze again on the scant grass between the rocks. She would never again give milk to the tug of Mary's firm fingers.

"Why, what could have killed her?" asked Mary.

"Perhaps it was too cold," said Jock, choking.

Mary's eyes filled with tears. As she looked, she re-

285

membered the calf which she and Jock had brought in
the boat from Goat Island. She shivered with cold and
turned away. As she stumbled back toward the house,
she heard voices and looked up. At the corner of the
cottage she saw, as in a dream, two horses and, upon
them, her father, mother and the children.

"There is no milk for the bairns to drink," she
thought, and the knowledge stabbed her like a physical
pain.

Soon they were all in the house, warming themselves
about the kitchen fire.

"Oh, Ma!" cried Mary. "What is it? What is the
matter?"

Although it was good to see them again, Mary knew
at once that something was wrong. She could tell by
the strained look on her mother's face.

"Come, Mary," said Cousin Jeanie, gently, "pare the
potatoes. "We shall need a big pot of chowder to-
night."

Almost at once, Cousin Tom came thundering in,
stamping his great boots heavily on the floor. He had
seen the horses at the door and he frowned heavily.

"What! The family and all?" he shouted to James
Clark. "Ye needn't think ye can come and live off me,
after neglectin' your farmin' the way ye have. I'll not
have the lot of ye in my house, a-eatin' my food and
a-drinkin' my drink. Go back to the woods where ye
came from!"

"Tom, Tom!" begged Jeanie. "What're you saying?
You don't mean a word and you know it."

Mary looked from one to the other in dismay What

would Cousin Tom say when he knew that the cow was dead?

"I mean every word I say," roared Tom. "It's too big a burden to house a whole family. I told James years ago he was makin' a mistake to go out in the wilderness and try to bring up a family a-choppin' down trees, when there was plenty of fish in the sea fer the catchin'. . . ."

His shouts echoed through the tiny cottage and set the hearts of all the listeners quaking. Mary began to wonder where they could go. She had never seen Cousin Tom so angry before.

Tom Martin planted himself before James Clark and pointed an accusing finger at him. There was silence in the room as every one looked at James, expecting not

287

a tiff, but a quarrel which would end in a fight. But there was no fight left in James Clark. When he spoke, it was in a feeble voice.

"I'm beat, Tom," he said, keeping his eyes on the floor. "I made a mistake that I'm sorry for. 'Twas greed for the gold in the masting-business got hold of me. I thought 'twould be easier and quicker than planting corn. If I'd listened to my wife, we'd be better off. I'm sorry I've got my family in these straits. We'll go at once, but God knows where . . ."

"Oh, don't, Pa—a!" cried Mary, in a wail of anguish. "Oh, Cousin Tom, don't send them away!"

"Tom, Tom," cried Jeanie. "They'll starve. They haven't had food enough for days. Look into their pinched faces. How can you be so hard-hearted?"

"I'm hungry, Ma," whimpered little Georgie, at his mother's knee. The baby on Elizabeth's lap began to wail, but Elizabeth did not speak.

"I'll go . . . I'll go and sleep at the almshouse, if you'll let them stay, Cousin Tom," begged Mary. "Ma can sleep in my bed."

Then Cousin Tom surprised them all. He took James by the hand and bade him make himself at home. "I'll have none of my kin-folk sleep at the almshouse, while I've a roof over of my head. I spoke hasty. I said what I did not mean. There's only the floor for the bairns to sleep on. . . ."

"Oh! We're going to stay, we're going to stay!" shouted the small boys.

"But there's plenty of fish for everybody to eat," added Tom.

"I shall never say again that I do not like it," said

James, humbly. "I shall eat it and like it and thank God for every mouthful."

Then Mary remembered the cow. Distressing as the news was, she could keep it to herself no longer. Even if it meant that the family had to go, it had to be known sometime.

"But . . . the cow," she cried, unhappily, "the cow is dead! There won't be any milk for the bairns to drink!"

The announcement was very upsetting. Angry shouts came from Cousin Tom, blaming the Clarks for this new calamity.

"But there's our cow at Nutfield!" said Elizabeth quietly. "We've already arranged for Silas Gregg to bring her the next time he comes to town."

"And the dead cow's hide will make shoes enough for all the bairns," added Jeanie, practically, "and for Mary and the boys as well. I hardly know who needs them most."

So the calamity was straightway turned into a blessing. At the mention of the Clarks' cow and the new shoes, Mary was cheered again. That evening, after a generous supper of nourishing fish-chowder, both families gathered about the great fire and listened while Elizabeth told of their difficult experiences:

"We could scarcely believe it when James came home from the Bank and said there was no corn to be bought. So many of the settlers had not planted a single hill, because of timber work. Johnny and I went out hunting in the fall and took a number of raccoons and beaver and we dried their meat in smoke, the way Lean Wolf taught us. The children all helped gather acorns, beechnuts, ground-nuts and lily roots. These we dried and stored. We ground acorns and corn-cobs with the last of the corn in the mortar. Some-times we added lily-roots to make it last longer. For a time we lived on the fish James had brought. Finally we were reduced to game only and the children be-came ill from eating nothing but meat.

"The big snows came and there was little game to be caught. The cow went almost dry and I boiled maple-syrup with the little milk we had. I cooked elm-bark, hazel-nuts and lily-roots together, and it filled our stomachs, but it gave us no strength. The children became thin and cried continually.

"I think I was at my lowest point the day the In-dians came—Lean Wolf and Blackbird. I wondered what I could find for them, without depriving the children. Then I saw they were behaving queerly. They peered into the pot where the root and nut mix-ture was boiling and made gestures and grunts of dis-gust. When I offered them a taste, they turned away and walked about the cabin, hunting in vain for more palatable food. I was out of patience with them, God forgive me. . . ." The tears came into Elizabeth's eyes at the recollection. "They went out the door and I thought they looked morose and angry and might do us some harm. And then . . ."

"I know!" cried little Georgie. "They came back in with presents for us—all kinds of good things to eat."

"Yes," added Elizabeth, "all kinds of good things which we had been without for so long. It was not much in reality, but it seemed a great deal at the time.

They brought a leather bag full of corn, some venison and a beaver leg. We made a large corn-cake and cooked the meat, and nothing ever tasted so good. The children laughed as they had not for days and kept on asking for more.

"I had misjudged the Indians. They brought their gifts out of gratitude to Mary. . . ."

"To me?" exclaimed Mary, in astonishment.

"Yes, child," said Elizabeth. "I can see now that it was God's providence that you should come to the Bank when you did. Often, after we began to be short of food, I was thankful that you were here with Jeanie, where there was plenty of fish to eat. I knew you would never be hungry. Then when Lean Wolf told me that you had saved his life and Standing Elk's, I knew that it had all been in God's plan, so that we should not starve."

"Mary saved Lean Wolf's life?" cried Jock and Jamie together. "Why, she never told us."

"No," added Jeanie, "she never said a word."

Then the whole story of mad Marm Pecksniff's attack came out and Mary insisted that she had done only what any one would have done. Her face flushed at unaccustomed words of praise.

"It is often said," Elizabeth went on, "that an Indian never forgets an injury, but I think it is still more true that he always remembers a kindness. When the food that the Indians brought was gone, we were forced to give up. We knew we could never go through the winter in Nutfield. We knew we must come to Strawberry Bank, where there is always plenty of fish to eat."

"Eh! Come down to fish at last, have ye?" growled Cousin Tom.

And every one joined in a hearty laugh.

The next day Mary and Jock loaded the dead cow's hide into the wherry and took it to tanner Tedworth to be cured and made into shoes for all the children. Upon their return, they hurried into the cottage.

"Mary's found corn!" shouted Jock.

"What's this, Mary?" asked her father, in amazement.

"There was a leak in the wherry," said Mary, breathlessly, "so we pulled up at a wharf. Jock told me to look for a piggin to bail the water out of the boat. It was cold and windy on the wharf and when I noticed that a small back door of the warehouse was ajar, I walked in. It was warmer there and . . ."

"Then what?" asked her father, anxiously.

"I found nothing downstairs, so I climbed up a small ladder. Then I saw that the loft was full of corn. I felt of the sacks to make certain. I came down quickly and Jock had found something and was bailing the water out. I asked him why we didn't buy corn from Merchant Pomeroy and Jock said the merchant must be saving it for shipment to the West Indies. I thought, Pa, you'd be glad to know where you can buy some . . ."

"Was it the Pomeroy Dock, are you sure?" demanded James Clark, almost fiercely.

"Yes, Pa," said Mary, "it was the third wharf south of the Town Dock. I noticed particularly. I could see the Sign of the Mortar and Pestle when I came out . . ."

James Duncan listened to Mary's story with a serious face. Then he looked at Tom Martin and whispered a single word, "Hoarding!"

Mary could not understand why her father did not go at once to Merchant Pomeroy and buy corn. She had forgotten that he had already been there and been refused. Nothing more was said about her surprising discovery, but a few days later, a group of Nutfield settlers gathered with James Clark at Tom Martin's cottage.

One morning, not long afterward, Mary was roused from her sleep by a rude shaking. The sun had not yet risen and no light came through the windows.

"Wake up, Mary, wake up!" cried Jock. "We did it! We did it!"

"What do you want, Jock?" asked Mary, sleepily, as she stumbled to her feet.

"We did it! We raided the warehouse," Jock went on. "We took all the corn!"

Mary was surprised to see that both Cousin Jeanie and her mother were up and dressed and a fresh fire was blazing brightly on the hearth. They looked as if they had been up all night. At the word *corn* Mary woke up.

"Do you mean you stole it?" she cried. "Why, I thought Pa would go and buy some . . ."

"All the corn is on its way to Nutfield, now," cried Jock eagerly. "Not a grain is left. I went as far as the stockade gate and saw the men and horses waiting for it. Then the Indians loaded the bags on the sleds . . ."

"Indians!" gasped Mary, feeling that she must still be dreaming.

"The men dressed like Indians, I mean," explained Jock, hastily.

"Didn't the night watchman catch you?" asked Mary.

"We heard him call, 'All's well,' in the distance, but he was afraid to come near," said Jock.

"Don't interrupt, Mary," said her mother. "Let Jock tell what happened. Now begin at the beginning."

"Jamie and I waited behind a shed at the Ark Tavern till the men came out the back door," said Jock. "Then we saw that they were dressed like Indians, so no one would know who they were if they were seen. We all walked down Queen Street toward the warehouse. Some of the men began to talk and laugh a little as we reached Water Street. It seemed so easy. But that was the time they made a mistake. As we passed the Sign of the Mortar and Pestle, an upper window burst open and a woman with a large, white cap put her head out . . ."

"That must have been Marm Pecksniff," interrupted Mary, nodding her head vigorously. "She's afraid of the Indians. . . ."

"I should think she is!" exclaimed Jock. "She screamed as loud as she could, 'Indians! Indians! The Indians are coming!' I never heard any one scream so loud, and it sounded worse because the night was so still. You should have seen the men run. One man said, 'Poke-Nose will soon be after us.' We hurried to the warehouse, climbed up the ladder and took the sacks of corn on our backs. All the men were silent now, for we knew we were in danger. One by one the men came down to the lower part of the warehouse and waited. We all went out together. It was dark outside and we could not see much. We started up Queen Street, all moving along together.

"Suddenly, we saw lanterns swinging back and forth in a cross street, and we heard foot-steps and excited voices. One man in our crowd said with a laugh, 'It's Poke-Nose! He's brought the night watchman and Merchant Pomeroy!' Another said, 'And the Select men and the constable and the Justice,' and some one else added, 'Maybe even Dunbar himself!' Then they shouted, 'Who's afraid of Dunbar? Who's afraid of Dunbar?' Nobody seemed afraid at all and it was great fun. Whooping like Indians, we ran until we reached the Parade. Lights began to be seen in the houses and heads were thrust out of the windows. The lanterns followed us, then stood still as if the men were afraid to come near. We rested a while, then saw that they were gone.

"'Poke-Nose is discouraged and has gone back to bed!' the men said. We all laughed because we knew we were safe. Then we met the sleds at the gate and the men loaded the corn on, while I came home. They wanted to get their Indian clothes off before dawn. Oh, you should have seen them. . . ."

The raid on the hoarded corn was a great success. Every one in town soon learned all the facts. Master Pecksniff had indeed roused both Justice and constable, who were not only fearful but powerless before so large a group of men. The memory, too, of the recent timber riot was not conducive to action. It was rumored that Merchant Pomeroy had appealed to Governor Dunbar, but he, knowing that his Council was at odds with him, had refused to act. Others said the hoarding had been done with the Governor's consent and approval. There was nothing for the merchant to do but suffer the loss of his corn. Public opinion was against him and he was accused of holding the corn for extravagant prices, knowing the settlers would be forced to buy rather than starve. No sympathy was wasted on him and every one was relieved to know that the corn had gone to the suffering Nutfield people. There was a great deal of gossip as to the way the corn had been discovered, but no one thought of associating Ocean-Born Mary with the occurrence.

During the winter months, Mary had little opportunity to see her friends. After her family's arrival, she helped with the extra work and cared for the small children, while her mother and Cousin Jeanie did the spinning and her father took turns with Uncle Sandy at the weaving.

One day, while returning from Aunt Becky's on an errand, Mary stopped in at Susannah's, and there met Madam McFarland. She was glad to find Susannah looking better and to see the basketful of good things which Madam McFarland had left at her bedside.

They came out the door together. The day was blustery and a strong wind was blowing. Winter was in full swing now, and from the chimneys of low frame houses throughout the town, clouds of smoke poured forth, evidence of blazing fires within. Like every one else, Madam McFarland had heard about the raid on the corn. She asked Mary about her family's need and was relieved to learn that they had come to Portsmouth for the winter. Then she noticed that the girl was thinly clad. "Have you no cloak?" she asked.

"It was too small," said Mary, "so Ma made it over for baby Ellen. I have a linsey-woolsey jacket. I wear it underneath," she explained with a laugh. "Cousin Jeanie made it so it can be fastened in front in summer and turned round to act as a chest protector in winter."

"You poor child," exclaimed Madam McFarland, sympathetically. "There's no warmth in linsey-woolsey for this wintry weather. No wonder your face is blue and your hands are like ice."

Before they parted, Madam McFarland's mind was full of busy plans and she had arranged for Mary to call at her home a week later.

On the appointed day, Peggy Fayerweather was already there when Mary arrived. Madam McFarland pulled a chair up before the fire and bade Mary warm herself.

"And then we'll have the fitting!" cried Judy, her eyes sparkling. "Everything is ready!"

Mary looked from Judy to her mother, extremely puzzled, but no more was said. It was good to be at the McFarlands' again. The house was warm and comfortable and made Mary forget the piercing cold outdoors. She never tired of the paintings on the stair walls or the Dutch tiles about the fireplace. They were as wonderful to her as on that day so long ago, when she had seen them for the first time.

Mary held out her hands to the welcome blaze and studied the tiles at the side, while Peggy went on with a story she had been telling.

"You remember I told you he has been in Boston for the last three months," she said quietly. "Well, he called upon us yesterday and Grandmother sent him away and forbade him to return!"

"But I thought she liked him!" protested Judy.

"She knew his family connections in England and said they could not be better," said Peggy.

"What will your father say when he returns from his voyage?" asked Madam McFarland, in amazement.

"Grandmother says he will understand," Peggy continued. "Well, it seems Lord Peabody lost a snuff-box . . ."

Mary sat up stiffly and her heart began to pound.

"He said it was not valuable," Peggy went on, "but had a sentimental value and he had sworn never to part with it. He insisted that he had left it at our house and Grandmother told him we should have found it if he had. Then she politely returned the fashionable hoops and other gifts and he took them away. Grandmother said she was glad to discover his real character and was thankful to see the last of him. He has returned to Boston."

"Oh, I'm so glad!" cried Judy. "I never liked the way he tilted up his nose or his tone of voice or . . ."

"I didn't like anything about him," said Peggy, "and now I am so happy."

Mary rose awkwardly to her feet and every one noticed that her face was pale. "What was His Lordship's name?" she asked in a weak voice.

"Philemon Sedgwick Prindle, Lord Peabody!" answered Peggy, dramatically.

"How dreadful!" exclaimed Judy.

"P S P—yes, it was his!" cried Mary. "I found his snuff-box!"

"You?" cried the two girls and Madam McFarland together.

Then Mary told the whole story of the snuff-box, her failure to send it away on a venture and her purchase of provisions from Maggie McDonald with it. Remembering the carver's caution, she did not speak of Goody Gregory's red cloth. Judy and Peggy decided that in order to drop the box in front of the almshouse, Lord Peabody must have taken a stroll about town.

"Do you think, ma'am," asked Mary, turning to

Madam McFarland uncertainly, "I should tell Maggie McDonald that I have found out the owner?"

Madam McFarland's eyes twinkled as she said: "I will speak to her about it myself. The snuff-box has served two good purposes. It has sent Lord Peabody packing and it has kept Goody Gregory from starving. Maggie will understand, I am sure."

"Then it need not be returned to its owner?" asked Mary.

"No, child," said Madam McFarland. "Maggie may do with it as she sees fit. His Lordship has gone away and we hope we shall never see him again. You need no longer think of the snuff-box. Now, it is time for you to come upstairs with me." Still mystified, Mary followed Madam McFarland up the broad stairs and both disappeared from view.

Black Peter entered the room, announcing Master Greenwood, who followed close at his heels.

"Oh, it's Nathaniel!" cried Judy. "We are so glad you've come."

"And you, Miss Peggy," asked Master Greenwood, "are you glad, too?"

"Why, certainly, Master Greenwood," said Peggy, shyly.

"I knew you were here," the carver announced boldly, "and I came to escort you to your home."

"That is kind of you, sir," said Peggy, "but may I ask how you happened to know?"

"Oh, a little bird told me!" laughed Nathaniel, looking about for Madam McFarland and noting her absence.

"I am sorry I cannot go yet, sir," said Peggy, "not until Mary is ready."

"Ocean-Born Mary?" asked the carver. "Is she here, too? I am always glad to see her."

"Come, have a cup of tea, while we are waiting, Nathaniel," invited Judy.

A few moments later, Mary entered the room, clad in a full set of new, warm garments. She wore a striped woolen shortgown, a quilted petticoat, a plain muslin apron and a neat kerchief folded over her shoulders. "Oh! Is Nathaniel here?" she cried.

"Nathaniel is here," cried Master Greenwood with a bow.

"Now, Mother!" cried Judy. "Let us see it."

Madam McFarland carried in her arms a hooded cloak made of soft, velvety wool cloth of a brilliant scarlet. She held it out for all to see.

"Oh, how lovely!" cried Judy and Peggy together.

As Madam McFarland turned toward her, Mary cried out breathlessly, "Oh, but it's not for me . . ."

"This is the reward for your unselfishness, my child," said Madam McFarland in a voice of kindness. "This is what the snuff-box brought you." She placed the cloak over Mary's shoulders and fastened the hood beneath her chin. Then she kissed her on the forehead.

"I . . . I don't know . . . how I can thank you . . ." said Mary, shyly.

"How fortunate that I happened in at this auspicious moment," cried the carver, smiling at Madam McFarland. "Just in time to see our little queen receive her crown. I would not have missed this for worlds. Mary, you are the sweetest, bravest child I know." He took her hand in his own. "Together, you and I are not afraid to brave . . . er . . . lions, are we?"

"No, sir," said Mary, gravely. Then to Madam McFarland, "You don't think any one will . . ."

"Will what?" cried Judy.

"Tell us the secret, too!" begged Peggy.

But Madam McFarland had thought it wise that no one but Master Greenwood and Mary should know that the cloak had been made of Goody Gregory's cloth. For this reason, Judy and Peggy were allowed to believe that it had been imported. Aloud, Madam McFarland said, "If any one asks questions, you may tell them that Merchant McFarland's wife gave you the cloak and they will say no more. Now, my child, you will, I hope, be able to keep warm."

"The color itself will do that," laughed Mary. "It makes me happy just to look at it. How can I ever thank you?"

"My child, there is no need."

Chapter XVI

"NO NEWS today, Mary?" asked Marm Moseley. "No sign of the *Golden Arrow?* When does the merchant expect her?"

The little Moseleys crowded close and pulled at Mary's skirts. "Merchant McFarland says, Marm," answered Mary, "she was due a fortnight ago, but he's not worried yet. There are many reasons why she may have been delayed—storms or . . ."

"O Lor' me!" wailed Joey's mother. "I never go to sleep but what I dream o' poor Joey, a-rockin' on the waves. I never hear the wind and rain, but what I see him washed right off the deck as plain as if he was before my eyes. O Lor' me, O Lor' me!"

"There is no cause for worry, Marm," said Mary, patiently. "Judy and Peggy and I go to the Point almost every day and watch. Sometimes we talk to Old

Cap'n Pete and he says ships are often driven out of their course and are delayed for weeks and months."

"It seems to me I've done nothing but wait, wait, wait for years," said Marm Moseley, mournfully.

"It's only been eight months, Marm," said Mary, in an effort to cheer, although she herself was as tired of waiting as any one.

"What's the matter?" asked little Ichabod.

"Nothing, Ichabod," answered Mary. "Joey's coming back safe."

"Joey's coming back safe, Mary said so," cried Ichabod, and the news was repeated in a chorus by the other children.

It was hard to leave the Moseleys. They depended on Mary more and more, for they knew that she was a friend of the owner of the *Golden Arrow*. Marm Moseley had never recovered from the abruptness of Joey's departure and even now that the time for his return was so close at hand, she could not be cheerful about it.

Finally, Mary succeeded in shaking off the children and hurried away. She was restless every moment that she was out of sight of the sea, for fear the brig might be sighted in her absence. She wanted to be the first to see it. Peggy had promised to take her and Judy up to the Captain's walk. The air was clear and it ought to be possible to see a great distance. It was a pleasant day in early June, with warm sun shining brightly overhead.

It was easy to forget all the rigors and hardships of the past winter in the satisfactions of the present warmth and sunshine. For welcome spring had indeed come at last, and with the breaking up of the ice, three small coasting schooners had arrived from the Carolinas, loaded with corn. Immediately, the shops and warehouses were generously supplied; there was plenty to be bought and the famine came to an end. James Clark and family returned to Nutfield in early April, as did many other settlers. Elizabeth's four children had thriven noticeably from feeding on cods' livers and fish. They looked stronger and more sturdy than before.

Captain Anthony Fayerweather's mansion-house stood above the waterfront, only a stone's throw from the McFarland Dock. Mary had seen it many times, but had never been inside. Nor had she ever seen Peggy's grandmother,  who, it was generally understood, led a life of retirement. A white picket fence with carved gate-posts enclosed the small front yard and an orchard of fruit trees behind. The house had a hipped roof, with a domed cupola, which was surmounted by a platform enclosed by a balustrade. This platform was known as the Captain's walk.

Judy and Peggy were waiting at the gate when Mary arrived. They entered the house, climbed several flights of stairs and entered the cupola. They stepped out a narrow door onto the roof.

"Oh! I didn't know it would be like this!" exclaimed Mary.

She looked about her and saw the town and harbor spread out like a map at her feet. Just below the house were the rows of parallel wharves along Water Street. Across the bay, dotted with its many islands, lay the Kittery shore and Mary could see a ferry boat making its way to Pray's wharf in the northern part of town. Above the tiny wooden houses, the spire of North Meeting House could be seen and beyond the stockade and the windmill in Rock Pasture, the heavy forest in the distance. The town itself was almost an island, with only a narrow neck of land between North and South Mill Ponds.

But Mary turned back again to the sea and it was the sea that held her. She could not look elsewhere except at the harbor with its wave-washed islands and white-sailed ships riding easily at anchor, and beyond —the blue, blue sea, running out to meet the sky. Mary breathed deeply and could not speak. An emptiness inside her was satisfied at last.

Judy and Peggy were talking but she did not hear. Then they thrust the telescope into her hands and she looked. The first thing she found was Goat Island and Goody Gregory's hut. She remembered the old woman's prophecy that it would not be long before she returned to Nutfield. Her heart filled with gratitude that she had been allowed to see the launching, and now—she hoped—the return of the *Golden Arrow* as well.

"I've waited so long," she heard Peggy saying, "sometimes I feel as if I have been waiting for years."

"You sound just like Marm Moseley," laughed Mary.

"Grandmother says I will grow accustomed to it in time, especially if I marry a sea-captain. . . ."

"Who? Oh, tell us, who?" cried both girls at once.

"But that is just what I shall not do," said Peggy, stamping her foot for emphasis. "It's bad enough with Father always going away. We may as well go down; there's no use looking . . ."

"Just one more look," begged Mary.

"I do hope Father does well with Nathaniel's guineas," said Peggy, thoughtfully.

"Why, you haven't forgotten our keeking-glasses, have you?" cried Judy. "Ever since Lord Peabody went away, you have talked of no one but Nathaniel."

Peggy flushed and turned away. "We may as well go down, there's no use looking."

"Wait, just a minute," cried Mary, still looking intently through the telescope. "I think I see . . ."

"Oh, do give it to me, Mary," cried Judy. "I can tell."

"There's a small speck on the horizon," Mary announced. "I can't tell yet what it is."

What if it were the *Golden Arrow*, coming back after long adventures in strange waters? Bringing back profitable ventures to Judy and Peggy and so many other townsfolk? Bringing back Captain Fayerweather and Joey and the beautiful figure-head? Mary wondered suddenly what a keeking-glass looked like.

Peggy and Judy took turns at the telescope and both agreed that the speck was a ship. The girls spent the rest of the afternoon on the Captain's walk, watching as the tiny speck grew more and more into the re-

semblance of a white-sailed ship. Then the sun began
to set, dusk fell and reluctantly they went down the
stairs, knowing it would be impossible for the *Golden
Arrow,* if it were she, to reach port that night.

All three, after restless sleep, reached the wharf
early the following morning, together with Nathaniel
Greenwood and Merchant McFarland and his wife.
The Town Crier walked the streets, announcing the
arrival of a ship from foreign ports. Boys ran through
the streets, screaming: "The *Golden Arrow!* The
Golden Arrow!" Word was hurriedly sent from the
counting-house to relatives of the crew. People appeared in excited groups.

Mary watched the ship come slowly nearer and
nearer. Before the sharpest eyes could make out her
name or distinguish her figure-head, the crowd began
to be restless. Beyond Great Island the incoming ship
passed, her masts plainly seen above, as if moving along
on dry land. Then she rounded the point and stood
out plainly in the sun. The people stood waiting and
watching in puzzled silence. The name, *Golden Arrow,* was heard no more.

"It's the *Morning Star!*" cried Nicholas Wiggin,
shipbuilder. Well did he know every line of every ship
which had been made by the cunning of his own hand.
He waved his hat aloft. "Captain Wainwright and
the *Morning Star!*" he shouted.

"Oh, no!" Peggy cried out in disappointment. "It
cannot be. It is Father and the *Golden Arrow!*"

"There, there, dear," cried Madam McFarland, putting her arm about her. The people continued to
shout: "The *Morning Star!* The *Morning Star!*"

But wishing did not make it true, and, like Peggy, Mary was disappointed. The tears came to her eyes, but she brushed them away. There was still hope. If this was the *Morning Star,* there would be another day when the *Golden Arrow* would come. Surely it could not be long now.

"Whose mistake is this?" cried the hunch-backed apothecary, bustling up. "Who sent false word about that it was the *Golden Arrow?*" He glared at Mary as if she herself were responsible.

But the lusty shouts of welcome for the *Morning Star* died down as suddenly as they began. When the waiting people saw that the flag was dropped on the sail, they knew it was a sign of bad news. Those who had friends and relatives on board waited with heavy hearts, preparing themselves for the worst—sickness or even the death of a loved one. The ship came closer and Mary saw that the captain and crew were gathered on deck.

She noticed that Merchant McFarland had not said a word. Straight as a ramrod he stood, ready for whatever might befall, ready for bad news as well as good. The arrival of a ship from a long voyage was always a sad as well as a happy event. Through years of experience, he had learned to steel himself for whatever came. His straight, brave figure showed courage in every inch, and yet Mary saw his face turn pale. She heard him ask his wife in a low voice, "Who is that standing beside Captain Wainwright? Does it look like Anthony to you?"

"Is it Father?" cried Peggy, torn between hope and fear.

Mary stared. Captain Fayerweather on the *Morning Star!* What did it mean? She looked from one to the other of her friends, puzzled.

"Something has happened," said Merchant McFarland to his wife. "He's back!"

"It's your father, Peggy," cried Madam McFarland, taking the girl into her arms. "He's back, alive and well, thank God!"

"What can have happened to the *Golden Arrow,* sir?" asked Master Greenwood, stepping forward.

"We must wait until Anthony tells us," said the merchant, slowly. He put his hand on the younger man's arm, as if for support. "He seems to have . . . lost . . . his ship . . . Something has happened . . . to the *Golden Arrow* . . ."

Boats were put out from shore by eager men and boys, to learn the news as quickly as possible. The time dragged slowly, and it seemed longer than it was in reality, because fear clutched at the hearts of those who waited. When the *Morning Star* finally reached her dock, to the amazement of all, Captain Anthony Fayerweather stepped ashore behind Captain Wainwright. A hush fell over the crowd.

Captain Fayerweather took his daughter into his arms at once. Lieutenant-Governor Dunbar, Merchant Pomeroy, Justice Puddington, Master Pecksniff and others rushed up to grasp his hand. A circle closed in about him and he talked for a short time, then with Merchant McFarland, proceeded to his home. Peggy and Judy followed with Madam McFarland.

Full of newly acquired importance, Master Pecksniff mounted a barrel with surprising agility. He

"'Oh!' cried Mary, with a sinking heart. 'It's not true!'"

rubbed his hands together and chuckled aloud. Then he held up his hand for silence. "My good people," he shouted, "Captain Fayerweather announces with regret that the *Golden Arrow* has been sunk by pirates in mid-ocean and now lies at the bottom of the sea!"

"Oh!" cried Mary, with a sinking heart. "It's not true!"

The apothecary looked down at her and scowled. "What do you know about it?" he cried angrily. "Of course it is true or I would not say so!"

The news spread through the crowd at once. "Pirates!" "Sunk by pirates!" came the cries. "The *Golden Arrow* sunk by pirates!"

Afterwards, Mary never knew how she lived through that first, dreadful moment. The word *pirate* itself seemed to stop the beating of her heart. She felt faint and made her way out of the crowd, not knowing where she went. She found a seat in a corner alone. The *Golden Arrow!* The *Golden Arrow* which she had watched from the time its keel was a log—a tree from Nutfield! The *Golden Arrow* with Nathaniel's beautiful figure-head! Suddenly she realized that the sailors' idea about their guardian angel was only nonsense, as Maggie McDonald had said. The figure was made only of wood. How could it save a ship from black-hearted, armed men? The words of the gossiping prophecies of the day of the launching came back to Mary clearly. How did the people know it was going to happen? Then she remembered Governor Dunbar's threats. Why did he not do as he said? Why did he allow such beautiful ships to be sunk?

Mary looked up and it was then that she saw Joey. She scarcely knew him, he had grown so tall. But the thing that made him seem so changed was the look on his face. The laughing, mischievous boy was gone and here stood a sober-looking youth in his place—a complete stranger. Then Mary remembered that she had promised to let Marm Moseley know when the ship came in. How could she go now and tell her what had happened? How would she ever dare face her again? Helplessly, she watched young Joey make his way through the crowd, accompanied by a handful of men who had once been a part of the crew of the *Golden Arrow*.

It was Nathaniel Greenwood who told Mary the whole story. Seeing her sitting alone, overcome by grief, he had come to her at once, to cheer her if possible.

"Everything is lost," he said quietly, "but we can be thankful that Peggy still has her father and that the men are unharmed."

"Is your figure-head . . . has it . . . ?" began Mary.

"My figure-head is at the bottom of the ocean," said the carver, calmly. "But I can always make another, so my loss is nothing. My guineas are gone, but more can be earned. The whole valuable cargo, picked up in the Mediterranean countries and in England, is lost and the ship is sunk. The goods were transferred to the pirate ship and the men were taken on board. From there, they were forced to watch the sinking of the *Golden Arrow*. Only as a great favor were their lives spared. They were put into a boat and set adrift. After two days out, they were picked up by an English sloop. Some were taken to Boston, where they expect to ship on other voyages. Those who wished to return were transferred to the *Morning Star*."

As she listened, Mary told herself that it could not have been Captain Babb. She thought of his kindness to her and she remembered how he had said that he would rid the sea of pirates. She remembered that he was Goody Gregory's son and she thought again of his promise to bring her a poppet. He was an honest sea-captain now. There were many pirates on the sea more wicked than he. She reassured herself—and yet there were facts that had to be faced.

"Could the pirate captain have killed them if he liked?" she asked, wide-eyed.

"Pirate captains usually do," said Nathaniel, frankly.

"Did he let them go as a special favor?" asked Mary, in alarm.

"Yes, so Captain Fayerweather says," replied the carver. "You are glad, aren't you?"

Mary remembered that it was Philip Babb who had once saved the lives of a group of helpless people whom he might have killed.

"Oh, he couldn't have done it! He couldn't!" she sobbed. "I will not believe it. I will not believe it!"

"What do you mean, child?" asked Nathaniel.

"I mean the pirate . . . I mean the pirate . . ." sobbed Mary.

"Why, Mary," exclaimed the carver, "what are you saying? You don't know any pirates. . . . You are tired and overwrought. Come now, I will walk home

with you and we will try to forget this dreadful
story."

But Mary did not forget for many a day. The whole
town was thrown into a turmoil and no one talked
of anything else. Captains Wainwright and Fayerweather, with Merchant McFarland, went into immediate consultation with Lieutenant-Governor Dunbar,
Justice Puddington and other officers of the Crown.
Governor Dunbar was roused as he had never been
since he took over the governorship. Their delibera-
tions were lengthy, continuing day after day.

One morning while walking in the Parade, Mary
saw a horse and rider dash up Court Street and then
turn the corner at the Meeting House. She watched
the horse gallop swiftly along King Street and disappear out the stockade gate.

"An express! An express! An express to Governor Belcher!" cried the bystanders.

Was it a message about the *Golden Arrow?* Mary remembered the letter sent by Lieutenant-Governor Dunbar on the night of the almshouse supper about the Exeter timber riot. She had heard her father say that the timber men had gone without punishment. She knew, also, that the men who had raided Merchant Pomeroy's corn had never been molested. She wondered idly if Governor Belcher ever answered the letters which he received.

Two men, near where she stood, were talking earnestly about the pirate. She recognized them as Master Griggs, ropemaker, and Nicholas Wiggin, shipbuilder. They walked to Queen Street and entered the Sign of Noah's Ark. Eager to hear what they were saying, Mary went round to the back door and explained the situation to Old Mammy Chloe. The good-hearted slave propped the bar-room door open with a chair and Mary sat down upon it.

"So Governor Dunbar has called a meeting of his Council at last," the ropemaker was saying. "He's been slow enough about it."

"Captain Giddings, president of the Council, refuses to act except on orders from Governor Belcher," explained Master Wiggin.

"Two Governors is bad business," said a third man, whom Mary did not know.

" 'Twas only at the insistence of the merchants and the Justice that Giddings consented to call a meeting," the shipbuilder went on.

"Did they vote anything?" asked the third man.

"I hear that Dunbar asked them to issue a proclamation, offering a reward to apprehend the pirate," said Master Griggs.

"Did they do it?" asked the stranger eagerly. "I haven't heard the Town Crier give it out."

"Even when he offered to pay the money for the reward himself, they refused to do it," Master Wiggin explained. "They insisted they could not act except by Belcher's orders. That's all because of Giddings' influence. He's a strong man and he hates Dunbar and opposes everything he does. Some say he is in Belcher's pay. Of course, Dunbar is suffering because of his unfair methods over the timber in the King's Woods."

"Didn't they do anything then?" persisted the stranger.

"They sent an express to Governor Belcher in Boston. We saw him leave Dunbar's house just now. They cannot do a thing until they get his reply," said the shipbuilder hopelessly. "I feel a sense of personal loss —I loved that brig, more than any ship I ever built. She was a beauty."

"I heard Dunbar was all for beating up volunteers to man a boat and go right after the pirate," said Master Griggs, the ropemaker. "It seems Fayerweather insisted the fellow was not far off Cape Cod somewhere and if there'd been a man-o'-war handy . . ."

"Dunbar's made many mistakes, but this time he's trying to do his duty by the merchants if he can," said the shipbuilder. "He says he'll get the pirate yet, and maybe he will."

"I hope he does," added the stranger. "Pirates is

devils." Something in the man's tone sounded familiar to Mary. She peeped at him again, but he had turned his face away.

"They say he's come back," said Landlord Drummond, joining the trio.

"Who?" asked the ropemaker.

"The pirate devil," answered the landlord. "He's been seen, first at sea, then actually here in town."

Here in town! Mary repeated the words to herself. Could it be true? Ever since the sinking of the *Golden Arrow*, Mary had been fearful of finding out direct evidence of Philip Babb's guilt. Now he was back again. Did that mean he was guilty or innocent? Mary smiled to herself, not because she had answered that difficult question, but because she had forgotten it. She had remembered something else—that he had promised to bring her a poppet! She peeped in again and saw that the third man had drawn back and was lighting his pipe.

"Just gossip!" exclaimed Master Wiggin. "People will say anything."

"How do they know what he looks like?" inquired the ropemaker. "How would they know him if they saw him?"

"I don't know, except that's what they say." The landlord put on an injured expression because his word was doubted.

"Why should he come back here?" asked the shipbuilder. "Out of a spirit of bravado, just to show off?"

"They say he's a local man," the landlord went on, undaunted. "He knows his way about in this province and on the islands. Probably he's heard of

Dunbar's incompetence and knows there's no danger!"

The shipbuilder and the ropemaker laughed, then rose from their seats and left the tavern. Mary peeped in again. The little man, the stranger, who had not spoken for some time, went to a corner and sat down before a table as if waiting for some one. Almost at once, the front door opened and rollicking voices could be heard singing:

" 'Go tell the King of England,
Go tell him this for me,
Though he reigns King o'er all the land,
I will reign King at sea . . .
Though he reigns King o'er all the land,
I will reign King at sea. . . .' "

Two young men came lurching in at the door, singing. The landlord was busily engaged behind the bar and paid no attention.

Mary almost fell from her chair. Though the words were muffled, she knew that she had heard that song before—on the pirate's boat, anchored in the harbor. Her heart began to beat quickly. Was it true? Had he really come back? Would he dare to do such a thing?

Mammy Chloe came over, pulled the chair away and closed the door. "Honey chile," she said, "you don't want to listen to them men no longer. It's 'nough to send cold shivers down your spine to hear 'em talkin' 'bout them wicked pirates. How come you want to hear so much? I reckon it's 'cause you was born on de ocean and I tells you it ain't healthy, neither."

"Just a minute, Mammy," said Mary.

She pushed the door open inch by inch. She must

know who was singing that song. Wider and wider she pushed it, until she could see. Yes, there in the corner, at the same table, sat the peddler and the juggler. They were talking in low whispers to the little stranger who had asked so many questions of the shipbuilder and the ropemaker. Mary had no doubt, whatever, of their identity. Since the day when they had sat in the stocks and talked to her, she would have known them anywhere. They were Mink and Weasel. They looked just the same and yet different. She wondered what was changed. Then she noticed the peddler's wig. It was a new one, of light brown hair, which, like the black, reached to his shoulders to cover his cropped ears. But it would take more than a wig to deceive Ocean-Born Mary.

She continued to stare at them as they sat at the table. Then she noticed that it was the little stranger who was doing all the whispering. The two others were listening. Was he telling them all the things that the shipbuilder and ropemaker had said? Of course he was. He was one of Babb's men, like the other two. He had come to the tavern to listen to the gossip and find out what was happening in town. He was the squint-eyed Rat! Why had Mary not thought of it before? She pulled the door to and turned away.

"Did you see what you expected, honey?" asked Mammy Chloe.

"Yes, Mammy," answered Mary.

She had seen and heard much more than she had expected. She was frightened, yet happy, too, for it meant only one thing. The rumors were true. Philip Babb had come back.

Chapter XVII

OCEAN-BORN MARY walked proudly along Queen Street. In her arms she carried a poppet. Stiffly made of wood, its hard, round head had a painted face, from which two large glass eyes protruded, staring. Its arms and legs were crudely jointed to the body, but these could not be seen because of the clothing. It wore a blue silk brocade gown, outspreading sideways over hoops; gold ear-rings hung below its dainty lace cap and a gold necklace round its stubby neck.

It was a doll of character, a doll which any child would have delighted to own, a doll far more beautiful than the few others of that day. In Mary's starved and empty heart, it had already found a home. All the fears which she had suffered since she had learned the fate of the *Golden Arrow* had faded away. Her happiness was complete. She stopped every now and then, held the doll out before her and looked at it. Then she smoothed its lace cap, adjusted its skirts and set it once more in her elbow. Her face glowed with unusual enjoyment.

She went first to the log gaol. In accordance with the carver's suggestion, Mary had visited Susannah as often as possible, in defiance of Master Pecksniff's orders. She willingly ran the risk of incurring the apothecary's displeasure, for Susannah's sake.

The side door stood open, for it was a warm day in midsummer. Mary walked quietly to the room where Susannah still lay in her bed and found her sleeping. She looked so pale and still, lying against the pillows, motionless. Was she dead? Mary's heart skipped a beat.

She spoke her name softly, "Susannah!"

Susannah opened her eyes. "Oh, I had such a good nap," she cried. "I dreamed I was out in a field, picking daisies, running and running, and you were with me. . . . Oh!" She stopped abruptly when she saw the doll in Mary's arms. Her breath came quickly as she asked, "What is it?"

"A poppet," said Mary, holding it out with both hands.

"A . . . pop—pet!" exclaimed Susannah, delighted. "Is it yours?"

"Yes," answered Mary, proudly.

"Oh!" cried Susannah. "Is it real?"

"It is made of wood," said Mary.

"It has a cap and a gown and a necklace and . . ." cried Susannah in wonder.

"It has hands and feet underneath," explained Mary, "and two shifts."

Susannah feasted her eyes on the wonderful sight. Like Mary, she hungered for something beautiful to love. Impulsively, she stretched forth her arms and asked, "Could I hold it?"

"Yes," answered Mary. "I brought it so you could." She handed the doll to Susannah.

"I won't muss it," said the sick girl. "I'll only hold it for a minute." Carefully in the crook of her arm she placed it. She looked down and a radiant smile transfigured her plain face.

Mary sat on a chair beside the bed. The girls talked casually of different things, of the little Moseleys, of Maggie McDonald's shop window, of the weekly market. But all the while they were thinking of only one thing—the beautiful poppet.

"Here, you take it!" cried Susannah. "It's your turn to hold it."

"Oh, no," said Mary, unselfishly, "I like to see it in your arms. I can watch it from here. Keep it till I go."

Then Marm Winslow came in. "Is it you, Mary?" she called. "I thought I heard voices. I went out to the garden for a moment while Susannah was sleeping. . . . Why, what have you brought?"

"See, Mother, see!" cried Susannah, holding out the poppet with both hands.

"How beautiful!" cried Marm Winslow. "Where did you get this, Mary?"

Mary hesitated, looking downward. "It was given to me," she said simply.

"Ah!" smiled Marm Winslow, "Merchant McFarland, no doubt. He is such a kind, generous man."

Mary said nothing.

"How unfortunate it is about the loss of his ship," the woman went on. "Joseph says he hopes our gaol is strong enough to hold that wicked pirate, when they succeed in catching him."

"Would they bring him here, ma'am?" asked Mary, in surprise.

"Yes," said Marm Winslow. "Years ago, when Susannah was quite small, there was a pirate by the name of . . ."

But Mary turned to the doll in Susannah's arms and scarcely heard the words. Even her worries over Pirate Babb's safety seemed to fade away when she looked at the doll which he had brought her. The doll was evidence enough of the man's goodness. What did it matter about the other things of which people accused him?

At last Mary took leave of Susannah and her mother, promising to come again soon. On her way to the almshouse, she stopped at the door of the Moseley cottage. All the little children crowded round.

"You must not touch it!" cried Mary, holding the poppet high out of reach. "Look at it, but do not touch it!"

"Oh! Oh!" "It has eyes!" "And feet!" "And ear-rings!" cried the children.

Marm Moseley, disheveled as ever, came to the door. She wiped her eyes with a corner of her stringy apron.

She did not notice the poppet. "Joey's gone again," she announced sadly.

"Joey?" gasped Mary. "Gone . . . again?" She had wanted to talk to him ever since his return on the *Morning Star* and tell him how sorry she was, but she had never dared. Now it was too late.

"He went with Baker Matlin to Boston," said Marm Moseley, mournfully. "He said there were too many children here. He was discontented-like, said the house was too small and his Pa had oughter git it shingled and . . ."

"What did he go to Boston for?" asked Mary.

"He's a-goin' to ship before the mast," said his mother, as if accepting the inevitable, "on another long voyage. He said he likes the sea better than the land. He said he's not afraid of pirates and there's more ships to choose from in Boston. He said he warn't never a-comin' back." Marm Moseley wiped a few tears from her eyes.

"Never coming back?" echoed Mary, stunned. "But how about the cows?"

"Oh, Jacob's cow-herd now," said Marm Moseley in a tone of resignation. "We need the pay he gits, to feed so many mouths. He makes a better cow-herd, too—don't go a-runnin' off like Joey did. I reckon it's all for the best. Jacob's been a-doin' it ever sence spring. Ain't you never noticed?"

No, Mary had not noticed. She had not been thinking of the welfare of the town's cows of late.

At the almshouse, the monthly washing was going on. The kitchen was full of hot steam and Tilly and Hetty were thumping the pounding barrel with great gusto. Aunt Becky dried her hands on her apron and stared hard at Mary, as she stood in the doorway with the strange object held tight in her arms.

Then she marched into her own room, pushing Mary ahead. "What next?" she demanded.

"See! Just see, Aunt!" Mary held the poppet out and smiled eagerly. But her smile and her enthusiasm died away when she saw the look on Aunt Becky's face change from ordinary kindness to incredulous horror.

"Ocean-Born Mary!" she cried in a shocked voice. "Where did you get *that?*"

The tone implied that the object was some base, hateful thing, too dreadful to be touched. With an instinctive impulse of protection, Mary gathered the precious doll tightly into her arms.

"Did you steal it? From one of the shops? From Maggie?" cried Aunt Becky in solemn tones. Even as she spoke, she knew that Maggie McDonald's shop had never seen the like.

"No, Aunt," said Mary, firmly. "It was given to me. For my very own. To keep. It's . . . a poppet." She hugged it more tightly. "I always wanted . . . a poppet."

"Who gave it to you?" The harsh words were hurled like stones from Aunt Becky's lips.

"I . . . cannot tell," said Mary, faintly.

"Who gave that

wicked, sinful poppet to you?" demanded Aunt Becky again.

"I cannot tell," said Mary again, feeling more and more miserable every moment. She closed her lips firmly. Then she looked down into the doll's staring eyes and was reassured. Even if the poppet brought trouble, it would be worth it, just to have it to hold in her arms. Then she realized that Aunt Becky was speaking.

"You need not tell, then," she said. "Not that it will do you any good, for, of course, I know where it came from without your telling. There is only one place it could have come from. You have seen him somewhere and he has forced this evil thing upon you. He is not drowned as I had hoped. He has come back again, hasn't he?"

Mary said nothing. She stared at the doll in her arms.

"Where is your hornbook?" demanded Aunt Becky suddenly.

Automatically, Mary felt at her side where the hornbook always hung. It was gone. Had she left it at home? She remembered having had it the day before. "It's . . . gone!" she gasped. "I must have lost it when . . ." She put her hand hastily over her mouth without finishing the sentence.

"Lost it! Just as I thought!" snorted Aunt Becky. "That's why he has come back. As long as you had it, you were safe."

Aunt Becky's horror knew no bounds, based as it was on her conscientious desire to assist poor Jeanie in the child's proper bringing-up while she was away from her mother. She knew that Mary had, in spite of all her efforts to make her hate him, formed an attachment for the wicked pirate. No, not an attachment, simply a sentimental regard for him, because he had saved their lives. She reproached herself bitterly that she had not heeded Governor Dunbar's reprimand and restrained Mary more severely. She had been too soft-hearted, for she had grown fond of the child and it was hard to be stern. But it was not too late to save her. She could at least destroy the object which he was using to contaminate the child. It would burn quickly in the hot fire in the kitchen.

"Hand that pirate poppet to me at once," she demanded.

Mary clutched it more tightly. "It's mine," she said in a steady voice. "To keep."

There was something in the child's face which startled Becky Armstrong and made her draw back the hand which reached out to seize the poppet. Suddenly she saw her clearly—a child who had been made old for her years by her hard life, made harder by her parents' difficulties to get food and clothing enough and by her father's timber troubles. With so many younger children, Mary had had no childhood of her own. Becky had hoped, for these very reasons, to be able to make Mary's life happier since she had come to the Bank to live. She had not thought it necessary to impose restraints, for she had trusted the child, knowing her instincts were right and good. She had tried to understand her. Every girl was a little mother by instinct, she knew. What harm would it do if she kept the doll? What harm, even if that wicked man's hands had stolen it from its rightful owner and soiled its beautiful gown with his touch? Becky Armstrong stared at the poppet and came nearer to forgiving Philip Babb in that moment than ever in her life, before or after.

She turned away from Mary quickly, so the child would not see the tears that had gathered in her eyes, or realize that under the hard front, she was soft and pliable beneath.

"Run along home, Mary," she said, in a shaking voice. "I'll come and talk to Cousin Jeanie about it as soon as I can."

Filled with amazement, Mary left the almshouse and walked toward the Parade. She looked down at the poppet again and smiled. Although she did not realize how near the poppet had come to destruction, yet she felt that every one was bound to love the doll as she did. It was when Aunt Becky saw how beautiful the poppet was that she forgot the pirate and stopped scolding.

Mary hurried to the water-front, anxious to reach the carver's shop. Her feet skipped along lightly and she hummed a little tune to herself: *"Go tell the King of England . . . go tell him this from me . . ."*

"Ma-ry! Ma-ry!" cried a shrill voice overhead.

The girl stopped short. She was passing the apothecary shop. She looked up and saw Marm Pecksniff leaning out of the open window, with her ruffled night cap flapping up and down. She waved her long, skinny arms. "Please come in, Mary," she begged. "I want to see you. Please come in."

Mary smiled. She stretched her arms high and lifted

the poppet up toward the woman. "See what I have!" she cried, eagerly.

"*He's* gone away and I'm all alone," said the woman, in a loud whisper. "Bring it in and let me see it. Walk right in through the shop and come up the back stairs."

Mary did as she was told. Marm Pecksniff's bedroom was very untidy. Under the large canopy top, the bed was unmade. Clothes lay about in heaps. The old lady came forward.

"Well, if 'tain't Ocean-Born Mary!" she cried, with a broad smile. She stared at the poppet and instantly held out her hands. "Can I hold it?" she asked, as eager as a child.

Mary put it into her arms. The old lady carried the poppet as carefully as if it were a sleeping baby. She took a shawl from a chair and wrapped it round, then she sat down. She cuddled the doll and began to hum a tune to it. She rocked her body back and forth. Mary watched in amazement. Did the poor woman think it was a real baby? Did it remind her of some of her own babies, now lost in man and womanhood?

Mary waited patiently. She was anxious to go to the carver's and yet she did not like to disturb Marm Pecksniff. "Could I take it now?" she asked timidly. But the woman did not hear.

Mary waited a long time. At last she began to despair. Then she heard the opening of the shop door below and the sound of footsteps. "I must go now," she said. "Could I take it, please, Marm?"

Still, Marm Pecksniff seemed not to hear. The footsteps came closer, mounting the stairs, and Master Pecksniff entered the room. The apothecary looked at Mary with eyes of hatred. Well did he know that she had been visiting Susannah Winslow in defiance of his orders.

"What's this?" he cried. "What are you doing here?"

"Take it, Mary, take it!" the old lady cried, thrusting the doll into her arms. "He always scolds me," she added, starting to whimper.

Mary had no desire to speak to the apothecary. She held the doll close and tried to slip past him down the stairs. He blocked the way and she could not stir.

"Oh ho!" he jeered, sarcastically. "A poppet! A poppet! Where did you find that?"

"It was given to me, sir," said Mary, trembling.

"Given to you, ha, ha, ha, ha!" cried the apothecary. He snatched the doll from her arms. "Any one who knows anything, knows there's not another poppet like that in the whole province! Any one who knows anything, knows that poppet came from France or Holland or . . ."

"Will you please give it back to me, sir?" cried Mary, in alarm.

"Any one who knows anything, knows that such a fine poppet as this could only have been brought to you by . . ." the apothecary continued.

"Give the poppet back to Mary!" ordered the old lady, advancing with uplifted fist. "Give Ocean-Born Mary's poppet back to her at once or I'll . . ."

"Very well, Ma," said the apothecary, abjectly. "Ye

needn't shout so loud, I can hear ye. I'm a-giving it back to her. Now don't you go to fretting!"

"Ocean-Born Mary shall have her poppet," screamed the old lady, her eyes blazing, "and nobody shall take it from her. I've taken quite a fancy to Mary and . . ."

"I know you have, Ma; I know you have . . ."

As Mary ran down the stairs and out into the street, she could hear, through the open window above, the old lady still shouting and her son trying to placate her. Mary smiled again and patted the doll lovingly. Once more the poppet was safe. Marm Pecksniff loved it as much as she did. How could any one help loving it?

She walked in the direction of the carver's shop. Just ahead, she saw three men emerge from the door of Merchant McFarland's counting house. They were

Merchant McFarland, Captain Fayerweather and Justice Puddington. They stood on the corner, talking, and she saw that she must pass them. For a moment she thought of turning to avoid them, then her courage returned. A poppet was nothing to be ashamed of. Every one who saw it would love it as she did. She set it up stiffly in her elbow and advanced. She was nearly past, when Merchant McFarland called her back.

"What have you there, Mary?" he asked kindly.

Mary faced them unafraid. Two of the men were her friends, but she had never spoken to the Justice. She wondered if they had ever seen so beautiful a poppet. Of course, merchants were always buying things in foreign countries. They might have seen many poppets more beautiful than this.

"It's a poppet, sir!" answered Mary, proudly.

"May I look at it, Mary?" asked Merchant McFarland.

Mary handed the poppet to him. He examined it carefully without saying a word. He handed it to Captain Fayerweather, who did the same. Justice Puddington had turned away, indifferent.

Captain Fayerweather nodded to Merchant McFarland. Both men knew at once that the doll could only have come from Europe, that it was, indeed, one of the finest to be had there. Something of the incongruity of the situation struck them. This handsome, European creation in the hands of a poor, backwoodsman's child. Had it not been that the implications were so serious, they could have laughed aloud.

"Where did you get this, Mary?" asked Merchant McFarland, gently.

334

Mary was beginning to be annoyed by the intense curiosity which every one showed. Why could she not be allowed to enjoy her poppet in peace, without answering questions? Then she remembered that Mr. McFarland was her friend, and that Captain Fayerweather was Peggy's father.

"It was given to me, sir," she said in a low voice.

The next question followed as surely as the first. "Who gave it to you, Mary?"

"I cannot tell, sir!" said Mary, flushing to the roots of her hair. She looked from one to the other of the men anxiously. Why were they so serious? Why did they wish to know everything? She saw the merchant nod to the captain significantly.

"Will you take a look at this for a moment, deacon?" the merchant went on.

Justice Puddington took the poppet in his hands gingerly, as if he were afraid it was alive and might squirm. He handed it back at once. "Just what . . ." he exclaimed, but his sentence died away.

"Bring it around and show it to Judy sometime, won't you, Mary?" said the merchant, as the men walked away.

Mary received the poppet back gratefully. Once more the doll had worked wonders. Every one admired it, even cold-hearted Justice Puddington. Mary laughed and hurried on.

Master Greenwood looked up as she entered the shop. Again, a great pine log stood before him as he sat on his high stool, tools in hand. The base was covered in chips and shavings, but as yet no definite form could be discerned.

"What is it?" cried Mary, eagerly. "Another figure-head? Has Merchant McFarland given you an order? Is he going to build another ship?"

"I hope so," answered Nathaniel. "In fact, I am certain he will in time. Yes, I have started to carve a figure-head for him, though he doesn't realize it. And do you know, Mary, the strangest thing has happened. All my grief over the loss of the *Golden Arrow's* figure-head has disappeared. I am so keen over what this new one is *going* to be, that I've forgotten the other entirely. It's as if I were a snake and had shed my skin and . . ."

Suddenly he saw the object in Mary's arms. He jumped lightly from the stool and took it from her. "Now what," he exclaimed, chuckling, "can be the meaning of this? Isn't she lovely, enchanting, gor-

geous? A lady of the world, from Paris—or is it London?—has descended upon this humble province! With ear-rings and necklace and the latest fashions, she seems quite capable of traveling far. Mary, where did you, of all people, find her?"

The carver, his eyes sparkling, sat on the bench and pulled Mary down beside him. "Now, tell me everything," he insisted.

Mary had intended to keep the story to herself, for she remembered the pirate's injunction. But somehow, it seemed easy to tell the carver, and once told, she could forget about it. For, underneath her pleasure over the poppet itself, there lay this gnawing memory. Her faith and trust in Nathaniel Greenwood were complete.

"He sent a message to me by Old Turtle," she began slowly.

"Who is 'he' and who is 'Old Turtle'?" asked the carver, with a bewildered look.

It seemed strange that the carver did not know of Mary's friendship for the pirate. Both men had been so much a part of her life at the Bank. It was a little difficult to explain. Mary told as well as she could how it had come about.

"Do you mean the pirate who sank the *Golden Arrow?*" asked Nathaniel, frankly.

"I don't *know* that he did that," said Mary. "There are other pirates more wicked than he. All I know is that he saved our lives, long ago. Old Turtle is one of his men, and then there's Rat and Squirrel and Mink and Weasel. . . ."

"Do you know them all?" asked the carver, in amazement.

"Only those," said Mary.

"Do go on," begged Nathaniel.

"He sent word by Old Turtle to say that he would come to Puddle Dock just after curfew—last night, it was," said Mary. "And for me to meet him down on the beach, because he was back and had brought something for me. Of course, I knew he couldn't come in daylight, with everybody hunting for the pirate who sunk the *Golden Arrow*; they might think he did it and put him in gaol. He had promised to bring me a poppet when he returned from his next voyage and I wondered if he had remembered . . ."

"So you went?" asked Nathaniel, listening carefully.

"Yes," answered Mary, "as soon as I was sure Cousin Jeanie and the others were all asleep. He was there, waiting on the beach, and his boat—a gundalow—was there, too. It was moonlight and I could see his face plainly. It was kind and his voice was kind, too, so I wasn't afraid."

"Didn't you know that was a dangerous thing to do?" asked the carver, gently.

"Oh, Nathaniel," cried Mary, earnestly. "You won't be like all the others, will you?"

"I shall be as different as I can," said the carver, seriously, realizing his responsibility. The thought flashed through his mind that it was Mary who had brought him his first figure-head and had brought him Peggy's friendship as well. He hoped he might be worthy of her confidence.

"You must believe me, even if no one else does,"

insisted Mary. "They've always said he was so wicked, but if a man promises to bring a poppet because his little sister had one, he must be good, don't you think so?"

"I wish I could believe it as you do," said the carver, "and I shall try. Did he give you the poppet then?"

"No, he said he wanted me to come with him, so I climbed into the boat. He told me he hadn't brought the poppet with him and we must go and get it. He said also he wanted to show me something. The boat was a gundalow and he put up a sail. He had Old Turtle with him. I remembered he had once careened his brigantine on Goat Island and I thought we were going there and I might see Goody again. We passed under Swing Bridge and out into the harbor. I remembered that Goody was his mother . . ."

"His mother? The old woman with the chip basket?" asked Nathaniel, in surprise.

"Yes, Goody Gregory. I thought I would see her, but we didn't stop at Goat Island. We kept on going and the sea was very rough . . ."

"Were you frightened?" asked Nathaniel.

"I was sea-sick, we rocked so much. I was wet and cold and covered with spray. I wished I had brought my cloak or had stayed at home in bed. I was too miserable to think where we were going.

"After what seemed a long, long time, we came to land. When Rat and Squirrel and the juggler and the peddler all crowded round me, I was frightened. Then the captain took me away from them for a long walk and showed me what we came for. He told me some things I must not forget or tell any one. I was so tired and frightened that I cried."

"Did he . . ." began Nathaniel, in an angry tone.

"No, he was very kind all the time and even found one of the men's capes to put over me. Then we came back from our walk. The captain went aboard his brigantine which was anchored there. Then he came to where I was waiting by the gundalow to be taken back. The last thing before I climbed in, he put the poppet into my arms. It was moonlight and he smiled and said, 'Do you like it?' and I said, 'Yes, sir!' He was as pleased as I was. I could see its ear-rings and neck-lace shining. I could see its bright eyes staring as if it loved me. I was so happy I forgot all about being wet and cold. I thanked him and climbed into the boat. Squirrel and Old Turtle were waiting. As they pushed off, he said, 'You won't forget, Ocean-Born Mary, will you?' and I said, 'I won't, sir.' I had the big cape over me all the way home and I didn't get a single drop of salt water on its brocade gown. I don't know what time it was. They brought me to Puddle Dock, just below the house. I hurried in and went to bed. I slept with the poppet beside me."

"And what did Cousin Jeanie say when she saw it this morning?" asked Nathaniel.

"She smiled and said, 'I think I can guess who gave it to you. It was Madam McFarland, wasn't it?' And I did not say a word."

"Did she know you had been out in the night?"

"No, she never thought of such a thing," answered Mary. "I had been to the McFarlands' yesterday and she knew they often gave me things."

Nathaniel Greenwood did not speak for a few moments. His eyes had a far-away look as if he were lost in thought. At last, he said, "I think I would take the poppet home, Mary, and not show it to people."

"Oh!" laughed Mary. "Everybody's seen it already."

"Everybody? Who?" asked the carver.

Mary named over the people who had seen it. "They all thought it was the finest poppet they had ever seen. All except Aunt Becky. She didn't like it much."

"Ah!" said the carver, smiling faintly. "Then you did not bring it to me first." Knowing that the harm from which he wished to guard her, was already done, he added, carelessly, "No matter. Take it where you please."

"I think it is nice for people who have never seen a poppet to hold it for awhile, don't you?" asked Mary, earnestly.

"Yes, I do, Mary," answered the carver.

He looked at her thoughtfully. He could tell how much she loved the poppet, and yet—that harmless stick of wood, decked out in gaudy show, might cause a deal of trouble. He was thankful in his heart that he had merited her confidence. He made up his mind not to mar the child's happiness by needless worry. He could only stand by and be ready to help when she needed him. From the doorway he watched her make her way down the street. As she turned and waved her hand, Nathaniel Greenwood said to himself, "What an amazing child she is!"

Loyalty to a Friend

Chapter XVIII

"OUT at the mouth of the harbor, when the fog
lifted, we saw a ship a-ridin' at anchor . . ."
a loud voice was saying.

Mary hugged her poppet tight and pushed through
the crowd.

"Did she fly a black flag?" some one asked. "Did
she fly a Jolly Roger?"

"No," said the first speaker. "She looked like a fish-
trader and there was only three or four men aboard."

"We hailed 'em," shouted a boy's shrill voice. "We
asked 'em from what port they'd come and they said
from Barbadoes, loaded with rum and sugar."

"The captain shouted down that they was in need
of provisions," the man's voice went on, "and if we'd
get some for him, he'd pay us handsome. He says,

'Let one of them boys come aboard for a minute and I'll tell him what we need.' "

"What did he look like? Did he wear a mask?" inquired a curious bystander.

"My boy mounted the deck, 'cause we didn't have no reason to suspect nothin'," the man continued. "Then this other boy here, he went up behind 'im. I waited below in my boat, wonderin' why on earth the captain was a-keepin' the boys so long. At last the second boy come down alone, with gold-pieces in his hand—here's a couple on 'em. . . ."

"Pieces of eight! Pieces of eight!" cried the people, pushing forward to see.

"The boy had them gold-pieces in his hand," the story-teller went on, "and he told me what provisions the captain wanted. I asked why t'other boy didn't come and he said the captain was a-goin' to keep him there, to make sure we'd come back. I shouted for Jock to come. . . ."

It was Cousin Tom and Jock. As Mary heard the boy's name, she knew. She could scarce believe her ears. Cousin Tom and the two boys had gone out fishing as usual that morning at dawn. When two hours had passed beyond the usual time of their return, Cousin Jeanie became worried. Mary had set out at once to try to learn news of them, and this news was startling, to say the least.

"But he didn't come and there warn't a soul to be seen on board," Cousin Tom went on. "Then I knew 'twas that wicked pirate devil . . ."

"Did you see a name on the ship?" asked a woman, timidly.

"There warn't no name as I could see," growled Cousin Tom. "We started off to get the provisions, leavin' Jock, this boy here, aboard. We come to the Town Dock and got 'em as quick as . . ."

"Why didn't you tell folks about it?" "Why didn't you report to the Lieutenant-Governor? Everybody knows he's a-tryin' 's hard 's he can to find the pirate."

"Hain't I a-tellin' ye, now?" roared Tom Martin, angrily. "I was a-hurryin' to get back to Jock before the pirate hurt 'im. . . ."

"Did the pirate hurt ye, boy?" "What did he do to you?" All eyes were turned on Jock.

"Nothing," answered Jock, in a disappointed tone. "There were four sailors there on the fore-deck a-playin' cards. They put me down beside 'em and they went on a-playin'. It seemed a long time to wait. I thought Pa would never come."

"Did you see the captain?" asked Mary, who had at last edged her way through the crowd. "What did he look like?"

"I didn't see him," said Jock.

"What did the ship look like?" some one asked.

"Just like any ship," answered Jock.

"Then how do you *know* it was the pirate?" demanded Mary. "He *might* have been an honest fish-trader out of provisions. . . ."

"This young lass seems to know a great deal about the pirate!" announced a penetrating voice. Everybody heard and looked in her direction. Mary had not noticed him before, so she was surprised to see that the apothecary was standing beside her.

"My good man," asked Master Pecksniff, addressing Tom Martin, "do you think it was the pirate?"

The whole situation was puzzling to the poor fisherman. This thing of being in the center of a curious crowd was upsetting. Tom Martin shook his head and said, "Wall, honest men ain't afraid to show their faces in port, seems to me. It looks mighty queer, a-holdin' a boy to force his Pa to do somethin' like that. . . ."

Just then, Pompey, the apothecary's Negro slave, came running up, shaking with terror. "Oh, massa, massa," he cried, "I seed him, I seed him!"

"Who, Pompey?" asked the apothecary, calmly.

"I seed the pirate hisself," said the Negro, rolling his eyes. "He rode into town on a bay horse."

"When was this, Pompey?" asked the apothecary. He rubbed his hand together. Things were shaping nicely.

"This mawnin', sir, 'bout two hours after daylight, sir," said the Negro, his teeth chattering.

"You saw him ride into town in broad daylight?" asked Master Pecksniff, contemptuously. "Do you think he is fool enough to do that?"

"I seed him with my own eyes, sir," persisted the Negro, "a-comin' right along King Street from the Highway. I was up at the town pump in the Parade . . ."

"Gossiping with all the other slaves?" interrupted Pecksniff, sarcastically.

"They was a-fillin' their pails, sir, when he come a-ridin' by as bold as you please. His horse had a great long tail and . . ."

345

"How did you know it was the pirate?" demanded Pecksniff.

"We seed sparks a-flyin' out behind his hoofs, sir; yes, sir, we seed sparks a-flyin' and then we knowed 'twas the pirate devil hisself and we all ran fer home as fast as we could go!"

The crowd laughed heartily.

"Which direction did the horse go?" asked the apothecary.

"He swished round the corner headin' right for the Ark," said the Negro with a grin. "Likely the pirate war thirsty from ridin' so fast. Leastways, that's where the bay horse is right now. I jes' been back to see."

"The Ark Tavern! The pirate's at the Sign of Noah's Ark!" cried the crowd. "Let's go and see him!"

The apothecary at once took on an important air. "We must report this to the Lieutenant-Governor at once!" he shouted. "Where's that fisherman? Where's that lass that knows so much about the pirate?" He looked round, but they had disappeared.

"Poke-Nose is a-goin' to report to the Governor!" cried a bystander. "He's a-goin' to send the constable to the Ark Tavern to capture the pirate alive!"

The apothecary hastened away from the dock, with the crowd at his heels. They passed up Queen Street to Ark Lane. Then they stopped suddenly. There, tied to a post in the yard, was a bay horse. The crowd looked across the street in astonishment. The Negro was not such a fool after all.

Master Pecksniff took but one look, then scuttled round the corner to the Lieutenant-Governor's mansion, as fast as his short legs could carry him. The

346

crowd waited opposite the tavern, in order to miss
nothing. They looked at the familiar building with
wonder, for it was transfigured by romance and imagi-
nation. The pirate was inside, drinking flip, no doubt.

Mary stared, too. She had taken a back street and
had arrived at the tavern in time to see the apothecary
disappear round the corner. She breathed freely again.
Although she remembered what the pirate had told her
regarding his whereabouts, these alarming reports were
most convincing. Although she knew he could not
possibly be there and had no connection whatever with
the bay horse, yet the excitement of the crowd was so
contagious that she would not have been surprised in
the least if the pirate had opened the door of the tavern
and stepped forth. She found herself wishing that he
would hop on the horse and gallop away before the
constable came. Then she laughed, remembering how
false the clue was and how ridiculous the situation.

The bay horse pawed and stamped restlessly. But its
rider did not come to take it away, nor did Landlord
Drummond appear. A whisper ran through the crowd
that the landlord must be an accomplice of the pirate,
since he allowed his horse to be tied up in his yard.

Then the constable came, followed by a group of
Dunbar's men. They went to the tavern, opened the
door and walked in. The crowd waited breathlessly.
After a few moments, the constable came out again—
without the pirate. They turned away, disappointed.

Master Pecksniff, who had rejoined the crowd, hastened to meet the constable and find out what had
happened. They talked together in low voices, with
their backs turned toward the crowd.

"Landlord Drummond said the man came in shortly after breakfast and tied up his horse," said the constable. "He took a drink, stayed only a short time and went away, saying nothing. When I asked Drummond which way he went, he said it was not his business to spy on his customers."

"H-m-m," grunted the apothecary. "Looks as if he knows more than he cares to tell. What did the pirate look like?"

"He didn't say."

"What about the bay horse?"

"I've left some men there to watch," said the constable. "If any one comes to look after the mare or take her away, they will seize him and bring him to me."

"Good!" said the apothecary. "Did you hear about the fisherman who claims he saw the pirate and his boat out in the harbor?"

"No," said the constable, "when was that?"

"This morning," said Pecksniff. "There was a big commotion at the Town Dock just now. I told Dunbar but he only laughed. He said fishermen and sailors are so superstitious, it was a waste of time to bother with them. Then I told him about this smart young lass who has been carrying a Dutch poppet about in her arms. Do you know her?"

"Can't say I do," grunted the constable.

"Well, she knows more about this pirate than any one in town. She has seen the man since he returned, for he gave her this poppet. The Governor told me that if this was a false alarm at the Ark Tavern, we

348

should find the lass and bring her to him. There she is now, on the other side of that fat woman yonder." He nodded his head in the direction indicated. "Dunbar's doing all he can while waiting for word from Belcher. As soon as the express returns, the proclamation will be given out, assuming that Belcher consents, of course. Dunbar is furious over the delays. . . . In the meantime, he wishes to question this girl."

It was indeed evident that Governor Belcher in Boston intended to take his own time about replying. Did the delay mean that Belcher was conniving with or at least attempting to protect the pirate, as he had played into the hands of the timber men,—to bring about Dunbar's downfall? Would his personal dislike of the man go so far as to endanger the personal lives and cargoes of merchants on the seas? Dunbar believed that it would, for the hatred and jealousy of each other's power, was mutual. He had decided to do all he could without him.

The crowd had become restless with waiting for something which never happened. Even the bay horse failed to hold their attention, so they began to scatter.

Mary had been listening with interest to the various conjectures made on all sides. She had seen Master Pecksniff engaged in earnest conversation with the constable and had assumed that he had forgotten her presence. The scene had lost its novelty and she was about to return home, when two men suddenly appeared beside her. To her astonishment, she saw that they were the constable and the apothecary. One took her left arm and the other her right.

"Why . . . what . . . what is the matter?" she cried, weakly.

The poppet was jolted out of the crotch of her arm, but she caught it in her hands. She looked from one to the other of the two men, incredulous.

"That's the lass!" cried one of the bystanders. "Ocean-Born Mary, she's called. She knows the pirate, they say."

Mary was hustled quickly along. She saw the remaining people point accusing fingers at her. In consternation, she begged for an explanation.

"Governor Dunbar wishes to see you, lass," said the apothecary with a cruel smile. "He gave orders to fetch you at once. He wants you to tell him all you know about the pirate."

"All I know?" gasped Mary, in distress.

"There's no doubt about it," said Pecksniff to the constable, "she knows more than anybody else and she must tell what she knows." With these words ringing in her ears and preparing her for what was to come, Mary entered the Governor's mansion in the company of the two men.

"Fetch the lass in," said the Lieutenant-Governor, when she was announced.

Mary entered the high-ceilinged room, clasping her poppet tightly in her arms. After a hurried glance at the heavily curtained windows, the rich furniture and the group of men standing about the Governor's desk, she looked down at the doll in her arms. She was not frightened, but she felt herself trembling and could not hold still.

"We searched the fisherman's cottage, sir," one of Dunbar's men was saying. "It was small and there was no place for a man to hide. We also searched a cow-shed but it had only room for a cow."

Mary looked up, startled. Had they been to Cousin Tom's?

"Any signs of anything?" asked Dunbar. "Any signs of illegal goods?"

"No, sir," said the man. "The poppet was not there. The woman said the lass had it with her."

"Were the fisherman and the two boys there?"

"They came, sir, and told about seeing the pirate in his ship out in the harbor. They insisted, sir . . ."

"Yes, I've heard all that nonsense," said Dunbar sharply. "You may go." He turned to Mary. "Where did you get that poppet, lass?" he asked. His voice had an unnatural, wheedling tone as if he were trying, against his nature, to be kind.

"It was given to me, sir," said Mary, steadily.

"Who gave it to you?" asked Dunbar.

"A friend, sir," said Mary.

"Will you tell us who the friend was?"

"No, sir."

"Why not?"

Mary did not answer. She pressed her lips firmly together.

"Now, Ocean-Born Mary," said the Lieutenant-Governor, frowning heavily, "we all know who gave you the poppet without your telling us. We all appreciate the fact that you wish to be loyal to your friend. We also know that your friend is not far away. What we do not know is where he is hiding. That is what we want you to tell us. It will make it much easier for us and it will save time if you will tell at once. You know that he is an enemy of the King and of our province. You know that he has sunk the *Golden Arrow*. You know what a great loss that has been to Merchant McFarland and Captain Fayerweather as well as to other townspeople. You know that, do you not?"

"I have heard it, sir," said Mary.

"You know the difference between right and wrong, do you not?"

"Yes, sir," said Mary.

"Do you believe that it is right for a pirate to steal the cargo from an honest merchant and sink his ship?"

"No, sir," said Mary.

"What do you think should be done with such a man?"

Mary looked down and said nothing. She remembered that Marm Winslow had said the gaoler expected to keep the pirate in the log gaol when he was caught; she also remembered that Governor Dunbar had threatened to hang all pirates by the neck. She shivered.

"I will tell you," said Dunbar. "He should be punished to the full extent of the law. But how can we punish him, if we cannot find him?"

"I don't know, sir," said Mary.

"Will you tell us where he is?" asked Dunbar.

"No, sir," said Mary, firmly.

"Why will you not tell?"

Mary closed her lips and refused to answer.

"Ocean-Born Mary," said the Governor, sternly, "I have seen you many times on the streets and wharves of the Bank. I have sometimes thought that you were an idle, mischievous, loose-tongued child. I have changed my mind. I believe now that you are good and obedient and that you wish to do what is right. Is that true?"

"Yes, sir," said Mary.

"Will you tell us where the pirate is hiding, so that he may be punished for the wrong he has done?"

"No, sir," said Mary.

Governor Dunbar threw up his hands. With a baffled look, he cried, "Take her away. Let her wait in the back room."

The back room was small, with only one window. It contained a table and a few chairs. Mary sat down beside the window, where she had a narrow view toward the side street. She sat without moving for a long time. At times she could hear loud voices in the next room. At other times, the sounds were only a mumble. She did not fret or worry, for she had her poppet to comfort her.

After what seemed a long time, Merchant McFarland came in and closed the door behind him. Mary was glad to see the face of a friend, for she had felt lonely among the cold strangers who surrounded the Governor. She was anxious for the strange proceedings to be over, so that she could return to Cousin Jeanie's. She felt that the merchant would be the very person to help her out of her difficulties. But as soon as he began to speak she knew that he had banded with the others, against her, for, like the Governor, he begged her to tell all she knew.

"I cannot, sir!" cried Mary, with tears in her eyes.

She thought, with a pang, of the merchant's constant kindness, of the generous gifts she had had from his wife, of her love for Judy. She realized, as never before, that they were her best-loved friends. But even if it meant the sacrifice of that friendship, she could not betray the man who had given her the poppet, the man who had saved her life as a babe. He had saved hers and now she must save his, no matter how difficult it might be. No matter what happened, she was more determined than ever not to say the words which would send him to the gaol and to the gallows.

"You loved the *Golden Arrow* as Judy did," said the merchant, sorrowfully. "Do you not think that the man who sunk her should be punished?"

"But you do not *know*, sir, that he is the one who did it!" protested Mary. "There are other pirates more wicked than he. Old Cap'n Pete says the sea is full of them!"

"My child," said Merchant McFarland, "I wish I could spare you and I would if I could. But I cannot. Do you remember the day when we met the pirate captain in the shipyard? All that Captain Fayerweather has told me about the man who sunk my ship confirms my belief that he is the same man. The man we talked to there had a white scar from left ear to chin and so had the man who sunk my ship."

It could not be true! It must not be true! But, even if it were, there still remained his kindness which

355

she must not forget. "But he is a kind man, sir!" cried Mary, with a feeling of despair. "He . . . gave me my poppet!"

"If you will tell where he is, Mary," said Merchant McFarland, "I will buy you twenty poppets on my next voyage."

Mary dropped her head, ashamed. She knew she could not tell.

Merchant McFarland left the room, only to return later with his wife, Judy and Peggy. Mary stared at the little procession they made as they filed in. They all asked her to tell and pleaded with her, but she sat like a stone image on her chair and refused to speak. She did not look up, for she could not bear to face them.

Then, after a long time, Aunt Becky came and with her, Cousin Jeanie, trembling and nervous. Was the Governor sending for every one she knew? Were they all against her?

Aunt Becky bustled into the room in a determined way, as if she thought it was about time things were put into her capable hands. She felt sure she could manage Mary better than any one else. She came with a heart full of love and devotion and anxiety, but it was the sight of the pirate poppet that made her lose patience. It signified that that wicked man had a closer hold on the child than Becky Armstrong, her mother's oldest and closest friend.

Aunt Becky did not beat about the bush. "Do you know where that man is hiding?" she asked, directly.

"Yes, Aunt," said Mary.

"Where?"

Mary refused to speak.

"Why, Ocean-Born Mary!" cried Aunt Becky, impatiently. "Tell me this minute where he's gone."

No word came from Mary's lips.

Aunt Becky leaned over, with an awed, almost frightened look on her face. "You know, Mary, Governor Dunbar stands in the place of the King. When he commands, every one obeys. Do you realize that Governor Dunbar himself is out there, waiting for you to tell? That all those men are waiting to hear? Just think how pleased they will be when you tell them!"

"Yes, I know," said Mary, faintly.

"If your Ma was here, you'd obey her, wouldn't you?" Aunt Becky went on.

Mary did not answer.

"Elizabeth asked me to be a Ma to you," continued the woman, wiping a tear away. "I've tried to do the best I know how. I've always found you good and obedient. You're not a-going to start bein' wicked and wilful now, so that I shall have to tell your Ma, are you?"

Still Mary did not answer. She kept her eyes fixed on the poppet in her lap.

Then Cousin Jeanie spoke and it was her gentle voice which brought the tears. "Tell Cousin Jeanie, dear," she said, gently. "It will make it easier for the Governor and it will be better in the end for us all."

Cousin Jeanie so seldom asked or demanded anything of Mary, had given her for so long the freedom which she desired, that Mary felt like a selfish beast. She fell into the woman's arms and sobbed. Aunt Becky stood beside the table with a grim smile on her lips. Now, at last, Mary would give in and tell. What a determined child she was—Aunt Becky could not help but admire her—and the whole town waiting, too. Well, perhaps Jeanie's gentle way was best, after all.

But Mary did not tell and Aunt Becky and Cousin Jeanie went away in despair.

Then Parson Flint came. He told Mary what a dutiful and industrious child he had always known her to be. He reminded her again that 'one must labor without ceasing that good may overcome evil.' He said he knew she was anxious to help punish the wrong-doer. He talked on and on, ending with a threat of eternal punishment. His words mixed themselves up in Mary's tired brain, so that she scarcely heard. Still she stared at the poppet on her lap. At last, he, too, went away.

Then Governor Dunbar came to the door. "We cannot let you go, Mary," he said coldly, "until you tell us." He closed the door and she was left alone.

Mary waited. She saw the sunlight fade and knew that it was growing late. She saw the long shadows stretching out over the field across the street. She saw groups of men coming and going, sometimes stopping to talk together. She saw Aunt Becky and Cousin Jeanie hurry past, as if intent on some important errand. Why was Aunt Becky going away from the almshouse just at supper-time? Mary felt strangely desolate to think that they had left her.

Inside the house, all was still. She waited patiently. Now and then she heard the rattle of dishes and was conscious of the appetizing odor of food. Forlornly, she held the poppet close for company. Then, all in a moment, she hated it. It was only a stick of wood, cold and lifeless. Like Nathaniel's figure-head, only a stick of wood. She hated its unseeing eyes, its painted smile, its gaudy trappings. It had brought her nothing but trouble. She thrust it away heartlessly and it fell to the floor with a sharp thud. She stared at it as it lay there, but she did not pick it up.

Darkness fell and she began to wonder if she would have to stay where she was all night. Then the door opened. She steeled herself for another ordeal. They would try to make her tell again. Didn't they know by this time that it was useless? Couldn't they guess that she would never, never say the word which would send Captain Babb to gaol and to the gallows? She was tired now, after the long siege, more tired than she had ever been in her life. It would be harder to resist them. But she set her chin stubbornly.

Then she saw that it was Nathaniel. He carried a lighted candle in a silver candle-stick. He set it down on the table carefully. She flew into his arms.

"Oh, Nathaniel," she cried, sobbing, "I wanted you to come! I wanted you to come so badly!"

"I came as soon as I knew," said the carver, gently. "I only wish I had known sooner, to have spared you all this."

"All afternoon," she cried, "all afternoon, they've been trying to make me tell where Captain Babb is.

If I tell them, they will kill him . . . if I tell, they will . . . kill him!"

"I know, dear . . . I know," said Nathaniel Greenwood, holding her tight in his arms and letting her sob until all her pent-up emotions were spent.

After a time she looked up again. "How did you find out they had brought me here?" she asked.

"Aunt Becky and Cousin Jeanie came and told me," said Nathaniel.

Then they talked together quietly.

A half-hour later, they left the room together and were conducted to the Lieutenant-Governor's presence.

"I have something to tell you, sir," said Mary, gravely.

"Has she come to her senses at last?" asked Dunbar.

The carver did not reply. He gazed steadily between the brocade window curtains at a patch of deep blue sky.

In Mary's eyes there were no tears, but her face was pale as she said bravely, almost proudly, "Captain Babb is hiding on Goat Island, sir."

"Good!" said the Governor. "We will go at once."

A man rushed into the room hurriedly. "The bay horse is gone from the Ark Tavern, sir," he said, breathlessly.

"Who took her? Why didn't you seize him?" demanded the Governor.

"We couldn't, sir," said the man, hesitating. "Er . . . er . . ."

"Why not, if I may inquire?"

"He was . . . he was the express . . . returned from Boston, sir."

"Express from Boston?" shouted the Governor. "Where's he been all day with his horse tied up at the Ark Tavern?"

"Visiting his sick wife, sir," answered the man, with a smile which he could not hide. "He'll be here as soon as the horse is stabled, sir."

"Is that the way my important messages are carried?" shouted Dunbar. "Is that the way . . ."

Nathaniel Greenwood took Mary by the hand and led her out of the Governor's mansion. Clasped against her breast, she held the pirate poppet, and as she looked down at it, she smiled.

Safe at Last

Chapter XIX

LATE the following afternoon, Ocean-Born Mary walked up Queen Street, carrying her poppet in her arms. She crossed the Parade, passed the Meeting House and came to the gaol. She tarried a moment to look at the iron-grated windows and the double-barred, oaken door. She trembled, for she knew that Philip Babb had been captured and now lay in confinement within the building, only a stone's throw from where she stood. The whole town had been stirred by the news of his arrest and people had stared at her curiously as she walked through the streets. They all knew that she had played an important part in the man's capture.

But Mary did not notice them. She kept repeating over and over to herself the words she must say. She knew she must not forget or make a mistake, for everything depended upon her. The sun—a dull, red ball—was sinking below the stockade in the west as she stood waiting beside the door. It would be almost dark by the time she came out. That would be just right. She looked at the poppet in her arms tenderly. She touched the lace cap and the brocade with loving gentleness. Then the door opened and she went in.

A half-hour later, a heavy fog had begun to drift in from the ocean. Mary came out of the Winslows' door without the poppet, smiling. Glancing about, she saw that the street was empty. She flew down the path, like a bird released from a cage. She came to the carver's shop. The door was barred and the shutters were closed. She ran to the end of the wharf, dropped into the row-boat there and under cover of darkness, climbed up the back door and entered. Inside, alone, she waited in the dark. After a time, she unbarred the front door and tried it to see if it would open easily. Satisfied that it would, she closed it again, but did not put up the bar.

She waited patiently and the time seemed interminable. The fog had grown dense and soupy and Mary was thankful. She heard the night watchman call the hours one by one, sometimes near, sometimes at a distance. She lay down on the wooden bench, pulled a shawl over herself and dozed intermittently. Now and then she woke up with a start, worried and fearful. What if things did not go as she hoped? What if some difficulty arose? What if he did not come? But she never quite gave up hope.

She knew it was long past midnight when she heard

a sound. She sat up, alert. She heard muffled footsteps coming nearer and nearer. She did not move. She saw the door open slowly and cautiously, and although she had been expecting it to happen, the reality was so disturbing that she put her hand over her mouth so that she would not scream. A dark shadow filled up the opening and a man entered, hesitating. She rose to her feet and said in a low voice, "I am here, Captain Babb."

Mary knew it was he and her heart leaped up within her. She knew that Susannah Winslow, for the gift of the poppet, had unlocked the door of the gaol with her father's key, while her parents lay sleeping. She knew that Susannah had remembered the instructions she had been given and had told him where to come. She knew that he was free—the fog had shielded him. She never thought once of the beloved poppet or regretted the sacrifice. She had been forced to betray the man—to tell of his hiding place and cause his arrest—but she had been able to free him, too. She went to the door behind him, closed and barred it.

Philip Babb did not speak. A dim light shone from the night sky through the back door, which, overlooking the water, stood open. He walked to the middle of the floor, with his hand held to his head, as if stunned. His breath came thick and fast, the breath of the hunted fugitive. He knew he had no time to lose, but first he must think.

Mary brought bread and put it in his hand. He gulped greedily as if he had not eaten for a long time. Then she handed him a pitcher of water and he drained it.

"I tried to keep my promise, sir," whispered Mary, "but they forced me to tell where you were hiding and that's why they came and took you. So I had to think of some other way. . . ."

"When I heard the key turning in the lock," said Philip Babb, slowly, almost painfully, "I thought I must be dreaming. When I saw the lass with the key in her hands I thought 'twas you and I was dreaming still. Only when I saw the door standing open and no one to block my·path, did I come to my senses and listen to what she was trying to tell me. . . ."

"I was fearful something might happen," whispered Mary. "The gaoler might wake and hear her, or some one might see you leave the gaol. But . . . you are here. . . . The boat is there at the bottom of this ladder waiting. . . ." Mary pointed. "Oh, sir, you must go at once!"

Philip Babb looked down at the girl before him. "Why have you done this, Ocean-Born Mary?" he asked, huskily.

"You saved my life once, sir," she replied readily. "I wanted to help you if I could. You must go quickly, sir. They will come after you at once when they find you are not at the gaol. Please hurry!"

Still the man looked at her. The light from the open door fell on her upturned face and he could see her features plainly. He stared down at her and put out his hand for a moment.

Then he let his hand fall. "I must be off at once," he said. Hastily he fumbled, then drew a heavy gold ring, richly ornamented with carving, from his first finger.

"Do you remember, Mary, when I showed you this ring at the Ark Tavern, that day so long ago?"

"Yes, sir," said Mary, "I remember."

"It is a magic ring to bring good luck!" he said softly, thrusting it into the girl's hand and closing her fingers over it. "It is for you."

Mary stared at it in her open palm. "But, sir," she cried, "you will need it! Oh, please do not go without it. You said that as long as you wore it, you would be safe—you would never go to the bottom of the sea!"

But he paid no heed to her words. "Do you remember what I told you about what is on the island?" he asked gruffly. "Do you remember the instructions for finding it?"

366

"Yes, sir," said Mary. "I will not forget. But the ring, sir. . . ."

"I shall not need it. Keep it always, to remember me by," he said, climbing out the door. "It will bring you luck."

Philip Babb slipped down the ladder and disappeared in the darkness. Mary heard a few splashes of the oars and he was gone. She stood at the open door and looked out through the heavy fog. She looked at the gold ring in her hand and turned it over tenderly. She knew she would never forget.

She went back to her hard bench, overcome with exhaustion and relief and fell asleep at once. When she awoke she was surprised to see that the sun was shining through the upper window. It was mid-morning. Stiff and sore, she rose to her feet. Then she saw that Nathaniel Greenwood was hard at work on his high stool, making the chips fly.

"I thought you would never wake up," he said, teasing.

"Have you been here a long time?" asked Mary, yawning.

"All night," he said, gravely.

"All night?" asked Mary, astounded. "Do you mean all night?"

"When I say all night, I mean all night," laughed Nathaniel.

"Were you here when . . . ?"

"Yes, I was here when . . ." echoed Nathaniel. Then he explained: "I could not let you stay alone and I did not want Captain Babb to know I was here, so I kept very still in the corner. Mary, you have been wiser than the rest of us. You have seen only the good in him, while we others allowed it to be covered by the evil. I know now that there is good in him—he spoke to you from his heart—and he will be a better man because of you. I am glad we have been able to give him one more chance."

"And now he is safe!" cried Mary. "You were so good to think of this way out of it. . . ."

"Hush, Mary. You must never mention it," said Nathaniel. "Remember we had no hand in his escape. We must play our part well. What we did last night was easy. Now comes the hard part, to guard our tongues. If the Governor or any one in authority asks you about the pirate's escape, divert them by telling about the buried treasure. Can you remember? Can you be strong and brave?"

"Now that I know he is safe," said Mary, "it is easy to be brave . . . but what is that?"

Loud voices were heard in the street. People were running about in great excitement.

"The news is out," said Nathaniel.

"Oh!" cried Mary, "do you think he has had time enough to reach his ship at the Shoals?"

"Ample time," said the carver. "He must be far beyond by this time. We will go out and see what is happening. Remember now, be brave."

Mary looked at him trustingly and they went out the door together.

At the corner of Queen and Water Streets, Nicky Newton, Town Crier, had planted his grotesque figure firmly on his bow-legs. He rang his bell lustily. Then he opened his mouth so wide that the upper part of his face folded itself into heavy wrinkles. "Hear all! Hear all! Hear all!" came the words in tones of thunder. Men, women and children crowded round to hear. Doors and windows were thrown open. From a long document in his hands, he read:

> " 'By the Honorable Jonathan Belcher Governor of the Provinces of Massachusetts and New Hampshire, Greeting . . . A proclamation for the suppressing of Pirates, whose leader . . . Philip Babb by name . . . has committed Divers Piracies and Robberies upon the High-Seas adjoining our Plantations . . . which hath occasioned great Damage to the Merchants of this province and others trading in these Ports . . . whosoever shall discover or seize any one or more of said Pirates . . . so that they may be brought to Justice and convicted of said Offense such Person or Persons . . . shall have and receive as a Reward for the same the sum of One Hundred Pounds . . . which said sum the Commissioner of the Treasury for the time Being is hereby required and desired to pay accordingly . . . Given at the Province House at Boston the twenty-seventh Day of June, 1733 . . . The Honorable Jonathan Belcher . . . God Save the King . . .' "

The moment the Town Crier finished, excited cries rose from the throats of the people: "The pirate has escaped from the gaol!" "He bribed the gaoler!" "He broke the locks!" "They never captured him at all —it wasn't true he was in the gaol!" "He's gone—the bird has flown!" "We are not safe to walk abroad!" "He'll plunder more ships!" "Let's find him and get the hundred pounds!"

Mary looked up at the carver questioningly.

"It's a reward for his capture," said Nathaniel in a

low voice. "His escape has been discovered. The express who came yesterday evidently brought Governor Belcher's permission to issue a proclamation under his name and offer a reward. They've acted fast."

"Will they . . . ?" Mary began.

"No," said Nathaniel, firmly. "Now, do not worry."

The news of Gaoler Winslow's neglect and the pirate's escape spread rapidly through the town. All the excitement of the previous days was as nothing to the turmoil now created. People were gathered in taverns and on street corners, talking and speculating. Mary and Nathaniel listened.

"I hear the Governor's called for volunteers," cried a ropemaker's apprentice. "He's manning a boat to go after the pirate immediately."

"Who's a-goin', I'd like to know?" snorted a shipwright. "Who's a-goin' to go out and git murdered? It's all right to put down piracy, but who wants to meet a pirate face to face?"

"Pirates is devils!" came the cry and every one seemed to agree.

The Town Crier passed on up the street. As Nathaniel and Mary watched him go, Peggy, Judy and her mother appeared.

"I cannot understand a word Nicky Newton says," cried Judy, in vexation.

"He's calling a reward for the pirate's capture, but they'll never find him," cried Peggy. "Father's given up hope."

"We are all so sorry, Mary," said Madam McFarland, "that they made so much trouble for you. We can understand how torn you were in your loyalties."

"Mary told them where the pirate was and they captured him and let him go away again," said Nathaniel. "Rather careless, eh?"

"Well, if I didn't know how to keep a pirate locked up in gaol," said Judy, with spirit, "I would not capture him in the first place."

Mary looked at Nathaniel, but said nothing.

"We want you to come and see us as soon as you can, Mary," said Madam McFarland, turning to pleasanter subjects, realizing that the girl had been on a severe strain. "There will be so much to do to help Peggy get ready for the wedding."

Her words had the desired effect. "What wedding?" cried Mary, her face brightening. She looked from Peggy to Nathaniel. "Are you two . . . ?"

"Yes, we are," said Peggy, slipping under Nathaniel's arm.

"But not until this pirate business blows over," added Nathaniel.

"Oh, I'm so glad," cried Mary, happily. "May I come?"

"Certainly," answered Peggy. "Judy's father is going to build a new ship for Nathaniel's figure-head and after we are married, we want you to come and visit us and . . ."

Mary paused, thoughtfully. "Thank you," she said, "but I cannot do that, for I'm going back to Nutfield soon."

"Going back to Nutfield?" cried the others in surprise.

The decision had come over Mary all in a moment. She had a strong feeling that her days in Strawberry

Bank were ended. She felt she had to go, she must go. "Yes," she said aloud, "Cousin Jeanie doesn't need me any more and I am homesick for Ma and the bairns. But I will stay for the wedding."

On the afternoon of the day following, Lieutenant-Governor Dunbar sent for Ocean-Born Mary again. When she saw the constable with his tipstave coming toward the cottage, she was hardly surprised.

"Oh, my child," cried Jeanie. "Run and hide while I speak to him."

"I'll send him away," growled Cousin Tom. "He shan't start questionin' ye agin."

Mary knew that they wished to protect her because they loved her, but she told them she must go. "I can answer his questions now," she said. "I can tell what I know."

Amazed, Cousin Tom and Jeanie wondered at the girl's courage. They watched her walk willingly away, beside the constable, with her head held high.

As she entered the Governor's mansion, she told herself that the first question would be regarding the poppet's whereabouts. Mary was ready to confess her part in the pirate's escape and suffer punishment for the same. She made up her mind to take all the blame upon herself, to free Susannah. She would tell about the buried treasure, too, as Nathaniel suggested. Perhaps that would stop the search for the pirate, or at least, give him more time to get away. As she remembered Nathaniel's words, she determined to keep up courage.

But the Governor began without noticing the poppet's absence. "The pirate captain has escaped," he

said solemnly, studying Mary with penetrating eyes.
"The gaoler reports that through no negligence of his
own—but through the unaccountable action of his sick
daughter, who has just died . . ."

"Died?" cried Mary, with a sinking heart. "Susannah?"

"Susannah Winslow died yesterday," said Dunbar
bluntly, "after a lingering illness. . . ."

Mary felt suddenly weak and faint. The objects in
the room swam before her eyes. Then some one
brought a chair and held a cup of water to her lips.

"Do you feel better now?" asked Dunbar. "Then
we will proceed. You need not rise. I will let you go
as soon as you answer these questions."

But Mary did not hear his words. A thought flashed
through her mind that Susannah was beyond punishment and it comforted her. She remembered that
Nathaniel had said that Susannah could never get well
and all that any one could hope to do was to bring her
a little happiness. Susannah had loved the poppet and
had had it for her own. . . . Then Mary heard the
Governor speaking.

"You told us, lass," said Governor Dunbar, "that
Pirate Babb was hiding on Goat Island. That was cor-
rect, because that is where we found and captured him.
Do you know of any other hiding place of his to which
he might have escaped?"

"The Isles of Shoals, sir," said Mary, half heeding.
Susannah was beyond punishment and sickness, now.
The words kept going over and over in her mind.

"On which Island?"

"Appledore, sir," said Mary.

Suddenly Mary felt that she must see Susannah's mother as soon as possible. Perhaps what she had done had made Susannah worse and had hastened her death. In order to get away quickly, she must heed the Governor's questions and answer them.

"Did he ever take you there?" asked Dunbar.

"Yes, sir," said Mary, remembering the treasure again. "He showed me where he had buried his treasure, sir, and he told me if . . . he never came back . . . I was to remember . . . because he wanted me to have his treasure."

At the word *treasure* Governor Dunbar pricked up his ears and looked at Mary with some surprise. What an unusual child she was! Her eagerness now to answer his questions puzzled him, so great a contrast was it to her previous silence.

"When did he tell you this?" he asked.

"It was some time ago, sir," said Mary.

"Did he often speak as if he might never come back?"

"Sometimes, sir," said Mary. "He said, also, in case anything happened to him . . . in case he should be captured or . . ."

"But why would he want you to have his treasure? Why would he not leave it for his men?" persisted Dunbar.

"He had divided it up long before, sir," explained Mary, "and this was only his own share which he buried on Appledore Island. I think he never wanted to see it again, sir, for he meant to become an honest sea-captain and begin all over, sir."

The Governor smiled, but did not dispute. "I see,"

he said, "and he wants you to have it. Did he tell you how to find it?"

"Yes, sir," said Mary. "He told me the directions."

Governor Dunbar looked at the group of waiting men and smiled. "If we cannot find the man, we may at least take his treasure!" he said in an undertone. The men looked forward eagerly, hanging on every one of Mary's words.

"Can you tell us what his directions were, lass?"

"Why should I tell, sir?" cried Mary, impatient to go. "It is his secret and mine."

"You realize, Mary," said Dunbar, in a serious tone, "that all this trouble over the pirate has cost the province a great deal of money."

Such a thought had never entered Mary's mind. She said, "I did not know that, sir."

"Now if we can find the pirate's treasure, it will repay us for all that we have spent. Do you understand, lass?"

"Yes, sir," said Mary. Eagerly she wished that they might go at once to hunt for the treasure. That would give Philip Babb more time to get away. "I will give the treasure to you, sir."

Dunbar looked at his men and they laughed heartily. Then he turned to Mary again: "Will you tell us how to find it?"

"Yes, sir," said Mary, readily. "He made me say the directions over a great many times so that I would not forget. 'On Appledore Island, not far from the mouth of the creek, there is a clump of bushes growing on top of a rocky ledge. Behind them is a group of pine trees, one of which is much taller than the others. Go to this pine tree, then go twenty feet south by east half east and drive a peg. Return to a shelving rock not far from the pine tree and go one hundred feet east half north and you ought to cross your former angle just at the peg. If you do, that is where the treasure is buried."

During the clear and unhesitating recital, the men looked at each other in surprise. There was no doubt about it, the child had learned her lesson well and in all likelihood without an error. The fascination of hidden treasure began to show itself on the glowing, eager faces. The furor of hatred against the pirate cooled noticeably and the reckless determination to capture him at all costs had been deflected—as Mary had hoped.

"Do you remember the spot?" asked Dunbar. "Could you go with us and show us where to start and give us the directions again?"

"Now, sir?" asked Mary.

"No, later. I will let you know when we are ready to go," said Dunbar. "The information which you have given us is astonishing and I may add that you have been most generous." He looked at her almost affectionately.

"Is that all now, sir?" asked Mary.

"Yes, you may go."

Mary hastened at once to the log gaol and found it overflowing with people. It was only a moment until she saw Marm Winslow, who led her into the little room. As she looked at the still form on the bed, it seemed as if Susannah were only sleeping, for a half-smile played upon her lips.

"She looks so happy!" cried Mary, clinging to Susannah's mother.

"She is sick no longer," said Marm Winslow, calmly.

"But, oh, ma'am," cried Mary, "do you think that what I asked her . . . what she did for me . . . made her worse . . . did I . . . ?"

Marm Winslow put her arms about Mary and looked at her earnestly. "My dear child," she said, "you gave Susannah the greatest happiness each time you came. She was always better for seeing you. And when she was going, she bade you farewell and asked me to give you back your poppet. She loved having it for her own. I am sure she was glad to do something for you in return for all the happiness you gave her."

She led Mary from the room and put the poppet back into her arms. As Mary went out of the house, she met Master Pecksniff coming in. He looked questioningly at the poppet in her arms.

Mary met his gaze steadily. Had he suspected her part in freeing the pirate? If any one suspected, it would be he, for he hated her and the carver, too.

Then, all at once, she was overcome with relief that Susannah was free and out of the man's power at last. She would never have to taste his drugs again. Mary felt free, also, even as she knew Susannah was free. She would never be afraid of the man again.

But the apothecary was thinking neither of the poppet nor of Susannah nor of the carver. "My Ma," he said, in a perplexed and worried tone, "says she has taken quite a fancy to you and she wonders why you don't ever come and see her any more. . . ."

Suddenly Mary saw the apothecary in a new light

and she felt sorry for him. He had a poor, crooked soul, because of his poor, crooked body. Poor Marm Pecksniff must have cried over her poor, crooked baby in those terrifying months after the Indian massacre. And now he was a helpless man and had his hands full, caring for his half-mad mother. Mary wondered how she could ever have misjudged him so.

"Tell your mother, sir," she said, kindly, "that I am going back to Nutfield to live, but I will come and visit with her before I go."

A week passed by—ten days—a fortnight, and the pirate was not re-captured. Then one day, Mary went with Dunbar's men to Appledore Island in the Isles of Shoals. She repeated the well-memorized directions and they were followed step by step. Everything was found to tally with the description and the digging began. Several heavy stones were lifted, but no treasure came to light. The directions were repeated over and over again, different spots were tried and the whole of the Island seemed in danger of being upturned. Was there some mistake or had the pirate intended this?

Would the treasure ever be found? Had the pirate made its exact hiding place uncertain, so that through the centuries to come, men might go on digging, forever hopefully digging? Would the ghost of Philip Babb hover over them and laugh?

While the men worked, Mary stood on a high bluff and looked out to sea. On a linen thread about her neck, hung Philip Babb's ring. Mary took it in her hand, wondering if the loss of it had brought him ill luck. There had been many conjectures about him since his escape. Some said that he had been captured, taken to England and hanged on the gallows. Some said that his ship had been wrecked and that he and his men had been drowned. Others said that he had reformed, gone to some remote island where he had taken on a new identity and was leading an honest and useful life. Mary hoped that this was true. She had never forgotten the promise he had made to give up pirating. She believed in him more than ever. She turned the ring over in her hand and watched it flash in the sunshine.

Then she thought of Goody Gregory's words, spoken so long ago—Goody, who like herself, saw only the good in the man. The old woman's words came back clearly: "Remember that whatever happens, you will always be a friend to those who befriend you." She meant her son, the pirate, of course. "When the time comes for you to go away from Strawberry Bank, you will be ready to go, yes, happy to go. But you will never forget the sea. You will remember it to your dying day." Mary let the ring fall upon her breast. She opened her arms wide as if to embrace the sea and hold it close.

"The rest of your life will be spent far away from the sea—but you will love it the more for having lived with it here." Ocean-Born Mary watched the sun set over the town in the distance and its radiant glow spread over sea and sky. She thought of the McFarlands, Peggy and Nathaniel, Aunt Becky and Cousin Jeanie, Cousin Tom and the boys, and she knew that she loved them dearly, so closely were they bound up with her life. She remembered all the many exciting and interesting adventures which she had had in the sixteen months she had lived at Strawberry Bank. If she had to live it all again, she would not wish anything changed. But it was over now and she was filled with longing for her home and her mother. She was ready to go back to Nutfield again, without any regrets. She was ready and happy to leave the sea, for she knew that she would hold it, for the rest of her life, safe in her heart.

The end

AFTERWORD

Ocean-Born Mary was a real person, the daughter of James and Elizabeth (Fulton) Wilson. She was born on the ocean on July 28, 1720, during a passage from Ireland to this country.

Parker's History of Londonderry, New Hampshire, gives the following account:

"*Tradition says that in* 1720, *a company of emigrants, on their passage from Ireland to this country, were captured by pirates, and while in their hands as prisoners, Mrs. Wilson was delivered of her first child, which so moved the pirate band and particularly the captain, who had a wife and family, that he permitted the emigrants to proceed on their voyage, bestowing upon Mrs. Wilson many valuable presents, mostly articles of wearing apparel, among which was a valuable silk dress, pieces of which are still retained by her descendants as memorials of her peril and of her deliverance from piratical hands. The pirate captain obtained a promise from Mrs. Wilson that she would name the child Mary, for his wife, that being her name. This signal deliverance from the pirates was commemorated during a generation by the annual observance of a day of thanksgiving by the people of Londonderry.*

"*Ocean-Born Mary's father died in Boston soon after landing. His widow brought the child Mary to Londonderry, New Hampshire, where they had land laid* out to them by reason of the father's being a grantee of the town. The mother married James Clark, and had four sons and one daughter. The child Mary resided with the family until her marriage to James Wallace in 1742."

These are all the known facts about the early part of her life.

Cogswell's History of Henniker, New Hampshire, gives the following information:

"Ocean-Born Mary resided in this town for many of the last years of her life and died Feb. 13, 1814, at the age of 94 years. She was buried in the center buryingground, amidst many of her descendants. She was represented as being quite tall, resolute and determined; of strong mind, quick of comprehension, sharp in her conversation with a strong brogue and full of humor. She was florid in complexion, had bright eyes and was elegant in her manners to the last of her life. Her younger experience was wonderful in toil and hardships; but her last years were sunny and happy."

On a wind-swept hill in New Hampshire, a few miles from Henniker, stands the Ocean-Born Mary house, where the latter part of her life was spent. It is thought probable that it was built after the year 1767, as a number of Scotch-Irish families migrated from Londonderry to Henniker at that time.

A great many traditions and stories are still told about Ocean-Born Mary and the house which she occupied. Architects say that the house shows every evidence of having been built by ship's carpenters. Some people like to believe that it was built by the pirate or at least paid for with the pirate's gold. Certainly it is a much grander mansion than other houses built in the same locality at the same period. The house is reported to be haunted by the ghost of Ocean-Born Mary. Some people believe that whenever the house is in danger, her spirit sends some one to save it; that she comes back periodically to try to point out the treasure which the pirate may have buried on the premises or beneath the house. It is believed by some that Ocean-Born Mary knew the pirate all through her life and was the recipient of frequent, costly gifts. It is difficult to say how much truth there is in these stories. One fact only we can be certain of—that Ocean-Born Mary was a marked woman all her life; and continues to be so, more than one hundred and twenty-five years after her death.

The Ocean-Born Mary house, now (1939) owned and occupied by Mr. L. M. A. Roy, contains a fragment of the green silk brocade which the pirate gave to Mary for her wedding-gown.

There is no indication that, as a child, Ocean-Born Mary ever lived in Portsmouth. It might have been possible for her to do so, as the people of Londonderry kept up constant intercourse with Portsmouth, which was the port of entry and customs, the place of exchange and the seat of government for the province of New Hampshire. I have taken the liberty of placing Ocean-Born Mary in Portsmouth for one and one-half years. My story is, of course, entirely fiction. I have made use of the early, original names—Strawberry Bank for Portsmouth and Nutfield for Londonderry.

The Isles of Shoals were for many years the convenient hiding-place of sea rovers and pirates of the New England coast. Star Island was long known as "Smugglers' Isle," the paradise of free-traders. Appledore Island has for two centuries been haunted by the specter of Philip Babb or "Old Babb," who is said to have been a pirate, one of Captain Kidd's men. The legend is that he was murdered by his shipmates, so that his ghost might guard their hidden treasure. Repeated searches have been made for his treasure, which like so many treasures, has never been found. I have taken the liberty of appropriating his name, but the character that I have built up, is imaginary.

The Boston News-Letter of July 9, 1722, states that "sundry goods left by pirates on board the brigantine 'Rebecca' were to be sold at publick vendue at the house of Captain Long in Charlestown." Among the goods listed, one item of particular interest is: "5 Horn books."

For the background of my story, I have attempted to give an accurate picture of life in a New England seaport town fifty years before the Revolutionary War; to show the closeness of backwoods and seaport and their dependence upon each other; to describe concretely the early West India trade of this period and to suggest some of the dangers of shipping on the high seas, caused by piracy.

I have also tried to show the strong hold which England had on the colonies at this time and the difficulties which resulted from enforcement of "The Pine Tree Law"—that most odious of all oppressive measures, *which did so much to unify the people of New Hampshire in active resistance against Great Britain and which was one of the strongest contributing causes of the Revolutionary War.*

The facts regarding the mast question, Dunbar's questionable practices, the rebellion of the people are taken from New Hampshire State Papers. Dunbar's speeches are actual quotations. It is interesting to note that in the Exeter timber riot, which took place on April 23, 1734—forty years before the Boston Tea Party—the settlers disguised themselves as Indians.

I am deeply indebted to Miss Dorothy Vaughan, Assistant Librarian of the Portsmouth Public Library, for her generous help in reconstructing accurate conditions in Portsmouth in the 1730's; to Mr. Gordon Grant for his supervision of nautical details and to Mr. R. W. G. Vail of the Antiquarian Society Library of Worcester, Massachusetts, for invaluable general help and encouragement.

LOIS LENSKI

Greenacres, Harwinton, Connecticut
May 1, 1939

BIBLIOGRAPHY

Adams, Nathaniel—Annals of Portsmouth, 1825.

Brewster, Charles—Rambles About Portsmouth, 2 vols., 1859.

Chapelle—The History of American Sailing Ships, 1935.

Charnock—History of Marine Architecture, 1802.

Coffin, Charles—Daughters of the Revolution, 1895.

Cogswell—History of Henniker, New Hampshire.

Dow and Edmonds—Pirates of the New England Coast, 1923.

Drake, Samuel Adams—Nooks and Corners of the New England Coast, 1875.

———— The Pine Tree Coast.

Earle, Alice Morse—Home Life in Colonial Days, 1898.

———— Curious Punishments of Bygone Days, 1896.

Ellis, G. H.—The Portsmouth Book, 1899.

Fassett—Colonial Life in New Hampshire.

Foster, Sarah—Portsmouth Guide Book, 1876.

Fry, W. H.—New Hampshire as a Royal Province, 1908.

Gurney, C. S.—Portsmouth, Historic and Picturesque, 1902.

Mathes, Frances A. and Hazlett—Historical Calendar of Portsmouth, 1907.

May, Ralph—Early Portsmouth History, 1926.

Morison—Maritime History of Massachusetts, 1921.

Northend—Memories of Old Salem, 1917.

Parker—History of Londonderry, New Hampshire, 1851.

Pierson, Helen—Vignettes of Old Portsmouth.

Rogers, Mary C.—Glimpses of an Old Social Capital, 1923.

387

Rowe, Wm. Hutchinson—Ship Building Days in Casco Bay, Maine, 1929.

Scott, Miss—Journal of a Lady of Quality, (1773).

Wallace—Wooden Ships and Iron Men.

Weeden, Wm. B.—Economic and Social History of New England, 1891.

Willey—Book of Nutfield.

Also: various histories of New Hampshire, volumes of "The Granite Monthly," New Hampshire State Papers, 1730-5, books of Scotch folk songs, pirate songs; and other volumes.